STUCK ON EARTH

STUCK ON EARTH

BY WAYNE KAATZ

ARCHWAY
PUBLISHING

Archway Publishing books may be ordered through booksellers or by contacting:

Archway Publishing
1663 Liberty Drive
Bloomington, IN 47403
www.archwaypublishing.com
1 (888) 242-5904

ISBN: 978-1-4808-3280-0 (sc)
ISBN: 978-1-4808-3281-7 (e)

Library of Congress Control Number: 2016909713

Print information available on the last page.

Archway Publishing rev. date: 07/18/2016

CHAPTER ONE

A fter seeing the gorilla in church I expected it would be there every Sunday, a part of our religion like the talking snake which was all I remembered from a year of Sunday school. Graduating from Bible stories in the church basement took me upstairs into a wooden pew deep between my parents. When they stood with the rest of the congregation I stood on the bench seat, then remained standing as they sat down. Past the men's Saturday buzz cuts and the ladies' hairspray sculptures a gorilla stepped out of the vestibule, hunched behind the pastor reading at the lectern. Some of the audience chuckled and coughed and some grumbled in the low murmur of prayer voices. My parents jerked me down onto my heels then pulled my legs out straight, whispering that our shoes don't belong on God's furniture.

The next week I waited eagerly in a stiff suit and bowtie, eyes sliding right and left like a ventriloquist dummy, trying to sit tall enough to see something other than the hymnals racked to the back of the pew ahead, but the hard wood was oiled and slippery and my butt slid out from under me. Slouched low with my chin crushing the tie into my adam's apple, all I saw was the pastor's bald head bobbing high in the pulpit, catching the light at certain angles that made what wispy hair was left glow like a halo. The ape might have danced below during the entire sermon.

1

By the time I had words enough to ask why the gorilla wasn't in church anymore, my parents said there never had been a gorilla, it must've been my imagination or I was remembering a dream, but they were wrong. I didn't have an imagination and hadn't started dreaming yet.

At Christmas my dad lifted me up to see a sheep in the pageant, thinking any animal in church would excite me, but I couldn't stop looking at the girl with angel wings.

There weren't even enough memories to be confused about. I didn't know that people saved thoughts, putting them in storage in the head to be pulled out like an old movie and played again. Except for the gorilla the only thing I remembered was being stuffed in the back seat with two wicker and iron lawn chairs, staring at my white and wrinkled thumb. The flavor had been sucked out and I was giving it some air to get the taste back. I stood up on the hump in the center of the car floor where I could see out the windshield.

The hood of the car was round and it looked like it was eating up the road. I leaned against the top of the front seat, holding my thumb out so it wouldn't touch anything while still wet. My dad asked if I was thumbing for a ride and mom yelled his name as if scolding him for saying something bad, but it was because the car was eating up grass instead of road. There was an exciting sound and I was in the air tangled with the chairs, still trying to keep the thumb from touching things. All motion stopped with punishing weight, my face flat against a back window.

Though I had the choice of either side window in the back, leaning any cheek against the glass to get it knocked away when a tire chunked through a pothole, usually enjoyed the panoramic view ahead from that hump. Now my head was against the glass, upside down and with a smear of blood.

The car was almost sideways in a ditch overgrown with tall grass through which I watched sun sparkles on brown water a few feet away past the blood. I wasn't scared until I saw how scared my parents were.

People didn't wear a seatbelt back then unless you raced cars or were an astronaut. There was so much smoke in the car with the windows rolled up it might have been healthier to crash. We hadn't smashed into anything, just a near collision that pulled off the back bumper with a metal shriek and gave me the scar through my lower lip, but no memory of a hospital or chewing the stitches.

My mother wouldn't drive for ten years. Still nobody buckled up. We were survivors of vehicular natural selection, and our descendants should be immune to crashes and wrecks.

Those were my toddler memories and I never dreamt them or versions of them. My parents agreed I had the accident correct in my mind but when I said the word gorilla they went into a zombie trance, unable to hear or see me. Those intervals of invisibility took years to get used to and gave me the idea of wearing a gorilla suit, that and some episodes of The Three Stooges in which the ape never fooled me, and I expected the guy in the suit would take it off at the end as part of the story.

In school there were two other kids with weird lips, one a girl, and it gave me comfort having her around for when we all started kissing, which I thought might have been going on secretly already among the better looking beginning students, but when I asked the guys that stood next to me in line for the bathroom, line to the playground and the lunch line, none admitted to it. In the few years of watching black and white television on a screen that had varying snow conditions, the picture tilting crooked or rolling up and down while dad turned little knobs to solve the problem, there was a guy after a girl, or two guys, or a monster, but always some kissing. Either it didn't happen everyday at school or somebody was lying.

Before bed, moments of the school day replayed in my mind, the parts with girls, and that was when I began keeping a memory stream, and when I had my first dream. It was confusing until I woke up, and then there was no confusion. When trying to explain it to mom she must have smelled the ape word on my breath because she changed the subject to scrambled eggs and if I wanted to learn how to make them. It wasn't more dangerous than cooking rubber bugs in metal molds on a toy hot plate, or using a hammer at the curb to explode an entire roll of caps, which left chip marks and gunpowder stains on the concrete but no new scars on me.

I had seen big kids hammer the caps. They were dangerous things, big kids. If not walking to or from school I was allowed only to the end of the street and looked out on the rest of the world from there. I'd seen them with other little boys, acting nice and asking names but each time it turned to teasing as if unable to help themselves, throwing fake punches, bumping them into bushes, knocking stuff out of their hands and dry-spitting into their hair that felt so real the kids had to ask each other if there was a snot ball on their head. If any ran away crying the big kids laughed as if they'd conquered giants, throwing stones at the ground so they'd skip up behind the kid, more of an insult than trying to hit him but better when they hit him.

The first summer vacation after kindergarten I walked the curb in front of our house to the driveway then followed heel toe along one of the tar-covered cracks in the street damaged by the war between summer heat and winter cold. Used as baselines or goal lines, the tarred cracks crisscrossed the length of the street, and we used the intersections for four-square if somebody had the right kind of ball. At a section where the sun had been shining the tar was so hot that sticky black strands pulled back on my tennis shoes until one came off, so I got a stick from the gutter and dug out a shiny glob that looked like licorice but tasted bad enough that I worried about poison and spit until the taste was mostly in little white specks along the pavement. There was a firecracker bang, some chinking sounds then another boom that pulled me to the corner, stick and tar ball still in my hand.

It was natural to hide behind the wooden pole of the street light though it smelled like the garage floor where the car dripped something yellowish brown, leaving a stain that slowly grew through the years until it was wider than the vehicle, and I never let my foot touch it because of seeing the blob movie, a little afraid it might consume me. The corner gave a view of a parallel street where the big kids were messing around and as they changed their position I moved around the pole so I was always hidden exactly on the opposite side. If they came close I'd run to the front steps of our house as I did the day they passed with shovels. I asked them what they were doing and they said they were going to bury the president. That's all the news I remember about Kennedy being shot. Days later I snuck down into the ravine and saw a large hole they had dug into the hillside, a cave fort. They never used it again and each rain would wash away more of its edges until there was an open wound in the landscape, the roots of trees exposed like tentacled creatures of the dirt.

This time they were exploding cap rolls with a hammer that had a loose head. One guy tried to hit the red paper roll while positioning his head away from that business as far as his neck would stretch, so after a few misses that chipped white scars into the gray concrete, the iron claw flew off the end of the cracked handle, almost hitting the red curly haired head of another guy who was leaning in too close as if he might learn some secret of destruction from the bang. The hammerhead clinked to a stop in my direction and the chubby third kid who scuttled after it saw me peeking around the pole and pointed me out like a dog sighting wild game. They only chased me because I instinctively ran, triggering some pack mentality, maybe superstitiously blaming me for the hammer's defect but probably something more primal, eat anything that runs away, anything that moves but the stuff running away tastes better.

If I made it home they would pretend it was just a race and pat my head in front of my mom, telling her that I was a good kid, fastest on the street, but it was a race I was going to lose and be force fed something random and within reach from nature. Before they caught me I dropped the stick with the tar and went up a maple. They stopped to inspect the tar on the stick, uncertain if it was valuable, giving me time to climb. Knowing they had me treed like a raccoon they did a primitive dance around the trunk howling and whooping while I kept going up. Two climbed into the tree after me, the chubby kid too weak to pull his own weight off the ground so he played with the tar ball which stuck to his fingers and seemed to be eating his hands like the blob again.

The redhead got tired and confessed to the cap hammerer that he didn't know if he could get down. The third kid reached the bendy branches and caught the scared kid's worry, backing down until they were both stuck about halfway. They argued over foot and handholds but with gravity guiding them were able to find the lowest branches near the ground. I swayed in the breeze with the treetop, enjoying the view of roofs and chimneys and tv antennas pulling in Jungle Jim and Zim Bomba the Jungle Boy, leftovers from Tarzan movies.

The neighbor came out of his house and the chubby kid with tar-covered hands ran away as the gray haired man told the big kids to get out of his tree and play somewhere else. They slid down the trunk getting bark burns on their bellies where their shirts got pulled up, became polite and walked away, turning back once to give him and me the finger before running across the street and around the corner. Mister homeowner never saw me through the leaves.

Later mom yelled my name from the back door and I climbed down for lunch, salami sandwich and chicken soup. She told me I had tar on my shoe and asked what I had been doing and I told her nothing, just playing. Later I took the caps out of my cap gun, licking the end of the barrel because it tasted good though not like food, then snuck the hammer out of the junk drawer and went to the corner where I exploded the roll, losing hearing in my right ear for several minutes and my hand smelled like it had burned but it was fine. Mom saw me sneaking the hammer back into the drawer and asked what I needed it for and I told her nothing, just playing. She leaned out the back door and looked around for things smashed or broken, even glancing into the trees against the thought there might be a miraculous tree house in one of them, telling me it wasn't a toy and not to take it again without permission.

From then I got away with stuff. The corner was never the edge of my world, just the length of my leash which I slipped to explore the wilds of the next block, taking the hammer for protection, hiding in trees but unable to swing from one to another because the vines only grew on the trees in the ravine behind our house. There was a moment when mom saw me suspended in one of those treetops as if lounging in a big green hammock. She screamed that I didn't have the brains to fill my father's shoes. Because of the accident she was afraid I'd get hurt again. My leash might have reached only to the corner, but with the basic cleverness of a monkey I adventured out into big kid land alone and survived.

My parents kicked me out of bed many mornings, saving wear on the twin mattress. There was a belief that sleeping anytime toward noon was bad, probably featured in a story and sermon about biblical ruination, or maybe only denounced by the Sunday school teacher who also made the school lunch so she smelled like school lunch, though decades later after she had been retired for many years I passed her on the street and learned that those meals long ago had nothing to do with it. Friends with school enough had already left town to learn and work and breed, so when I returned home with no sort of degree or engagement and no job my parents soon kicked me out of the house. Not out of the family, just out of the home, maybe to save wear on the floorboards and doorknobs and toilet seat.

It was a humid Sunday evening, the air heavy enough to pin the dog down, tongue surrendered to the pine slat flooring in a pool of white spit, its teeth showing in an opossum smile. It had taken a year of whining even to get a dog because dad claimed he had a puppy in childhood that was swallowed by a catfish. We never ate catfish either just in case it might be a relative of the culprit, sharing some blood tainted with digested pup. The ceiling fan croaked with each revolution like a broken record of a laughing frog. It aggravated the air making loose hairs of fur dance in circles with punctuation marks of dust on one section of my bedroom floor as if demonstrating the origins of the solar system. It caused me to remember making my bed once, fluffing the top sheet to billow it out over the fitted sheet, but the sheet hit the fan and was pulled around like a ghost decoration for Halloween. It was the last perfect moment of contentment and contemplation because angry voices preceded the door being opened quickly enough to destroy the dancing dust world, and caused the dog to raise his head fast enough to make his tongue produce an audible pop as it became detached from the floor.

Dad told me that mother and he just had an agreement. They never called them arguments. The person who won the argument could label it an agreement at the end. You need to get out, he added, not saying which of them had won this time.

The dog clunked his head back down, tongue unfurling, knowing its own position wasn't threatened. I nodded to my dad, thinking that he had never gotten over me quitting church. If I had gotten up early and worked at something as an alternative it wouldn't have mattered, but my sleeping until they came home with the Sunday paper made it something against several of the ten commandments. Told him I got up just before breakfast same as they did, only at a different time. He said my logic was thin as the skin on a weenie and then he evicted me.

Acting like an adult requires energy, pretending to be responsible when the mind and body desire all things irresponsible. The most energy I ever had even as a kid was when the neighbor wrapped me in a long orange extension cord to turn me into the electro-magnetic boy. My hair was already standing up because of the butch-wax. I might've pulled nails and keys to my fingertips but my arms were tied to my sides, and I did not attract girls any more than I did small steel items even when my arms were free. They were of a polarity that repelled them from me toward hairier boys who began shaving in the eighth grade and took long showers in the locker room so I couldn't avoid standing near them in embarrassing comparison. The showers were mandatory by coaches who were coached themselves to promote proper hygiene along with sportsmanship in several sports dependent on balls. My mind was just as hairy and sweaty as others but in the locker room it seemed shriveled and bald, too white reminding me of my first guilt from over-sucking my wet shriveled too white thumb.

If you are soon enough you can sneak back into childhood. Two years of theater classes were an extended vacation no different than if I had wandered a thousand mile circle during that time. The bedroom was intact, not yet a walk-in closet for the parents' odd sweaters and old golf clubs. Science fiction paperbacks still stood like a cityscape across the shelf. Clay and rubber things posed patiently on the dresser, surrounding a plastic puddle of fake puke ordered from the novelty page in the back of comic books that were piled under the bed next to the Mads and monster magazines. Brilliantly slipped between them was an old boob mag that featured a girl in a leopard skin bikini captured by a fake gorilla, then the girl without the bikini.

Maybe a third year of college would have changed me into something that couldn't go home again, instead of crowding Dad for a piece of his territory as a baboon might. Could have become handy with tools and learned to enjoy the cave-like confines of a grimy garage, but I saw a movie about hippies that gave me the idea to drop out. The new world was going to be different, so I didn't have to play along with old world rules. No more waking up too early to carry a heavy stack of overpriced textbooks. There were too many slaves to education with enough books to stack into a pyramid that would dwarf the ancient wonder. They had us competing for a chance to get up too early and go to work for the rest of our youths, Saturdays off for chores, Sundays to get up too early to sit still, shut up and listen in church about an invisible superhero and magic land for the dead if I obey the rules. And I couldn't afford another year of student loan debt.

Back home I felt like a wild variable introduced into an earth family as an experiment. My earth family felt that way also. They didn't like that I ate meals off the refrigerator shelves, at night illuminated only by that little bulb light casting my shadow so big it bent up onto the ceiling. The electric hum of the cooling action clicked on at a pleasant frequency, a note good for digestion.

The single bar of soap we shared would get left in a watery dish, soft and squished into an asymmetrical blob so I would drain the dish, dry the soap then carve it back into bar shape.

I became a clipper, collecting favorite ads and pictures from the newspaper and tv-guide leaving rectangular holes in the schedule or articles on the reverse side of the page.

I neatened the trash. They casually tossed garbage and debris into the open bin and it filled up quickly then overflowed. It was my chore to take out the trash so I'd nest as many containers as possible, shift garbage into left over spaces, uncrumple papers and lay them flat against each other, getting twice as much refuse in each load saving bags and trips to the galvanized metal curb can. Seeing me regularly digging in the trash gave them worry over what other disgusting things might fascinate me.

When the blue jays fought the ravine tree squirrels for mulberries in the morning waking me up with their screechy threats I shot at them through the window screen, the BB's leaving holes several times larger than the screen's tiny square spaces, which allowed a wild grape vine to reach a tendril through the screen and grow behind the window. The scenario depressed mom so much she donated the gun to a church rummage sale, a fundraiser for feeding some kids who had their own invisible magic super hero but for some reason no parents to sell their BB gun for food. It sold to one of the preacher's boys. Coincidentally many of the picture windows on their street became starred with tiny conical fractures as if hit with a pebble, and because the glass would've been too expensive to replace for a single spot of damage, those scars remained when I moved home back from college.

I returned with dirty laundry, every piece of clothing weeks unwashed, and an oversize tribal mask made in scenic arts. The girl I didn't bring home was panhandling for homework assignments to copy in our dorm where she wasn't allowed but we allowed her. She was so attractive she could set up a kissing booth and guys like me would give her money just to watch her laugh at the idea she'd ever kiss us. I auditioned for a play to get close to someone like her and it turned out to be her exactly. We were cast as a couple in a comedy so old the laughs to fit it had become almost obselete, but theater audiences are polite and chuckle in the appropriate places to prove they get the pun or tired sexual connotation.

The young actor who played to lead role of the old man had a cast party at his parents' cabin on the big lake, serving a mixed drink made from Hi-C and whatever liquor was left in the five bottles locked in a liquor cabinet that could be unlocked with a paperclip bent into an L. It was mixed in a galvanized pail and he told us it was called sucker punch because you didn't know when it was going to hit you. It was sweet but still triggered my gag reflex so I invented reasons to turn away from people each time I drank a sip. Bad songs played from a cheap old radio, and I thought it was the local station's fault but later realized we were in an era of bad music.

The director of the play stood on the rise of the first stair leading to an overhanging loft that held two twin beds, the pine knotted ceiling slanting down to meet the mattresses on one side. He made comments to people from there, just conversation but shouted out as if he were still giving directions from his script station in the theater seats. He wore a bowtie that looked like a small bat sucking on his neck. His one-sided smile from always smoking on that side of his mouth made him look off balance.

He was thin as a dancer and preached that the best actors were lean and mean, though many in the cast weighed as much as both of us together. You can always act fat, he said, that's what costume and make up are for. The overweight people in the play pretended not to be insulted and nodded as if they knew that already and would be thin soon as possible. He moved one part of the body at a time, a finger then the hand, or he'd look up with his eyes then head from a chair, finally bringing the rest of the body after it. It was trick to rivet the audience taught to him by a partner of a famous mime who caused our single generation to have an unprecedented number of mimes expecting celebrity. It didn't happen and mimes became an easy laugh for stand-up comedians, almost killing the silent art among young entertainers, but unfortunately didn't.

He told me I moved like an ape and that if I had any hope of working in this business it was to learn to dance, take ballet. I told him that ballet seemed like mime with an orchestra only funnier. He almost didn't laugh but it was a party and let out a token heh-heh then told me to go ahead, act like an ape the rest of your life. Then he lifted one leg in preparation to walk away as he always did before making an exit, and either my joke or the spiked punch made him truly off balanced because he forgot he was on a step. He gracefully moved that foot forward and set it down where he thought the floor would be and instead it dropped the extra seven or eight inches, and to keep from falling he had to run to get both feet to catch up with the weight of his upper body, lurching across the cabin like Groucho until he found one of the heavy cast members to grab and right himself.

Everyone laughed and he took a bow as if it were planned, then exited properly. I turned toward the punch bucket and almost crashed into my girlfriend from the play. She told me I moved like an ape while handing me her empty plastic cup. I dunked both our cups into the bucket then wasted moments setting them down and fumbling for a napkin to dry them and my fingers. By the time I turned back she was sitting on the steps to the loft. Deliberate drunkenness had not been the plan, but my gagging had stopped and after another cup we had somehow climbed the stairs one at a time while sitting and ended up sharing a twin bed. She was wedged between my body and roof that smelled like floor cleaner. I had been anticipating sex for so many years that I expected it to change my life, bringing adult powers. When her moves made it clear this was going to be the electric moment for me, feared I might be glowing in the dark, giving away my expectation.

The one thing I was not prepared for was that there wasn't an actual hole between her legs, a neat circle like on a drill bit gauge, hopefully one with a diameter that matched my diddler as grandpa called it once when we peed against the side of his cousin's barn in the moonlight to avoid the stinking outhouse after dark at a family reunion.

The peeks at old issues of Playboy poorly hidden by a friend's father did not give the anatomical specifics, and as we took turns being lookout while the other flipped through pages to see as many pictures as possible my eyes always focused on the breasts. Neighborhood dogs demonstrated the basic procedure but I remembered Jeff Deal telling me in seventh grade that girls had three holes, so a medical volume with illustrated directions would have been more help than any centerfold but his dad didn't have a real library, just a box of magazines inside a dusty suitcase on a closet shelf. But nature and a college girl took me by the hand and shoved me through the entrance of no return and I said out loud, oh I get it, and she made a sweet little purr of agreement that I never have heard exactly the same from anyone else.

Feeling like a newlywed I warned her about meeting my parents, and she asked if they were coming to the party that night. I said no, that I was hoping she would eventually go home with me, home to their house and meet them, and she told me she was engaged to an older guy back home in Chicago. I pictured a guy with shoulders big as a Sandberg poem and wanted to throw things but pretended to be adult about it and drank another cup of punch, a bad taste in my pants. Later I thought maybe he didn't exist, that she invented him at that moment for my sake, as if being rejected by a single woman would be worse, but later heard it was true. They got married but it didn't last much longer than my return stay at home. We worked on other shows together and took the same classes but didn't have sex again. Last time I saw her she was standing at the depot, waving as I walked back to campus. It was closed and the last train had gone through years before, but she suggested we say goodbye there to have a nice picture in our memories.

The heart mends slowly unless you transfer the break onto someone else, so I planned to feed like a vampire on eighteen and nineteen year olds' feelings until I felt better. Needed to back up and start where I had left off at graduation with a girl like the one I broke up with to have a season of freedom before college, a summer of love. She didn't get angry because she never got angry, just a little sad as if expecting it, maybe because of her voice that made her more insecure than I was over my lip. She spoke in a voice so high it sometimes rose out of my range of hearing, which caused conversation to crumble and nearby dogs to bark, and often her father was suddenly looking for something in the vicinity as if answering an alarm he heard from the opposite part of their large house. Though I was crazy horny, especially during class lectures which accounted for my mediocre grades, she was satisfied with making out and letting me work around her bra. It was so tight she couldn't have gotten much pleasure from me forcing my hand under the cups at awkward angles but it sometimes brought her voice down half a note.

When dad gave me my eviction notice I went directly out into the heat. He hadn't been that serious since the time I stole a check from his checkbook to send away for a live monkey. He didn't lock the desk drawer because it was perfectly organized, so he knew at a glance someone had been in his private space, though I was certain nothing could have moved more than a sliver. Maybe he taped a secret hair across the back or left a fine dust seen only under special lighting, but he noticed the breach, figured out the last numbered check was missing and tracked my hidden letter down before I could find a stamp and mail it. I was grounded for weeks, which was ironic with the current punishment of being forced out.

Took a walk hoping to meet a blond just out of high school and bring her home to impress him into changing his mind. Some guys don't care if a girl is blond, heard of a couple in Texas alone, but I craved blond hair like lunch. Rarely one around when you need it though so I returned home hoping the situation was not so serious as a mail order monkey. The doors were bolted from the inside. Knocked but nobody answered though I could smell dinner and knew they were inside sharing my portion. Tried to find an open window but even with the temperature still sweaty they had closed and locked the windows. I pounded and kicked the house, then climbed the young maple to get on the roof but the chimney was only for the furnace and not a fireplace. I had snuck in and out my bedroom window for years but it was locked and had a note taped on the inside that read go away.

One of the older neighbors must've have noticed my siege and called the police because a patrol car pulled into the driveway at an angle that pointed the grill directly at me where I stood on the lawn so if I ran it would run me over. I put up my hands and told them it was okay, that I lived there. One told me to stay where I was while the other rang the doorbell then knocked too. The door cracked open and after a quick conversation it opened wider and the officer waved me over and waved his partner back to the cruiser. My dad stepped out and waved me inside, telling me that evidently it was illegal for them to kick me out, for thirty days anyway.

I still was evicted officially and had one month to change their minds, maybe find a mate and a job to become better company, a desirable breeding member to advance the family unit, but that weekend they got rid of my room. Spent most of a day prowling around just to be away from the house, kind of looking for work but mostly studying window displays for stuff I'd like to have, same as at the beach desiring local girl graduates summering before going away to college, maybe never to return. Opened the door to my room and the roof and walls were gone.

The framing studs that held the windows stood like weird art but only the wood flooring was left, tan worn sections at the door and center but darker toward the edges, a pattern that reminded me of a grub when I was younger. Dad snuck up behind to ask me what I thought about the renovation, adding a new wing to the house for relatives to stay at Christmas. Told him that it was weird. He said that he and mom had pretended to be normal for my sake, but that they secretly were peculiar and didn't need to hide it any longer.

Without a room I didn't live there anymore. My stuff was boxed and stacked along one side of the garage, leaving no space for me even to sleep on the floor when the car was parked inside. There was no basement because the house itself had been moved by the previous owners onto a lot-sized yard bought from the previous neighbors but for some reason they preferred the front of the house to face east which caused the front door to open toward the other neighbor's yard, so since we moved we had been living sideways. The new construction would include a new entrance that fronted the street. With me gone the home would be properly adjusted.

As my mind toured the rest of the house looking for a space to squat in legally, dad began singing an old country song. It was to inhibit any further conversation. They raised me not to be rude and he knew I wouldn't interrupt, waiting for the end of the song. The only other time I remembered him singing when not in church was during a feud with the neighbors behind us, though that meant they were on the opposite side of the house than the end with my room toward the street. An old elm had grown into the corner of the shed that we used for a garage that came with the property, reached by a long driveway that passed the length of our house. It hung menacingly over that neighbor's fence and when they hired a tree company to prune those branches the weight shifted back onto the shed, turning the rectangular opening into a rhombus. It was Christmastime so he had us go around the block to carol them with several long and slow holiday favorites, horribly sung. They stood in the cold doorway with rictus smiles while my father sang loudest and worst. They were too polite to interrupt.

Now the car was in the leaning garage past our sideways house so it couldn't be used as my living space. He rarely parked there because of a hose or bike in the way, and even in the winter he'd have to wait for me to shovel the drive, but until I was gone he would use it every night. Squeezed past the car to dig out a sleeping bag and camped out that night on the bedroom floor under the stars, waking up once for a meal at the refrigerator then again to use the bathroom. In the morning woke up a third time to a tapping sound and when I tried the door to use the bathroom discovered it had been nailed shut. Peed in the privacy between the lilac bushes and went back to the garage to pack some of my stuff.

CHAPTER TWO

In Pummern my great grandfather Yanitch went into the forest with a borrowed axe. He had to fell a tree large enough for lumber to build a cabin in which he and his bride would begin their family. The local forests had been worked for hundreds of years through many generations so he had to spend at least one night sleeping among lesser trees to travel far enough to find a massive tree. The larger the tree, the longer the trip, the bigger the cabin, the better the man. The distant old growth forest still had an occasional wildman, a Pummernian who hadn't finished the task so was ashamed to return and breed, a failed breeder gone hairy.

When a successful man returned, the men of the village would follow him back to the fallen tree, reduce it to lumber then haul it home, the entire process fueled by oak kegs of warm beer, the empties left behind to make room for the fresh cut beams, and one only partially emptied in payment to the wildman for continuing diminishment of his new lonely home.

The marriage ceremony occurred atop the platform of stacked wood the first morning after the men's return, hangovers the source of the humble solemnity, and by nightfall there was enough of a building to house the honeymoon couple.

Staring at the clothes and books piled in the driveway, too much for one person to carry, and wondering which friend might allow me to stay with them, I decided it was best to get out of town. My grandfather told me an old Pummernian saying: in a dump the top rat eats garbage, in a castle even the lowest rat eats cake. It would not be to my advantage competing with laborers for a local smoky girl, even if my leaving meant becoming the distant wild man.

After moving the pile back into the garage, found my canvas backpack and stuffed a few things into it. Had a used car picked out, but buying it would use all my cash. My old paperboy bicycle was up in the crossbeams, rusty and flat tired. Chose eating over driving or riding and walked away, eager to meet reality but unready if the world was not like books or movies. Idle hours alone with a radio smaller than a sandwich was no preparation either. It didn't take up much room in my pack, but also did not teach me how to shake an ironsmith's hand beneath the ringing church bell to know the secrets of powerful men, or which season to bury a fat lady carved from soapstone in the cornfield to grow another inch taller. I envied island boys diving from trees with their feet tied to vines, and the jungle boys piercing themselves with bamboo while passing a jug of fermented goat blood.

Our local ritual was sneaking out to swim at midnight, diving off the rounded tops of old wooden pylons that used to support a dock for homegrown boats made in a nearby shipbuilder's lot that now was a tall stack of apartments for the elderly, many who had worked in the textile factory on the next lot but it also had been shut down then torn down to make space for a park with an expensive sculpture of wind and water next to a wooden bench that cost more money than all the factory survivors together had. Those old boats were lake buses with cheap pine plank benches that toured the scenic waterways by day and smuggled liquor at night, for which much of their pay went.

Older kids knew of tides and which old post to jump from, choosing nights when the water was high. I jumped from a wrong stump between waves on the wrong night and unexpectedly hit the lakebed, jolting my spine that gave me a pain, which forced me to walk with a stoop. After the pain left I kept the walk, having become used to looking at my feet and the ground. In high school lifting my head to view the wide horizon made me suddenly dizzy, so other kids mimicked my walk when I passed, grunting like something primitive. I learned that the ravines divided the town into sections and worked as short cuts, so I traveled them to avoid attention.

With the transistor radio playing muffled music out of my pack I jumped off the dead end of our street and followed a worn path that angled down the hillside. We called it an indian trail though it came out of the trees conveniently at the factory entrance below and probably had been a short cut for workers in the neighborhood before the steel barrier and yellow diamond shaped sign were installed. Before there was a town the entire area had been wooded, not an indian village, but the settlers from the old country found the river that fed the giant lake. They drove out any local wild men then used axes to turn the trees sideways for shelter. The streets made a crossword puzzle pattern around the ravines, the town an unburied time capsule from the 'forties and 'fifties. By leaving it I eventually would enter the future. Though the fashion and music of the 'sixties were seen and heard, it wasn't until the 'seventies that hippies were common enough not to get beat up and given alleyway haircuts by street barbers.

Past the factory I crossed the bottomland park with custom-made giant toys. Same as with the lack of seatbelts, the giant swing-set dared us to survive both it and the towering slide next to it. They were taller than the trees around them. The newly planted trees were better protected than kids, tethered to stakes all around like a captured beast, automobile tires around their bases as bumper guards against groundskeeper Rudy's primitive riding mower that was a small tractor difficult to steer pulling a row of push-mowers with the handles removed.

One afternoon he had begun mowing the first patch across the center of park lawn vast as a prairie then stopped, sitting unmoving for so long that we followed the cut path to the back of his grass-eating machine and called out in our elfish voices if he was alright. He turned to tell us that Jack Benny had died, and that he didn't know what was going to happen. About what, we asked. He wondered aloud, who will they get now? A part of his world was gone with nothing to replace it.

Rudy was at work before the park opened each summer morning dressed for whatever weather would arrive that afternoon, a walking forecast. He would be laughed at in his yellow raincoat and rain hat under the morning sunshine, but later that day we'd huddle out of the rain in the crowded shelter, watching him continue working across the park. When it didn't rain he set out giant sprinklers that shot fire hose streams of water. It looked fun to run through but knocked us over and left bruises, the spanking mechanism bringing it back to attack again.

Thunderstorms flooded large sections, the water flowing across the road to connect park and river. Catfish crawled through the two-inch deep waterway following some instinct for adventure. They became stranded in puddles that lasted for days in the outfield of the softball diamond until one morning there was nothing but dew to keep them alive for too short a time to learn to walk. By the time of the late morning softball game they were frozen in mid crawl, curved to one side or the other and the outfielders had to watch where they stepped so they didn't get fish guts and scales on the bottom of their Red Ball Jets. Stepping on one burst the lungs with a pop that stopped the game because the other kids could not help themselves against the reflexive laughter caused by any disgusting sound.

One time the weather cooled suddenly and a cloud floated up out of the puddle area and sat just above the ground as if fallen from a picture book. When I got close to taste it and try to climb it like a pile of cotton candy there was only fog and I got my shoes wet, which got me in trouble because we were visiting a relative that evening and I had outgrown my school shoes and had to sit on the front steps while my parents visited.

The toys looked normal from the road but only when you walked up to them and under them could you see they were giant, twice the size of the same swings and slides of other parks. There were big kids who had outgrown playing on them properly, like Rex Ronco, but he would climb the support poles and hang by the backs of his knees from the high crossbar. He said that a family with big heads owned the land when it was still mostly swamp. They were part indian and all of them huge. When they sold the land to the town to be drained for the park, the toys were built especially for all the kids in that family and it was a large family. For the first years if any big-skulled family kids were around they wouldn't let anyone else on the swings or slide unless you brought something to eat, or some beach glass, or did a painful stunt they invented.

I never had seen one of the rumored family members but by the time I was a kid Rex had taken over. He was too old to waste all day everyday at the park, but bullying us made it worth showing up occasionally when bored of hurting cats or stealing from unlocked garages. When he got in trouble his dad shaved his head as punishment, which happened so often it constantly looked like a man's chin with five o'clock shadow. Then one day the police came to the park looking for him so he escaped up the hillside through the wild blackcap bushes and hid in an old lady's garage, bleeding from scratches. After an hour of the pain getting worse, throbbing with each heartbeat, he gave himself up and they had to take him to the hospital before jail. Then he went into the army, the only guy who wasn't humbled by the army barber's buzz cut. My haircuts only seemed like punishment because mom gave them to me to save money even though she didn't know how.

Thick approaching weather caused static from my little radio though the sun was out, and the park was open as I crossed it, a summer daycare, the utility building staffed with a supervisor and assistants to hand out sports equipment and games to another generation of little kids, but Rudy was gone, replaced by a rotation of city workers. The giant swings in action squealed over the dry waves sound of cottonwood leaves busy in a high breeze.

The fat trees had been huge back when the big heads first found a dry spot to settle on, the levels of the lake and reach of swamp in decline ever since the flood at the end of the ice age. The steely groan went up a half note as the swing swung forward then dropped back again as it returned, a factory sound that would prepare many for a working life later at a lathe or on an assembly line.

A guy my age was pushing a little girl so high it probably would be considered child endangerment in the future and why the swings eventually were taken down. She swung until her back was parallel with the ground. Swinging like that gave the swinger a flying gut feeling at that moment of weightlessness, the chain losing some of its tension so there was a second of freefall until your weight pulled the chains taught again. I got the feeling in my gut just watching, the girl producing a tiny squeal in harmony to the metal shriek above her, thrilled to flirt with danger.

When the girls would swing the boys stood directly in front, our noses inches from their pumping feet, pretending to do it as a test of bravery but we were peeking under their skirts, back when girls played in skirts, and though there was nothing to see the thrill of getting away with something was real. The guy gave me a nod as if he knew what I had been looking at years ago, so I stopped thinking about it even innocently in general. I looked around instead to see if there were a sign yet to warn kids off the poles or against swinging so high they might bump the moon, but it was still play hard at your own risk.

Hey, Neat, the guy said. It was somebody I had known from school, just hairier. He always called me Neat, short for neato keen because that was his insult first time we me because he didn't like the look of me and hurt me. Enough, he asked? Thought that was meant for me, something he used to say when knocking me around. That single question word had always been rhetorical, though. He never stopped until he had enough. But he had been talking to the girl.

He stopped pushing and when her pendulum motion allowed it safely, she jumped off at the forward end of the swoop, the long chains slackening with a rattling and clacking noise. Thanks, Daddy, she said and ran over to rock herself on the toy elephant mounted on a spring. Even in school he was hairy in a plaid shirt and looked like a lumberjack. When I wore plaid it looked like big pajamas. Hey, Steve, I said and wow, you're a daddy. In my mind he was Stick, the guy who showed up late for school, a couple years late.

It was only second grade when his family moved to town but he would be that new kid to us the students who had gone through kindergarten and first grade together without him, long years and most of your life if you didn't remember much from when you toddled. And we already had two Steves, a Steve and a Stephen, so a third one made our minds uncomfortable with the change and confusion, but the teacher told us to call the original Steve Stevie because he was small and the stranger would take over as Steve. We didn't like it but hadn't learned to protest yet so just called Steve Steve in the hall or on the playground, avoiding calling either Steve by name during class time.

Besides stealing Steve's name we didn't like him because he ripped the little loops off the back of our shirts, the loops for hooks if you had trouble with hangers which most of us did. He called them fruit loops and us fruits if we had a surviving loop on any of our shirts. At first I called the third Steve Extra Steve but he became Stick when they paved the dirt parking lot with gravel, turning our playground into half an acre of hazard. After skinned knees and punctures in the heels of our hands we stood around carefully instead of playing tag or kick ball. A windstorm brought down a dead branch. Those of us who turned at the sound stared at it like it might be the beginning of something more exciting, a miracle maybe or the end of the world.

Extra Steve rushed over and picked it up and in my mind came an instant desire for that stick, with sadness for the missed opportunity to grab it first. It was long enough to make a whoosh sound as he swung it like a sword with both hands. I knew I could get it to make more noise if I had the chance. He swatted the fence pole and lost a piece off the end. It looked like great fun so I asked him for try. He held it out to me but when I opened my hand he swatted it, so I cried to the teacher who had been chasing a piece of paper caught in a little whirlwind. She opened her hand for the stick, and Extra Steve waited an extra moment

that gave us time to wonder if he'd crack her palm with it too, then he
handed it nicely to her and she flung it over the fence. I changed his
name to Stick, and after that I called every guy who was mean a stick.

After school there it still was, but the magic gone out of it. Slammed
it against a tree twice to break it into three pieces then threw the last
piece across the street into the opposite gutter. It had never been the
stick itself, just that somebody got it first and wouldn't share.

Stick held a grudge against my tattling and one future rainy evening
after he had dropped out of high school he stopped me at McDonald's
wanting to fight. I probably could have handled him because he was
drunk, but I had a puppet inside my coat to keep it dry and thought that
handing it to my friend to hold while I fought would give Stick an unfair
mental advantage, even if he couldn't make a list of one-letter words in
his condition. I shrugged him off and walked past him. He reached out
with his fist just enough to touch
my chin as if to wipe off a bit of food. My first punch, anticipated
almost as much as my first kiss and just as frightening and numbing. I
bounced off the trashcan to pretend I had been socked firmly but kept
walking toward the door. There was a flagpole in the mini lawn at the
front and the flag popped in the breeze sounding like one hand clapping
for the winner as I went inside and ate a sad burger. I was quick to cry
as a kid and tried to toughen myself by stepping on black pinching
beetles big as my thumb, but it felt bad so I apologized and stopped.
Remembering that splat of black shell and green guts though kept me
from tearing up over my fries.

That winter when we first had three Steves I got the finger of my
knit glove caught in my coat zipper and the teacher couldn't pull it loose
or unzip the zipper so she said we'd have to cut it off. I though she meant
the finger because it was still in the glove so I cried in front of the class.
Had to carry my lunchbox in one hand and my book bag in the other
so I couldn't put the one with the naked finger tip in my coat pocket. It
froze on the walk home and I felt like crying again but thought of the
car crash that time.

In the summer we weren't allowed in the park after the workers
went home because there would be guys like Stick hanging around,
dropping cigarette butts in the dirt beneath the giant toys. This is
my daughter he said as if it wasn't shocking that after being raised by
two monster parents he would rush into fatherhood. Maybe being
knocked around gave him the knowledge of how not to raise a kid
and he would parent by process of elimination. It seemed to have
taken the bully out of him anyway, not punching me in front of his
daughter. He was proud of her and of himself. Isn't she a doll, he said,
not expecting an answer.

How'd that happen, I asked, meaning how was it she didn't have
fangs or two heads from having a stick as dad with inherent monster
blood, but he took it literally and answered, you remember Arch don't
you. Vy Arches was a legend from the sand dunes and even I felt one
of her boobs once while another guy was feeling the other. Told him I
remembered her but didn't mention the memory. She dropped out of
high school, rumored to be pregnant. I was jealous at the gossip just
knowing some guy got lucky with her, thinking it was probably an older
guy raiding our generation, a mechanic with automotive stains on his
work shirt like scout badges. Didn't know if this was that kid and was
afraid to ask.

Told him it was great they got married, and he told me not yet, and
that he heard I had left town. Told him not yet but give me a minute.
I lifted my pack as evidence and he nodded slowly as if impressed,
or maybe just wondering if I had anything worth stealing in there.
But there's something I gotta do first, I told him, setting it down and
asking him to watch it, then climbed the ladder to the giant slide. It
was still nervously tall and I might have backed down if Stick hadn't
been there. My hipbones touched the sides and though I went over
the edge worrying I'd end up on my back with the wind knocked out
of me, instead I screeched to a stop at the hump in the middle, pants
legs crinkled up my calves exposing the white socks that were always
considered queer in grade school. Used my heels to pull myself to the

STUCK ON EARTH 27

bottom then shook my pants down around my ankles like a tv comedian shaking something wet down each leg.

He asked if I knew the tool factory over there by the river, and I asked if he meant where we broke out the windows. Nine years old and he told us it was okay to throw rocks through the windows, that the building was condemned. It wasn't. The police pulled up behind us as we were throwing so we couldn't even lie to them. They put us in a cell but didn't close the door, the old kind with actual bars. They asked us our names and phone numbers and again lying would have done no good. His dad told the cops to keep him but his mom eventually claimed him. I got spanked with my own little belt that went with my church clothes when I was six. It hung on a nail behind the basement door like a religious relic for penance.

He said that yeah, the Veeks turned it into a club and I bartend. C'mon down tonight before you head out and I'll buy you a beer. Live band, Twist and those guys from the Catholic school. A date with Stick, music, and who knows what immoralities might be included with the Veek brothers running the fun.

Shrugged and told him maybe, and he offered his hand. I shook it. If his kid were a boy, I thought, he'd be showing him how to kick my butt. An olive branch is also a stick and could be used to beat peace into a guy's head.

See ya, Sti … Steve, I told him and walked away past the second set of monkey bars and gave the red pump merry-go-round a push. Two kids would pump it into motion while the rest of us played Dropped-it, Got-it with a stick. Disrupted some honeybees working a patch of clover growing with the grass, then lurched up the sled hill where the squeal of the swing-set began again but faded away.

Before the hill met the street there was a path that went behind the houses above, one of them with a garden terrace with giant stalks of rhubarb I used to steal and cut into bites then salt and eat like popcorn while reading Heinlein. Pulled up a small stalk and bit a section out of the middle, the sour juice making glands in my jaws ache for a moment.

Tight-roped along the top of the concrete retaining wall while chewing the fibers like cud. To one side were staked tomato plants where my falling would mean impalement, and a patch of poison ivy on the other. It covered the ground and stretched from tree to tree, growing up their trunks with vines like green veins. The risky route took me to a hole in the steel wire hurricane fencing meant to keep kids from getting to the park down through private property and the ivy, but same as at school the fences had been bowed out from the tons of snow and frozen slush smashed into from the three months of winter street plowing. That created a space for us to slide beneath it down a convenient dirt trough scoured out over years by the butts of jeans from that repeated action. With a little more effort I crawled up it, climbing out of my childhood, and crossed the street toward the alley behind the library.

CHAPTER THREE

Instead of an allowance my dad gave me a ride to the library and back every other Saturday. Walking there was easy but coming home with a stack of books was work, big kids thinking that knocking them to the ground was as much fun as stealing their parents' cigarettes. Had a paper route and mowed lawns to earn enough for comics and magazines but not the kind of books the library loaned out, especially all I could carry. The stuff they forced on us in school almost ruined reading for me, another chore, but I skipped school to sneak to the library. If the church had been filled with thousands of books I would've gone to extra services, but it had that one book and a hymnal. Be ever learning, my grandma told me, sounding old world wise though it came suspiciously soon after she put down her Reader's Digest.

When I had only a children's library card I snuck up into the adult section pretending to search for my parents, wandering lost down deep and high dewey-decimalled aisles that leaned in over me, considering whether I was worth being crushed with good words. Up there out of my reach was probably pornography and books of curses, maybe one on how to change water into gasoline, or something well illustrated about what other kids did during that hour we church children sat in pews waiting for the gorilla, or something more wonderful that never arrived.

The closest thing to those and luckily on a low shelf was one that showed how Houdini did his trick escapes, the milk can, the water torture cell, and his metamorphosis. Didn't even have to look up that word because I received an insect guide for my birthday years before. I stuck the magic book down my pants and smuggled it back to the children's desk then checked it out on my kid card. No alarms sounded so the next trip I smuggled down an art book with nude paintings. It didn't work any more than the medical volume that had photographs of naked female patients with assorted conditions, and also depicted several stages of pregnancy.

The book checker outer asked where I had gotten it and I pointed toward the table with oversized books open and standing upright in a display of distractions for those who liked only looking at pictures. Kids would grab one for illustrations of elves or puppies in clothes only to be lured into having to look at text integrated into the artwork, tricked into reading. But I remembered just looking at the pictures until my first Batman comic, finally needing to know the story.

She concluded aloud that a parent must have set it down there and forgotten it. I soon received my adult library card and checked it out anyway, earning access to Latin words and almost sexy clinical photographs. In high school I visited the downtown bookstore to browse the expensive bestsellers, read a few pages to rate their crappiness on a one to ten scale, then continued to the library and stand before the aisles as if in a grocery store and starving, hungrily thinking that all this is free.

Crossed the library lawn with card in wallet. Turned off the radio in my pack thinking that I could check out an atlas and mail it back when I reached my destination. Went past the keep off the grass sign to peek in the window, not worried about a security guard because there is no reason to guard free knowledge.

The older library lady who went to our church could've scared me away, the same way she used to scowl my wandering eyes back toward the pastor during his sermon. I had been appreciating the carved wooden beams arcing gratuitously toward heaven, my head against the wooden back of the pew, and if I rolled my eyes up could see the upside-down faces of the congregation behind me. It looked like she was smiling until I turned around with my head right side up. Every service after I would glance back and she was still giving me that face forward or go to hell look. The gorilla could have been sitting behind her and I never would've noticed.

While flipping the pages of a movie book, looking for scandalous pictures of nineteen-twenties actresses before the decency code was passed, found a grocery receipt used as a bookmark. It was dated from years earlier and only a few days after the check-out stamp on the fly leaf in the front of the book. Nobody had checked the book out since. The reader had stopped reading sixty-two pages in and may have stopped to eat some of the stuff rung up, eleven dollars and twelve cents worth. I randomly began pulling books and flipping through them in a search for other bookmarks. Most had a couple dog-eared folded corners but soon I had a little pile of torn pieces of notebook paper and newsprint, a small Kleenex. Also found an actual bookmark printed with a calendar of events at the library for the previous winter, a discussion group, a guest speaker and other activities appropriate for active but lonely minds. There were notes, some on the subject of the book but others were reminders, lists, doodles, seemingly random numbers and vague phrases but no confessions.

A librarian saw me speed-searching one book after another as if not only had I forgotten something in a book, but had forgotten even what book it was, like maybe I had read all of them, which would have been weird because I happened to be going through the sewing and knitting section.

She did the skinny walk they learn from passing others regularly in an aisle only wide enough for one and a half people, like a flight attendant or shoppers at the mini market.

In school she had been two grades ahead of me, and I remembered her completely different in those wide hallways wearing a sweater vest that made her breasts look bigger than when she wore only a blouse. She stopped to whisper that she knew what I was doing. Evidently finding out of place things was a library normality same as dry cleaners searching the pockets of evening wear, everybody looking for dollar bills or bank robbery plans or maps to hidden treasure. There was coffee on her breath and she wasn't wearing a sweater vest so I gave up trying to think of something to say, just nodded knowingly for being let in on a world secret and returned the crochet guide back to the space that made the shelf look like it had a missing tooth.

Browsed some of the movie books that I had checked out. Noticed even as a kid that most gorilla suits were originally made for some kind of drama, but always ended up later in comedies where the lack of realism worked as if they were meant for funny stuff. That's when I decided it was time to make my own, to become funny and popular.

That's where you were conceived, I said to the suit using up most of the space in my pack, then walked downtown. There was a bar and grill that hadn't been there more than fifty years, just run down enough to look like maybe it had, like a historic gathering place of founding drunkards. Stopped to eat one of their famous burgers, thinking the name was redundant because burgers were already well known before the place was built. It wasn't as if their burgers had gone to the moon or starred in a film. Even Big Macs were more famous than a Famous Burger, or maybe infamous for not being good for you according to my parents, but they were beef, bread and salad same as my mom's home cooked meals except you could hold it in your hand.

When I told that to Mom she broke down, admitting she was jealous I would choose a stranger's food over her hard work on a plate, making me guilty. She cheered me up by making burgers and fries as good as McDonalds that caused me to wonder if she hadn't snuck away to the drive through, but there were potato peelings in the sink so I didn't complain that it was still more fun to eat with friends and strangers than at home with the family. Didn't want her to start being amusing at meals, whatever that might involve.

When a McDonalds finally opened on the business strip in south town it felt like our city had crawled through the television screen and finally entered the modern world. Biting into the Famous Burger was like cheating on a girlfriend but I got over it and looked out of the side of my eye at Olie who sat at the bar every day, who had never eaten at McDonalds. He had a free newspaper, a bottomless mug of draft beer, and his choice of channels on the little tv mounted up in a corner. That little turn up to the left in his neck had become a permanent condition causing him to walk crooked out of the bar more than the amount of beer. One day there would be a report of his passing away on that stool, elbow on the bar with his twisted head resting in the crook. Even the mortician wouldn't be able to straighten him for the viewing, the body posed as if turning away from the mourners as if he couldn't be bothered with his own funeral.

Stood next to him to pay my tab. His smile was a canoe, no teeth showing. I learned to walk and talk like a normal person at home, but there were variations for school and the street either to go unnoticed or to attract attention, but there was another way to walk in a saloon. If you were used to seeing me walking across the living room for the tv guide you might not recognize me crossing the floor of the bar, something like an orangutan doing an imitation of John Wayne, staying off the toes and keeping the hands below the waist.

People may not want to pick on you but if you smile idiotically and move around like a balloon twister at a kids' party they sometimes feel forced to do something. Found out the hard way when I turned eighteen, the drinking age back then. Was given sips of beer when I grew up and liked the taste so sometimes bought the non-alcohol beer called Zing and drank it with Suzy-Q's, the cakes with whipped lard in the center. When friends offered to buy me my first legal drink we claimed a booth, skipped the famous food and chugged a schooner of Blatz.

Three guys hunched over drinks at the bar were trying to forget the last eight-plus hours of what the unemployed called good factory work.

Something about us bothered them, maybe because we were teenagers who never had paid rent and didn't know what it was like to owe rent and not have it. Maybe it was because we smelled like pimple cream and chocolate milk instead of assembly line and dead hopes. As we laughed in unison they took turns looking over their shoulders with that church lady's glare. Got up for the bathroom and smiled at them, tiptoeing past with my hands against my chest. One of them shoved me along from the back so hard I got a little whiplash in my neck, even hearing it pop like a big knuckle. He said if I didn't wipe that stupid face off my grin he'd do it for me. I wiped it off.

Knowing better these couple years later I put on a tired face and eased away from the bar as if something pained me below, hip, knee or groin. Olie and others nodded in sympathy. Had an urge to take that stool at the end of the bar and order a beer. Later I could meet up with Stick then find a good factory job, maybe get a younger girl pregnant and start paying rent. But that would put me in line of eventually replacing Olie. He lifted a finger as if to wave and I nodded back and told him about going to California. He said he thought I'd left a long time ago.

The street was hot so I purposely went the wrong direction, taking a cooler route to the lake. At that section of town you could drop a marble on the road and it would slowly roll in the direction of the water. The foundations of houses slipped that way one thirty-second of an inch each year, leaving the structures imperceptibly rhomboidal as if an imaginary neighbor had cut the branch off an invisible elm. Walked past a fence with a knothole knocked out where a dog's nose filled the gap, sniffing me pass its world, smelling my slight fear at being a stray. The rule for playing outside as a kid was staying within shouting distance to hear mom call me home. Already I was too far, outside that fence and no longer sniffing at the world through a hole.

Other paperboys used the little green rubber bands supplied by the distributor to bind each paper into a tight throw-able bundle, but that added half an hour to delivery time. I kept the rubber bands but looped them together into a chain that stretched half a block from our house.

That's what leaving felt like, stretching to the point of breaking, the tension growing until it either would pull me back like a paddleball or snap. I felt the snap like a whip cracking me on the butt, hyah giddup.

As the heat entered their houses through osmosis the porch people popped out onto their rockers and gliders to get what little breeze the back and forth motion simulated, the equipment sawing and creaking along with grasshopper and cicada noise, a late summertime street orchestra. A person nodded and another waved, knowing me from delivering their papers, but one old lady stared because I climbed her crab apple tree to steal the sour fruit, throwing apples to kids waiting in the alley. The fruit never turned completely from green to red, just in one spot as if a cheek were blushing. We assumed that too much of them had made her similarly hard and sour, disapproving of humans in general. She already was old the first time I saw her but over twenty years her skin turned chicken-foot yellow and her hair white as an Eskimo's butt. Her head shook up and down a little as she stared making me wonder if she knew I had been kicked out and was nodding to say could've told you so.

I pictured the word embarrassed in my mind as am-bare-assed, turning quickly at the corner onto the street that spanned the railroad tracks. Dropped from public view down over the side. The tracks paralleled the shore all the way to Chicago so I walked along the rails where the humidity was thick as if I were walking in a strange variation of water. It was muggy enough to make mosquitoes itch and fish were swimming well above the surface of the lake. Felt like something in a terrarium as I turned to look back up at sudden sounds of traffic. An old farm truck snored its way sleepily up the hill followed by a growling motorcycle angry at slowness.

Walking the crossties like stepping stones I remembered seeing a train derail but never had told anyone in case they might blame me. Was sitting in the long Johnson grass waiting to throw a few rocks at the train in an attempt to get one through the gap of the sliding doors left open by hobos. An older guy came along the tracks and stopped to drag a hunk of wood across the rails, a gray and splintered old weathered crossbeam for power lines that had been taken off the pole and replaced. I sat still as a statue while he walked past and up onto the street the way I had just come down. He must've heard the train coming but didn't look back as it crawled around the bend, chunk-chunking low and heavy before it could throttle up on the straight away. The front end of the engine bumped up onto the lumber rolling it apart into giant splinters, but the wood held together long enough for the wheels of the train to leave the iron and when they came back down they missed the rails. The engine dug into sand and gravel as if plowing a row in a field. The metal yelled and screeched followed by ground shaking thuds as cars behind buckled into a zigzag of major damage. They tipped but didn't fall over, just crunched into each other as the last of them caught up with the accident. I crawled up the bluff and through somebody's yard then went to the corner where a few others were rushing as if they were in a Godzilla movie. The derailer-guy was not among them.

Delivered the next day's paper with the headline about it, reading the front-page article during the short time between houses. Nobody was damaged but the dollar amount was large enough to be beyond a boy's understanding, just a big number. Every time I saw the guy who did it, in the street or at church, I imagined him locked behind bars instead, wondering if he'd give me money not to tell on him but also afraid he'd just kill me. Maybe he had seen me throwing rocks before and knew I was in the weeds, waiting for me to make a move, then would turn me in as the derailer or demand money and start me on a life of burglary and mugging. I never told anyone.

It happened not far from the shoreline amusement park that used to pull tourists to the town. The train crash was a month before it closed. That last day of the park we rode the roller coaster free five times in a row. It felt and sounded as if it were falling apart as the seven linked coaster cars ratcheted up that first hill, the high curve seen from downtown that created the momentum for all the rolling and coasting, sounding like my great uncle rattling those yellowed false teeth in his mouth before taking them out to bite at me in a weird act of puppetry. The coaster was built of wood and had become rickety, each run more noisy and shaky, turns wider and looser, the thrill of the extra gravities gone but replaced by a dangerous excitement over our chance of hurtling beyond its built-in safety features. It didn't crash then or for later other free riders but fell apart during winter storms, looking like the remains of a sea monster washed ashore. After that it existed only on postcards, a new version of fossil evidence.

The funhouse was made of wood same as the carousel horses and the kiddie boats and most of the ferris wheel, crisscrossed with a geometry test of struts and braces. Even the mechanical clown out front was carved oak

with a wooden mocking laugh as you entered, forced to stumble drunkenly across the buckling wooden teeter-totter walkway. Inside was an upside down plate made of wood that simply spun and all you had to do was hold on but without anything to hold except other slipping people. The person at the center didn't have a chance, too many slippers grabbing an elbow, foot or bellbottom. A wooden barrel tumbled paying guests. A pit of spinning wood pinned them to its walls. Wooden stairs led me up to the start of a wooden slide where you could almost touch the wooden ceiling, it's waxed wood waves held together by smoothed over pegs and dovetail joints, everything hand-hewn at the beginning of the twentieth century by men with mahogany pirate legs and George Washington teeth who ate sawdust sandwiches washed down with root and bark beer.

There were pictures on the library walls of the park when it opened, people in silent movie swimsuits along the boardwalk that still smelled of shavings and varnish. The sawyers had toppled old growth trees too big for Ojibwe axe blades of chert and flint, the lumber hauled in wagons drawn by imported European farm horses that snorted at model A Fords. Trees that had lived for centuries fearing only forest fire were reduced to planks menaced by waves, tides and blowing sand, in the end taken by time. Time was finished with the amusement park, which bothered me so my mind and I wandered away along the beach. Walking on it was exercise enough to show up in bad dreams about trying to run away from villains and wild animals.

The beach was dotted with cig butts, all parks doubling as ashtrays back when smoking was allowed everywhere. Dad made a sandbox for us under the back porch, shoveling the trunk of his old car full of sand from that section of beach but it instantly became the cat's poop box instead. The surf was light and made a hushing sound as if it wanted my feet to stop squeaking against the sand, then it sighed with relief where the sand ran out at the base of the clay cliffs and I was sliding as much as walking. A sign warned against trespassing past that point but the shore had been lost to the rising level of the lake over ten years, the private beach now part of Atlantis.

There were some kind of willows growing sideways out of the mostly clay bluff, the tips of the branches hanging down to touch the water as if fishing or testing the temperature. I used their trunks for footholds and climbed the greasy gray wall, grabbing tufts of grass with my free hand, never testing any with my full weight, knowing they sometimes came out by the roots jokingly to watch me slide and fall back down.

Crested the mucky bank on one hand and my knees, back in the world like a three-legged primate scuttling through the weeds onto a groomed tree lawn then crossing it to reach the lakeshore road. For all that time and effort, had traveled so little distance that my Dad was leaving the edge of our neighborhood on an outbound errand. Though I was walking in the same direction he didn't stop to offer me a ride, but saw me because he waved. A few miles later he passed me on his return, nodding proudly that I was well on my way gone.

Was tempted to knock on doors and ask for a ride, also needing a bathroom, but wasn't comfortable stinking up a charitable stranger's life even a little. Went into a stretch of woods that surrounded a scenic look out area and played squat tag. Never saw it move but when I finished with some wide leaves as toilet paper the sun was setting on the lake, shining through the maples, light scattered into green gold watery sparkles around the nervous fluttering leaves. This is how I will travel, slow like the sun, so slowly that when I cross a border nothing is strange because I will have acclimated everything by inches, absorbing the changing customs and language casually, passively. That is how I will age, maturing so slowly it will be painless.

With the sun sunk into the lake the scenery became evenly lit in those minutes before dark as if it were all indoors and artificial like a live size movie set of the world. That and the quiet, the day bugs' shift over and night bugs' not yet begun. It smelled like the Congo might smell, delicious, almost everything edible, maybe because I was hungry. My stomach growled and I almost could hear words in the gassy gurgle, something that would make sense if I listened more carefully, the way an English or Irish person seems to speak gibberish until you catch on to the accent. A large burp erupted, the famous burger doing the talking instead, sounding like something living low to wet ground, something homeless unless there was a rock to lie on.

After only moments alone in the dark the moon peeked over the roofline across the road, visible through the trees. Its edge had been nibbled away by something in the sky over that part of the world. The moon is a mirror so the sun can see what we're doing at night, reflecting lovers and burglars who think they get away with things. That meant the sun could see me, comfort against the night's darkening that turns being alone into being lonely. Five or six blocks toward the river Stick's invitation for free beer and live music was waiting, and I had three hundred dollars evenly distributed among my shoes and several pockets so didn't have to sleep in the woods, but despite my physical present presence, finally I was leaving town.

Sat against the lean of a tree and listened to the dark, prepared for sleepless hours of mosquito slapping and regrettable choices, but fell hard and quickly to sleep. Woke only hours later feeling good. Maybe beds were too restful, undermining the need for actual sleep. Wondered how many ancestors had soft warm beds or did they curl up on smooth

stones or in the crotch of a sweet gum tree. That short piece of sleep
was the best since I'd been off the nipple, or off the thumb anyway, the
patch of woods making me doubt the progress of walls.

I didn't like indoor plants, never knowing what they were thinking
since that was all they could do, sit still and brood about growing too
slowly for the human eye, wanting to stretch and sprout to music,
show what they were like inside. Mom had exotic tropical things with
big waxy leaves in terra cotta pots that sat on decorative plant stands
made of curlicued iron footstools maybe forged by elves, similar to
grandma's sewing machine treadle. It was an early model mechanical
sewing machine that folded up from inside a wooden cabinet, doubling
as a simple table when closed. Grandma used that also as a plant stand.
On it she kept a violet, geranium and pepper plant which one season
bore red fang shaped fruit that I couldn't resist fingering, then I must
have touched my eyes for some reason because suddenly I was blind
and crying with pain. She washed my out my eyes with water and that
began my suspicions about houseplants. The plants that surrounded
me outside seemed friendly, but if someone were to pot them then drag
them inside of four flat walls with pictures hung of outdoor scenery for
cruel insult, then others' eyes might burn.

Scratching my bug bites with one hand I peed in the out of the way
place I had pooped before sleeping, thinking of thousands of people
doing the same thing every morning before history. Some people who
lived outside, before inside even had been invented, would pick random
spots for that necessity but then some agreed all to go in the same area,
a single place they avoided so they wouldn't walk unknowingly barefoot
across someone else's mess. Others didn't care, same as now.

The pee flowed downhill like a marble, my personal saltwater
tributary. Grandma said that every river was the same size, two sides
wide. Locals were proud of the local water whether it was the lake, the
river, the ponds and creeks, or just swamp, all the wetness. It created
changing skies from blue to thunder cloud and rainy gray within
minutes. It created talk about the weather, especially for whatever

wasn't happening at the moment. Hope we get some rain soon. Where's that blue sky already? Think it'll freeze? This heat's gotta break. Looks like snow. Sat down again and dozed a few times until dawn when the best weather talkers also got out of bed, thickening the air with their got to go to work sighs. Little wonder the humidity.

I stretched, looking up with the motion to discover late ripened cherries. Couldn't reach them from the ground so shinnied up the leaning tree trunk that I had slept against and bellied out lizard-like on a thick enough branch, biting the fruits off the stems without using my hands, temporarily arboreal and wishing I had a tail, another appendage to hold the branch. When the cherries in reach were gone I became still, part of the branch, half plant half animal, a new genus though raised by humans. Lying front down with my knees squeezing the branch gave me an erection so I carefully slid to the ground and feeling atavistic smelled my way back to pavement.

Wind blew off the lake, lonely in its travels, which made it pull at everything to come along and keep it company. Fallen leaves crossed the road together like kids on a field trip. A wind chime struggled to hold onto its eye screw ringing furiously in alarm. It stirred a memory of a farmer relative who fought a tornado. He saved his life by holding on with his feet anchored sideways between the spaces in the porch railing, but it took his shirt and pulled out much of his hair. He felt lucky to survive and never complained about his bald spots, just took to wearing a hat. I let the weather take me and walked with the wind.

CHAPTER FOUR

Miles south of downtown along the lakeshore road there was a phone booth for broken down drivers and me. Dialed the number for time of day. It was a party line so if you spoke then anybody else listening for the time of day could hear you and chat back if they had the time. I told anybody who might be on the line that I was leaving town. A female voice asked if it was me. She didn't recognize my voice but she recognized that line. I'd been using it in place of conversation for years. She told me she thought I had already left which explained why I felt invisible all summer, hidden behind my imaginary exit. Who is this, I asked, erection returning. There was no answer so I said hello-hello, hoping she was thinking of inviting me over, her or anybody, but a car pulled up outside so I said bye and hung up to free the booth to anybody else walking out of town. It was my mom.

She said that Dad had waited until breakfast to tell her that I was wandering around out this way, and if I wanted a ride. Back home, I asked but she said no, somewhere not so close to back home, she didn't want the neighbors to see me homeless. I declined the ride but accepted a thermos she handed out while asking where I had slept. Outside, I told her. Looks like it, she said shaking her head, the seat of your pants is all dirty. I used my free hand to brush away what I could, puffs of brown cloud behind me. She hoped I had packed clean clothes, pointing to my pack still inside the booth. What I packed is clean, I told her. Good luck out there, she said with a sad smile, and call once in a while. I promised and waved as she did a five-point turn on the shoulder to get the car facing the way she came, then drove away almost hitting a tree ten feet from the pavement. I hoped she would catch up with me again at mealtimes for as long as I was in reasonable driving range.

When she was out of sight I sat on my pack in the shade and opened the thermos filled with a big puddle of soup. Her soup was so thick that it was soup only because she served it in a bowl with a spoon, but it was more like chicken and vegetables in gravy. Hadn't packed any utensils so drank it out of the cup using my finger to help it pour. Wouldn't have packed a spoon anyway, just taken the yellow handled spatula for sentimental reasons and maybe the steel nutcracker with knurled handles because I liked holding it, but didn't want to travel with a bunch of extra emotion. Finished the soup but was stuck with the thermos. Set it on the triangular shelf inside the booth. The next person to call from there would have something interesting to talk about. Years ahead I looked through Mom's photo album and saw this was the year that I was replaced in pictures by successful gardens, holiday meals, lonely Christmas trees and completed 5,000-piece puzzles on the old card table.

When I was eight or nine and she was busy making supper she sent me to the neighborhood corner store for milk and cigarettes with a permission note for the smokes. On my bike I didn't have to fear strangers or big kids, maneuvering from street to sidewalk to alley, weaving up and down driveways, jumping curbs at the perimeter of every block because the only wheelchair ramp in existence was at the new wing of the hospital. Same as carrying luggage before it had wheels, people eased wheelchairs up and down the stairs one step at a time. Also there was no annoying beeping when heavy equipment backed up. I rode into construction happening on a section of street, bricks plowed up and front-loaded onto a heavy-duty dump truck then replaced by concrete. Back tracking was too abstract for me at that age so I tried to sneak between two monsters of equipment, but the bike became stuck in the exposed layer of sand from under the bricks and the front loader backed over my front wheel. I was thrown off to the side and rolled to keep from being squashed by the tire with treads like factory gears. One of the other workers shouted to the driver to stop and the crew rushed over to make certain I wasn't injured, though I expected them to kick me around for getting in the way.

Had to walk the rest of the way to the store, then dragged the bike with one hand while carrying the paper sack in the other, stopping every twenty feet to rest and switch arms. My parents said I'd have to pay for the repairs, which began my walking the paper route. But I also had walked to school, the beach, to little league, across town to houses of school friends along this road, giving me a daunting estimate of how far I had to go so I began running.

I put the pack properly on my back and as my legs stretched I picked up speed, the soup sloshing in my gut and making me burp but it felt good, like traveling. Cars passed and at first I had been self-conscious of being seen during my humble exit, but soon I stopped seeing them, barely noticing when a joker honked a horn, so when the police siren bleeped I didn't look back and kept running. Then it blared for a couple cycles directly behind me, almost scaring me into the ditch. I stopped and a male officer got out of the car, asking me why I hadn't stopped the first time he used the siren. Told him I didn't think it was meant for me, then he asked where I was going in such a hurry and I answered that I didn't think I was going more then ten miles an hour, well under the speed limit. He asked what was in the pack and I told him it was just my stuff and he asked to take a look. Knowing what was in there and trying to remember anything about search warrants from tv shows, I hesitated. The guilty pause prompted him to take off his sunglasses then lean in and down at me to stare eye to eye, being much taller, and tell me that there had been some break-ins at summer beach houses in the area. I dropped my shoulders to let the pack slide down my back and swung it around to unzip it and offer the contents.

When he pulled my gorilla suit out to let it hang from his outstretched arm many people were going to work at the same place at the same time so the red light in the distance caused momentary slowdowns in traffic. He turned it one way then another like something off the rack in a costume shop. The mocking car honks didn't last long but I heard them for years. It looked like he was arresting my skinny wildman friend, interrogating him for old world secrets.

He looked at the pack still in my hand so I opened it to show him there was not much else. Evidently a gorilla suit was not on the list of items stolen so he tossed it back to me, telling me to have a nice day. He put on his lights and blurped his siren once more to merge among the commuters while I crouched to roll up the suit on my knees and stuff it back into the pack. Getting pulled over for running was one of many uncomfortable moments I called growing into your self. It felt like going to back to school in the fall at the start of a new grade, wearing stiff new clothes bought a size too big so I wouldn't outgrow them by spring, starting the school year stretching myself taller and holding my arms out wider, then at the end slouching with my elbows pulled in to cover my wrists and ankles so I wouldn't look like something from a hillbilly sitcom. Christmas was good not only for presents and two weeks off from school, but when clothes fit.

Every time I grew into myself for a comfortable couple of months either my body or my circumstances would change, forcing a personal evolution. I walked around some hedges along the road to get something between the public and me, feeling different than myself again, a new and maybe better version but feeling like an imitation, an alien replacement as part of their taking over earth, a remnant of the real me somewhere deep inside. I was at the front edge of somebody's lawn but there were enough trees between me and the set-back home that I was probably unseen by anyone looking out the picture window, an invisible trespasser. The wall of shrubbery made a perpendicular turn to frame

the lawn so I pushed through to the other side and emerged next to a
tow truck parked at the edge of a gas station corner lot, a car behind
it down on its knees. I'd seen that towing beast many times prowling
behind old beater cars as if it were stalking a sick wounded animal
falling behind the herd. There was an oversize rear-view mirror sticking
out wide off its side and I looked at my reflection for visible changes.

Gonna get hot, somebody said. It was a mechanic or a guy who
liked wearing greasy overalls. He was looking at the sky with his hips
slumped forward as if taking a long awaited piss. He had a big belly for a
skinny guy, like a snake out of hibernation that had eaten its first mouse
of the spring. The temperature was already good for sweating in the
shade so his prediction was probably just idle talk, the adult substitute
for conversation that I hadn't been able to force myself to try, thinking
I'd sound foolish. I looked up at the sky, ready to join in as part of my
adventure just as he added, wind pickin' up too. Darn, he beat me too it.
I had been thinking of saying simply, windy. Dangerous day for spitting
carelessly, I thought in rehearsal but he looked down at his shoes as if to
change the subject so I forgot about the weather and waited. They always
said I was a quiet boy, a kind of apology as if it were something that would
be remedied when a kid from the real world discovered a cure.

He told me I was Karl's boy then asked, aren't you? I nodded,
realizing that was what we were busting up here, the male umbilical.
It was a chance to earn my own name, become known for something
more than my parents' fertility. Someday my dad would get told, you're
Neat's father.

He pointed his chin at my pack and said, campin'? Leavin', I
answered.

He know? Not wanting to give away family secrets I told him the
rumor would find him after I'm gone, eventually, being redundant just
to show off. He looked me up then down, his chin pointing at my feet.

Walkin'? He turned his head a little to look at them with either eye
the way he might look at a pair of worn tires, judging how far they'd
get me. I told him yes and walked a few steps in place to prove it. As

if I had started something he marched toward the garage. I fell in step behind and followed him inside where there was breakfast for sale if you preferred chips, gum and candy in the morning. Didn't want to get down the road into a situation where I had to remember the place as my last chance for food, where starvation could have been avoided, so bought what fit in my pockets then found a bathroom at the side of the building.

Only the cold faucet worked, trickling at a rate that made the stream hit to one side of the drain, creating a stain there the color of dried blood. Threw away my sweaty stinking socks and used the cracked remnant of soap to wash myself one section at a time, a piecemeal cold shower.

Out front a car pulled away from the pumps. He put some money in his shirt pocket then reached for a black and blue hanky from his back pocket. It once was only blue. Without looking at me he asked, fall in?

Shouldered the pack and tried to think of something to say, beginning with the word well and a pause, but my mind was blank. It was like staring at a clean sheet of white paper rolled into a typewriter. He said if I was looking for work he needed someone on the tire machine. Didn't know what one was and told him thank you, but that I had promised to get myself out of town. He looked down the road and nodded, maybe thinking about coming with me, then told me I could find some cardboard out back and make a sign, sit in the shade there with it as long as I didn't bug the customers at the pump. Thanked him and he added that Dad had told him to keep an eye out for me.

Didn't want a ride but didn't want to insult his keeping an eye out, so I drew my vorpal pen and searched the trash pile hidden behind a row of fifty gallon drums past the bathroom. Picked a box that once held a dozen quarts of motor oil and split it down the corner seams, then spent a few minutes blocking out the letters of CALIFORNIA on the unprinted side of a one-by two-foot section.

People threw me skinny wary glances as if I were a dog on a chain or sitting in for one. Those who turtled their heads closer to read the sign reared back in fear as if the word might suggest a new religion. Some thought it meant money and offered me spare change, which I accepted. Went back for the other sides of the box and wrote PRETZELS AND COKE, but it got me nothing. Wrote CARDBOARD MIRROR, then FREE SIGN. Learned you can get a paper cut from cardboard. An employee arrived loudly in a Chevy Nova and parked between the public and me. The owner left in the tow truck. I tried to spin the cardboard on the tip of my finger but the wind caught it and it rolled crookedly along its corners like the original wheel, the one that failed before someone got the idea to make it round. I chased it, stomping it flat. It was dirty with bits of gravel embedded in the corrugations. You're only as good as your signage and I didn't want a ride with anyone who would give one to a guy with such a crappy sign. I frisbeed the sign toward the row of drums and it hit one with a hollow dong, my village bell.

Walking again I passed an open field and paced a tractor plowing the hay stubble under. It must've turned up worms because it was followed by a plume of white that looked like a bridal train in the wind, hundreds of gulls flying behind and swooping low to feed on suddenly exposed wrigglers. Then I also was surrounded in white, afraid the birds were attacking, but it was a blizzard of parachuting seeds blown from a row of cottonwoods grown as a windbreak. They did not trick my mind into forgetting the heat but they cued a memory of winter when Grandma sent me out to play, telling me to catch her a snow fly. I looked up and down tree trunks and under the bottom row of siding and under the back porch steps until my face froze then went back inside. She moved a chair for me close to the oil burning stove and brought me a grilled cheese sandwich from homemade bread with crusts so hard it cut my gums. I told her there were no flies and she asked what gave me the frost bites on my cheeks, then brought me a cup of healing soup. When I asked years later what it was made of she said it didn't matter, whatever she had, so asked what made it heal and she said just the fact that she made it especially for me, though her healing liver sausage on crackers never was as effective.

Despite the cooling memory it was so hot that I looked around to see if things nearby were on fire, but it was just the day burning. On the other side of the road near the state highway was a bigger, newer busy gas station that inspired me to try another cardboard sign. I printed HOLLYWOOD? A girl appeared around the corner from the back of the store wearing the green and white paisley checkout blouse of an employee of that chain of gas stations, undoing the buttons on her cuffs and one at her neck then un-tucking the shirttails from the waist of her knee length green skirt. She passed behind me where I sat on the curb of the raised walk that circled the building, then jumped down and wandered out far enough to allow her a peek back to read the sign. I lifted my nose to get a whiff of her but smelled only gasoline and hot shrubbery because of the decorative planters at the forward corners. She turned around, still moving away but walking backwards and told me that if I didn't get a ride there was a bus later.

I hadn't thought of buses. The only buses in town were school buses. I opened my mouth in preparation to say something but again had no words, only dirty thoughts. That dramatic pause stopped her walking backwards and we both waited for what I might say. I wondered how much a bus ticket might be, then braved the great leap to say what I was thinking, and asked her how much. She shrugged and turned away. In my mind was another bad word.

On the news I saw a teenage guy who sailed across the ocean alone in a sailboat a little too big to float in a claw foot tub, bored, excited and lonely all at the same times, his eyes searching for another shore. That's what it was like for me thinking about girls through every hour of every year, my mind bobbing up and down on waves of desire. I yelled after her, asking if she could give me a ride. She stopped and turned again to ask which way was Hollywood from here. I pointed south along the road south and she waved me over, saying that she could give me a ride as far as she was going, adding that she usually didn't pick up hitchhikers but that I looked okay. It was an insult, though she didn't intend it to be, and I thought of mean things I might do to reveal her poor judgment, but I was too nice a guy so she was right.

Her teeth matched her yellow white hair and her eyes changed from blue gray to just gray as she got into her off-black Pacer. She moved crumpled bags of used lunch from the passenger seat to the floor in back. Her uniform was splattered with grease stains but I didn't want to know how that happened, especially in a clean convenience store. Wondered if she would offer sex for money, or hoped, then wondered if I should offer. She drove a mile down the state road then took the curving entrance into Libertyville, a sprawl of three separate trailer parks better known as hillbillyville. There were about one thousand people there but most had the same ten or twenty last names. If I hadn't stopped to try another cardboard sign and kept walking I already would have been far past the area. Polish jokes were altered and told about the place.

She parked where a lawn should be in front of a mobile home that had a carport but it was filled with a kid's bike, a half deflated wading pool and a Big Wheel missing one end of the handlebar. She smiled like a spider and grabbed the pack from between my knees, telling me to come on in, that I looked thirsty. Two boys were jumping from a beat up couch to an old stuffed chair as they watched a soap opera on tv. Get down, she said and they landed and sat still, but mumbled things to each other as if saying bad words. Because judges and sheriffs had been the most regular men in her life for the last ten years she named her boys Judge and Sheriff. When they came of a troubled age somewhere between seven and ten then got arrested for the first time, going to court would have something funny in it for them. They acted as if they were used to me being there, same as any strange guy. Thought that I was being seduced but was afraid it wouldn't involve sex. I wanted a wild woman to drag me home for a reckless night, not a single mom luring me into her overpopulated life.

She went somewhere to change. From the outside it didn't look big enough to have more than one room. I didn't want to get to know the

boys if that was her plan so I wandered into the sink and hot plate area
hoping to see her in an awkward moment of undress. The worst that
could happen would be getting kicked out and back on my way. There
were two doors and I opened one to discover a bedroom where an old
lady sat on a small bed covered only in one fitted sheet patterned with
yellow smiley faces. She shattered me with an exhaustive list of bad
words. For half a moment I thought maybe it was the girl wearing a
rubber Halloween mask and making a joke, but sheet lady stood up
and brought her face close enough for me to smell a mix of ashtray and
hairspray but no latex. I backed away saying sorry, sorry, sorry in my
head because I was afraid to speak out loud. I would've yelled for paisley
girl but never had introduced myself or gotten her name and didn't want
to shout hey paisley girl.

She appeared anyway and met the old lady face to face with the
same vocabulary, backing her down again onto the mattress lacking
its happy sheet. Without taking another breath she turned and told me
that was just her momma, don't take her the wrong way, then what's
your name sweetie?

Her mother smiled at me now that she knew I was a friend of the
family and told me her name was Hap, that it was from an old cowboy
movie. I put out a hand to momma Hap and asked which movie. She
took it in both of hers and pulled herself back to her feet then just shook
her head and said that maybe I should call her Loretta. She whispered
with the same smells that Hap was sort of a nickname, that her real
name was Winnie. I asked why they didn't call her Winnie and she
said because her daughter took over the name, they couldn't have two
Winnie's in the same house 'cause nobody would ever know who was
talkin' to who. I turned to young Winnie, noticing then that she had
changed into a tube top and short shorts. I said Winnie, huh? She
nodded and snapped gum she hadn't been chewing earlier, sending me
a whiff of red-hot cinnamon. She must've changed in the bathroom
because there wasn't room for a second bedroom unless the thing had
a basement.

Young Winnie pulled as her momma pushed and the three of us
moved back through the tiny kitchen into the tv room. The boys were
in a trance watching a commercial about powdered cleanser because
it had a cartoon genie turning a dirty toilet into a shiny white throne.
I tried some math in my head, approximating the older boy's age and
how old Winnie might have been when she was pregnant. The number
was too low, in the illegal range. The boy saw me looking at him and
made a face at me that gave him a cramp in his cheek. He dropped to
the floor holding his face saying bad words. His mom massaged the
cramp away and told me he was not allowed to use bad words unless it
was something serious. The other one laughed so hard that milk came
out his nose, which was weird because he wasn't drinking milk.

Loretta was clinking things together near the little sink and I turned
toward the sound. She waved me over and I expected to be asked to fix a
faucet or something but she shoved a full beverage glass into my hand.
It smelled boozy, or she had forgotten to rinse soap out of it. I avoiding
taking a sip by looking back toward Winnie and her crampy son, but
the other boy was behind me pushing on my butt cheeks, telling me to
sit on the stool at the short counter that divided the kitchen from the
entrance. Momma almost crawled into the little refrigerator and dug
around, emerging with a few tiny ice cubes in each hand. She dropped
a share into my drink, splashing whatever it was onto my hand. It didn't
burn much. Winnie squeezed between us to steal one of the other
cubes, then got a glass out of the sink. The pushy boy tried to climb
into my lap so I slid off the stool and told him he could sit there, but he
wasn't interested in sitting and tried to hang from my belt. Winnie and
Loretta raised their drinks and chugged while I tasted out of curiosity.
It was some kind of liquor maybe mixed with green kool-aid.

Lightning lit up the windows and the almost instant crack of
thunder that followed saved me from having to fake another sip. It was
so loud and close there might have been one less trailer in the park. The
boys made whining sounds as they rushed out the door, good only that
it wasn't raining yet. Loretta said that they were inside the last time

lightning struck the metal unit. Winnie said their teeth tickled and their ears buzzed for two days. She couldn't get their hair to lie down and demanded haircuts, which she couldn't afford so she sent them over to the vet where her sister cleaned cages. She shaved their heads with the electric razor used to prep animals for spaying and other surgery.

She still had gum in her mouth and it danced into view as she spoke, looking like a pupa. My eyes wandered around the home, noticing items that seemed manly for two women and boys, a large trucker's cap and pair of work gloves, a package of loose tobacco, aviator sunglasses. Dust covered snow boots on a shelf above the door, and I wondered if they belonged to one guy or many, maybe men who had gone missing in the area.

Donchlikerdrank? Winnie was refilling their glasses and Loretta was pointing at my glass thirstily. I replayed what she said at a slower speed and nodded, pretending to sip a swallow but not letting it past my lips. There was a fluorescent flash with more distance from its lesser crack of thunder. The boys came back in and the one with the tweaky cheek said he felt a raindrop. The light from the open door of the refrigerator attracted them to each side of their mother where they got into an elbow fight grabbing for snacks. She slapped their hands away from forbidden foods. Loretta became impatient waiting for her refill and jammed herself into the mix like a fourth tag team wrestler.

I looked out the screen door in time to see the front edge of a wall of thunderclouds roil in from the lake, eating the last of the blue sky directly overhead. The temperature dropped along with a heavy rain shower that broke loose from the ceiling of sudden gloom. Fat drops made chinking sounds on the metal roof, which grew into a steady patter like food being fried. It reminded me of the grease stains on Winnie's uniform and I felt a mix of hungers. I could get a job on the tire machine and have the boss tow the trailer into my parents' back yard right up to where my room used to be. Hiya, folks, meet the family. Going out for a few beers with Stick. Back by suppertime. Go easy on the grease.

I pushed the door open to let in the better smell of rain and a pinch on my butt cheek sent me just past the doorway where water streamed off the overhang of the roof. I turned to get back inside but Loretta had moved forward half a step onto the threshold. She was pointing her finger inches away from my nose and said something like pitchangwa. It could've been Chinese but Winnie squeezed into the door opening next to her and turned her finger so I could see a cut on it, swollen and un-bandaged. I stepped back into the rain where it was half as wet as under the runoff from the roof. Winnie told me the finger was cut on some picture hanging wire, that the painkillers were making her act out. Together they pulled me inside. The boys were back on the furniture eating pieces of cold chicken held in their hands, no napkins. Loretta took my glass, which was more full than before because of all the water. I dripped on the throw rug that had been thrown too many times, watching a cartoon show that had replaced the soap opera. Winnie snuck up behind me and tried to dry my hair with a dirty dishtowel but I ducked away and blurted that I had to go.

Both she and Loretta stopped moving as if their switches had been turned off. I looked back at the boys and the tv to make sure the entire world hadn't stopped. Both ladies came back to life and said something about the rain as I sidestepped toward the door, and at that moment the sun lit up the horizon past the low hanging butts of the last of the storm clouds. I watched the line between the clouds' shadows and the sunshine move toward us from the west.

Winnie asked why I had to go. I picked up my pack at the side of the door and said that I had come in just to get out of the rain. She reminded me it had not been raining as I opened the door and rushed through the curtain of drops still coming off the roof. If I don't leave now I'll never get to Hollywood, I told her honestly. She whispered, take me with you … I'll drive. She stepped outside and let the spring loaded door slam behind her. It was a thought and I stopped to consider the offer, but one boy opened the door and yelled that Sheriff stuck a chicken bone up his nose. She darted inside and I escaped.

Her trailer and its row of six look-a-likes sat above the end of another ravine and I realized I had walked this far before by following the wooded cuts with friends. We were afraid to hike across the trailer park because of stories of escaped prisoners hiding out and married couples shooting it out. This was the last ravine to the south anyway, the edge of the flat world. The roads inside the park weren't paved and now were twin rows of mud and puddles, my shoes getting heavier with each step as the wet clay filled the threads of my shoes then became layered like extra soles. I scraped the muck off against the edge of the asphalt of the state road then walked down its wet shoulder wishing I had fixed my bicycle. I did some math in my head. If I spent a day walking back home to get it working I'd still get farther the next day by riding, theoretically passing myself. I didn't even look back, just walked out into the flatlands, remaining my theoretical self.

CHAPTER FIVE

I t was the wrong side of the road for hitchhiking but I walked forward with my thumb out in a southern direction. It was traditional and polite to walk backwards in the right lane so the driver at least could see your face and make a judgment call, but I made out with a girl named Christian who got run over while hitching, so I wanted only to walk forward. Maybe she turned and showed her thumb lazily at the last moment surprising the driver, but they both ended up in the ditch.

There were long shallow puddles on the road where recent rain proved the blacktopped surface wasn't level, made uneven through the heats and freezes of opposite seasons. Standing rainwater temporarily stuck on earth splashed like wings off the tires of passing cars so I kept a safe distance from the pavement in case one might hydroplane across lanes. Stared at the ground watching my steps along the dirt shoulder that had become muddy, careful not to slip and pratfall into the wet ditch without anyone to laugh.

Occasional paranoid frogs jumped from the bank to ploop into brown green water that smelled like the family reunions out on some distant cousin's hog farm. My pace was steady and mildly hypnotic. From reflex or boredom I thought about the gorilla in church, wondering if an assistant pastor had rented a costume to illustrate something about creation versus evolution, or if the church janitor had a pet monkey that had outgrown its cage and wandered into my line of sight while all other eyes were on the stain glass Jesus holding a shepherds crook in one hand, imagining themselves as the lamb held in the natural crook of his other arm while considering both damnation and Sunday dinner, which would make it easy to miss a big monkey for the instant it changed hiding places.

A VW van driving toward town slowed as it passed me, a student-driver sign mounted across the roof. I heard its tires leave the pavement but it didn't get airborne, just skidded to a stop on the dirt, kicking stones into the ditch water that made the same ploopy sound as the frogs. Kept walking to demonstrate I didn't want a ride that way, curious if stopping for hitchers had become something taught in drivers ed. The German horn bleeped weakly and I paused to turn and point south, making my direction clear. The van drove back onto the pavement, made a u-turn and stopped again on the opposite shoulder ahead of me, then bleeped again. The driver's side window rolled down and a guy with long black hair, beard and mustache and sunglasses smiled and waved for me to come over. Decided then that if I wanted to get to California, strangers would have to be potential friends I just hadn't met or gotten to know yet. Very few were probably cannibals or contagious with a deadly disease. This one called me by name. It was my old friend Jayo grown hairy.

Jackson Overstreet and I met in gym class in junior high. A few weeks into the school year our phys-ed teacher died. The substitute was a football coach who hadn't gone to phys-ed college and didn't have a degree in gym, so every day when we changed into our shorts and t's ready for tumbling or wrestling he told us to play dodge ball. Same as with any activity the big guys with little mustaches punished us smaller guys, using the sport as an excuse. We went to the showers with different size ball marks on our arms legs and torsos where we had been hit hard with the chili red acne-scarred kick balls. Jackson and I hid behind braver players for as long as they lasted, talking about things we hated such as standing against the wall at the end of the gym like targets in a shooting gallery. When the hiding was over we split up and dodged for desperate moments, getting some exercise.

One of the winners gave a victory howl and punted one of the balls into the iron girders that arched forty feet above the basketball court, but their ends curved down between the windows at the top of the bleachers, the textured glass covered in steel mesh to protect it from flying objects, also giving it the appearance of a reform school security measure to keep us from escaping.

A spontaneous game began of throwing and punting the rest of the balls toward the stuck one to knock it loose. I went up the bleachers and climbed out along the girder easily, setting my feet along one bottom lip of the I-beam, using the bolted cross struts as handholds. The substitute didn't look up until he noticed the chaotic noise and movement had ended, everyone silent and still as they watched me risk death by monkeying my way along the dusty ledge. Wasn't scared until he yelled for me to get down. I knocked the ball loose and nobody moved to catch it. It bounced a dozen times, each time less high like a working model of radioactive half-life, then rolled in a wobbly semi-circle until quietly settling neatly within the half-court jump ball circle. My punishment was to sit out the next game on the blue foldable wrestling mats stacked at the end of the bleachers, excommunicated from dodge ball, but as guys got hit and had to leave the game they gathered around me, sitting on the blond wood of the floor below my feet in sweaty honor.

In the locker room I bragged that my intention had been to wrap my legs around the girder and hang upside down, that the teacher hadn't given me time to show off. Jayo said that I showed off pretty good anyway, nobody else had the guts to climb out there. The made me feel as if I had grown a little more pubic hair and I braved the shower, wondering how many girder climbers there were per average gym class.

Jayo was artistic, or at least had the reputation of being an artist solely based on his spending classroom time drawing an eye patch, mustache and cigarette on every face in his textbooks, sharing his work with other bored students in other back rows. He quoted George Carlin and Cheech & Chong as if the lines were his own, and used phrases learned from his divorced mother's dates, the first one I heard causing hilarity in our corner section of study hall when we were told to study, something about trying to squeeze honey from a monkey's butt.

Once you're off the toys there isn't much for a boy to do except get into what my grandma called mischief. By ninth grade I was a natural tag-along. If anybody had a chore or errand they didn't want to do alone they'd ask if I wanted to come. Jayo often had errands because it was just his mother and him at home and she worked and dated most of the time. When ravines couldn't get us there we used alleys instead of streets. They rarely had traffic and there was stuff to find, and not just trash left next to the garbage cans.

Garage doors were left open and a partial roll of any tape was always useful. Loose nails of all sizes could be pocketed with little guilt. Cans not full of paint with rusted lids almost begged to be taken but were left behind, unwanted even by us. The twist-off bottle had just been invented and there were hundreds of bottle and can openers next to buckets of bottle caps and pull-tops that could be woven into chain mail or hippie door curtain. Bamboo fishing poles were stored across rafter beams, hooked lines wrapped around their lengths like spider web peppermint stripes. Many town residents had grown up on farms where they used everything at least twice before the word recycle existed. They saved stuff that hadn't existed earlier in their lives, Styrofoam meat trays, plastic bread bags and the paper-covered wire twist ties to reseal them.

Partner in crime he called me as I crossed the street by tiptoeing through a shallow puddle, the rubber front of my tennis shoes keepings the canvas sections above the water line. Told him I thought hippies had gone extinct years ago. Up close he didn't look healthy but I kept smiling and looked across his vehicle as if it were a shiny new car in a showroom. He asked how I liked the j-mobile and I nodded yes though

I was unemotional about automobiles and confused why owners named them.

He asked if I needed a ride and I told him I wasn't going into town, I was finally leaving it. Hop in, he said, I'm going that way. I reminded him which way he had just been going before the u-turn and he said he had been going back for something but didn't really need it, might as well just get going. I looked down the straight line of the road to the horizon, feeling all the steps it would take to get there. Somewhere farther the walk would be harder where the road dipped and curved and rose over hills. It would be a slow long roller coaster of a walk and I felt it in my guts.

I got in. It smelled smoky but not as strong as the odor of his patchouli oil so thick it was almost visible. Just like the old days, he said and started to laugh but it became a coughing spell that ended in a hock of phlegm that he spit out the window, hanging his head out there for a moment as he gagged, swallowed then turned back inside. Thought I was gonna puke again, he said, too much of last night last night. He shifted into low gear and the van lurched slightly as he let out the clutch. It had a hard working engine that let you know it, humbly making a foreign sound. My thoughts had been going in circles, but tagging along with Jayo felt like going in other circles but at least their diameters were larger.

There was a billboard on the other side of the road that welcomed traffic to Ravinia. My dad was parked behind it. He must've been waiting for me to hike past. I waved though he couldn't see me. Jayo asked why I was waving at that cop. Told him it was my dad looking out for me. He said no, undercover narc, been sitting there for an hour. I asked how he could know that and he said he had driven by earlier and spotted him, you could tell because the government had a contract to buy Pontiacs which kept the car company big enough to elect presidents. It reminded me he had a book in junior high with a recipe for making a bomb in your kitchen, but the couple times he tried it got impatient with measuring or looking for a thermometer for whatever extra ingredient needed cooking.

You should've been down at the Veeks' last night, he said, and I asked him what went on. He said they hired a band that had played Chicago and South Bend, huge horn section. I asked him how the Veeks ever got their own club, they never had money or even a job that I could remember. Investors, he said, the Veeks are promoters. Y'know there's no such thing as money unless we all play along, believing a worthless piece of paper has the value of whatever number is printed on it.

I had heard it before, confusing but still entertaining. When Jayo met with his career counselor he said he didn't care what kind of work he did as long as it involved having sex with large breasted women. Counselor Barnes wore a dark gray shirt with a large white collar that somehow earned him the nickname the flying nun. He dug into a drawer without comment, and Jayo held his breath for a moment wondering if there really might be something for him, hoping his grades would be good enough for large breasted women. Counselor Barnes handed him brochures on different kinds of schools, none mentioning sex, at least not on the covers. After high school he got work at a pet store because of the snakes.

The first time I tagged along to his house after school he showed me snakes he kept in a basement window-well covered with a ragged piece of plywood, three brown and gray Dekay's about thick as a nickel and almost two feet long, twice as big as any I had ever caught. A big kid on our street wanted a snake for science class so I talked my grandma into letting me find one down the hillside though I'd never seen one before. When I returned empty handed she was waiting at the screen door to say I told you so. Like a magician I pulled four baby DeKay's out of my pocket. She told that story until she died.

From metal shop at school we stole thick leather welding gloves that protected the wrist. Fat water snakes would sun themselves on rocks and overhanging branches along the river, but when our footsteps alerted them they reflexively dropped into the water, so we stalked in slow motion then from a blind spot grabbed them by the tail, which wasn't difficult because besides their head they were all tail. They whipped their heads back biting, getting teeth stuck in the leather so we could use our bare other hand to pinch them behind the neck.

In the next window well were feeder toads. He had them for pets, but they were sacrificed for our evolution as any pet owner moving up the food chain, hoping someday to own a wildcat, then maybe a wolf, and finally a monkey or baby chimp.

Jayo and I didn't drift apart as friends, just quit. He always was smoking and tried to light a cigarette in my bedroom so I sprayed air freshener at the flame of his lighter and burned his hand. He picked up an empty coke can and threw it at me. It dinked off my front tooth and knocked a corner of it into the back of my throat. I coughed it onto my tongue and spit it at him. He thought I was spitting spit and left angrily at the insult. The chipped tooth matched my weird lip and I hated my reflection but couldn't stop looking at it every few minutes.

We hadn't driven past more than a dozen farms and their fields of corn and orchards of fruit trees and vineyards heavy with sour green unripe grapes when he said he needed gas money, that he didn't have money, not gas money anyway. I asked him what he had planned on using before he picked me up. He inhaled deeply as if he were smoking, then held it in as if it were pot, then used the lungs full of bad breath to admit quickly with run-on words that he had heard from Steve that I was leaving town on foot and he needed to get out of town himself but didn't have gas money and had used up what was left in the tank driving up and down several roads searching for me thinking it would be a trade off, that his wheels needed get out of town juice and I needed get out of town wheels.

Asked where he was going and he told me he had a job in Chicago. It was on my route and the van could get there on one tank of gas so I told him I'd fill the tank for a ride that far. The needle on the gauge was close to E but he thought it would get us to the next station. We almost made it.

Luckily we were on a slight downgrade and were able to coast toward the next burg. An older lady in a cream-colored Hudson Jet crept up behind us. She must've feared the traffic gods because she wouldn't pass in the opposite lane, just honked until we pulled off the pavement to get out of her way, the wet dirt of the shoulder stealing our momentum. Jayo yelled for her to get a horse and laughed, not because it was a funny line but because it was funny to yell at older people. He lit a cigarette to catch his breath then told me to go get a can of gas, volunteering to stay with the van as if that were the tougher duty. The lady was far down the road and I ran after her waving my arms, but she never had learned how to use the rear view mirror. Walked down the center of the road wondering why the get a horse line ever had been funny, probably propaganda against the newly invented automobile, maybe by churches that believed man shouldn't go faster than anything off the ark.

At a little service station the attendant was pumping gas into the Hudson. He spoke using extra shwa syllables. Uh, can I, uh, help a-ya? Told him I ran out of gas, speaking crisply to set an example. He pointed me toward an old metal gas can, once fire engine red but now turned maroon from a coating of oil and dust. It had a bendable metal spout that looked like neck bones. As I unscrewed the spout he motioned me over to one side of him, blocking the lady from view as he pumped me five gallons of gas on her tab. He whispered that she uh never tips, ma-uhn, stuh-ingiest lady in uh town.

I thanked him and said I'd be back in a few. As I headed down the road I heard him tell the lady, uh see ya at uh home, mo-uhm.

The wind thrummed the power line above my head, then I heard the muffled falsetto of Jayo singing. He had slid the side door open and was sitting on the floor of the van wearing my gorilla mask with a hand rolled cigarette in its mouth. The rest of the suit hung off his shoulders like a fur cape. I pretended not to be angry, tonguing the space of my snaggle tooth in anger. He gave me a big cool nod, working the head, probably having rehearsed in the tall side rear view mirror. He pulled off the mask and wiped sweat off his forehead, which meant there was sweat inside my mask. He had so much hair it was almost funny that he looked wilder without the mask. I asked why he was in my stuff. Just looking for contraband, man, he said. He offered me his smoke and I automatically shook my head no, rolling up the suit and putting it back in the pack. I shoved it behind the back of my seat and slid a cardboard box over to secure it. Something in the box made a fragile breakable clink and Jayo told me if I broke it I bought it. Beneath some newspaper pages folded down and around them were pieces of ancient writing the size of an open wallet, framed between pieces of glass. They had price tags from five to ten dollars though they all looked the same. I asked if he had broken into a museum or something.

Before he broke my tooth we had a secret campsite at the marina where we went snaking. There was a soggy path we could walk through a swampy area that led us to a tree-covered mound of dry land like a private island. We had seen snakes bigger than any we caught and their legend grew that winter along with a scheme to burglarize the boats docked during early spring, when the nights were too cold for owners to sleep over on them. Jayo's motto was all you can get and all you can get away with, tempting words to a tag-a-longer. Maybe it was church but more probably Batman comics that changed my mind even before my tooth was damaged, intending to chicken out of the stealing and leave both the secret island and the legendary snake to him.

He said that was a bunch of shit, and I didn't know if he meant my question or the stuff in the box. I picked one out but recognized only a few letters of a different alphabet. He elbowed me and explained they were ripped pieces of brown grocery bags crumpled and soaked in bleachy water to age them. He used a tiny brush to copy words from books in Greek and Latin, random words that looked best, not even copying words in a row that by chance might be a complete thought. He sold them at the flea market. Some people bought them for a joke, others for religious reasons. Keep it, he said, but I put it back in the box.

It took both of us to lift and pour the gas into the tank, taking longer than it would to pump it. He told me he learned the fake antique trick from his little skinny grandfather who had moved to Florida, Fritz.

During Fritz's first hurricane watch he loaded survival kit supplies out of the back of his station wagon into a plastic tub on the driveway. The tub was large enough to bathe in. At the bottom of the driveway, a bundle of four by eight sections of plywood were stacked for boarding up his windows. He stopped for lunch then washed it down with a few beers and took a nap, waking up to the hurricane knocking on his door. He hurried out to get his supply kit but was knocked onto the pavement by the wind, which also sent the tub hydroplaning down the driveway on shallow rapids of rainwater.

The tub pinned him against the stack of plywood where he held onto its strapping, calling for help but the neighbors couldn't hear him over the crushing sound of the wind and a spring training game on their emergency radios. Hours later the storm passed and they emerged like munchkins checking for witches under thrown houses, fearing extreme damage. They heard repeated triplets of someone tapping out S.O.S. in Morse code, eventually wandering over in annoyance at the knocking to discover their small neighbor half drowned and exhausted from the ordeal.

He started a company selling the kind of kit that saved his life, claiming that without his tub of supplies he would've been carried away by the storm.

Jayo asked me to drive as a kind of work for your supper deal but the only stick-shift I'd ever driven was a Cushman cart one summer at the golf course, mowing its big grassy hillside by lowering a mower on ropes then hauling it back up like a sailor I had watched heaving line on a reproduction of Columbus' ship Pinta harbored off the pier that year. On the first attempt I stalled the van and Jayo helped me find third gear a couple times but we were back at the gas station to top off the tank not more than a few minutes longer than it had taken me to walk the same distance. The pump guy uh-thanked me for the uh-dollar tip, and I lurched the van through town that might've been a speed trap if the VW had the ability to accelerate faster than that old Cushman.

Jayo shouted at random things out the window, making no sense, but there was a flaming eyeball decal on the windshield that stared at me, daring me to criticize his behavior. He yelled at an empty corner fruit stand, bragging that he was hated for being a nonconformist. It had taken me a few years to realize he and other nonconformists who skipped classes and made animal sounds during pep rallies dressed alike, spoke alike and forced rookie nonconformists to do the same, mocking any original rebellious behaviors. Jayo lived as if always on the way to another Woodstock because he had missed the real one.

We passed one orchard where all the old fruit trees had been cut down and piled in a tall dead tree stack in the distance. Jayo said he drove this road in winter and the neat rows of stumps in the snow made him think it was a cemetery with a chapel behind. He seemed depressed it was only a graveyard for trees, telling me he had thought it would be a good spot to be buried instead of in town, and now he'd have to find another place.

The sunset cheered him up again, or rather the darkness did. He said that people underestimated the egg sandwich as a meal, and he redefined the word aftermath as having survived algebra and the teacher who insulted any student confused by letters in a numbered equation. His favorite guitar was the Les Paul but he pronounced it lay-pow as if it were French instead of the name of the inventor who built the prototype out of wires, magnets and a four by four chunk of lumber outmoded by plastic furniture.

He asked are you getting tired, but before I could answer he said good, keep rolling till we wake the rooster. Asked him what time it was and he said he refused to wear a watch. Ten seconds went past before I asked why. He said if it was so important to know the time, what if the damn thing stopped, so then he'd have to wear a second one just in case, and there was no way he was going to walk around like a geek wearing two watches. I said that sounded like a gag from the Three Stooges and he told me of his belief that Shemp liked all the Moe pain because his comedy takes went toward the abuse instead of flinching down and away as Curly did.

I was picturing Shemp doing that familiar jerk forward off his toes, and though I was cruising at the pace of a turtle winning a race, was surprised by a curve in the road and veered onto the slippery shoulder while slamming the clutch and brake to the floorboard at the same time. The van's butt slid around but we stayed out of the ditch. There was a clunk sound and out of the corner of my right eye I saw a flying saucer. There went the hubcap, Jayo told me. He opened the glove compartment and grabbed a flashlight that used up most of the space. We got out and he shined it along a fence that was covered in hundreds of hubcaps like the wall of a fantasy fortress, reflected highlights jumping along the many variations of curves and edges.

The ditch was thick with cattails and froggy grasses and the light was swallowed up by dark water. Mosquitoes floated up, almost a swarm, their buzzing like the noise from a radio tuned between two stations. Jayo told me not to sweat losing it, that this was where he got his hubcaps in the first place during colder seasons when you could cross the dry ditch and creep up to the fence and help yourself quietly, when every little noise sounded like the click of the hammer on a shotgun being pulled back into firing position.

He got into the driver's seat and reached for the nub of his rolled cigarette to relight it, and only then did I realize it was the roach of a joint and he had been high since I went for gas. He shouted the word revolution at the lost hubcap and drove on, without headlights. Most of a moon was up and everything was an eerie silver green gray. The lights of a car coming the other way took an edge off the danger until we saw the official seal on its door. The dead light on the middle of its roof burst alive into swirling colors that ironically meant the party was over.

Jayo swallowed the dirty butt and kept swallowing nervously, saying shit over and over, sounding like the mimeograph machine back in junior high. Once he had snuck in to use it, copying some anti-war hand-outs for the big town parade the first Saturday every May, but he didn't know how to work it and came out with his shirt splattered in blue and smelling like a new test.

The air was deliciously clean with farm fresh oxygen off the fields around us, making obvious the oily reek of pot leaking from Jayo's pores as he sweated fear and paranoia. The cop's flashlight beam shone first on his face then mine as if it were some kind of game to see which of us would cry first or turn into a werewolf or something. Jayo did. His eyebrows and the hairs of his beard and mustache stood straight out, perspiration glinting like dew drops. He faked a smile that featured his canines, the way chimps do when they're angry, revealing some connection between pain and comedy. The sharp beam of light caused his eyes to close halfway in a feral squint. When the officer finally spoke Jayo gave an involuntary bark. The officer waited for another outburst then asked to see Jay's license and registration. Jayo reached up to the visor and pulled down a baggie of marijuana, handing it over as if it identified him better than paperwork.

As the officer cuffed him Jayo looked at his dirty shoes and asked the cop why wasn't he out arresting muggers and rapers instead, then he looked up at the stars and answered his own question, that society must be protected from a peace loving Buddhist. As the cop led him to the cruiser Jayo said that weed was part of his religion, didn't he have freedom of religion, then looked back at me said to call his mom. The weird thing was that the officer was a sheriff so Jayo would end up back in Ravinia in the county jail.

I was feeling the gravity trying to pull me back. The cop shined his light into each of my eyes, smelled my breath, examined my arms for needle marks then checked my pockets for paraphernalia. He investigated the box of fake parchments and pulled my gorilla suit out of the pack, finally concluding I was an innocent passenger, or at least not guilty of anything evident.

The van wasn't impounded so Jayo gave me permission to drive it, telling me to pick him up when his mom made bail. Instead of turning around and following the cruiser I drove ahead and found another lonely phone booth. Back then the phone company placed them in lonely places intentionally, far from where there would be any other free phone you might ask permission to use. Phone booths were good business. I asked information for a Mrs. Overstreet hoping she still had the same last name. She was the first divorced person I ever had met, always rushing around with a lit cigarette between her teeth, dressed in sexy clothes as if late for a dirty magazine shoot, but she worked as a cocktail server and though I knew it meant waitress I imagined the specific title included something pornographic.

When I tried to explain who I was she got angry thinking I was clumsily asking her out, so I blurted that Jayo had been arrested, that I was his snaking friend from school and was stuck with his van. She was more surprised it was me than that he was in jail. Her voice was edgy like the rolling scratch of a glass-cutting wheel as if she were almost about to crack. She told me she was not going to bail him out again, that she had only one parking spot at the apartment and there was no overnight street parking, could I please hold onto the van until he got out. I promised I'd take care of it and she said thank you thank you thank you.

Repacked my suit while thinking about what to do, knowing I wasn't driving back to town. Drove ahead to a used car lot on the edge of a short strip of business, everything closed for the night except a motel with a blue neon vacancy sign. There was a cow chain across the entrance drive but it wasn't padlocked. I lowered the chain and drove in as if I belonged there and knew what I was doing. Not looking around to see if anybody was watching took all my strength, but I hooked up the chain behind the van then found an empty space between a truck and a car with prices soaped on their windshields, backed in neatly, camouflaged as a used vehicle for sale, rhyming with the surroundings.

A couch took up most of the back of the van with moveable cushions to make it a bed. I closed the curtains on the windows and the one that screened off the front seats, pushed one cushion to the floor and turned the other sideways to use as a pillow. Stretched out for a nap and tried to sleep, wishing I were back under the cherry tree but thinking about sleep is worse than caffeine at bedtime. I still smelled Jayo. I took the suit out of the pack and used it as a layer between the upholstery and me but the pot smell permeated the mustard colored naugahyde so I unzipped the cover to remove it and use just the foam rubber inside. Inside a hollow carved out of the foam were several pounds of marijuana, three packages of stash neatly wrapped in cellophane as if awaiting postage.

CHAPTER SIX

Never smoked anything but grew up in a world of smoke. Family, neighbors, teachers and preachers smoked everywhere. New school clothes, Christmas presents, my lunchbox and even lunch smelled of something burnt. Friends at thirteen smoked whatever they could get and when caught laughed off lectures from smoker parents or teachers, a solid foundation of the rebellious years.

I wasn't going to smoke Jayo's stuff and didn't want to get caught with it. Any trashcan would solve the problem, or the continuous ditch. Thought about it so loud that I kept myself awake worrying about a night watchman or a nosey person shopping after hours for a Volkswagen. I sat hunched over in the dark as if already in a cell, looking guilty. Traveling thousands of miles with enough marijuana to support a reggae band was too risky, but I decided not to dump it for Jayo's sake. I would hide it nearby.

Took out my suit and crammed the bundles in the knapsack, then suited up to sneak out into the dark and stash it somewhere. Because Jayo had smoked in the mask it smelled similar to the stinkier part of my childhood. Dark and hairy seemed reasonable for prowling anytime but especially at night. It had worked for bears, skunks and my uncle the trash picker who knew the garbage truck routes for every neighborhood in several cities and salvaged enough junk to start his own dump. I would move silently from shadow to shadow, stash the dope then hightail it out of town though I didn't know what hightail meant, the thought appearing in my mind as a series of comic book panels with that word inside a thought balloon above my head.

Peeked through the curtains in every direction, my breathing inside the mask loud as a sound-effect for a scuba-diving movie scene. Held my breath and carefully opened the sliding door just wide enough to get out noiselessly, leaving it open. Crept away in a crouch and waited a moment between two pick up trucks, listening for surprises. The bottoms of my gorilla feet were made of rubber pulled from a mold to look like the bottoms of bare feet, so they barely whispered like anything close to footsteps as I slipped into the shadow of a hillbillyville-type trailer used as a sales office.

There was an alley behind the lot, a high wooden fence on the other side stretching away in both directions. Through a gap between the slats saw that it was an auto graveyard, probably a connected business for car parts. I would locate a junker too rusty for retrievables then stash the contraband in some corroded cranny. Sang the words corroded contraband cranny in my head.

Seeing through the eyeholes eliminated peripheral vision. Eyes front to hunt, eyes side to hide. My science teacher taught me predators had forward vision, that and how to dissect a frog, an unused skill because the need to provide a frog heart or liver for any reason never occurred. And gorillas had forward vision only to find wild celery. I didn't ask questions out loud and hunted by looking forward to pizza, cash and girls.

Under a layer of cloth and fake fur my real hairs stood up on my neck and arms, pushing against the underskin of fake fur, alerted by an unused skill of nerve endings becoming aware of something before my word-filled mind had a clue. I heard toenails and wet breathing then turned around to face three dogs. Their eyes were not to the sides. One thing in common was that each had a frayed piece of leash hanging from their collars. It meant they were drop-offs disguised as beloved pets broken free of their tethers. Owners moving away or tired of keeping them would leave them humanely near a shelter with the leash cleverly attached to disguise them as escaped lost dogs, but the tags always had been removed so they couldn't be returned.

Kibble would be left out at the shelter to keep strays in the area so they could be rounded up before they became a pack of dog pirates. Our town had a half-drunk ex-deputy sheriff working animal control. The job was a bone tossed to him by his ex-wife who kicked him out after three kids when she was elected to the city council but still needed child support. He chased strays in a renovated delivery truck, grinding gears as he listened to the police scanner, reflexively chasing their nearby calls too, criminals knowing to run and hide if they heard or saw the dog truck because it meant a patrol car was on its way.

Kids would go after the hounds with BB guns and slingshots, putting accidental spider web cracks in car windows all along County Road 49, but each winter with the wind chill off the frozen lake when it got so cold that people had to blow on their soup to keep it warm, the opossums and raccoons got the kibble bait, so the dogs surrendered hungrily to be sheltered. Evidently that hadn't worked in this town because this was an old pack of hungry dogs that probably lived on opossum and raccoon through winter.

They were confused, not knowing what was trapped against the fence. A middle sized black dog volunteered to taste me then let the others know in which category I belonged. It lunged and got a muzzle full of rucksack over which we fought a tug of war. The other dogs came closer either to get a better look or to help so I swung the black dog back and forth like a weapon to change their minds. The flap was pulled open enough for one of the packages to drop onto the gravel of the alley, and thinking it might be edible the black dog let go of the canvas and chomped onto the bundle, slinking away along the fence. The other dogs assumed the brave one had scored something worth abandoning me for, chasing after it. I tossed the pack over the fence then scrambled up and over too. One dog looked back at me with respect that not only had I escaped them, but had conquered the secret of the wooden wall, gaining access to the other side.

I pulled off the mask and let it hang off the back of my neck, then sucked in air and its delicious flavor compared to the mix of exhaled CO_2 and sweaty smoky latex I had been breathing. There was no junkyard watchdog on that side because there was nothing worth guarding. All the wrecks were ancient and useless, the fence there simply to hide the depressing endless mess from anybody buying a used car in slightly better condition.

It was darker there so while I waited for my eyes to adjust, the dogs began scratching at the hard packed ground below the fence. They were back from learning that pot wasn't dog food. Unable to jump the fence their brains only worked the dog thought of digging under. They use their front paws same as their back feet despite seeing the advantages of human hands. Gorillas are ahead of both of us, not just having hands as feet, but using their feet as extra hands. It's a skill that could be taught to children in honor of our primate heritage. It should be a class in school like phys-ed. I saw people without hands on tv typing with their feet, shaving their faces, signing their names to petitions to clean up public restrooms, though how they managed in the toilet never was revealed. Extra credit could be given in art if you drew a picture with a pencil between your toes. As a school fundraiser the student council might wash cars using only their feet.

The rubber gorilla toes stuck out farther than the ends of my shoes, so the natural length of my stride was wrong for where I thought I was stepping. Tripped continually over nothing, painfully falling to my knees, stopping the fall with a hand but banging knuckles against fenders. I stumbled bruised through wet weeds and unidentifiable rusty remnants of ancient crashes, crashing into them again. A hillock of tires that never would roll again rose above the rest of the wreckage like a monument to breakdowns. I transferred the drugs from the pack deep into the pile, and to hide them completely from lazy or lucky treasure hunters, lugged a bunch of shredded and therefore useless tires onto that section. The burial site of Jayo's stash was memorialized by what looked like big black wreaths.

Walked back along the inside of the wooden fence to find a way out. It ended at a corner where a steel wire fence began. There was a droop in its mesh where people had climbed over before, the neatly interwoven squares crunched down into surrealistic Dali shapes. On the other side was a group of trees on an undeveloped lot along the alley. Back at the alley I peeked around the wooden fence post to see the dogs impatiently waiting, two still clawing ground then biting at the back of each other's necks. Put on my mask then peeked again.

By some dog sense or animal fate they were looking at me, the little bit of me showing. They came running, happily barking like laughter. Unable to outrun them I searched for an escape tree, one with a low crotch. In one leap I was up in the gap of a maple split with a double trunk. The yapping of the dogs sounded much like the words get 'im, get 'im, so from there I jumped again to hug one of the trunks with my arms and legs higher and hopefully out of doggie reach. The smallest dog jumped across the back of the biggest one and leaped into the crotch where it became wedged, wriggling and whining, rolling its eyes up with a why is this happening to me expression. I felt the same way, shimmying up to grab a branch.

Somewhere a door slammed open against an outer wall. A man yelled and whistled and banged on something else. The dogs went quiet and I held my breath. There was distant muttering and the snapping of sticks being walked on. I heard the sound of a train whistle, about as far away as I wished I were. When the door closed again I slid down the tree, my rubber foot touching the little wriggling dog. It snarled and bit into the rubber. By pulling my foot up I freed it from the tree's pinch, so it stopped biting to fall then run away, disappointed with its dog's life.

Waited in the crotch and heard more footsteps. Looking hard in the direction of the noise I could see movement but no flashlight. Had to be that same guy so before he got any closer I got down. Picked up my empty pack and backed away in the other direction to put tree after tree between us. Behind a fat one I sat on my heels. Not hearing anything for minutes I straightened up and looked around the trunk. The flashlight went on and I was looking directly into the beam. Other guys my age were getting married, putting in overtime, joining a benevolent brotherhood, voting for a presidential candidate, but I was hiding someone else's drugs and running from a stranger's flashlight while trespassing in a gorilla suit.

Veered around some evergreens and fell into a dip of ground, belly-flopping onto layers of leaves from previous autumns. Instead of stopping, the guy kept running as if I were somewhere ahead of him. In seconds I was across the alley and near my van. From between the two trucks I looked back. The black dog was behind me carrying the bundle of weed in its mouth. I lunged at it with a gorilla growl and it jerked back as if playing keep away, then took a step forward as if it wanted me to try to grab again. Instead I moved low on my hands and feet to the van. Turned back to see it was following as if imitating me.

Quickly and quietly went inside and slid the door almost shut, then peeled off the costume wet with sweat. Peeking out for a mob of angry villagers I saw only dog and marijuana. Didn't want to leave any evidence behind so slid the door open and said c'mon doggie, moving back to give it room. In one neat movement as if it were jumping through a circus hoop the dog was inside the van. Among the trash along the top of the dashboard was a package of beef jerky, so I offered a piece to the dog. It dropped the pot to eat.

After stashing the package back inside the cushion I slipped out and undid the chain across the driveway. Back in the van I waited a very long five minutes for any kind of movement, the painful kind of waiting like when someone else is using the bathroom. Drove out of that nice quiet town, and when I was sure nobody had followed turned onto a dirt road between cornfields and hopped out to pee, puke a bitter bit of something, then finish peeing as the night throbbed with noise from a less crazy species.

Black dog was sprawled on the couch, sleeping with its head against the marijuana pillow. The plastic package of jerky was now on the floor, chewed up and empty. Left the state road to drive the highway, but a parade of vehicles grew behind me waiting to pass when opposing traffic made it safe, or sometimes barely probable. The van could not surpass the speed limit, and barely could approximate it. Truckers took it personally and crept up close, giving the bumpers a chance to kiss before coming around, crowding me into the right half of the right lane and sometimes onto the shoulder. They collectively forced me off an exit from which I found the state road again with its dead motels and dying drive-ins.

Still got passed by impatient speeders but at a velocity that didn't make we wonder if I had marked the organ-donor box on the back of my driver's license. Get them while they're hot I said to the dog, young healthy organs. It must've heard, coming up between the seats to see if I were serious. I was afraid to undo the old collar, but to brave life I scratched its neck. It flinched then let me, so I undid the collar. It jumped into the passenger seat and tried to get a snout out the passenger window but settled for looking out the windshield. Saw it was a girl. Asked her questions about what was ahead but she had fallen asleep again, a trail of snout mucus down the side window.

Drove half the night then found a road leading back to the highway where there were all night things open for truckers. Used a bathroom while the dog peed then drank from a puddle. Gave her the option to run off or make the place her home but she jumped back into the van ahead of me, not knowing I was out of food. She let me curl up on a corner of the bed and we slept until it got too hot. At one of the all service places bought some breakfast jerky, juice and a quart of Coke.

After the jerky I needed some kind of water dish for the dog and found a Frisbee under the driver's seat. Chugged the juice then went back in to fill the bottle with water in the bathroom and poured it into the upturned Frisbee. Told her we could be friends but I wasn't going to give her a name because I wasn't her owner. She stopped lapping, looked around then drank again, almost unemotionally uninvolved as I.

We saw the country, much of it the same, passing through little towns that once were larger. I lost a fear of strangers, convinced they didn't judge me by the out of state license plate. We had weather in common but I didn't comment on the rain or shine, not to offend with my slightly nasal way of speaking compared to the more relaxed speech of those farther south and west. Who needs that zombie talk anyway, I mentioned to the dog. When I forced a hello or thank you I tried to imitate the locals but it sounded theatrical, as if hiding gum in my cheek sometimes in grade school where chewing gum was not allowed. Nobody minded me, just smiled while chewing their own gum.

Was afraid of a janitor who cleaned gum from the bottom of our school desks, a seasonal obligation using a putty knife. He'd scrape them off like barnacles until they dropped into his cupped palm, which was nothing to a man who picked up the solid chunks of student vomit with his fingers before wiping up the liquid with a rag that always hung from the back pocket of his railroad engineer coveralls. Because I swallowed my gum he was able to skip my desk each year, but back then there always was another year of school, which maybe was what I feared most.

Late in the day the black dog and I crossed a long scary bridge across the Mississippi to a parking area where you could lean on a wall with a view of the water. Vacation families stared and took pictures. I could have impressed them with a description of Lake Michigan but they might have planned this moment for months and I didn't want to spoil it.

The country flattened out with longer distances between random places, the more desolate the scenery the prettier the name of the town, Eden, Hope, Paradise, some kind of early advertising propaganda, but the rare river valley towns were named Bitter Root or Devil's Hole as if to save those oases for themselves.

A second fear was for the van. First I thought a tire was going flat, feeling the van tipping to one side, stopping several times to check but nothing was wrong. Then became painfully conscious of engine noise, that it might spit flaming oil or a part would work loose and freeze the motor, the sudden stoppage causing the entire vehicle to somersault. Night driving had built-in panics just from being afraid of the new and unfamiliar dark where anything might leap out and get hit, maybe an animal big enough to ram us, maybe an old prospector mauled by a cactus turned predatory by radioactivity.

There were turns that suddenly appeared no matter how slowly I drove because the headlights reached out with weak short beams unable to give fair warning for any washout or sinkhole big enough to swallow a vehicle entirely. Lightning bugs crashed into the windshield and when I finally discovered how to turn on the wipers through random fumbling, glow juice smeared across the glass and reduced vision to half and confused the yellow dotted line.

If the dog shared my worry she showed it by sleeping, running in her dreams on the couch, making me jealous and angry she didn't have to take a turn driving. When stopping for fuel I examined the front of the van for identifiable road kill, mostly bees and beetles but also a bat perfectly splayed out as if it were a hood ornament for the caped crusader's camper van.

I calculated the hour and day I could arrive back home if I turned around, passing the point where there was not cash enough. I could afford only to continue forward, running out of money at the western limit, my left arm two shades darker than the right from resting it out the sunny side of the van, a compass guiding me west.

Once I fell asleep at my desk, the only time, while the teacher chalked a chart about the population explosion, dragging the chalk across the board hard enough for it to screech and wake me. He drew stick figures that represented millions of people and went wild drawing them, each one less accurate until they were mutations with oversized circles for heads, scratches of white that were meant to be arms and legs but didn't connect to the vertical body line. I believed him because the graphics were so shocking they must've been inspired by reliable statistics. Where would we put everybody? Looking out the windows of the van at the wide empty stretches of America I found the answer. Put them here.

The dog panted continuously, the air driven in through the windows hot and gritty leaving a sandy feeling in the throat and lungs. With enough time there my face would have skin like a baseball mitt with the squinty eyes of a cowboy always wincing even when the sun wasn't shining.

Slowly climbed a mountainside road of rock surrounded by rock, considering the difference between geography and geology. The peaks, earlier just distant facets of blue green and pointed, became detailed with patches of translucent forest cut by white shining snow in shadowed cuts.

Couldn't see the cutbacks of a road up there so expected a tunnel or a cliff-edge drive around a shoulder of rocky outcrop, but instead the road eased into a canyon, winding down through a pass deep between the peaks until I was at the sunless bottom where foamy water ran fast and muddy like a cocoa river. The dog and I got out to visit it, not having seen water for over a day, catching up on old wet times and laughing at being worried over hundreds of miles of desert plains. After she drank I threw the Frisbee for her to catch but she only glanced as it passed over her head, eyes back to me waiting for a better trick. Found a stick and threw it next to her but she moved away to the side as if used to dodging thrown things. While I retrieved the Frisbee she got into the van and hogged the couch.

It was uphill again, a long slow climb out of the canyon at forty miles at an hour or less. The top of the hill wasn't a mountain peak and we coasted down to another day of dry driving that included long stretches without radio as the gas gauge needle leaned on the E, country music stations fading in to alert us that a small town might be ahead. The dog never worried even those short times she was awake. We did this longer than any time warp episode of The Twilight Zone.

In the middle of the night we climbed another hill, our line of sight directly at the stars, no moon, no clouds, just hundreds maybe thousands of little lights, and at the crest the horizon dropped away as it does at the top of a roller coaster, but here it revealed many more lights below as if the stars were reflected not only by the calm surface of a waveless great lake, but reflected in an infinite trick of funhouse mirrors. It wasn't water or mirrors. It was a super city made of dozens if not a hundred cities side by side with no space between, so large its skyline showed the curve of the Earth. We had reached Los Angeles.

When the black and white television went on the fritz a repairman would come to the house with a fold-out case full of tubes as if he carried a small crystal city stolen from a miniature planet seen on the covers of scifi magazines and in the pages of Superman comic books. That's what Los Angeles looked like from the high ground in the east. Because I stopped the dog woke up and left the couch to sit in the passenger seat, and together we stared at the panoramic array of lights above and below The road had no rest stop or ditch, just continued on as flat hard packed dirt with some humble vegetation that looked like props for a Mars movie. Too tired to drive I turned off the road and parked next to a scrubby tree for a nap, surprised by the cool summer night. Used the suit and the dog for warmth, dreaming of Hollywood, Oz and Mars.

CHAPTER SEVEN

We drove across the open ground to the road, leaving behind two puddles of pee and a set of tire tracks leading back to them. The road merged with larger roads that merged with a highway that paralleled the freeway, satellite cities merging with others until everything was paved, not streets and sidewalks the way pavement crisscrosses any populated area, but enough pavement that could keep a land of giants off what little grass existed. Nothing touched the ground, the concrete complete and unending. There were varieties of stunted vegetation but they didn't need a patch of dirt, just grew from cracks and seams or out of dunes of dirt inside the corners of or along the perimeters of parking lots. Trees grew from deliberate holes built into the sidewalks, and every twenty minutes a sign alerted me that we had crossed into another city's limits.

The fear of a flat tire returned because for all that road there wasn't a side of the road, just a concrete barrier to keep you from drifting into the merging lane, one every half mile. The concrete barrier seemed overly littered with shredded tire treads of every size. Anticipating the smell of burning rubber and the flapping sound of a tire shredding followed by the shriek of a bare steel wheel grinding against the pavement, I made whining sounds that were bothersome to the dog. She rolled her eyes at me either to say it's okay, or please stop that before I bite you.

The red and blue spinning lights of a police car turned my whine into a yelp. It's lonely to be in a sea of cars and the one pulled over like a hooked loser in a school of fish. Told the dog it was okay but she couldn't take any more of me and went to the back.

When I left home it had been to play along with the banishment, to enjoy the novelty and the lust that came with wandering, the possibility of strange women. I might've visited Chicago with Jayo and watch my first major league ballgame, or winter in Florida to swim at the beach for Christmas with other Michiganders, but way out here on the far side of the continent with a borrowed vehicle and a dog with no tags I was not only alone but invisible. It was the same as if I weren't there. If I had waved at all the people who had passed me along the way I might be a familiar face to someone in another car on the freeway, a travel companion to give me a thumbs up for good luck with the cops, but I was alone and invisible, except to that specific officer.

Almost scraped the side of the van against concrete with my compliance, pulling over as far as possible without the right-side tires riding up onto the barrier, cars passing inches next to him as he walked up. They didn't bother him as he stuck his butt out farther by leaning in my rolled down window. He glanced at my license but mostly looked around my seat and into the back, asking where's the fire, nodding a polite and professional hello at the dog resting across my pack, then added if I had noticed that everybody was passing me. I told him that the van was a long distance runner but not much for speed, and that they had been passing me all the way from Michigan. He asked what was in the pack. My gorilla suit I said without hesitation, brain sweating with thoughts filled for the first time of having marijuana, hoping it was for a short time. He said he was a Michigan fan, and I didn't know if that meant the state or a football team, then he suggested I take an exit and find breakfast, wait out rush hour before easing on down the road. I promised. He knocked twice on the door and added that there's always work for a guy with a good gorilla suit. It wasn't easy easing until finally reaching the exit ramp, then eased on up.

The streets were almost busy as the freeway, and not knowing where I was going took right turns first to circle a block, then every second street to circle four blocks, every third street so I always came back to parallel the freeway. When I felt comfortable with the area and a few street names, found a rare parking space that allowed two hours, hopefully enough time for traffic to lessen.

The dog's Frisbee was dry which was a good reason to explore, putting our feet on big city pavement. Made a slip knot of my belt around the dog's collar and we walked, the dog charging ahead as if it had a sled behind it, pulling the leash out of my hand but the moment it was free she stopped and waited until I picked up the leash then charged ahead again. I had to walk fast to keep my balance, each footfall more of a stop than a step, thinking she'd make a good plow dog. She stopped without warning to sniff nothing spots and pee a little at each, the stopping and starting giving me a headache. She ran out of pee but that didn't stop her stopping.

Other walkers were rare but I examined them carefully from the corner of my eye hoping to recognize a famous face from tv. We passed stores in foreign languages then like a miracle in the desert there was a drinking fountain in the lobby of an office building. Unable to tie her up outside we boldly entered together and I caught the stream of water in the toy then set it down for her to drink. She licked it dry so I gave her more while waiting for a security guard or an angry receptionist to yell at us to get out but people passing either smiled or didn't care.

We crossed the street and from there could see the freeway diminishing not into the distance but into a gray haze that consumed reality like a hungry cloud, maybe radioactive. Still there were more cars than I'd ever seen in one place, even the junkyard. Back at the van we shared some jerky and tried to wait the extra hour and a half but it became too hot so we drove the city street parallel to the river of cars flowing down the freeway, stopping and starting for stop signs and traffic lights as if the van had the dog on a leash.

The hotter the air the harder it was to breath, similar to but heavier than desert dust. There was a different radio station every few numbers along the radio dial and an oldies station playing wonderful stuff I never had heard. It almost took my mind off the smell of the engine, something burning. It stalled at an intersection and in the moments taking to start it again an impatient horn reminded me to move, a second blat more threatening. I turned the corner to get out of the way, driving away from the freeway and caught in the flow of lesser traffic, eventually finding an open left turn lane at the same moment there was a gap between cars coming the other way, able to turn west again without stopping and stalling.

It was a smaller street of houses and apartment buildings and thankfully little traffic. Did a rolling stop at a stop sign to get across a four-lane street, a car in the far lane of cross traffic braking and skidding to keep from t-boning the van. Floored the gas pedal to motorvate through, a new verb I had just learned from an old song, and in the wide-eyed breath-held moment expecting impact I saw the extra large street sign on the corner. It read Vine as in Hollywood & Vine, and though we weren't on Hollywood it was my first famous street, more exciting than my famous hometown hamburger. Looking for studios and actors I slowed down enough to earn another parade of angry cars behind me, engine smelling like the backyard grill on fourth of July extinguished by a sudden rain.

Made another right turn, again to get out of the way of the hurried drivers as the engine spit and coughed. I lied to it saying c'mon girl, you can make it, just a little bit farther. Didn't know the sex of the van but the motorvation seemed to be female, the engine finally clearing its throat to quit coughing and say instead jug-of-rum jug-of-rum jug-of-rum as it lurched ahead in that rhythm. Maybe it had made a self-adjustment that would keep us moving even with the limp, all the way to Alaska if needed, I hoped.

It broke down one jug-of-rum later, just died into silence but still moving. Using the leftover momentum I steered it to the side of the street, drifting to the curb like a dingy to a dock, no noise to distract anyone in concentration along the sidewalk if there had been anybody walking. The van was angled with its butt stuck out where a wide enough vehicle might kiss it platonically in passing. In neutral it was push-able and I got it straightened out by alternately shoving it a few feet one way, turning the steering wheel, then pushing it the other, a tedious manual-labor version of parallel parking, all the time looking for a passerby to ask for help but the sidewalks were walker-free, as unpopular as the streets were busy, which accounted for the continuum of cars.

The dog got tired of looking up from her nap of the hour and put a paw over the side of her head, unaware of or simply ignoring our situation. Street signage informed the public that the only parking restriction was between two and six a.m. on Tuesdays, and adding up the recent nights and days of the journey it was probably Wednesday. I popped the hood just to do something and there was no engine, then found it in the back on the second try while hoping nobody was watching from a distance to witness how much I didn't know about things.

I pretended to check the motor, wiggling connections and stretching my neck like a turtle to get head deep into the hot stink, spying hard for mechanisms hiding because they were guilty of stranding us in the middle of somewhere that wasn't any better than nowhere. Would've cursed any part of the engine if I knew the name of any. Listen hard, Dad told me over years when I left for school in the morning. Closed the engine cover and told myself I should have listened harder, though I hadn't taken auto shop.

Stepped onto the sidewalk empty in both directions, making me wonder if I were the first to put a foot on that specific concrete, but it was blemished with acne colored pieces of ancient gum walked-on into amoeba-shaped splotches. Went north toward the nearest intersection. There was a phone booth on the opposite and otherwise boring corner. Through an opening between the bumpers of cars wide enough for several people I dashed across diagonally, cars unnecessarily stopping and honking.

That morning heard more horns than the church basement during band practice. Learning the cornet during winter chapped my lips into looking like the wax candy treat at Halloween. Got into a habit of stretching them in a yawning motion which made me look as if I were gagging and caused the cracks to open and I'd have to lick the blood off during class. Didn't look a girl in the face that school year from Thanksgiving to April Fools Day on which I received a love note from a secret admirer, handwritten by a girl but dictated by a stick one grade up who sat first chair trumpet and hated me for my bad lips and worse playing. I waited on the corner long after school for a date that never arrived, just the stick and his buddies laughing as they pushed me back and forth between them while imitating trumpet solos with their healthy lips.

The telephone booth on the corner was scratched up and scrawled over and I had a moment of revulsion about touching any part of it, which I overcame by remembering I didn't brush my teeth everyday until school program sent a memo home. Called my parents collect.

Where the hell are you, Mom asked as if I had been abducted. It was the first time she ever said hell to me. They had been half-expecting to get a ransom demand, which was good because it put them in a desperately generous mood and I needed to borrow money. Dad took the phone from Mom and asked in a hushed way if I was in trouble, and that Jayo had been stopping by everyday looking for his van and to see if I had called. Told him I wasn't in trouble, just in Hollywood. In California? That's the one I told him. At eye level there was something white and dried that had been wet when it hit the glass of the booth so I twisted around to fold the door open. I ducked under the stiff cable of the handset and leaned my head outside, mildly nauseous and claustrophobic.

Looking north along the street through the same haze I had noticed down the freeway, the Hollywood sign hung from a hill above the city. I'm definitely in California, I said.

They thought they could wire money through Western Union, so I gave them the number of the telephone booth while they checked into it. There was a phone book fat as a bible, bound in a blue plastic cover chained to the metal corner shelf. Looked up Western Union and found a Hollywood address on Sunset Boulevard. There was a map of Hollywood among the first pages that also provided first aid instruction and seating charts for arenas and stadiums. Using Vine Street and the freeway as parameters it looked like I was south of but close to Sunset.

Jammed myself across the opening, butt against the folding door, feet against the doorframe, feeling thousands of miles in my lower back. Graffiti was inked and scratched about the booth, random numbers and misspelled sexual suggestions. Debating whether to call the number under a specifically lewd free offer I saw the black and white of a patrol car through the glass. It stopped in the no parking zone at the corner and the officer inside stared at me, waiting to use the phone I hoped. He slowly got out and adjusted the gear on his belt then waved me over and asked me what I was doing. Told him waiting for a call. Drug dealer? I said no. He looked down at his black cloddish shoes and wiped the toe of one on the back of his pants leg to get the shine just right.

The substitute gym teacher wore shoes like that instead of the expected tennis shoes. They left black streaks on the gloss of the wooden floor. The janitor would stand in the open doorway staring at the sub's feet wherever he walked as he took roll call before dodge ball, but when the sub glanced over to him the janitor smiled and waved, pretending he had been sweeping the hallway with a push broom wide enough to sweep an average kitchen with one push. When the sub turned his attention back to us the janitor went back to watching his every step, head slowly shaking with every scuffmark.

The officer asked where I lived and I explained the recent breakdown, pointing toward the van, and he wanted take a look. I shrugged as the phone rang, telling him it was my parents. He nodded and wanted to know if I minded him answering it. Shook my head no and prayed it wasn't some drug dealer by coincidence. It took him seconds to verify it was my parents and he waved me over and gave me the phone. Mom asked me what was going on and I told her the police officer was helping me because I was new in town. She told me they would get to the bank then wire me money in the morning.

The cop was almost to the van when I remembered the hidden pot. My guts curled up into tight ball. There was a big American made car parked in front of the van and though it looked normal to me it was out of place among the small foreign economy models lining the street. It was the kind of cars they use in movies when the car eventually gets shot to pieces before crashing, catching fire and blowing up. The windows were tinted, and there was a peace sign sticker on the driver's side triangular vent window like the one on the van. They let in limited fresh air on cold days for people who had to smoke when they drive. The cop opened the big car's door and searched it instead of the van.

He half sat on the driver's seat, his legs out and feet on the street, leaning over to check the ashtray and snoop inside the glove compartment. Hey, hello? It was a female voice. Hey, get out of there! A young lady came down from the front steps of a bungalow dwarfed in the shadow of a three-story apartment building. She stopped every other step trying to pull the strap of one of her cloggish sandals up around the back of her heel, making a click click, pause, click click, pause waltzing noise that grew louder as she came down her front walk until she reached the dirt of the tree lawn that separated the sidewalk from the curb where she tripped and caught herself with both palms against the passenger side window. The thud frightened the cop into tossing the wad of papers as he scrambled to get out of the car, reaching for something on his belt at the same time she slammed both her palms down onto the roof and asked him what the hell he was doing in her car.

I had jogged over to the corner of that block by the time she told him that he didn't have any right to search her car. He looked at me and I pointed to the van and shrugged. He told her sorry in an official voice. She got her shoe thing on and clunked around the back end of the car in two/two time. He suggested she keep her vehicle locked as she put her stuff back. She told him to shut up. He told me he'd still like to take a look in my vehicle and she screamed out from inside her car to tell him no. I was in awe of the Hollywood girl and forgot all words, including my favorite words, even articles and prepositions.

That had been a problem in lunchrooms divided naturally into boy tables and girl tables where the only form of communication was throwing a small piece of food without being seen. She wasn't attractive except that she had breasts, but the way she scared the cop then yelled at him with authority fascinated me to near silence except for a quiet grunt I hoped she couldn't hear. She climbed out, locked the door and slammed it shut so hard it rocked slightly on chirping springs. She looked at me saying what. Having no small piece of food to throw I faked a smile and shrugged. She kept looking, wondering even more what.

Sorry, I finally said, apologizing for the cop and told her he thought it was my car, gesturing to the van where the cop was looking in the window. She looked at the Michigan license plate and said don't be a complete tourist, clunk clunking back around the big butt of her boat-like sedan and up to her little house the color of brown mustard. The cop opened the sliding door and the dog was waiting there to scare him back a step, causing him that reflex motion for something on his belt again. He looked embarrassed for being startled twice within the same minute, which gave me the courage to ask why he was so interested in me. Cause you're a mess, kid. You look like you've been up for days. He let the dog pass to pee on the dead grass of the girl's patch of lawn. I wondered if the dog dug a hole would it reach more concrete.

The cop leaned in to reach for my pack as he finished his answer. You smell like a mushroom and talk through your nose. He smelled the pack suspiciously and opened it, pulling out my suit. It's the latex, I told him, smells funky after you sweat in it. He tossed the bundle into the van like it might carry disease, told me to have a nice day, then instead of going back kitty-corner, walked across one street between the painted crosswalk lines, then turned left to do it again, got back in his cruiser and motorvated toward the Hollywood sign.

The dog came over to smell the rear tire of the girl's car. It reminded me of a scene in which a dog pulled a salami patch off a repaired wheel, making me hungry. Tried to start the van hoping it had overheated and might run again now that the engine had cooled, but it was dead. Smelled my armpits and pulled the neck of my shirt out to see if the fertile smell was a good mushroom or a poison one. My crotch itched and felt inhabited by a herd of something microscopic slowly creeping across my skin, grazing on bacteria. Leaned my head back and closed my eyes.

When Jayo drove in high school he would close his right eye and drop his head as if he suddenly had fallen asleep at the wheel, peeking out his left eye to steer dangerously close to the centerline and on coming traffic. Even knowing the joke I couldn't resist grabbing the steering wheel to keep us on the proper side of the road, just in case by weird coincidence at astronomical odds he might have developed undiagnosed narcolepsy since the last time he did the gag.

I yawned and my ears popped causing a ringing. It stopped. Then it started and stopped again. I realized it was the phone in the booth. Jogged over through traffic less busy, thinking the call might be an important update for me, but there was a guy with long blond hair hurrying toward it from another direction. It stopped ringing before either of us reached it. I stood on the corner as he slapped the booth and put both hands into his pockets searching but they came out empty. He asked if I had a quarter and I touched the outside of my pockets knowing I had three left, needing time to make up my mind because he looked wild. As he moved three steps forward to save me the trouble of delivering it I reached in for one of my quarters. I wanted to run home but it was worth twenty-five cents not to be a coward in public. And he might be a fast stick.

He said thanks and slid the booth's accordion door shut. There was too much dirt and gravel in the track so a crack of opening remained that allowed me to eavesdrop just by pretending to be waiting for something on the corner, looking down the street expectantly, noticing for the first time it was lined with a row of droopy palm trees. That I decided was why the air was barely breathe-able, not enough oxygen, no forests of deciduous broad leaf trees, no orchards, no fields of crops, just concrete and palms.

I had seen him push buttons to dial a number but didn't hear him say anything. Used the corner of my eye to see if he were whispering. He was nodding as if listening, leaning his hand against the phone but with his pinky finger holding down the little hang-up lever. Then the phone started to ring, just long enough for the r if you were saying the word, and his pinky let go of the hanger-upper and he started talking. Somebody had called back and he kept my quarter.

Crossed back to the van to observe. Maybe it was a drug deal and I could turn the guy in for a reward. The girl, now in cowboy boots, shuffled from the house to the car and there was a long noisy grind before the engine awoke. She shifted it forward then backward trying to steer the big thing sideways out of a tight spot. I forgot about phone booth guy and got out to help. She turned her head back to scowl at me with a question mark look. I asked if she wanted me to do it. That didn't sound right so asked if I could help. She said I could help by moving the damn van. Damn Van was a good name for it.

Told her it was broke down and she winced, asking if I was gonna just sit there and live at her curb. Not waiting for an answer she turned the wheel as if it had a previous life on a pirate ship and escaped the space to drive around the corner with all the smoke and screech of a factory.

The dog paced inside the van like it was a circus cage, restless to be rolling again, missing the rattle of the van's bones, wanting better smells. I let her out to sniff the area, run away if she chose. She backtracked the Hollywood girl's trail up her front step and onto the little porch, ignoring my call and whistle, so I ignored her and walked a half block down to the entrance way of the apartment building, the Palms View, thinking maybe I was fated to live there.

The gate was locked but there was a phone-intercom with a button. A plastic strip from a label maker gun said it was the manager's button.

Got tired suddenly. Just finding it was enough work for the moment so I walked back. There was a cat inside the window watching the dog wear herself out looking for a way in to wipe that smug feline look off its face. Told the dog I needed a bathroom and to change my shirt and find food, yelling from the sidewalk because I didn't want to trespass, which was a good idea because the owner returned from her short errand and tried to parallel-park the big Pontiac back into the same space.

I had several good looks at the metal letters that spelled out Bonneville along the rear of the car as she backed in repeatedly at the wrong angle, hitting the curb. Couldn't move the van back another inch or it would touch the Honda, a model so small I worried that any contact would cause damage. It was boxy looking and reminded me of my cast iron bank in the shape of a safe, which I half filled with pennies until Dad borrowed it, the only handy thing heavy enough to weigh down the garbage can lid against whatever was getting in there and spreading our trash through the neighborhood. He suspected an opossum but I wondered about the neighbor lady. One morning the garbage strewn again across the lawn my penny-heavy bank was gone. Not the work of an opossum.

Offered to park house cat girl's big car for her but got no reply. After trying a couple more times she got out angrily saying bad words but left the engine running and the door open. Through gritted teeth she told me thank you but it also sounded like cursing. In the spare time of youth some guys shot free throws or threw pitches at the garage, but I practiced parking in spaces most people would pass on.

On her dashboard was a plastic robed figure but it wasn't Jesus. That might've been the problem because according to a guy back home in church Jesus was good with Pontiacs. I smoothed into the parking space, locked and closed the door and went halfway up the walk toward her waiting at the front step, unable to go inside without her door key on the chain, a metal octopus with lesser rings and extra appendages clipped to one large central ring, each key on the end of its own tentacle of links. I tossed her the bundle, the mess jingling through the air but she ducked and put up her hands as if being attacked.

It was a good throw and they landed balanced on her shoulder until she stood straight again, and they fell in the dirt at the edge of her plot of deceased grass. She asked what was the matter with me, the words harsh but accompanied by a nice Christmas sound the key chain made when she picked it up. Maybe she wouldn't mind me if I cleaned up. Before I finished that thought the dog gave up on the cat and trotted down to greet her. Get your dog, she growled, kicking at it. Told her it wasn't my dog. She said she saw it in my van. Told her it wasn't my van.

Took my belt off for a leash again and we touristed toward the big sign, hoping there would be stairs and we could climb and touch the letters. A few blocks up we crossed Sunset Boulevard where walkers were few, but a couple more blocks took us to Hollywood Boulevard where we found company, many shoppers for all the shops in a row but also tourists there to see the stars, the big stars in the sidewalk each for a different famous person though I recognized maybe half the names. People tightrope walked the border lines from one to the next, cameras aimed down at the plaque in the center of each, clicking a picture then jumping forward to avoid stepping on any sacred names. Most of the stars were clean and polished gold, but many were covered in grime and gum. The dog stepped on them all, pausing only to smell flavored stains.

A bus stop bench had a holder for maps of several bus routes. I sat and unfolded one to look for a you-are-here arrow and find my place in the world at that moment. An older lady sat down on the other end of the bench with such a thud that my end would have teeter-tottered up if the bench weren't bolted down. Without looking at me she complained about her new shoes, that the Japanese put some kind of rubber soles on them that were made to make a person trip, who did they think they were fooling? I asked her how much to take the bus and she said a dollar, and not to forget my transfer. I studied her profile, trying to match a younger version of it with old movie actresses. Asked her if there were any movie studios nearby. She frowned in thought and said she wasn't sure where they were but the theaters were just down the street, that I should ask at the Chinese but keep one hand on my wallet and don't hand my camera to a stranger for a picture because while I was down on my hands and knees in someone else's prints they'd run off with it.

A bus arrived all hiss and whine as if coming in for a landing, the sun reflecting down off its side too bright for the advertisement to be read. She pushed herself up off the bench with both hands and frantically searched several pockets, asking where was that transfer, had she remembered to get one, then found a slip of paper inside a folded hanky and waved it at the bus like a victory flag before climbing aboard. The bus pulled away with a roar and left me in the shade again breathing diesel fumes, thinking I should have asked her where was a bathroom. The dog was gone with my belt.

I jogged down the sidewalk irreverently stepping on stars while looking for the dog. The familiar yellow and red of a McDonald's eased my panic. The proximity of a bathroom made it impossible to ignore my bladder and bowels, they knew. It was so crowded I wasn't self conscious about using it without buying some fries first, and I didn't look worse than many others loitering at tables with nothing but cups of coffee. Swam through the delicious greasy worldwide odor but had to wait in a line of two at the bathroom door before getting my turn in the stall.

When I got in before soiling myself as old people used to say, ineffectively washed my chest and armpits with paper towels, getting my shirt blotchy with wet spots and my pants wet with a line straight across my zipper and thighs from leaning forward against the puddled counter of the sink to admire how the facial hair was hiding my weird lip. Stood with my pants low on my hip bones without the belt to hold them up, pelvis forward while rubbing the wet part with a paper towel in an attempt to dry it quickly, but impatient people were trying the handle of the locked door, and if anybody saw me I'd probably be arrested for some sexual public display.

On the way out I expected some of the kids in wild clothing to laugh at my water stains but I was invisible. Ached for a Quarter Pounder with Cheese but needed something more to get through the night and morning, so went around the large block looking for the dog then stopped at a gas station convenience store, spending my last two dollars and fifty cents on a can of Coke, loaf of bread, quart of milk, and a mini-jar of peanut butter. The low harsh light dried my wet spots but the direct sunlight made me sweat myself dirty again. The dog was waiting at the van, curled up in the dirt under the palm tree. Her tail wagged sideways, thumping the ground and kicking up dust though she didn't look up, just recognized my smell.

Put my belt back on then poured half the milk into the dog's Frisbee. Used my finger to dig a wad of peanut butter out of the jar and wiped it clean using a slice of bread, giving it to the dog. Pulled the bus bench map from my back pocket and though it had little detail there were streets labeled enough to be able to find my way around a greater area than between the van and McDonalds. Sat in the passenger seat eating a peanut butter sandwich and listened to the radio while it got dark, smelling my finger. Suddenly the Hollywood sign lit up.

CHAPTER EIGHT

----

he village of my forefathers in Pummern was money poor, each
family secreting their small horde of coins in the hollowed-
out wooden legs of furniture or in a hole under the big flat
stone used as a hearth. The custom was to lie about having any money
especially to the tax collector then let him look for and discover two or
three coins hidden where they could be found, the gangster extortion
business over for another year. People survived with a garden or field,
a goat or cow, hunting or trading services, any varied skill listed on the
tax rolls. The way a person survived became many families' surnames
distorted through generations of translation and misspelling.

Our last name is Loffelbak, its origin in clay spoons. There was a
knife in most homes, treasure, but people ate from wooden bowls using
wooden spoons, until a peddler arrived with ceramic spoons. One of
my distant relatives saw the younger generation wasting hidden coins
on them.

There was a layer of clay below the topsoil and out of curiosity or
boredom, or maybe tired of the taste of wood and getting splinters in
his tongue, made a spoon of clay and baked it in the fireplace, his own
brick spoon. The experiment worked and his woman showed it off to
the neighbors. Others tried but he had the talent and soon produced
spoons of white with green ivy vining around them, getting permission

from the mayor to fire them in the traditional winter solstice bonfire. For no specific reason everyone wanted one of those spoons.

They were delicate and hard to make without defects, bubbles, bends or cracks. Maybe it was how he cleaned the clay, or how it dried, or how long they baked in the good section of a proper fire. Others imitated them but he had the trick and it paid off well enough for the sons to open a business in a larger burg, allowing later sons to emigrate to America with the name of spoon-baker.

The guy at Western Union wanted to know where the name was from, priding his ability to guess any person's heritage, but Loffelbak was new to him and he had never heard of Pummern. He guessed wrongly while counting out the stacks of twenty-dollar bills and my pride grew, signing for the cash with a new affection for the family line. It wasn't free money and needed to be paid back, but it gave me the confidence lost when they took my room away. Almost ran to McDonalds but it was too hot, the morning sun in my face making me understand how sunglasses and Hollywood went together. The glare on concrete could make a person snow blind in ninety-degree heat.

The dog and I ate sausage egg McMuffins for breakfast. The Hollywood girl's sedan was gone so I filled the Frisbee from a faucet on the side of her house, at first afraid it wouldn't work because of the dried to death lawn, but there was running water and I stuck my head under the faucet for luxury. With chores finished I walked down to the Palms View gate and pushed the manager's button. The phone rang through the speaker but I also could hear it ringing from the building in weird stereo, ringing and ringing until I gave up and walked away, and then someone answered. I yelled hello so loudly that a stranger answered me from the other side of the street, thinking I knew him. I waved to him then jogged back to the gate yelling hold on, finally asking the intercom breathily is this the manager? He said yes, but it sounded like a question. I could hear his voice from a window at the same time it came through the speaker with a metallic effect and hard to understand, so when I told him I was looking for an apartment I said it loud enough for him to hear me through his window too. He said that was what he was there for, room 101, and the gate buzzed.

I pushed through and opened the door to the building just as the door of 101 opened in the hall. A round man holding a piece of paper stepped onto the threshold and asked if I yelled like that all the time, that some people liked to sleep around here. By coincidence he was rumpled as if rolling out of bed. He looked me up and down probably thinking the same about me. I stifled most of a yawn as I asked how much was the rent, sounding like I had a speech problem. He told me it was fifteen hundred to move in, five hundred a month, first last and deposit, then handed me the paper telling me to fill out an application and I'd be on the list, he'd call me. I took the paper and looked at it, wondering how long was the list but he backed into the room and closed the door before I could ask. The gate opened from the inside without the unlocking buzz and I yelled thank you toward 101's window. As the gate relocked behind me with serious chink, thought I heard a faint and tired yeah-yeah-yeah from the window.

My paper route included the old folks building fourteen stories high that had a locked entrance with an intercom to get buzzed in. I'd press the apartment of any customer and say I was the paperboy. Years later when Jayo and I were hanging around there bored I shared that fact. He tried it and we went in just to ride the elevator to the top and throw small things off the balcony of the community room. Anyone could get in claiming a delivery or pretending to be the Fuller Brush man. Mom let that guy in, a stranger with a carrying case who arrived unannounced. The case could have been full of murderous items but she was lucky. He had a variety of brushes for things you never would think needed brushing, a case full of everything bristled itself being creepy. Mom rarely bought a brush probably because there was no cash in the house, making him seem to pity us as he slowly returned the samples to the box as if they were mink coats instead of something off a badger for scrubbing tubs and toilets.

Wanted to tell him we all used one royal brush handed down for generations, brought over the ocean from Pummern and made of wildman hair. He gave my mom a complimentary basting brush so small it might have been to embarrass us, make us regret not purchasing anything from his fine line, to imply we probably could not afford a turkey big enough to warrant a basting brush of respectable size.

The breeze was pleasant but smelled of parking lot and a fireplace gone cold. The dog was sitting in the driver's seat with her nose out the four inches of open window. Dogs were doubly blessed, for the ability to smell a thousand times better than humans, and second for not being bothered by the smell of rotting flesh or other dogs' crap multiplied by a thousand.

The dog scratched on the glass and barked just loud enough to be heard, wanting out of the too warm van as the phone began ringing. I opened the door for her but before I could get my belt off she ran up to the house looking for that cat. Not my dog I said to the house and worked my way to the phone, cars politely stopping for me but also honking. I answered on maybe the fifteenth ring wondering if it might be my parents or a drug dealer calling the guy with my quarter, or maybe the cop for some kind of law enforcement prank.

Jayo said hey man, but said it like a jazzy musician to sound cool. Then he said a couple swear words which he always used to begin a sentence whether glad or mad. Worried I had hung up he asked if I was still there, using personalized profanity, and I told him his mom gave me permission to borrow the van. He said that was great, now unborrow it, and a little piece of advice for no charge, don't do anything to get pulled over by the cops. Too late I told him, and I think he used the phone to bang on his forehead or maybe something more valuable. He told me you don't know what you're driving there, kid, but I told him yes I did, and he was lucky the van hadn't been impounded and searched.

You found the uh ...?

Found it and stashed it for you. It's still in the county.

Suddenly I was an angel though he still preferred vulgarities as modifiers. Told him I'd get the van running and probably be back for the holidays, leaving it vague which holidays. He got serious again and whispered that he wasn't just in trouble with the judge, then almost too breathy for me to hear he said that none of it belonged to him, not the stash or the cash.

What cash?

He was silent except for some swallowing noise then quickly asked where the stuff was, so I told him about the burg and the car lot and the pile of tires in the junkyard. He left to find something to write with then had me repeat everything in detail. Instead of thank you or goodbye he ordered me to get back there and hung up. Walked slowly to the van and opened the trunk in the front, looking for hiding places. It wouldn't be in the hubcaps because we lost one and that hadn't bother Jayo. Searched his box of framed foreign phrases. Looked at the bottoms of the seats and on the cot in the pop-top roof. There was no secret compartment in the little closet. Lifted the mattress but there was nothing under it. Maybe he didn't mean there was cash in the van, just cash from the deal. But that would be stupid.

Tried to sleep, but opened my eyes to stare at the green color of the backrest that matched the mattress, green like leftover peas. Too easy I thought, but there in the foam of the mattress was the money in four neat bundles probably wrapped by the same person who had packaged the pot. I left it there, pushed the cushion back against the frame and laid down on my back using the crook of my arm behind my head as a pillow, trying to remember the ten commandments and which number was the one about not stealing, thinking that the first one about having no other gods before me sounded self serving and insecure for an almighty creator.

The air was crowded, city air jostled by too many people and cars, too much construction, hard to breathe which interrupted thought. It reminded me of the air in classrooms, each delicate bit of information fighting for the attention of wandering minds distracted by the crowd of other students fidgeting, doodling, daydreaming and playing eye tag. Blamed the teachers for not forcing knowledge into my head with brilliant tricks. If there were a switch in the brain simply to alternate between transmit and receive I would have switched over to knowing everything instead of the pleasures of not knowing.

Didn't know my pillow arm had fallen asleep until I tried to scratch my nose and poked myself in the eye. There was noise outside the van and I panicked that Jayo had local connections. Peeked through the plaid curtains at the screened windows, the louvres almost allowing ventilation.

There was a guy in a new red sports car double-parked. He opened the trunk and I expected to see a shotgun but he pulled out two buckets, one with suds, one with water. He washed the Hollywood girl's big sedan, calling toward the house that he was sorry, really sorry. When he finished drying it with a chamois he went up her walk, got down on his knees and bowed with his hands stretched out on the pavement toward the front door where the dog had been sleeping on the welcome mat, her head now up with curiosity. The cat was in the window watching but I didn't see the girl. The dog went down to sniff at the guy's fingers, which still held the chamois. The guy looked up to see the dogs muzzle and backed away carefully but painfully on his knees. The dog followed the chamois.

The guy got up and emptied the buckets into the gutter, limping because of his knees, his posture similar to the wet rag. The phone booth cop was writing a ticket and slipped it under the wash guy's wiper blade who threw the buckets in separate directions and kicked his car, setting off an alarm, a lonely bleat-bleating cry that well expressed the moment.

I opened the sliding door to let the dog into the van, loneliness being contagious. Ironically you have to be near another person to catch it, and as the guy drove away with ticket still on the windshield, the front door of her house opened enough to let out the cat.

I told the dog about the money and gave her a slice of peanut butter bread. She dropped the wet chamois to smell then swallow the bread and lick my finger clean. Took her much longer to lick the residue off the roof of her mouth, keeping her busy until it was again naptime three minutes later. Seeing all that soap and water made me want a clean shirt. Promised to bring her water later and left singing drugs and money honey, drugs and money honey.

The air was warm but the setting sun was hot. On Hollywood Boulevard I studied what everybody was wearing, then shopped for something black and cheap with long sleeves but couldn't resist a Hawaiian shirt instead, wearing it loose over my dirty t-shirt. Went to the golden arches for a cheeseburger and paper towel bath, then crossed the street and hopped a bus for a buck, learning that the transfer cost an extra dime and that the drivers didn't make change, which exposed me as a first timer to the regular riders. I hoped they wouldn't get mean like on a school bus where big kids bullied us out of boredom.

The seats all were taken so I stood in a lightly populated area holding one of the many anchored hand-holds, that feeling of holding the phone returning as my palm sweated lightly, my out of town germs meeting and mating with those left by strangers. We passed the Chinese Theatre and I resisted an urge to yell stop, waiting instead until there was a stop with nothing of interest for a tourist to see so got off there. Back at the theatre the imprints in cement were more exciting than real people. This was where movies met the concrete. The civilized world had thousands of years of mortared buildings and paved roads, but movies were the same age as an old human, and in that single lifetime they brought visions of everything that ever happened, all of it visible to anyone with the price of admission. If it all disappeared there still would be evidence of the miracle, imprints in concrete more rare than ferns or ammonites from hundreds of millions of years before.

Instead of crossing America's dirt, felt as if I had crossed a mythical plain and now stood in paradise. I had died and gone to Hollywood. There was a guy doing Charlie Chaplin, working hard in the heavy vintage suit and sweating through his black and white make-up. I got close enough to notice he smelled like a wet closet, almost stinky as I.

People were having their pictures taken next to him, often tipping. He was nobody. They could've dressed up the little neighbor man with a mustache back home and saved themselves the airfare. He wasn't funny as much as brave to make a fool of himself, and his shtick wouldn't have worked in normal clothes except to get him arrested for bothering women.

A gorilla would be better. Waited about half an hour until he did a walking backwards bit, waving goodbye and falling into a backwards somersault, tipping his derby as a goodbye then instead of it returned to his head it sat up on the end of his cane. He chased after it like a carrot on a stick and disappeared behind a kiosk selling Hollywood mugs and shirts.

I was the only person who left the patio of prints to watch him walk quickly up the side street where he ducked into the back of and old station wagon. Off came the jacket, tie, mustache, derby and wig. He used a dirty towel to wipe off the make-up, which left an average guy around thirty years old. He counted the money from assorted pockets and as I caught up with him he went to another pocket and pointed a small gun toward my feet as if he didn't have the strength to raise it, but I believed he was being careful in case it went off. That worried me because maybe it fired accidentally often.

I raised my hands like it was a stick-up and asked him, can anybody do what you do? He said that Chaplin was pretty good at it, then he added why, do you do Charlie? No, I said. I meant are there other characters and do you need permission? He put the gun in his waistband without a worry about it misfiring and I suspected it was a prop. He said that nobody lets anybody do anything, that I'd have to take my chances same as the rest. Then he asked who the hell did I do?

Gemora, I told him, adding that Gemora might have worked with Chaplin. He put on a leather jacket while obviously thinking hard, trying to place the name and not lose the respect of Chaplin's spirit. He pointed his finger at nothing as if the answer had arrived but asked me if I wanted to get a drink. I said okay and he waved me into the passenger seat. He muttered Gemora Gemora, it's familiar but maybe I'm thinking Sodom and Gomorrah.

He checked the lane for traffic then pulled out with a little squeal of the tires to show me the wagon had some power and wasn't just a dork-mobile. He sniffed the air and asked, is that smell me or you? A little of both I think, then told him that Gemora was the guy with the gorilla suit in old movies, that I had a gorilla suit.

He laughed hya hya hya, as if karate chopping three things in quick succession then stuck his right hand out. I looked out the windshield thinking he was gesturing at something but he said his name was Roy and I realized I was supposed to shake it. Shook it and told him my name. He pronounced it laugh-back and told me I was new in town. He was proud of my surprise and continued, telling me I had driven cross-country to get there. I asked if he were a detective and he said no, a cab driver, then pulled up his left sleeve to show me his extreme tan line, rolling down the window and resting it there. You got a left brown arm and a northern accent, he said.

He got into the habit of driving with the window down instead of using the AC because all that did was circulate the smell of his stinky fares. Rolled down the passenger window to give us both more relief, thinking of when I used to shower and change into clean clothes every day. Now it was like being a famous cowboy on tv, in the same outfit for one to six years depending on the success of the series.

Roy used the alleys and quiet streets off the main grid bragging that he could get from Los Feliz to Pico with only two stop signs and two rights on reds. It was getting dark so he parked under a street light in front of an electronics store that stayed open late, saying the light wouldn't stop a dedicated thief but there was a chance, a skinny chance.

We walked a block toward the Pantages, its sign colorful and though it wasn't lit, almost bright. Before we could pass under the sign Roy reached to his left and found a door in the dark, opening it to let a ray of light onto the sidewalk, smoke visible in the yellowed air. Neon tubing flat across the front the building said it was Bob's Frolic Room, also unlit. There was a martini glass up there with it, and I was afraid it would be too ritzy for me in dirty jeans regardless of my palm-patterned rayon over-shirt. The bartender nodded at us, Roy giving him a weak wave back that did double duty offering me a stool as if it were his to offer. The bartender made a quick drink in a short glass and set it in front of Roy, then asked me for ID. He leaned back to look at it, catching some extra light reflected off the mirror and from a glowing beer sign, squinting at it as if memorizing everything on it then he handed it back to me and asked me what I needed.

Back home the drinking age was eighteen though we all drank something by twelve. When I turned eighteen, maybe because of the draft and the war in Viet Nam, they raised the legal drinking age one year more for the next three years until it was twenty-one because the draft and the war both were over. It didn't matter to me because of a hangover when I was fourteen. It spoiled the taste of beer for the next seven years. I thought people drank warm liquor because they enjoyed the flavor same as with other nasty things like coffee or liver, and when they got drunk it was from accidentally drinking too much. Only recently I figured out they originally had to force the booze down to get drunk, getting used to the taste and eventually liking it. I ordered a beer, pointing to the handle of the tap that advertised Budweiser but could've been connected to a keg of anything. Forced it down hoping I'd like the taste again. The price seemed high until I learned I was paying for both Roy's and mine.

Asked Roy did he ever see any famous people in here? He told me to turn around. My eyes had adjusted to the gloom enough to see that the upper half of the wall behind us was a mural the length of the bar, a nightclub filled with movie stars, caricatures of so many that some were unrecognizable having lost their fame somewhere among the decades, now appearing as nobodies who had snuck into the artwork.

As I admired the mural Roy asked, so Laughback do you have representation, all on the exhale after inhaling his drink then toasting the bartender with the empty glass, signal for a refill.

What, like an agent? Tried to gulp my beer but the throat still closed on it so had to spit half of it back into the glass. Nobody noticed, all looking into their drinks or up at the television, which allowed me a second attempt that was successful.

Yeah he sighed, that was his problem too, no representation. Said he had an agent in Whittier, could I believe it? Whittier! Said that she got him bookings at store openings and blow-out days at car dealerships. Said he spent most of the day driving to Orange County and back. Orange County! He had to take a leak, slamming his empty on the bar and walked to the back like a hockey player just off his skates, legs wide and shuffling on flat feet, arms crooked and chugging as if miming a locomotive, nothing like Chaplin unless he was doing the tramp crapping his black baggy pants.

Forced the rest of the beer down and toasted the bartender Roy-style but he wasn't looking in my direction so I set the glass on the bar heavily and got his attention. Went along the wall until I found Chaplin, drawn from the back and squeezed in among other comedians, segregated from musicians and sex symbols. Seemed right the funny men were separated and scattered, using unfunny celebrities as straight men and women. Planned to impress Roy with my comedic insight and went back to where my fresh beer was waiting with Roy's third drink. Looked up at the lights and almost was certain one of them had been used as a spaceship in an old scifi movie. Roy skate-walked back to his stool and for a change sipped his drink, silent and thoughtful as if contemplating how well or badly the peeing had gone. So Roy, I started to say and he looked at me as if I were a stranger who had just walked in. Know of any jobs for a gorilla suit?

He shook his head and I thought that was his answer, but after another long sip he said in a low reverent voice, kid, a gorilla suit is good as gold, the question being is how good is your gorilla suit. We laughed and between my nasal chuckling and his series of hya hya hya's he finished that drink and there came the bartender as if something terrible might happen if Roy ever went dry. He must've gotten drunk because he started paying for drinks.

The room got thick with smoke and customers looking like tough guy extras in a bar scene because of a tattoo, scar, motorcycle jacket, or sunglasses at night, but in conversation they spoke softly, mild statements about their latest troubles, confusion over things in the news, getting animated only about the Dodgers or a beer commercial featuring women on the silent tv screen, but especially a rock anthem on the jukebox that played louder each time around, which was every fourth or fifth song. Hours were lost and no person frolicked. Two women entered, faces that might have survived the dust bowl but earning a hundred glances in the first minute as they paused to look all of us over then taking stools offered by two gentlemen, five other galahads too slow in surrendering their own, one standing up so clumsily he knocked his over backwards causing a group chuckle.

Asked Roy if many women usually came in and he prayed god I hope so. The music was so loud I almost had to shout into his ear, asking him why Chaplin was portrayed in the mural with his back to the room. Maybe because he was mostly an ass, he yelled back, laughing a single weak hya. People lined the wall, standing two deep behind those with seats at the bar, ordering drinks over our heads and paying over our shoulders causing Roy to lose his good mood. He sipped an imaginary last drop from his long-empty glass, the good service lost to the crowd, stood and pushed through the late comers without apology and no word or signal to me. Sat there for a few minutes to prove I wasn't afraid of the dark then politely worked my way past a new bunch that had entered looking much wilder than the evening rabble, my bright aloha shirt making me feel like a target.

Roy was crawling into the back of his wagon. He noticed me and apologized that he couldn't drive me home, needing a nap. Told him I was fine, just point me toward the Chinese Theatre. He said just keep walking. I felt polluted but the night air cleaned out my lungs.

Had used the bathroom in the bar several times, each trip more difficult past the boots, knees and elbows, always a wait and someone waiting behind me so I had held it in the last hour. Now painfully needed to go. It was many blocks back to the van but knew I was getting close when I heard the dog barking. She was happy to see me but only because she also needed to go. With beer bravery I peed against the side of the palm tree on the side shadowed by the corner streetlight then snuck to the house faucet and filled the Frisbee, the dog sniffing around the porch. She wouldn't get back in the van until I offered her peanut butter. Toed the back of my shoes down off the heel and kicked them in the front where I wouldn't have to smell them, then remembered to take off my new shirt before I fell on the bed to sleep. The dog used it for a pillow.

CHAPTER NINE

hicken pox gave me a fever when I was eight. Elves mined my pillow for the stuffing, taking it away in tiny wheelbarrows. They were much like the seven dwarves except they didn't whistle or sing, but I didn't know that until later because I had never seen the movie. Back then it wasn't on tv, only re-released every seven years and even then in select theaters. Either elves existed and had been seen by Walt, or my overheated brain produced cartoons similar to those produced by Disney's brain, each idea fascinating as the other. The elves did not return, but I would get excited over catching a cold or flu or the measles, anticipating more elves or something else as good, but it was a one time thing same as the gorilla.

The dog woke me with scratching and flea nipping and heavy sighing, the van hot and grimy from a night's worth of both our bad breaths. Felt sick, wondering if elves had stolen from the cushions. A thin layer of liquid was left in the Frisbee but mostly was dog spit. That it was wet made my thirst almost painful. My great uncle had a bleached white fish skull nailed to the side of the barn from when he caught and skinned a sturgeon. That's how my head felt, nailed to the barn.

Pulled at the aloha shirt to stretch out some of the wrinkles then switched it for my t-shirt that now was fifty percent cotton and fifty percent dried sweat. Outside there was a tasty breeze that wrapped around my head like a cool bandage. The dog ran off with a plan so I locked the van and went to find water and a bathroom. Despite the headache a few gears turned and I used the giant phone book in the booth to look up libraries. One block up and two blocks over, a knight's move away, was a blessed branch of the Los Angeles public library. It was cool inside, quiet and patient like a church but with knowledge, the congregation in hushed awe of free information.

The bathroom was a honeymoon suite for soap and me. Clean and well watered I was normal enough to speak humanese again, telling a librarian I was new in town and if I could get a card. She told me I needed a California driver's license and an address in the district. Didn't have an address so couldn't get a license so I would have to read in house. Strolled up and down the aisles thinking of aspirin.

Walked to the gas station store for some edible junk, and when I pulled out money to pay discovered a crumpled napkin mixed in with the dollars. There was a steel and concrete trash receptacle outside the door so with the useless receipt I tossed the napkin, noticing something written inside its folds before it disappeared down the bin. Couldn't see in there and I didn't want to dig around blindly, so figured out that the steel top was a sleeve and could be slid up and off to expose the barrel. As I bent over the side to retrieve the napkin a driver-by honked twice long and loud, I instinctively waved until I realized they were honks of mockery.

Somebody thought I was fishing for breakfast, below the standards of a person with the luxury of a working car with a working horn. Wanted to shout proudly that I wasn't living on the street, but was living parked neatly on the side of one so I grabbed the napkin silently and put the trashcan back together. On one side of the napkin was Roy's name and a number for leaving a message, and on the other side the name of Leely with a different number. An almost memory came back to me of Roy talking under the music and me pretending to hear him. It was after the dust bowl women had a drink and I was straining to see if they might be looking at me through their cigarette smoke, not for anything to happen, just wanting attention.

At the van I called and whistled for the dog, pouring part of a pint of milk into the Frisbee. I also had a can of tuna, hoping she liked fish. Wondered if Hollywood had dogcatchers, thinking it must because dogcatchers were written into old comedies, always dressed in white with comedy size nets. Looking for her toward the girl's house I heard a confusion of cars and she came running through traffic from across the street, maybe happy I was back or maybe escaping trouble over there.

Also had bought a can of chicken noodle soup without thinking of a can opener, a handy machine taken for granted in the real world. Messily opened the tuna and the soup with a small flathead screwdriver from the glove compartment. It was an adventure but made the undiluted and unheated soup worth the effort. Washed down a double dose of aspirin with an almost cold can of Coke and went back to bed, gas building up in my chest every few minutes making me have to sit up to let out a burp, but my head felt better.

It was almost dark when I opened my eyes not knowing where I was, coming out of a grueling dream about walking endless hallways looking for an elusive classroom in high school, but while still dreaming I remembered graduating so knew it was a dream, which returned me to consciousness. Looked around in the heat, the inside of the van momentarily unfamiliar with a strange dog looking up, whupping its tail against the floor dreamlike. The streetlamp at the corner suddenly lit up, on a timer or sensor, and the extra illumination brought back my memory, remembering I had a surprise for the dog, a box of dog biscuits. She took one from my hand but dropped it on the floor to smell it then looked back up at me as if to ask what, no jerky? Told her no and she settled for the chew, gobbling it down. Let her out and she disappeared in a trot toward what she knew more than I did about something in the night.

Was exhausted from sleeping all day so rested in the passenger seat drinking a warm coke and listening to the radio. The apartment manager walked past dressed in a neat light gray suit with a bowtie, bouncing up off each toe and coming down on the opposite heel as if the bottom of his feet were arched the wrong way. Caught myself scratching my facial hair, not full enough to call a beard, maybe a ten o'clock shadow. Everything else also itched, feet, crotch, belly, butt and even the top of my head, but the hand always went back to the chin. It went with thinking, something going back to the first tool makers who hadn't thought to use the razor edge of a broken chunk of obsidian to shave yet, just scratched their hairy chins in thought over how to attach that dangerous chunk to the end of a stick, maybe win a fight without busting any finger nails or knuckle skin.

Didn't want to spend money on an electric shaver and have to carry it to the library, but I wasn't good with a razor and shaving cream, always leaving minor wounds around the lips and Adam's apple as if pimples weren't bad enough. Jayo had a different problem. To hide a hickey given to him by a neighbor he sandpapered his neck to hide it from his girlfriend, telling her he had an accident fake fighting in woodshop. Mongolian boys at sixteen steal an eaglet from a nest on the side of a cliff to enter manhood, but I was still afraid to shave with a safety razor.

It was dark and the days of sitting in dirty air had left a layer of pollution on the windshield. The streetlight shone on the outside of the glass turning it from transparent to translucent, bringing out the greens and grays of bug splats and bird droppings. It was the time of year that mulberries ripened, the birds eating them then crapping purple on the neighborhood, hitting more white cars than mathematically probable. There didn't seem to be any mulberries trees in the area, but I hoped the apologetic carwash guy would come back and try to impress the girl this time by cleaning the van.

The last swallow of Coke tasted like can and as I walked up the street began a shopping list in my head with toothpaste at the top, wondering if grocery stores sold water in a bottle or jug like milk.

From across the boulevard I could see Roy still at work, walking on his heels like human metronome, but then I saw another Chaplin, uncertain which was Roy. There were tourists enough between them that neither saw the other, both busy trying to impress any person looking at them, but eventually one saw the other and charged over yelling something that got the other one's attention and they had a cane fight, hats knocked off, the crowd thinking it was rehearsed and hilarious, encircling the event but at a safe distance. A punch connected but instead of that cartoon smack sound from the movies there was a fleshy thud that I felt from across the street. The crowd all oohed as if it were a rehearsed reaction of extras.

Weaved through the slow moving cars to help Roy though it turned out he had won the scuffle by throwing the punch. He was recognizable up close because he had lost his hat and wig. With just the square of mustache he looked like Hitler though the raging eyes helped. The other guy had hound dog eyes and no wig, his hair naturally curly, not surprising because Roy's knuckles had wiped the white make up off his cheek revealing he was a black person, freckled but black. He was cursing at Roy, trying to make it a fight but some grinning tourists held onto him as a cop approached. I told Roy he should run but he didn't care, waiting to see if the black Chaplin was going to pull lose. The cop didn't bother with either of them but walked up to me and asked me my name and for my identification, then issued me a ticket for jay walking.

Asked him if he was going to do anything about the fight and he said that he didn't see a fight, he only saw me crossing two cars in front of his. I turned for support from Roy but there were no more Chaplins. Several people took pictures of him giving me the ticket, one asking the officer if she could have her picture taken with him. He seemed flattered and took off his cap to smooth the sides of his hair. She shoved the camera at me and I had to fumble around to hold it and my ticket both while looking through the viewfinder and blindly hunting for the shutter button with my finger, their cheesy smiles captured with an instamatic click.

Found Roy at his car around the block, already out of his work clothes. I waved the ticket and told him that running across the street to help cost me twenty dollars. Roy whined that the cop writes a ticket for every time he gets in a fight with his boyfriend or finds a fingertip in his donut, that he had written him up for being a public nuisance and panhandling, then without a pause between asked if I was drinking tonight, walking away. Didn't answer but followed. The thought of more beer made me shiver so I said I was hungry. He stopped and told me over his shoulder that he felt like something with cheese. I caught up with him, thinking that wouldn't rule anything out then asked if the Frolic room served food. Nah, he said, we weren't going there two nights in a row, gawd they'd think we were dating.

He led us away again as I asked who was the other Chaplin. He shook his head and had no idea, but doubted he'd be back, not as Charlie anyway. I imagined two gorilla suits fighting for territorial rights over squares of cement, earning one movie star at a time.

We cut back to the boulevard and Roy stopped me from stepping off the curb though the cross traffic was light, telling me to wait for the walk signal. I told him there was time between cars to get across and he asked if I wanted another ticket, that I could sooner get away with selling drugs on the street than stepping out and stopping traffic. It was the sure sign of an out-of-towner. Why did the tourist cross the road? Because he didn't know there was a law against jay walking. Hya hya.

A few blocks up was the Musso & Frank Grill where he saluted a guy holding menus but passed him and the booths and tables, heading straight toward the bar where the bartender had his drink prepared by the time we sat down. As I scanned the room he stilled me with the back of his hand and told me not to look in the back, that if Demerest saw us we'd have to listen to him gripe about his love life. The bartender raised his eyebrows at me expectantly so I shrugged inside and ordered a draft beer. They got a good steak here, Roy said, and I wondered if that meant it came with cheese.

So did you reach Elise? I thought he was talking to the bartender but he finally looked at me and asked, well?

No, I told him, covering my confusion by forcing down a few swallows. His glass was already empty and I saw the future as far as the next morning with its pain. Took another guzzle then straightened the coaster under my glass, noticing a neat tower of them next to a stack of cocktail napkins that had been decoratively twisted into a rising spiral of corners. They reminded me of the crumpled napkin in my pocket. Leely must be Elise. Finished the beer and suddenly had more memory of the night before. At some point I had lost all inhibition and imitated Roy's walk and laugh, getting laughs in turn from the regulars. Then I did my ape walk and climbed onto a stool as if I were in costume, auditioning for Roy's approval of me joining him at Grauman's. That was when he gave me the number to call about a job.

Demerest stopped by on his way out to ask Roy for a ride up to Big Bear, which made Roy stare into his fresh drink as if looking into a crystal ball that revealed only bad things. Demerest coughed a hard laugh and was gone. Roy glanced sideways at me and said that he and another guy offered the first taxicab service up in the mountains but they didn't know the roads well enough, many unpaved, and even with chains on the tires they got stuck or lost so often the business didn't survive even the busy ski season. With the drink gone he raised the empty glass high above his head like a victory trophy and began a better story about the time he taxied four actress/dancers up for a ski weekend, but his attention went looking for the bartender who was talking to a female employee at the end of the bar, his back to Roy. The employee alerted the bartender to Roy's dramatic statue of liberty pose. They shared a what can you do look and both went back to work, the bartender grudgingly pouring Roy another in slow motion as if used to it and pacing himself for a marathon. I never heard the rest of the interrupted story, so maybe the ladies were still up there, wherever Big Bear was.

I put the napkin with the number on the bar and smoothed it out with my palm. Y'gotta call her, he said, before another gorilla gets the job. Finished a second beer and remembered the other lady in the bar, heavy make up and an obvious wig, Roy warning me to stay away, that it was a guy. So who is Leely again, I finally asked, hoping it wasn't wig man.

She's with Disney.

The studio?

The land. She was a dwarf then a chipmunk, but now she's in charge of talent at the new fun-park.

The extra beer kicked loose more memory. A rollercoaster park was opening way out somewhere, opening as a scare park for Halloween but also would be open for Christmas then have water slides by spring. They couldn't afford to license famous cartoon characters so they were looking for people with costumes. It was called something like Laugh Land, which is why Roy thought my name was funny.

Carefully folded the napkin and put it in the little coin pocket above the regular pocket, lucky I hadn't thrown it away and lucky for drinking with Roy both times. The place was filling up for dinner and I was about to mention cheese and offer to buy dinner as a thank you but I recognized somebody at a table, familiar as a friend from home but it was an actor I had seen in everything, movies, westerns, cop shows, not so famous for me to remember his name but I knew the wild bushy eyebrows and the way his nose ended in a bulb like a Christmas decoration. I elbowed Roy who was talking to his drink. He finished his sentence and gave me his attention. Told him not to make it obvious but to look at that guy over there, did he know him? Roy made a big turn as if the effort used all his strength and looked right at the guy, asking me what guy, did I mean old Lou? The guy caught me staring and I shrunk down in embarrassment, drinking the rest of my beer, feeling like a tourist who had just been caught jay walking on a barstool.

Roy grunted with the effort it took him to turn back to bar saying, aw don't mind him, he's a drunk on his fourth marriage. Pays more alimony than Carson. I had crossed into a larger reality where the TV Guide gave no guidance and reminded myself not to piss my pants every time I recognized an actor. To get back near normal asked Roy if I could use his shower.

Ain't got one.

Your tub?

He shook his head. Ain't got one. My place is too small.

What do you do, wash in the sink? Maybe he had a trailer.

No room. You've seen where I live.

I laughed. He also was living in his car, but at least it ran.

I could hear the beer rushing between my ears but wasn't feeling it, not in a good way and the thought of a steak hurt my stomach. The place was full of well-dressed people casually brushing against each other, touching each other's elbows and shoulders with relaxed fingers, the mix of deodorants and colognes thick as a department store perfume counter the day before Christmas. Nobody brushed against me or tapped my shoulder to lean past. It seemed I had developed the mutant ability to produce a personal force field. Roy had a similar power, keeping people away with mean eyes that growled.

Snuck out with the intention of returning in better clothes, when people might be glad to see me or at least not mind, some night when I hadn't pissed away my pride at the curbside with the dog, after a hot shower. On the walk I passed a shopping cart on a corner. A truck pulled up with a train of carts nestled together in the back. A guy jumped out to drop the gate then heaved the corner cart into the back of the train. He slammed the gate closed and drove down the street. The truck disappeared into darkness then reappeared in the cone of light from another corner streetlamp. The brake lights flashed red as he got out and rattled another cart into the collection, the slam of the tailgate echoing off something. Watched him stop along the street for blocks, the echo of the slam tolling his repeated success and making me jealous.

CHAPTER TEN

When tourists put money between my clumsy gorilla fingers I had no place to put it, so Roy worked up a bit where he tricked the money away from me and I chased him around, but the heat and the minimal supply of oxygen inside the mask limited how often that was possible without collapsing. Did mostly picture posing, my heavy raspy breathing working with the costume, leaning in against nice looking women's breasts. Kids were more menacing than the pack of stray dogs and loved to kick. Reacting honestly in pain amused their parents. My tunnel vision through the eyeholes kept me helpless, turning around quickly but never catching who did it, though a Japanese boy with three cameras looked suspiciously innocent. Roy got a few back with humorous Chaplin kicks that seemed harmless but let the kid know he wasn't joking, and they were too embarrassed or afraid to complain.

A Groucho appeared, duck-walking through the vacationers, something weird about him so I got close enough to see his face was coated in a light colored pancake make-up but the back of his hands were dark brown. It was the black guy in the same Chaplin tailcoat but with his hair slicked and parted down the middle, a cigar and a greasepaint mustache instead of the little paste-on. He moved to put distance from Roy and me, the crowd swelling like a tide toward him so we quit for the day because I had to drive to my audition. We used the van as a dressing room, now parked there on the side street.

In the morning I had walked to the gas station store to use their restroom and buy some junk for breakfast, asking the clerk if they had a mechanic. A Mexican with a tow truck drove me back to the vehicle then towed it to the garage. While I took a bath in their sink the Mexican got the engine running, its rattle bouncing between the old fixtures inside the bathroom, both shining clean, clean as the library, cleaner than McDonalds. While I listened to the mechanic speak Spanish and gesture around the engine, a kid in a dirty green jumpsuit came out of a dark corner of the garage to translate, his hands covered in so much grease it looked like he was wearing shiny new gloves. The engine had overheated and burned up some part. Told him I had driven slowly, not much of a choice.

Slow bad, the mechanic said in English, then finished a couple sentences in Spanish. The young guy told me it was an air-cooled engine, to drive fast if I could, that the mechanic also had covered the rusted-out heater box and it should give me some warmth now. Paid ninety dollars and drove away delighted, wondering where greasy gloves washed.

Went back for the dog but she had a secret life of her own, so with the sedan gone I filled the Frisbee at the house and left it and a peanut butter sandwich next to the palm tree. Went to the booth to call Elise and there was a message on the inside of the glass written in lipstick, telling me to call J.O. Dialed the number on the napkin instead and explained I was Roy's friend with a gorilla suit. She wanted to see it and meet me, sooner the better. Feeling ambitious I waited for Roy at Grauman's then went to dress for work. He wasn't in a good mood, probably hung over or mad at me for ditching him, but when he saw the suit he smiled and said to stick with him, I'd go far.

Later at the van he counted out all the money we made and gave me half without comment or argument. Back on the sidewalk he pulled loose a flyer stapled to a telephone pole and drew a map on the back,

directions to the fun park. Before leaving I went back to the kiosk in
front of the theater and bought a clean t-shirt with Hollywood U.S.A
across the chest, using the money I had earned performing there.

It was a thirty-minute drive up one freeway then across on another,
traffic setting the driving time as much as the mileage, but there was
less of it the closer I got to the park, MacLoughlin Park, not Laugh
Land any more than my name was Laughback. The audition was simply
me showing off the suit and a short interview in a trailer at the back
of the park property that was Leely's office. She had a list of rules on
a piece of paper, some of them crossed out along with the Disneyland
letterhead at the top of the page, but I could read it through the felt pen
ink, that and rules about length of hair and no mustaches or beards.
One remaining rule was not to retaliate if a guest got physical. I told
her about the kids on the walk and she promised to protect me. She was
maybe one inhale above five feet tall.

The park would have its grand opening for Halloween but there
would be a couple half days of pay for park orientation and parade
rehearsal at an hourly rate a token amount above minimum wage.
Didn't know who else would be working there besides Roy but I agreed
simply at the hopeful thought that some would be female. There wasn't
any paperwork yet so she made me promise to be there.

Drove faster on the way back, working the coolinator, not able to
speed like many of the other vehicles but keeping pace with traffic.
Parked in my old spot for the sake of the dog, the water and sandwich
gone but so was she. Walked back up to the boulevard feeling local,
passing a sex shop with lingerie in the windows, fantasizing already
about my unmet new co-workers. Wanted to enter but couldn't
force myself even to slow down and look through the glass door,
continuing past as if I had a destination anywhere but there. Any
person watching would think I wasn't sex obsessed, could report to
my family that I was being a good boy, and to my future wife that I
wasn't a pervert. That's what church had done to me, made me afraid
to enter a sex shop.

Snuck into an R-rated movie at thirteen only because I was with Jayo. We picked up stubs in the parking lot for proof we had paid then waited at the side exit doors. When the doors were pushed open from inside we held them as the audience busted out squinting, blinded by the light of day, then we darted inside and fell into seats, scrunching low so our heads wouldn't be visible from the lobby doors. When the theatre began to fill again we moved to better seats, all to see some nudity though the movie was more violent than sexy, more bad than good.

Next to the sex shop was a used book store with so many shelves and such tiny aisles it seemed from the doorway that an average sized human must browse sideways like a literate crab with a good chance of getting stuck in a rarely used section and endure his or her final hours with nothing except an abundance of food for thought. Intimidated and needing a bathroom I walked instead to the library.

Behind the reference section, an area even quieter than the front of the library where tall skinny windows gave a view of parked cars, there was a big-haired guy in the end chair of a three-chair unit, an open book between his thighs, kneecaps obscenely poking through holes in his jeans as if giving birth to bald twin babies, his head slumped down as if to show off the mess of hair long enough to cover the knees but it wasn't affected by gravity. I gently sat in the chair at the other end and put my stack of books on the middle seat, taking the novel off the top.

I choose a book by the title then give the author a few paragraphs to get the heart beating as if reading it is an emergency. If the writer backs into the story wasting time with life running out, I slam it shut and toss it disrespectfully. When I slammed that one the hair guy woke up with a snort and wiped away a thin web of drool that connected to the page he had been sleeping over. He was surprised to see me there, the other chairs empty when he had dozed and it was a shock to discover reality altered in a subjective moment. He stretched, bones popping and whispered during a yawn if any of the library workers had seen him sleeping. Told him that nobody could tell he was sleeping, that he was a great fake reader except for the drool. He flipped the book to wipe the page clean against his falling apart dirty jeans and said that he usually woke up a few times an hour to turn a page because if he was caught sleeping he'd get kicked out for a week.

When I didn't flinch he looked at my stack of books then shared with me the three rules, no loud talking, no sleeping and no stinking. He learned the last two through experience because he had recently been homeless. I recognized him awake, the guy from the phone booth maybe calling for drugs.

Leonard came from Chicago with a rock band and they had been somewhat successful, had a manager and got free equipment from Washburn but couldn't get a recording contract and became bored playing little clubs and arguing over whether to wear eyeliner or designer costumes. He told me this as I paged through an actor's biography looking at the photographs, then added the fact that he knew where to get happy hour draft beer for fifty cents. I left the books for another time and we went to a tiny asian restaurant with three tables and fifty-cent beer, and happy hour was two hours long. I spent five dollars on eight beers with a dollar tip then we went to a strip bar where I spent ten dollars on two beers with a two-dollar tip for my first stripper, learning that if a girl were willing to dance naked, being pretty was not required. Before she appeared I had been anxious over my clothes, worried I wasn't dressed well enough for a lady with nothing on, but she was harrier than expected with several distracting moles dotting her belly as if she had survived a shooting. A sick mix of sweat and perfume drifted toward us on the breeze she created spinning on one butt cheek, her name Exotica.

When the name of the next entertainer was announced Len made a face of disgust and waved me to follow him out, leaving me to wonder how much worse looking a woman they could offer without driving out the other six customers. He suggested we hop a bus down to Barney's and I thought it was a great idea, the beer rushing between my ears, the continued movement, having a friend. We bussed west on Sunset into the sunset. Len said his band was named Threex and after a few moments when I didn't ask why he told me anyway, that it was based on those words you can't say three times fast, the original name being Three Times Fast but it was already being used so they called themselves 3X, but that was used, so they spelled it out and pronounced it Threex. I said it sounded short for three geeks and he thought about it then said that three times fast and said close, but no.

Their demo tape had the original song titles Early Oiler, Clear Clean Creek and Her Rear Wheel. I asked if the lyrics limited them to only ballads. He said no, thought about it a while then laughed and called me a smartass as a compliment. As we got off at our stop I noticed other passengers silently wording those phrases three times fast.

Barney's was the beanery, an old restaurant with big platters of food. We sat at the deep end of an attached barroom where Len could watch games of eight ball in the small poolroom even farther back. The bartender was a black haired woman with so much black eyeliner I think she eye lined her hair with it too, that same deep black dimming any light reaching her face. Didn't matter because her forced cleavage drew the eye more than colliding billboards.

Wished she had been that stripper, and when she turned her professional breasts away from my stare I worried if she had read my mind. If god were a man he would have put women's eyes on their chests to save men humiliation. As she came back to take our order I kept my eyes high, asking the top of her head for two beers. She slid a menu in front of me and I looked down quickly to avoid getting distracted by the scenery. It was a menu of beers, a list of more varieties than I knew existed, all strange. I pointed to the nearest draft spigot and turned away, escaping any more awkwardness for thirty seconds until she brought the drinks over.

As she made change I looked up again to notice the wall was covered in old license plates. Maybe they had belonged to movie stars though they weren't labeled, or maybe it was because this was the end of the road for many, with space left for mine.

Len asked if I played and I told him okay, assuming he meant pool. There had been a short lived youth center back home in the temporarily donated space of a building for rent, run by Pastor Zilchy who was given the duty to keep our just confirmed teen souls on the lesser road, luring us in by playing pop and rock records with hit songs that mentioned Jesus who had gained a reputation as the original hippy. Zilchy was not divinely groovy but he was the youngest on staff so was given youth ministry duty. His years at a religious college had erased any accidental cool he might have inherited genetically, but he salvaged a Sears pool table from a member of the congregation's garage where it had been stored one winter too many, and for that single act we liked him.

Those equally weathered cue sticks were twisted and needed tips and the table felt was an obstacle course of repaired rips, waves and brown stained dead zones, but after we got the table almost level and a rack of balls to sit still long enough to break them, we played every minute of every hour the center was open. No betting or bad language was allowed but you could swear by faking a quick prayer for the ball to stay on line long enough to drop.

The building eventually was rented as a flooring showroom and we were evicted for racks filled with sample squares of faux brick and marble linoleum, shag and out door carpeting, so pastor Zilchy moved youth nights to the church basement. The pool table didn't make the move so we stopped attending.

At Barney's Lloyd asked me to put a quarter against the undercut of a rail to challenge the next winner. Our victor had a tattoo of Alfred E. Neuman on his forearm and carried his own cube of blue chalk in a silver holder hanging from a chain on his belt. He called himself Madman and told Len the game was straight eight, call your shots. Len played and lost then I played and Madman lost by scratching on the eight ball. He got angry as if suspicious for years that life is a conspiracy against him and losing again finally was proof. He wanted to play me for five dollars even as Len worked the coin slider to drop the balls from their confinement in the windowed slot. Madman went to the end of the table and grabbed the racking triangle, slamming it down on the felt. I was feeling good and told him I thought he was Madman because he liked Mad Magazine, you know, what me worry, pointing to his arm with the cue stick. That's right, he said angrily not getting the joke and began racking the balls.

Len found his almost empty glass of beer and went back toward the bar. I imagined what it would be like winning again and trying to collect the five bucks, deciding it wasn't worth the trouble, leaning the stick against the wall and telling Madman it was against my religion to bet, that it was his table. As I followed Len out of the room, two guys had a foot race across the six feet between their booth and the table to be the next opponent.

Len swallowed a last gulp of warm beer and I wasn't certain it had been his glass. He told me there was a good place to go on a Monday night. I couldn't believe it was still Monday. We jay walked side streets and I asked if there were many fights over pool back there. No, only over women he told me, but not very often. He asked if I had seen who was sitting in the corner watching us play, the Irish band with the number one album. I didn't know who had the number one album but I had noticed them because they had hair like Len's.

We went into the side door of a brick building that could have been the back entrance to a factory but it was boxy space with a small bar corralled to one side with a railing as if to keep out livestock, empty. Len said we were early though it had to be close to ten, but I was on a drunken roll like the carry along you get from a wave when body surfing.

Up on the forty-second parallel the summers were hot enough to turn Lake Michigan shores into temporarily tropical beaches where locals got rid of their winter white skin for a few months, camping out on towels in the afternoon and around bonfires at night half expecting the Beach Boys with guitars and surfboards to appear from around a mountainous sand dune. I asked Len if we were near the ocean and he asked compared to what? He borrowed a quarter for a video game that provided the only light in a dark corner. I asked him how far was the beach and he said half an hour but didn't say if that was by foot, bus or car.

I found the bathroom, a dirty little room with uninhibited graffiti and a small mirror with copper colored corrosion eating away at the silver backing, my reflection veined with the pattern like a biblical disease removing my face. I hoped it was the corrosion and not my face and touched my cheeks to feel for damage. The toilet had its own patterns of staining so I tried to hold my breath for the length of the piss, but had to let it out as I fumbled with my belt, skipping washing so I could get out the door before inhaling again. There was no clean air in the main room either, immediately smoked up by two guys crossing the empty floor with equipment, but I had my too much beer smile burned across my face and enjoyed being another place new to me.

I ordered two more from the bartender, a slender asian lady who moved like a dancer and also had an appreciation for black clothing, then found a stool and tiny table in the dark next to the video game. Why isn't there anybody here I asked Len, and he said things didn't happen much until midnight. I watched the smokers set up band equipment as a third guy arrived to gather them into a short huddle before he went to a sound board at the back of the room and knocked around for a moment. Suddenly there was music from the sound system, a pouty voice with punkish noise. As if on cue a few other customers wandered in and a waitress appeared to bring them drinks, returning to lean across the bar and share whispers with the bartender. I felt like the sole audience member attending a play in the round, something we did in college for an evening of one acts.

Len finished his game and drank his beer in one long back bending feat, caught his breath then told me it would be cheaper to buy a pitcher. As we worked our way through it a few girls crowded around another small table near the raised stage in the corner, probably with the band. There were hums and pops and thumps as the instruments became electrified, the guy in the shadowed back of the tiny room calling out checks for one thing then another. The waitress found us and asked if we wanted a second pitcher, ignoring all the beer still in our first. I was drowning from the inside, losing my education, forgetting everything except how to sit and eat and there was nothing to eat.

Told Len I'd be back but he was bird dog focused on the ladies, tail in the air, so I learned to walk again on the way out, not well but I got to the corner where there was a liquor store. Ate some jerky and a candy bar to help me continue the night's journey. On the corner I could see the sign for the club, a small lit marquee with no letters, no printing, and below that a door with a sign featuring a curved arrow and a printed on paper notice to the public that the entrance was around the side. Across the street was The Whiskey, big sign all lit up and a crowd around the door and I wondered what was I missing, why had Len brought me to the poor side of the strip? Back at the side entrance there also was a line forming. I passed twenty people on my way along the hallway to the inner door where a doorman was now charging a cover and told me to get in line so I went out again and waited my turn, paying four dollars to reenter.

It was darker and louder but filling up with people in black clothing. Len said he didn't think I was coming back. There was beer left in the pitcher but he had been saving it in case it had to last the night. He immediately filled his glass to the brim again now that I had returned.

The band was announced and they played something close to a song, not trying to fool the audience that it was supposed to be a song, more of a statement with attitude. I yelled in Len's ear asking if this is what he brought me to see but he shook his head and put out both hands in a calming motion to teach me patience. Maybe there would be an all stripper band.

There was a regular flow of people into the club, finding position around the tables and against the walls leaving only an irregular space of dance floor where nobody danced because the oddity of the music, but it felt like a community, one I might squeeze into without feeling like a spy sent to report on regular humans. Many seemed slightly off-human too, street weary maybe or a bit beat up, and tired from the weight of their layered clothing with clever accessories. Cosmetics looked to have been applied nervously in a worry that they might fade before the night ended and allow faces to become visible. I yelled across the table at Len to ask if he knew anyone. He pointed to a plain looking girl except she was almost armored in metal and leather, yelling back that she came down from the valley to hang, and the zombie dude near the stage was a student up from Orange County. Two other regulars were at the crazy busy bar in baggy shorts and combat boots, surfers from a beach city with wet suits in their car.

I yelled who were Hollywood locals? He shrugged then raised his hand to point at me as the band finished wildly with extra agitation and volume, the inattention of the crowd equally thunderous. It was an awkward silence for all of us so I clapped respectfully, echoed by some others in the room though it never caught on. Len said he and his band had played there and did I want to buy his bass guitar. I drank in baby sips to stay conscious and said I didn't think so, that I needed a room to rent if he new anybody with an apartment looking for a roommate. He said his place wasn't big enough but that I should check it out anyway.

The stage was dark and somebody packing equipment stumbled into a cymbal causing the murmur of the crowd to pause as if something were starting, then the rhubarb as we called it in college theater began again. I asked Len for some three times fast words and he gave me depth perception and missing synthesizer. We were having such fun saying them that others around us also tried.

We were interrupted by the hoot of a saxophone but it didn't come from the stage where there was still only one guy at the drums in the dark. The sax blurted a phrase over by the side entrance, and the cymbal sounded again but it was being played this time, the tsss-ts-ts-tsss jazzy riff that accompanied a stripper doing a pelvic driven slide-step in spiky high heels. I thought maybe a fight was breaking out because I could see bodies suddenly moving, or maybe somebody fell over, but the saxophone kept playing jumpy little phrases, getting loud as a lonely goat.

Maybe a street performer smuggled his saxophone in under a trench coat and was pushing his way into the club through the audience, which now filled the place wall to wall. When he was inside far enough I could see long black hair and gold reflections off the brass of his instrument bobbing and weaving with the honking. The sea of people was parting for him. It wasn't until he got near the stage that I saw the short guy in front of him, white-framed sunglasses, ear to the bell of the horn, able to chew gum, snap his fingers and shake his head to the beat all at the same time. He turned to jump on stage still wagging his big head to the groove and I realized the crowd had parted for him.

The corner became lit with a row of stage lights hanging from a bar over the stage, fresnels same as the performance area we used in the basement of the commons. Len nudged me and nodded his head up at the event as if I hadn't been sitting there watching, but I noticed there also was a keyboard player now knocking out boogie woogie and a younger clean-cut bass player keeping up lazily as if it were easy. A Henry Fonda looking guy in long brown hair stepped up unnoticed to play a simple guitar as if he had drunk the blood of Chuck Berry, chasing his memory up and down the fret board almost violently, threatening to break every string on his instrument of naked wood, kind of clunky with no pick guard, no trademark, and before the first song ended one string was hanging lose and dancing as if taking early bows.

The short guy whipped off his glasses and showed his teeth to mimic a smile, singing a rocking rhythm and blues number with lyrics a few beds just this side of the psych ward. He finished and told us thank you so much, then fell directly into another one equally wild. The originally static crowd was dancing, not only on the dance floor and around the tables, but against and up the walls. I wanted to dance, to chew on a partner. I wanted to join the tribe and regretted having no years in the jungle for future primal moments. I had a sudden love of growls and howls and wanted to pound a hollow log, thinking of old records thick as my thumb, southern radio stations drifting north on the static of humid nights, poems written on a cell wall above the toilet, and Moe Howard practicing syncopation against his brothers' heads.

There was no talk between songs about what they meant or how they were written, the way most guitar people tell you in soft self-reverent voices as if reading from a diary during therapy, their testimony propping up an average ballad. The songs were thrown at us as if they were unloading the day's catch of tuna or shark at the dock. The set ended the way it had begun, extremely cool with the singer and sax man exiting through the big squeeze of fans. The lights came on and the remainder of the band packed up their own gear. The crowd was sucked toward the entrance as if the space were being drained.

Len and I were caught in the flow as everyone went into the night, all partied up with nowhere to go. We stood on the corner of the liquor store still open and waiting for us, but instead of going in we waited for any females in the crowd to smell our need to inseminate something. A breeze blew delicately from the southwest and I could smell the thick wet air of Africa where our ancestors had the same urge with more success.

Told Len I was all drunk and asked if the busses ran by there. He said it was too late for a bus, so I got Roy's card out of my wallet and used the store's payphone to call a taxi. He was off shift but they sent another driver who arrived in one minute. Five dollars later we were back at Sunset and Vine, another corner where we stood like two stray dogs. Len offered to show me his place but I finally was tired enough to wonder if he wanted anything more than free beer. With slight fear I told him good night and walked home. He stood there and smoked. At the next street I looked back and he was still there watching me. I waved and he waved back and walked in his own direction.

Stepped sideways into the next alley to pee and in the still moment of waiting, noticed how quiet the city was at night, my splash suddenly noisy. Aimed it at a different angle against the wall but it only changed the tone, and it was taking too long. It was the longest piss I ever had taken, worried about being alone and vulnerable in an alley, using my gut muscles to force the stream to speed things up but it made more noise and I had to back out of the shadow of the building to escape the creeping puddle. Across the country guys my age were long into a night's sleep, resting for another ambitious day of sales, interviews and investments, lifting loading and trucking, manufacturing and constructing. I was trapped in a dark Hollywood alley by an act of prolonged urination.

I had parked close to my old space, leaving the big sedan girl extra room for her parked life, but a different car was there and her sloop was backed in crookedly behind the van, the right rear tire up on the curb so it looked more beached than parked. Her cat was rolling in the dirt of the lawn so I looked around for the dog and found it looking out at me from inside the window. The cat finished its dirt bath and sat down heavily on the step, thinking what can you do?

CHAPTER ELEVEN

M y conscience woke me up, screaming about how much yesterday had cost. Drove to a street that was a huge wall of a building on one side, parked then slid the side door open to puke down a storm drain while reminding myself about having a good time. Waited through the after-gags in case anything else wanted to come up, wondering what kind of building uses an entire block. Washed my mouth out with warm Coke, and because nobody was around I peed a pretty arc down the drain from the inside of the van.

Drove around the corner where there was a drive-in entrance with a security kiosk and an arching sign above that announced it was Columbia Studios. Slowed down to a creeping speed and someone honked behind me so I drove around the block. It was entirely walled and fence in, the storm drain side a continuous building. Drove again past the entrance hoping anybody was allowed including even tourists, because the lowly stooges had played and worked there. They probably had walked or staggered along that very sidewalk, maybe puking in the same gutter I had, wondering if their bosses ever got bruised or hurt while elbowing and jostling each other over the millions of dollars they made off the stooges' violence.

My Saturday morning memories involved the stooges as much as any family member or neighborhood friend. I believed there was a lost first episode that explained why Moe was forever angry and violent, that Larry and Curly had done something unforgivable which caused them to accept consistent abuse because it was deserved. Or maybe Moe had chronic heartburn from living on beef jerky and Coke, burgers and beer. Or the low California sun which wasn't cheerful or gold but more of a dirty white and always staring at the back of my head even when I was facing it, staring through my eyes at the inside back of my head.

Needed breakfast but wanted a beer. Wasn't certain if bars were open early in the day but it didn't matter because I would be embarrassed to enter one. It wouldn't be strange to buy a six-pack at a grocery store though, because people shopping in the morning would buy beer for later that night or week. Simply needed to buy other things so the employees and general public wouldn't suspect I was guiltily hung-over. During Roy's round about short cut I had noticed a small grocery store up on Franklin Avenue. Inside I discovered a bathroom in the back behind the swinging doors through which they brought out the cartons of stuff to stock shelves. It smelled of cold cardboard and cigarette breaks. I washed but ignored the mirror.

Surrounded the beer with sugary things that might be delicious later when I felt better, but there was no reason to worry about being judged by the cashier at the ten items or less lane because she looked like she drank something worse than a bunch of beer, blood maybe. She had a horror movie face made worse with blue make-up and her hair could have been a clown wig dyed several colors.

Her orange and white stripes lessened the shock value by making her look more like a clown. The nametag claimed she was Aphrodite. In my mind I nicknamed her Aphro. There was a Dianetics paperback next to the cash register but that didn't make it hers. I smelled chocolate on her bad breath from across the counter. She was quietly humming along to the piped-in music, very slightly mouthing the lyrics, but she had to interrupt the moment to monotone robotically at me a how're you. I said fine with an equal amount of sincerity then said the name of the song. She looked up to see me but shook her head as if she didn't know what I was talking about. It was a wimpy song someone like her never would be caught knowing the lyrics to. She handed me my change and bag and we were done. I wondered if married guys my age considered most every cash register girl as a potential sex partner. I did.

Drove back to my parking space and popped the top of an almost cold can of beer and sucked a few gulps. It took half an hour to merge back into the drunk lane and by noon I was asleep again. I dreamed grandpa was driving a tractor along some railroad tracks, knocking along, but the sound was real and woke me up. The house girl was outside the van waiting for me to answer the door, not deliberately peeking in the window with her face up against the glass but she was rocking at different angles to get a view of something. I rubbed the sleep off my face and out of my eyes and slid open the door trying to smile. Her eyes went straight to the beer cans, which made me smile. She accused me of having fun while she fed my dog. I promised her it wasn't my dog, that it had been hitchhiking, but offered her money if she was feeding it.

Why are you here, she said as an accusation. I looked around and told her that I was just here same as she, what was the difference? Dug into my pocket and gave her a bunch of dollars. She grabbed them, straightening out the wrinkled bills and turning them so all of George's heads were facing the same direction, satisfied either with the amount or her neatening. She told me there was a message for me in the phone booth. I asked her how she would know that and she confessed that she didn't have a phone at the moment. Asked if she needed a roommate to help with rent and she thought about it then told me no.

The message was the old message circled three times in a different shade of lipstick, to call J.O. but with OR DIE added with exclamation points and a number. Somebody was going to want me to buy them a new lipstick. Dialed the number, put in extra quarters for long distance and Jayo's mom answered by screaming to stop calling this number then she hung up. Others must've have dialed for fun despite the expense.

Went to the library to use the bathroom, daring a look in the mirror. I was shaggy, the light hair of my beard and mustache long enough to trim with scissors but looking theatrical like crepe applied with spirit gum. My hair was molded from pushing it off my forehead and behind my ears with grimy hands. I grunted a hmm and went out to read, finding a book about Columbia Studios that inspired me to apply for a job there.

When I saw the security guy in his neat blue uniform with a badge I regretted going there on impulse instead of washing the van and buying a hairbrush. He could've insulted me or bullied me away like other bums and nuts who had crashed the gate, but he smiled as if I owed him money then asked my name. He checked it against his clipboard then sadly shook his head as if he'd been rejected himself. Told him I was looking for employment and he happied up again, able to help by directing me to apply at the front office, that the doors were on the Gower Street side. A car pulled in behind me so he waved me through so I could turn around and leave through the exit side of his hut.

Drove past the Chinese Theater but didn't see Roy so kept driving. Hollywood merged with Sunset and I recognized that empty sign at the club from last night, and the one across the street. Another sign announced Beverly Hills and suddenly the world was green again and the air seemed thick with the smell of movie stars until I noticed I was following a delivery van for a deli so it was probably the sandwiches.

The road twisted and lulled as if approaching open country but instead it crossed a many-laned freeway and on the other side everything became crowded again, the air different, almost pickles and olives or some other garnish. The traffic became stop and go then just stop as I dead-ended at the ocean and that was the smell, salt and fish with a hint of China.

Turning onto a city street all the parking spaces had been claimed and the drivers behind me felt the speed limit was only a suggestion, or they loved the back bumper and got close as possible without actually mounting my rear. Turned down side streets with less congestion until reaching an industrial area with a few gaps between cars and felt I had won a round of musical chairs.

It was a long gritty walk to the beach through what seemed to be graffiti war territory. Many blue and yellow hippy murals had been painted over with names in cartoon lettering like trump cards. The gutters were filled with sand blown from lawns of sand with special sand plants instead of grass. I could hear several different sources of music that didn't blend but weren't fighting each other either, as if arguing different opinions about the same subject. Across the street from the houses was a row of little businesses. Passed a burger counter with such an intensely good smell they might be mixing chocolate into the meat.

Some of the music was coming from a gift shop's entrance trimmed with a dozen different kinds of wind chimes. No breeze was cutting through the store but everyone who went in or passed reached out to run their fingers along the strung metal and wooden tubes and dangles like pickets of a fence. The girl working inside had eyes like a baby bird and chewed her gum so fiercely she might have been trying to generate some noise to dampen the constant tinkling of fairy magic. I called over to her, asking how she could stand the music, my heart feeling rubbery enough to take rejection from someone I'd never see again, but she smiled as if I had come to save her, so happy that I had to look down to see if roses or diamonds had appeared in my hands.

She said the chimes were fine though she'd rather have the radio on. The owner had told her radio signals would counteract good vibrations, as if they didn't exist until you turned on a radio. Asked her how to get to the beach and she laughed, so asked if I could get her a Tommy's burger and she told me no. She was craving fries from smelling them all day but they used lard in the fryer. I hadn't known there were options for frying. Maybe her dad had invented a new type of grease.

My mind stretched and I accidentally bit the tip of my tongue. Somebody buying a kite stepped between us, but as she went behind the register she wrote something down on paper then waved it in the air like a free wind-thing to promote the store before handing it to me. Forced myself not to look at it until I was around the corner. She had written her name, Cricket, and her number. I waved it in the air like a flag and looked up to see the ocean, realizing why she had laughed at me asking directions.

The surf was hundreds of yards away across a giant beach, complete with the giant swings and slide of my hometown. This was where giants had gone. They had come here to play.

There were a thousand people who had the day off, some in the water but most of them drifting up and down a concrete pathway between people vying for their attention and dollars. It was like a reverse parade with the onlookers doing the moving and the attractions lining the sides. It made the patio at the Chinese theater seem smalltime. This was the Venice Roy had griped about and I realized it was because he probably went unnoticed as Charlie, appearing normal against the daily mardi gras, especially the roller skater in top hat and tails playing a piano on wheels who would make Roy appear more like a homeless bum than a silent film star.

Bought a light cotton shirt made in India and a pair of three-dollar sunglasses then sat on a wall that divided the beach from the concrete boardwalk to keep the drifting sands from burying it on windy days. A gorilla would fit the menagerie but the back of my neck was burning from the sun and sweat drops ran down my back. I would be dead inside the suit, drowned.

A shirtless guy with body builder muscles strolled by looking like the after picture in the timeless comic book ad that promised those exact results in six weeks, and I feared he might be on his way to meet Cricket but he met up with another guy who kissed him. I expected him to throw an "it's clobberin' time" punch complete with sound effect appearing as the word "whoomp" in heavy ink, more Marvel than DC, but instead he kissed the guy back. I had never seen two guys kiss. Looked around but didn't turn my head, only moving the eyeballs to see other people's reactions but there were none.

The sun's glare off the surf and sand plus the look-at-me crowd gave me a headache so I bought one of those burgers for the road and tried to find Hollywood, again.

Got caught up in some hills and canyons. Burned a bunch of gas finding my way back to the coast road but never was there a coordinated gap in traffic both ways to allow a left turn so finally turned right, going in the wrong direction just to be moving. I thought that traveling in the wrong direction but making good time would be good in a song and I wanted to write it down, but with a burger in one hand and the other on the wheel I was having enough trouble shifting gears. Didn't know if I'd ever be back on that road again so decided to see where it took me. The fuel gauge disagreed with the plan but with such serious traffic I told it to relax, that there should be a gas station ahead. Turned up the volume on the radio hoping sound waves would propel the vehicle forward and save gas even if only negligibly.

The song was self-dated to over twenty years old but new to me, Buick '59. Traffic slowed then stopped and the gauge pointed its needle at the E to say I told you so. A traffic light turned red about thirty cars ahead and a tall gasoline sign at the corner peeked over the car roofs. Snuck up the shoulder to pull in at the pumps, got out and threw away the burger wrapper and paper bag because the smell of them so good before eating was equally bothersome at the other end of the meal, stinking up leftover air in the van.

There was an attendant but that meant a tip so I did the work as he watched me. I thought he was going to mention the weather so I went first and asked how he was doing, practicing my small talk. He confessed that he hadn't seen his wife in over a year, not since she broke his toe moving a plaster statue of Assisi and that it still hurt like a monkey smuggler when he wore his church shoes, so he stopped going to church, and now he heard she got a house though how he couldn't imagine, not unless they agreed she could pay with her food stamps.

Not wanting to write that down in front of him, and having nothing to say to answer it, I looked at the sky and said we could use some rain.

He shook his head and asked me if hadn't I heard, when it rains it pours, pointing across the side street to a gap in the hillside. He said there used to be a gas station on that corner too. See that hill of dried mud there? That was it. He looked like he missed a friend so I let him keep the change.

Drove the road intercepting the one I had been on, the van struggling up into hills, more burro-power than horsepower. The landscape was bleak and scrubby and reminded me of Manson followers. If the van broke down I would become my own cult, a secret society of one and pushing the van would be my initiation, my discipline. If a flood came I would survive by using the mattress cushion as a floating device.

The road twisted, dipped then climbed again, drop-offs on one side then the other getting deeper and steeper. The worst part was that it was happy hour and I was a long way from fifty-cent beer. It was the time of day when there was no music on any station, only news of murder and political scandal, the day's scores and weather report, all for use in polite conversation. Almost hit a coyote at the highest crest but didn't have speed enough so it walked out of the way. The van was in more danger from a car speeding up behind me. Pulled over to the shoulder, letting the setting sun shine a dirty orange beam onto the inside of the windshield, because that beautiful moment made it difficult to distinguish road from a cliff.

A convertible raced up and did a stunt stop, turning so it was in the other lane facing back toward the sunset. It had kicked up a cloud of shining dust that washed against the van. The driver told me he was sorry, they had just watched the sunset on the beach then raced up here to see it again. If you're rich and fast enough you can catch the same sunset. Then they raced back down into the previous dusk.

Crept back onto the road and minutes later a freeway appeared like a chute from Chutes and Ladders. I slid back down to Sunset and entered a procession of traffic back through Beverly Hills again thinking of hillbillies. Above the boulevard was a billboard featuring one giant blond in sunglasses with breasts rocketing toward the stars, daring all the little men below to climb her. It didn't promote a brand of liquor or the release of a film or record, just showed off the lady as a generic object of desire, the true Hollywood prize valued more highly than the Oscar. Roy would know what she was about and I looked for him at the theater but didn't see him so went back to check the phone booth for messages. There was a message but it was written on the sidewalk in chalk, the words: they don't know what they do. Farther along: I'm nothing, can your ego stand it? I didn't think they were for me because the last ones were: You killed me. Walked around the block looking for more but that was all. It looked like a girl's writing. Maybe she ran out of pages in her diary.

Hoping to find Roy I walked to the Frolic Room. There was a different bartender and he had an assistant in a white tuxedo shirt. The drinkers didn't act as if they recognized me from the week before but I gave everyone a smile in hope they were liars. There was an important baseball game on but the screen was too small and far away for details. Followed the game through the play by play comments, not from the announcer but from the drinkers, all of them barstool managers following each pitch and play with insight and criticism. They worked the bar top like a pinball game, hands working the edge as if flipper buttons were there to cue the swing of each batter.

The bar helper asked if I was a Dodgers fan and I confessed that I didn't know, but had nothing against them. He asked me politely to take my beer off the bar and I thought he was going to wipe it down or something worse to me, but he squirted lighter fluid along the trough that ran the length of the back and the bartender lit the bar on fire.

It was a seventh inning stretch tradition. He used a long fireplace match, touching it at my end of the bar, the fire traveling along its length like a ghost train. The room lit up with the color of the Christmas card of Santa drinking a Coke in front of a glowing fireplace like a drunken burglar. The bar fire burned out in fifteen seconds, only a special effect. Some of the guys down the row barely moved their beers away from the flames, veterans who knew it was mostly a magic trick, a tired half-smile on their face that gave them one rosy cheek in the warm light. A too-drunk guy had tried to light his smoke in the flare-up and his eyebrows were burned into small tight curls, his buddies more entertained by the failed result than the actual stunt. He was pleased.

I was burping onion from the burger earlier and the beer wasn't working so I left and walked back toward the van. There was a new chalked comment: asses to ashes, butts to dust. The van was sitting alone, that side of the street empty and I remembered it was the one night of no parking. Didn't need the key to open the door because someone had broken into the van and my gorilla suit was gone. The cushions were on the floor but the thief or thieves hadn't bothered with the zippers. The doors and glove compartment were open reminding me of that cop searching the sedan. There was a bent-out coat hanger on the driver's seat that must have been forced through the broken triangular vent window to catch and raise the lock button.

I threw up not bothering to find a drain, just bent over and filled the gutter. There were the onions in the foamy beer puke looking as if they might be read the way a gypsy reads tealeaves. Stared into the shiny mess for a message, what I was going to do, what could I be without my suit?

When I opened a new Famous Monsters instead of doing homework, wondered if guys in gorilla suits were trained, if there were a gorilla suit academy, or if the suits were passed down in a family of gorilla suit makers. Either way, thought I could make my own suit good as some in the magazine, maybe better. At the thrift store there was a not too stinky old fur coat with a label inside the collar announcing it was from Belle Bon Furs. I pronounced it belly-bone in my mind.

Didn't have enough money so I stuffed it through a window in the back that could be opened a few inches for air but not wide enough for burglars. That night I picked it up in the dark. It was lying there like an animal huddled in fear, but I felt a wild strength. It was fur twice stolen, first from the animal and now by me with no taste of outrage, but maybe beer and onions vomit. There wasn't fur enough for a suit, but I made gloves, shoe cover feet, and a head mask.

I used oil-based clay smuggled out of art class to sculpt a gorilla face and made a plaster cast of it, spreading black silicone sealant inside the mold to get a rubber version of the clay face and attached it to a leather aviator's headgear also stolen from the same thrift store. Glued sections of fur to cover the entire piece, brushing and trimming the hairs artfully to create a realistic great ape face.

Wore those pieces with padded coveralls and mowed a section of the lawn knowing the neighbor lady would be watching through her kitchen window. I even paused, pretending to wipe sweat off the mask's forehead. Drove in costume to my grandma's house and knocked on the door which she slammed shut so hard after seeing me I stepped backwards afraid it would come through the doorframe. Went home to call her and apologize but the line was busy because she was still on the phone with the police.

Found matching fake fur in a fabric store and mowed lawns enough to buy enough yards to finish the suit basing it on a pair of long-johns padded out with scavenged foam rubber, strategically sewing on tailored sections of fur.

While stitching one piece and watching television the doorbell rang, but when I stood to answer the door I couldn't set the suit aside because I had accidentally sewn through the fabric and stitched it to the denim of my jeans. Carried the suit over to the door then let it drop, hanging off my pant leg. At the door were Mormon missionaries, my age with crew cuts so short and fresh their hair seemed to be in pain. The boys ceremoniously opened a three ring binder thick with laminated evidence of angels guiding an American farm boy to buried golden tablets inscribed with of a new story of an intercontinental Jesus, and portraits of old white men who spoke to god with a capital G, information never mentioned in the religion classes or sermons from my memory.

The ape suit was in plain view hanging from my thigh but the boys were on a mission and politely ignored it, dressed up too nicely to do anything inappropriate such as mock, not if they didn't want to be mocked for the story they told. They asked if I would pray with them and study beginner Mormonism in weekly lessons, after which I would learn stuff more amazing, but they sounded too sales pitchy like the ads in comic books. I looked down at the suit and asked it what it thought. After pretending to get an answer I looked up at them and said sorry, we were Lutheran. They told me only Mormons get into heaven and left.

Now the suit was loose in Hollywood, maybe to be used in a robbery though that would be like wearing my underpants on their head, but it would be ten pounds of underpants that made every move heavy like walking through a snowdrift. It should be reported to the police so if a crime were committed I wouldn't be blamed and maybe get my suit back. Looking over to the phone I saw movement in the shadows where the circle of light from the street lamp ended. It could be the thief trying to escape in the suit using the darkness as camouflage. I ducked behind the butt of the van and watched through the windows. It was a low dark humpy shape like maybe the thief was hurt or drunk. I went backwards keeping the van between us, back near the apartment gate where I could cross over in other shadows, then crept up the sidewalk on the other side of the street, keeping behind cars and trees until I was close enough to see it was the note writer, the concrete diarist. It was a small female dressed in black and crouched down to chalk another message inside a paved square, duck-walking sideways to finish a line of writing.

I stood up and walked into view toward the booth, exercising my right to approach a weird person on a public thoroughfare, hoping it was an actual human person. There was a moment when the booth blocked my view and when I came around it the person was gone like black in the night. The note told me to look in the palm tree. I turned and saw it in the palm where I was parked, hanging from a frond like something lynched.

Backed up the van and drove it onto the curb, scraping the corners of the cut stems that passed for bark on palms, making them look like skinny pineapples. Stood on the roof and used the bent-out hanger to snag my suit, wobbling drunkenly as if changing a light bulb on a ladder one rung too short for the job, but I rescued it. It needed a name. Leely had asked if it had name, telling me it would be good for publicity. I wanted something in the Gargantua and Kongo range, something to attract millions, my own comic ad sales pitch to rival Mormons.

There was one space left on the other side of the street but it was a couple bumpers too small. I clipped another car trying to slip squeeze into the space and its alarm went off so I drove away, its repetitive accusation fading with each turned corner. The van would have answered sympathetically if it could.

CHAPTER TWELVE

----

*T*he guy who worked the newsstand told me it was nice weather, the first Californian to mention the universal subject, but he was being sarcastic because I had been too long reading instead of buying. I bought the Variety and Hollywood Reporter I had been paging through looking at the classifieds for a gorilla wanted ad. They weren't as large as regular newspapers but were printed on quality paper and the articles were like being backstage at a movie preview. A picture of me in the suit would be magnetic to the eye on a page that ached for something other than nice faced actors with over-worked hair. Needing the advice of professionals I went back to Musso & Frank.

Made a decision not to leave the suit behind in the van, not to part with it again so carried my rucksack inside. Eight or ten guys were schmoozing in the bar area and within fifteen minutes I had drunk enough courage to ask the bartender if the gorilla that worked with the Marx Brothers was the same one that worked with the Three Stooges. Everybody stopped schmoozing. Thought I might have broken a rule or stumbled upon a secret. The bartender's face was carved from a solid block of suntan sanded smooth, but wrinkles formed as he squinted slowly to help his thinking, taking the question seriously. Someone behind me said that those were different studios.

Turned and saw two guys in a booth. Columbia and Paramount, said one of them nodding in agreement so it must've been the other guy who had spoken first. The other guy shook his head and said it was Columbia and MGM. The bartender said that didn't mean the gorilla was under contract, he could've freelanced for both studios, and asked if wasn't one realistic and the other scary. Maybe the same suit had different heads, someone guessed. Like you, someone else added and laughed through his nose. The first guy in the booth told me that the Ritz Brothers made a movie called The Gorilla, a stink bomb. That caused a long pause of almost silent musing except for some hmm-ing and uh-huhing.

They were different guys, said a man older than the rest wearing an old fashioned gray hat, the kind every man wore in old movies. He climbed off his stool as if climbing down a mountain, straightened his suit coat and pulled up his slacks, then twisted his hat down tighter and very slowly walked heel toe down the bar towards me, adding that they were entirely different suits.

The bartender told him to slow down before he hurt somebody and chuckled at his own joke. The old guy looked up at me with his eyes only peeking out from under the hat brim and put out a small dry hand for me to shake, which I did, thinking of the story about the monkey's paw. Gemora worked with the Marxes, he said, and the other guy did robots, monsters, anything with a suit. He told me the Ritz brothers didn't stink then whispered that the future was not Hollywood but in desalination of water. He walked out slowly, thirty seconds to get around the doorframe and out of sight, nobody speaking until then, the bartender saying he hadn't seen him in such a lively mood since he didn't know when.

Was he somebody famous, I asked?

Only if you know him I guess, he answered, around here he's famous as lunch. I didn't know what that meant but thanked him and went out to get another look at the old man but he wasn't anywhere in sight. I went up the boulevard hoping to get lucky in that direction but didn't catch up with him so he must've gone the other way, but I kept walking because I remembered seeing a wall painted with the red Levis logo and a sign that promised bargains. Found it at Western and Hollywood and entered to get some new used jeans. The khaki army shirts were only a dollar but you could see the little perforations that outlined the shape of the rank patch that had been stitched on but eventually removed again.

Changed clothes in the van parked on an unfamiliar street, anxious to get back near my original spot. Still feeling good from the beer I drove to Gower and found the walk-in entrance to Columbia. Carpeted stairs led up to a lobby-like space with soft light from sconces between old framed photographs of famous or powerful people. There was an actress sitting behind a desk pretending to be a receptionist, at least she looked like an actress hoping the head of the studio would pass by in a gruff panic about being unable to cast the next box office blockbuster until he saw her shining out of the corner of his eye.

The usual desire overwhelmed me and I wanted to be close enough to smear her make-up intentionally. She was busily reading a magazine but found time for me, closing it around a pencil for a bookmark then setting it at the corner of the desk so its sides paralleled the edges of the desk exactly. I asked her if there were any jobs I could apply for to work at the studio. She said, you mean on the lot, and I repeated in the studio, not wanting a job out on the lot with the security guard. She opened a drawer and handed me a standard work application and told me to attach my resume'. Certainly, I said as if I had one.

She told me that the shows were cast through agencies and the crews were union, was I union? Pretended to think on it then told her not at the moment. Well fill it out and maybe somebody'll need a PA. I mouthed the letters P and A and nodded, looking at the form, even the backside. She said that was a production assistant, a runner, a gopher. A couple of sit-coms were starting full seasons and there was always turnover. She pulled her hands inside the sleeves of her sweater and hugged her self, complaining that it always was cold in there. She didn't seem to be bothered by my not leaving so I told her it looked like she was wearing a straightjacket. She said she had a gay friend in high school who played football and that he called his letterman jacket a straight jacket. I laughed a couple of schwa vowels but didn't get the joke.

One of the phones blinked a light at her. She sat up properly and popped her hands free of the sleeves to punch a button then lift the receiver and said, Sunset and Gower Studios, where may I direct you? Picked up my rucksack and waved goodbye, stopping to notice that the Three Stooges wished me luck from one of the framed photographs. One of them had signed the picture that way, Good Luck from The Three Stooges. I thanked them for the encouragement. The receptionist pressed another button, finished in her labor and also wished me good luck before getting back into her sleeves and magazine.

Drove back home as it was. A Jeep with a chrome grill and giant tires was brooding behind the sedan like it was waiting for mating season, parked on the original side of the street. I got in line back near the apartments gate.

Filling out my name on the application was as far as I got, stuck for an address and telephone number, deciding to use the girl's house and the corner booth. Walked up to get the telephone number and there was a new message posted above the phone unit addressed To Whom It May Concern, a printed warning from the city of Hollywood and it listed articles and statutes about graffiti, defacing public property, fines and terms of imprisonment. It also mentioned penalties for removing the notice. I picked at a corner to see if it would pull loose but it was laminated and affixed to the glass with some type of permanent double-stick tape. I put a quarter in the coin return for Len and walked back singing the telephone number in my mind so I wouldn't forget it.

Peeked inside the Jeep because it didn't have a top or doors, just snooping, and there was the cat asleep in the foot well as if it had done it before. I looked over to the house and wondered what the dog might be witnessing. My stomach made the noise of a car driving slowly over gravel and it woke the cat, which licked its paw then rubbed that over the back of its ear a couple times, distracted momentarily by the movement of the end of its own tail.

My parents had an older cat injured when I dove into a load of clean laundry that had been dumped on their bed, not knowing the cat had found space in there to nap. It feared me until I earned back its friendship. One morning I freed it from being trapped in the bathroom overnight where it had been wrestling the throw rug and accidentally shut the door. Another time a big tom that would chase small children in the neighborhood boldly came through the back door left open to let in a breeze. It ate our cat's food. I tried to pick it up but it stiffened and growled then went back to eating. My cat looked away in hopelessness so I sprayed the tom with water from the rinse gun in the sink. It left but the food also was gone.

I followed it until big kids cornered it against a house. They tormented animals when they couldn't find a little kid to bother. They took off their shoes to throw, but I taunted them and dodged shoes while the cat escaped. Was struck in the back with a penny loafer as I ran home in the other direction, but villains couldn't catch me in a shoeless race especially if they still wore their socks.

Our cat lived its final days in the basement, too mangy for the house, and one night I heard it fall down the wooden stairs that were beneath my bedroom. Dad buried it behind the garage the next morning. I dug for the bones in high school to build a skeleton for a science class but couldn't find the grave. The house girl's cat finished its lick bath and jumped up the seat and out of the Jeep, slinking toward the house like a section of snake looking for the rest of its body.

At the library I tried to find information on desalination, which led to unfamiliar numbers of the Dewey decimal system where I discovered a book about the Los Angeles River, not surprisingly made of concrete and flowing with water from Colorado. There was a section on the importance of irrigation for the origins of civilization. When apes left the trees, the jungle, the banks of lakes and rivers, it was time to start thinking or die. Ideas made us people. Smarter females preferred smarter, less brutish and less hairy males, all those pieces of sharp flint and obsidian found with the skulls of early man maybe used for shaving fur to make themselves more attractive, and as a result required the invention of covering their bodies, something light from woven grasses that could protect yet breathe, invention itself like breathing, a necessity toward surviving a changing world in which we no longer wanted to change. Went to search my thoughts when Len appeared looking thirsty and said hey, been searching for you.

He told me it was his turn to pay, leading the way to a bar on a side street. I had passed the entrance several times but never suspected the regular door was a saloon entrance, There was a neon sign behind a window that was unnoticeable when unlit in the daytime glare of the sun. The interior was equally drab but through the back was a small patio where you could sit in sunshine. There was an every night crowd who had given up parks and beaches, but they could happy hour on the patio in the low golden rays to get a hint of color in their complexions.

A lone white female wearing big sunglasses sat in the shade of a wall, her head and much of her face covered by a dark scarf but she still turned away as we passed to get in the sun. She might have been famous and didn't want to be recognized with a half-full pitcher of beer and an empty shot glass in front of her. I set my pack safely between my feet and Len paid for our pitcher. I asked him if he got work.

He asked me back if I ever saw the guys grouped on a corner near a gas station every morning, waiting for people to drive up and offer them work for a day, paying in cash. I told him no. Refilling his glass he said that word went out on the street of a time and place, and if you showed up you could work in a movie. My swallow of beer stopped halfway down and I choked on the foam, sitting up quickly to aim a cough of spray where it wouldn't hit anybody. I asked if that meant anybody could show up, like me. He said I'd have to clean up, but it wasn't the kind of movie I was probably thinking of. I got the next swallow down and asked if he meant dirty movies, quietly so incognito girl couldn't hear. Len nodded. I told him that didn't sound bad, trying to keep my voice from flapping its wings and flying around the room excitedly. It's pretty bad, he said, all guys. The mood crashed suddenly and for any compensation he told me not to worry, he wasn't gay.

Took a deep breath and drank swallow after swallow to empty my glass. Asked if he went to a studio somewhere, mentioning I was applying for work at a studio, not wanting to hear any details of what he did. He told me no, that they'd go to a regular house in a regular neighborhood, different every time, often in the valley. I turned to see if the girl was listening but she was gone, the pitcher empty, but the wall now had some light blue chalked graffiti that I couldn't read from the distance.

Len leaned back in his chair and set his feet on the patio railing, smoking and getting some color. I wondered if there were a make up artist for x-rated movies, if they applied base and highlights to naked actors' bodies, but instead of asking I told Len about the graffiti girl. He jumped up to see what she had written, and as he was leaning over the spot on the wall a skinny guy in a white shirt and black vest came out to grab the girl's glassware, noticing the scrawl himself as Len came back to our table. The worker looked over at us accusingly and Len held up his open hands to show he wasn't carrying chalk. He took a moment to read it himself as Len told me that she must want me to call her, that it was a telephone number.

Took out my little pencil and wrote the number on a coaster, not taking another chance on my memory except to remember the little bit of face that had been showing. The vest guy came out with a wet towel and daubed at it until there was only a blue ghost of a smear. Maybe he would call her too.

Len wanted to show me something, and though I was afraid of being recruited into the wrong end of show business there wasn't much else to do so I tagged along. We cut down an alley and squeezed through a section of steel fencing that had been cut open for that purpose, stopping behind an old tall building with fancy concrete trim around bricked-up windows on the upper floors and plain boarded-up windows on the first floor that framed a heavy back door that warned us not to trespass. A New York style metal fire escape made it look like a movie set and Len dragged a big rolling trash bin under the access ladder that hung several feet above his head, climbed the side of the bin to pull the counterweighted ladder down then pushed the bin away again so it wouldn't be obviously available to other trespassers.

He went up the corroded iron rungs, each footstep making them almost ring, and I looked around for a reason not to follow but there was no other adventure in sight. The rust left a dirty band across my palms. We went up two flights of iron steps where that exit door wasn't closed tightly because of small wedge of wood duck-taped across the opening in the frame where the tongue of the lock should catch. When the door closed it was dark inside but there was electricity and one bulb in the high ceiling at the other end of the hall, its light too weak to provide much more than two dimensions to the scene.

Len knocked softly on door number 314 then opened it. It was a single room apartment with a single window, though the panes were so dirty the window might as well have been boarded up or bricked over. A window shade would have been redundant. The room was divided by raw sheets of plywood with sleeping bags and blankets on each side on the floor. Len proudly gestured to his space, waving his hand toward the cheap clock radio and a plug-in light socket and bulb that hung from and extension cord draped over a nail in the wall. The other space had a thin blanket as a curtain for privacy but I could see past its edge enough to know there was nothing more special to his roommate's standard of living. It was an enormous rise above homelessness.

Len told me that some guy had broken in and did some creative wiring in the basement, connecting the old fuse box to a hot electrical line in the wall shared with the building next door, charging a little rent to chosen guys from the street people crowd, those trustworthy to keep the secret. One jealous and angry soul could get them all evicted if not arrested. Somebody opened the fire escape exit door and the hall was exposed as shabby and dirty, the air filled with a swarm of backlit dust motes, a lumbering man's shadow blocking most of the light until the door closed again. Len said, uh oh, thinking it might be an inspector or fire marshal. I was afraid again but it was another resident who mumbled hey as he passed.

Thanked Len for inviting me to his home and told him I lived in a van, then looked at his clock radio and lied that I had to finish my work application and be at the studio for an interview, still worried there might be a crew with a sixteen millimeter camera around the corner. He wished me good luck as I opened the exit door, assaulted by the bright sun. It made my eyes water and I sneezed some of the dust away. Back on the concrete I pushed the ladder up out of reach. It made the same sound as the giant swing back home.

Back at the van I wrote the proper numbers on the application then drove to the little grocery to buy food and use the bathroom, wondering if the plumbing worked in Len's building. There was a different check out lady, older but smiley with a twang in her words. She seemed to flirt and called me cutey, asking if I were single, but I had heard her say the same thing to another guy as I came in. Maybe she was used to working for tips at another job. When she asked if I had found everything all right I told her I wasn't able to find any pichangwa. She didn't understand so I said it slowly, picture hanging wire. She shook her head and gave the guy behind me in line a fresh smile and told him she got off work at seven. In the parking lot I made cracker sandwiches of dry salami and ate a tomato like an apple. I had given myself the option between a pint of chocolate milk and a quart of beer but drank them both, surprisingly good together. And I bought a map.

When you have no place to go you can go anywhere, Dad had told me when I was sitting bored on the front steps and whining about it, which was stupid advice to a kid confined to the distance between the house and the corner. Without those limitations of kidhood I drove uphill out of the grocery store lot hoping to find the Hollywood sign, working my way around the hill and even up through the pass into the valley, finally finding a route up the backside of the ridge. It weaved up through low hills then cut back on itself several times to make the steeper inclination manageable, climbing higher on each turn and giving me hope that I would crest the peak then coast down the other side to the back of the sign, but I ended up in a large parking lot bordered by a low wall, a patch of concrete serving a domed building with only the sky in its background.

The climb was difficult for the van grunting like a pig on the steeper turns, but there was lower vibration almost like a growl that worried me more, making me fear another repair, but as I eased between the lines of a painted parking space and shut off the engine the growl continued. It sounded like the hills were filled with wild roaring animals and as I got out to walk toward the dome saw that was almost true. There were several rows of motorcycles crouched noisily under their leathered riders, the mufflers inadequate. It was like suddenly realizing you are standing under a hornets nest and don't know if it would be better to stand still or run.

Walked toward the dome. Maybe it was some kind of temple and gods would take my side in a fight. There were huddles of normal people wandering the lot but I looked down at my feet so I wouldn't trip and appear as the vulnerable member of the herd easily taken down. Because of that I almost walked into the sign that declared the building was the Griffith Observatory. Turned back to appreciate the gamut I had just traversed, and instead of a pack of mean and threatening thugs I saw the riders relaxed and talking, smoking and laughing, stretching and scratching and maybe discussing constellations. Never looked at the stars again without thinking of those bikers.

The building looked like Ray Bradbury might live there. Over the bordering wall was a lower level for some exit doors, its concrete balcony suddenly recognizable as the location where James Dean had a knife fight. There were dark spots visible but too far below to be certain if they were fake blood stains. The view of Hollywood was in panavision, and with deer eyes I might have been able to see the mountains to the left and the ocean to the right at the same time, but

my predatory eye placement required not only a turning of the head to
see the entire vista, but even a twist at the waist like when looking left
and right in the gorilla suit.

Somebody had snuck up behind me, a couple in quiet jackets
though when I faced them could hear leathery whispers from the
strained movement at their shoulders and elbows. Both had long hair
and work boots though it took a moment to focus on something so close
after viewing the curve of the Earth. One asked if I had a cigarette, the
other if it was okay to look around inside the building. I answered no
and that I thought it would be fine, walking with them to the entrance
and into the lobby. We circled the space inside and they asked me a
couple questions that I was able to answer from reading the signage,
and I offered the James Dean and Natalie Wood trivia.

In return they volunteered that they had just crossed the country
on a motorcycle. Told them that was cooler than making the journey in
a portable bedroom which I just had done. They said they had thought I
was a local and worked for the observatory. Why? Because I was the only
person not taking pictures and too bored to look at the bikers. Outside
they shared a cigarette and I saw my reflection in the glass doors, my
new khaki shirt and shagginess giving the appearance of a parks worker
and stargazer. It also was possible that being in Hollywood for a week
made you a local, depending on the week.

Asked them, Mac and Samantha, to show me their bike but they
said the truth was that it had broken down in Kentucky, that they
caught a ride with a trucker, their motorcycle strapped to his flatbed
through the remaining seven states. They needed a ride back into town.

Sam flopped back down on the bed and rubbed her hands
hungrily across the cushions as if they were leather not naughahyde,
swimming in the luxury of something bigger than half a motorcycle
seat. They had ridden up the hill on the backs of two other bikes that
had left. Mac guided me down the other side of the hill to Los Feliz.
I told him it was Spanish for happy according to my midwestern
teacher, but Mac pronounced it like Felix the cat because that was

how his brother pronounced it who had been living there for a year already.

Sam said that the van was cool, that you could live in it and have sex anywhere you went. I didn't mention that I lived in it because I never had sex anywhere I went. Mac said he was attracted to Sam's dirty mouth. Sam said, oh please, that she was a mess from eating a melting ice cream cone and that was his brilliant line. She did have a dirty voice, low and scratchy as if a cough would make it clear.

After a couple of miles of turn here and go up to that light and take the next street they finally stopped me in front of a plain little gray house that probably began as white, several motorcycles parked on the patchy lawn. Mac invited me inside but first I waited to see if Sam was going in. If she stayed on the bed I was going to drive off with her. Followed them onto a porch furnished with an old plaid couch with jar lids for ashtrays on the armrests. A dog barked at our footsteps though we hadn't make any sound. One dog's bark was a heavy roomph that triggered lesser woofs from farther inside. The door was not locked but as it opened a huge dog with a head like a badly carved pumpkin filled the entrance and jumped up on its hind legs to greet Mac eye to eye. Mac danced it backwards as a spotted bird dog sniffed our legs.

There were people inside but the place seemed to belong to the animals, especially the comfortable furniture. The big dog jumped onto the couch to claim it before any of us thought of sitting, and a sad faced hound deep in a lounger wagged its tail happily against the backrest. I sat on a skinny wooden chair next to the stereo system and dropped the pack between my feet. A tiny yipee dog jumped onto the pack then into my lap, leaning into my stomach to get far away from the bird dog that circled the chair once then sniffed at my pack, almost inhaling it with interest.

Mac handed me a can of Budweiser but before opening it I asked if he was going to have one with me. He said it was the last beer. The little dog nervously twirled once, its paws digging into my crotch, settling back against me. I handed the can back and offered to get some. Mac shrugged and took the can, but before he could open it a big black bearded biker stole it from his hand, popped the top and guzzled most of it, then knelt down on one knee to flip through a row of records leaning against a short wall that divided the living room from the dining area, saying thanks as if angry about saying it.

Instead of a dining table the next room was half filled with a drum set and several amplifiers. A lean muscled guy wearing a jean jacket with the sleeves ripped off that covered none of his tattoos came over to shake my hand in several ways, looking at my pack instead of my face and asked if I was on the run. Told him no, that I liked to keep some stuff close. He nodded his head back and said that was cool and that they call him Racer, then asked me whachunaman? He said it so fast it sounded like something in Cherokee but I realized he was asking for my name and almost answered him with Pichangwa. He pointed down at the big guy who was reading the song list on the back of an album cover and told me his name was Golly. Golly corrected him by muttering Goliath and elbowed the side of Racer's knee without spilling the beer or taking his eyes off the cardboard. There was a pop and a slight buckling but Racer kept smiling while he leaned in to grab the little dog by the back of the neck saying, exotic cuss ain't he? Exotic cuss, it sounded like a partner for the hairy stripper and I had the name for my suit, Exoticus.

The toilet flushed and a white haired girl passed on her way to the kitchen, looking at me out of the corner of her eye. Racer grabbed her by the upper arm and spun her around to face me, presenting her as Blanca. She said hey and backed out of Racer's grip, then from the kitchen she asked who drank all the beer, the tiles giving her voice a clean echoey quality almost as if she were singing. I set the dog down and picked up my pack, asking what everybody drank. They all said Bud.

Mac came out of hiding and offered to ride along. As soon as the door closed behind us on the porch I asked him if Blanca was with Racer or Goliath. He said neither, that she was with Chase, the guy in a band of course. He asked if I played. I asked, music? He said no, baseball, don't we all look like athletes?

Mac had long black hair and a feral look that reminded me of Sabu in Jungle Book. We bought a case of beer and a box of dog biscuits but instead of going back into the house he led me around to the garage where he unlocked the side door and motioned me to follow him inside. He turned on the light to reveal a motorcycle frame and engine propped up with parts all around on a blanket. He opened the case of beer and handed me a can then popped the top on one for himself. I said, so you're rebuilding it. He said no, this wasn't his broken bike, this one he was building bottom up from scratch to sell. He pointed at the motor to show how he had covered the bolt heads with silver skulls, a touch of voodoo to set it apart, having been into skulls since he learned to carve them out of soap in jail, though these were cut off cheap metal rings from a Melrose toy store.

Because he had shown me his I showed him mine, pulling out the suit and telling him it was made from belly bone fur. He said damn, was hoping you had a sack full of weed. I told him no, that was hidden in the van. His eyebrows went up but I shook my head as if just kidding. He examined the mask face to face and said it would be cool to ride around in this thing. Asked him where was the motorcycle he rode and he told me it was in his bedroom. My ride is my bedroom, I said, then told him about my job coming up and the application to work at the studios and that I needed an address and if I could borrow theirs. Why not, he said, it's a big ass mailbox.

There were a few more people inside and Samantha was playing a slow practice rhythm on the drums. Many hands competed to grab a can of beer at the same time, and I stashed a few in the back of the refrigerator behind a big yellow box of baking soda then took one to Sam and she stopped playing to accept it, surprised at the courtesy. Mac asked if I wanted to get high but I told him no, just drunk. The sun had set and it was dusk outside but dark in the house, the only light from the tv and the bathroom. Somebody lit a row of candles that sat on a board across a radiator. Goliath cranked up the volume on a fast and nasty guitar solo, not only recorded distorted but extra fuzzy through the blown speakers. He nodded his head almost in time to the music, but still looking at me.

Then it was twice as loud because a guy was playing along in the dining room. He yelled out, not that east coast shit, then began showing off by playing faster and outside the edges of the recording, laughing at an inside joke. Goliath surrendered and lifted the needle off the record with a zipper sound. Sam handed me her beer back and began playing again. Mac handed me his empty can, which I held against my chest. The guy with the Strat looked at me holding three cans and asked if I wanted a beer.

They played a song about rolling and tumbling, and the only reason I remembered is because later there was an earthquake.

CHAPTER THIRTEEN

hen I woke up the sun was forcing itself through the plaid curtains, light a hatchet to my eyes. Wished I were on the other side of the world because it would be dark and maybe cool. Peed twelve ounces into an empty beer can but had a couple ounces left, looking frantically around for another empty. Finding one bettered my mood despite the pain using up most of my head. The only bike left on the lawn was a Honda with a dented and scratched gas tank. Someone was sleeping on the porch couch or lying dead. Might have been the Japanese-bike guy and they killed him for that. I remembered seeing it last night laid down on the ground because it didn't have a kickstand, the Harleys parked around it as if they had stomped it down, hungry for rice.

Wasn't wearing my shirt and discovered it wrapped around two warm beers in the storage space. Forced one down around several gags then sat back to rest, building up strength enough to work the other one down past my hangover. My first Hollywood party and I had forgotten it. The second beer was easier and a long belch relaxed me until I remembered accepting a drug. When the beer began to work my memory crept back into my brain.

I was drunk at the kitchen breakfast nook across from Racer who took out two things, a tiny beer colored bottle and a big folding hunting knife. He poured out a pile of powder and dipped the tip of the knife into it then brought it under his nose and sniffed the stuff up one nostril. Then he dipped it again and stuck the knife in my face. Racer said the first time he went to jail was for shooting a chicken with a BB gun, and he subtracted the years he was in prison from his age so he was still seventeen. I felt like the chicken but the knife worried me more than the drug so I sniffed. Nothing happened. It wasn't like trying to swallow whiskey the first time, but later after the earthquake when everyone else had crashed or slept, I was wide awake in the kitchen alone, buzzed. In the sink was a dirty plate with food dried on it like barnacles, so I washed it.

The worst part was no women, not for me anyway. All the females could have been auditioning for a drive-in movie about chicks on wheels, but they were with somebody. There was a girl named Shortsie who seemed interested but Blanca came through asking where the dogs had gone. Somebody found two under the couch and then the shaking began, beer cans dancing across surfaces as a wave in the ground passed under us. One picture fell off its nail and slid down the wall, hitting the floor with a final crack of noise.

Shortsie followed most of the others toward the front door to see damage. Somebody said look, there was purple lightning coming up from the ground. I went to the kitchen because my beer was empty and maybe Racer was still there. I sat at the table waiting for the party to drift back into the house and kitchen, a thought-loop circling counter clockwise in my head. Don't know how long until I realized it was just the clean plate and me.

There were four beers left which I took to bed in the van to go with my brain damage. Drank two and in the morning life tasted as if I had a mouthful of mouse. Drove down an alley and stopped to toss the cans of piss into a garbage can. Parked a block south of McDonalds, grabbed my pack and hiked to the corner. Trying to remember how to speak human I mumbled my order around the dead mouse in my mouth, anxious to wash it down with ice cold Coke. Among the dollars in my pocket I found scribbled notes from the night, some legible but others might have been in cuneiform. Also there was a mystery telephone number. As I chewed my breakfast burger, the greasy goodness instantly rejuvenating me, I sorted the readable from the undecipherable.

For some reason I had written click bang what a hang. A phrase in quotation marks, "the body is a temple but what do I care about temples?" On one I claimed an ancestor of mine invented the note B flat. "They can hurt me but they can't scare me," was attributed to Racer who I remembered showed me the butt of a gun tucked into the waist of his black jeans. I assumed the other note with "you can't fight a bullet" went with the gun related one. This is how we pray (turn around, put your hands behind your head and interlace your fingers): "Please god, don't let them take me to jail."

I must have looked like an idiot writing everything down, and probably even when I wasn't writing anything down.

After causing a line to form outside the bathroom I was refreshed and didn't smell too bad from a distance, feeling good enough to cross the street and see if Roy was working. Maybe he wanted to carpool out to the park tonight or in the morning. Something furry was moving in the center of a group and I worried that it was another ape, considering other hairy possibilities from film, maybe a wolfman or cowardly lion, possibly Lassie.

A kid broke away from the throng with an autograph like it was cash money, leaving a gap through which I saw a wookie though it seemed about eighteen inches short of an adult specimen. It had a partner, some guy with acne scars dressed up as Skywalker who was getting so much sun on his cheeks they looked like orange peels. Beyond a kiosk was Roy doing a drunk bit. He tripped and his derby fell. Bending to reach it he put enough weight on his bamboo cane to bend it into the shape of the letter c and I was certain it would snap, but he caught the brim of the hat in his fingers and straightened up too quickly, losing his balance and stumbling backwards to the spot I was approaching. He must've known I was there because he pretended to fall back into my arms. Two older women were laughing and it was funny, but I almost dropped him because he was dead weight and I could smell that he really was drunk, though he probably didn't smell as bad as I did.

Got him upright so he could accept a lady's five-dollar bill, her smile big enough to hold a boomerang. Roy thanked her and I whispered for him to keep this bit, and he asked what bit? He leaned against me as we walked back to his car where he lowered the gate of the wagon and sat with his head between his knees to give puking a chance. The blood flowing to his brain sobered him up enough to tell me that Leely called to tell him that she might not be able to use him as Chaplin, that the park might get sued by the family or studio. He held up the fiver and told me that this kind of money wasn't going to cut it, crumbling and dropping it to the street. He ignored it for a few seconds before bending down, trying to reach it, and suddenly he puked, the bill catching some splatter so I let it lie, but Roy wiped his mouth then grabbed it in one smooth move, muttering the name of the lord in vain.

Asked him if he still were going out to the park. He said oh yeah, they weren't going to get rid of him that easy, especially for a paid rehearsal. He straightened out the bill and wiped it against his thigh, pulling out others from his pockets then sorting them as if arranging a hand of poker. Finally satisfied with what he had been dealt he asked if I was hungry. I told him no but he said to hop in, he'd drive us to the store. There was a rack with free classified ad papers in front of the grocery so I read one while leaning against the big window, the store's advertisements painted on the inside with wash-off paint bragging about whole cut chickens on sale.

There was a distant voice in the air, fading in and out. I turned and put my forehead to the glass, shading it with my hand to peek inside and see who was working check out. The express lane was nearest the door and the lady ringing up items never stopped talking as she slid each product with one hand, reading the price and punching it into the register using the other hand without having to look at it, like touch typing. The wafting voice matched her lip movements and I realized

I could hear her from outside. She must have been deafening to the customers, and what I hadn't noticed was how far they were standing from the counter, leaning away from her.

I listened carefully while reading her lips, and she was saying that her boy wouldn't bite into the front of a sandwich, that he always bit off the corners on the back first. She said that they rounded one edge of a piece of bread so you could tell the front from the back, and nobody ate a sandwich from the back. She was worried about her boy. She wasn't talking to any particular customer, keeping her attention on the prices, so each person heard only part of her ramble. She only would glance up at them and smile quickly before each order. When it was Roy's turn she refused to check him out, shouting into the air that her mother hadn't escaped Poland so her daughter would have to ring up neo-nazis. Roy looked like he had been shot. He ripped off his little Charlie mustache while apologizing and explaining that he wasn't imitating Hitler, that he was Jewish.

She calmed down and rang up his stuff. When he joined me in the sunshine I asked if he really were Jewish and he said nah, learning from experience what worked. He handed me a heavy bag of groceries so he could drive, and as we neared the driveway out to the street a Porsche entered the lot. Roy pressed the gas pedal to spin the tires and burn rubber to compensate for the wagon, but the breeze was faster and his self-made dirty cloud caught up with us, filling the cabin with its blackened stink. We showed him, I said.

He drove up into the area where I had been yesterday, leaving the perpendicular grid of roads for the snaky streets of the hillside, the twisting pieces of road like frayed ends of civilization. A sign welcomed us back to Griffith Park but instead of the Observatory there was a dirt trail past a graveled parking area that lead toward a rock-framed wilderness. It was that easy to get out of town.

I carried the bulky clunking sack as we trudged up the dusty path. Asked if we were going to the Hollywood sign and he said nah, that's over there more, waving his left hand as if erasing the question. At a fork in the trail he stopped and bent to put his hands on the tops of his knees, catching his breath. I asked didn't he know which way to go, but he shook his head and waved me over so he could reach into the sack, pulling out a quart of beer by the neck. Can't breathe up here, he gasped and tried to twist off the beer cap, but it wasn't a twist-off. He rubbed some of the pain off against his hip then inspected the damage. Shit in the sunshine, he said. As he looked around for a solution I tried to say shit in the sunshine three times fast.

Roy hit the end of neck against a rock a couple times, then one more time hard enough to break it off at the shoulder, spilling a good glug and losing more in foam as it erupted over the broken edge, but he carefully poured a choking amount into his mouth without touching or getting cut by the glass. He swallowed and coughed with beer running down his chin then did it again, smiling with the look of an adult who had just been baptized.

Able to breath again we followed the trail to the left, him saying the other quart was for me. Told him I was saving it for the surprise and he said well, there it is, pointing to two holes in the rocky side of the hill.

There is what, I asked and he said, don't you recognize it? I looked harder but it stayed unremarkable. Robot Monster, he said enthusiastically, toasting the view and drinking as much more beer as he could without losing a lip. My arms were getting noodly so I set the bag on the ground, seeing the capped neck of the other bottle rising above the other stuff inside and pulling it out. He reached down past my head to grab a torpedo of summer sausage. I stared at the beer cap then back at the caves, looking for a can opener, a little winded and light headed myself.

Roy gnawed the plastic off the end of the sausage then set his beer between his feet to dig into his pocket, finding a three-inch folding knife. He opened the blade with his teeth and cut the puckered butt off one end of the sausage and bit it off the knife blade like a chaw of tobacco. I told him I had done drugs last night. He stopped in mid-chew and mid-slice to look at me sideways and asked what kind of drugs. Told him I didn't know, that I was drunk. Jeez, kid, you don't want to start messing around with that crap, not now when everything is going your way. I asked to borrow the knife. He finished cutting a slice, handing me the knife and hunk of meat. I took just the knife and used the tip to pry each crimped curve of the bottle cap away from the lip of the bottle, then set the edge of the cap against an jut of rock and slapped my palm down on the bottle, the cap popping loose and dropping with a dull click against the hard ground.

Handed Roy his knife, picked up the cap and put it in my pocket, then took a few sips of beer and wandered into the cave. It was a tunnel chiseled through an outcrop of what must've been special rock. Behind me Roy grumbled that I must have seen Robot Monster, the words echoing like Blanca's voice in the kitchen. It was a goddamn gorilla suit, he yelled.

Then I knew what he was talking about, where we were. It was where they filmed the gorilla wearing a space helmet with a radio that blew Lawrence Welk bubbles, the alien ape that walked upright with an earth woman in its arms. That movie gave me the idea that the first ground apes walked upright not to reach fruit with a stick, not to see above savannah grasses or throw a rock at a lion, but to carry home a babe. The desire for a female was enough to steal one and carry her home, an evolutionary trigger for bipedalism that was only possible for the spine if a counterweight was held in both arms, a counterweight with the mass of a young ape woman.

Turned to toss my theory at Roy but he was back at the grocery bag, one leg on each side of it, biting into a bagel. I went over to him and said that I remembered Robot Monster but didn't know that was the title. He held the bagel between his teeth and reached down to get me one, slicing a section of salami and handing that to me. Around my own mouthful of picnic told him that I wasn't the hero type, preferring to be the villain and carry off the pretty girl same as King Kong. He said I was wrong, that Kong was the hero.

The beer was getting warm so after another swig I handed my half-empty bottle to Roy who didn't care, stabbing his knife into what was left of the meat so he could hold it and the bagel with one hand, and he drank the rest. He pointed the bottle toward the caves and told me that all the cardboard jungle sets were gone with many of the low rent studios, but right there is a landmark where they filmed a gorilla suit, most of one anyway, and it would outlast all the studios. A low almost growling sound came from one of them and I asked if there were animals up there. Coyotes, he said, but that was no coyote. He dropped the bottle and food into the sack, concentrating on holding just the knife. Another throaty rumble bounced off the stony walls and Roy backed away, tripping a little over the sack. I told him it might be a trick of the wind but he asked what wind, already walking away, looking over his shoulder to see what was coming to eat him, if it were coming.

I picked up the broken bottle then collected the broken bits of glass and put them in the bag, noticing two slightly smooshed Twinkies among the leftovers. The bag tinkled as I carried it, and I also looked back expecting to see a practical joker poke his head out from a cave. Caught up with Roy pissing on a big rock the path went around. He said we were safe, that no wild animal would pass by that spot now.

There were other cars parked at the trail lot that hadn't meant anything when we arrived, but somebody had probably gone up to the caves to get high or have sex. I tried that explanation on Roy and he said we should go back and kick their asses, but instead he got into the wagon and turned the key in the ignition. I told him yeah let's, I'm right behind you, then got into the passenger seat. He said the salami had made him thirsty and asked if I was thirsty. I knew he meant did I want to get a drink and told him I didn't care, fishing out a damaged Twinkie bleeding crème and eating it. I asked if he wanted me to open his, but he said no, just put the sack in the kitchen, gesturing toward the back seat. I turned and set the bag on a pile of clothes and asked how long he had been living out of his car. Since his wife kicked him out. Thought he had told me he wasn't married but maybe I had assumed it. Most of his money went toward rent on the apartment in the valley where she and their eight year-old kid lived.

It took me a couple blocks to get the courage to ask why she kicked him out. Years ago he did a couple seasons of voice work for a cartoon, usually a half day's work once a week for a few months of each year, then he lived on residuals for another year, getting too used to drinking by the pool all day with a neighbor who danced nights at the Hollywood A Go Go with Girls Galore. When his residuals ran out so did his lifestyle.

Asked why he didn't get more cartoon work. He had calls to audition but felt he shouldn't have to audition. Then there were no more calls. The checks in the mail were nice but he needed to find a way to make a living other than doing nothing. So, I said, can I go out with your wife? He fished around behind him muttering where's that gun dammit.

You should meet my kid though. You remind me of him only he's a lot smarter. He parked in a lot where there was a little set of concrete stairs that led to the back entrance of Musso & Frank. Past the bathrooms and kitchen we entered the bar room from the back end where the old man with the hat presided over the schmoozing. There were two vacant stools and as we sat I said, girls galore huh? He leaned into me and said that sex wasn't any better with a dancer, but she made masturbating fun again. I changed the subject by asking about the guy in the old fashioned hat at the end, thinking he was an old time studio head because everyone seemed to think highly of him. Roy laughed and said that he owned the sex shop down the street, the porno king of Hollywood Boulevard, that I should do a dirty movie in the gorilla suit, get work and laid at the same time.

The porno king caught me staring and gracefully raised his hand to point his boney finger at me. I gave him a low short wave as he slowly pulled out a long thin billfold from the inside of his jacket. If you want attention move extra slowly, it becomes hypnotic. He moved as if his batteries were running down and any moment he would come to a complete stop with his arms stuck in a mannequin pose. Eventually he drew a card from his wallet, held it up as if it might disappear, then gently set it down at arm's length in my direction and pointed at me again. Here it is, come and get it.

Roy was focused on the bartender's movements so I slid off my stool and stood by the card but looked at him, asking how everything was. Fine he whispered. Offered to buy him a drink but he waved a hand over his tumbler of tea-colored something and since it didn't transform into a bouquet of flowers I assumed that meant no. He was miserly with words so I took the card and read it, hoping it would explain itself. It said Catty's Attic and had a telephone number, the back blank. Call Catty, he said and I wondered if it were some sort of sex service, but as if he read my thoughts he said it was for any true student of Hollywood.

I thanked him and introduced myself then asked if he knew Roy. He said, certainly, that Roy was his best customer. He gave a musical laugh with both a wheezing in the throat and a whistling through the nose. I slid back down next to Roy who said not to believe him, he just knows me from here and thinks he's a comedian. Showed him the card and asked if it were a whorehouse or something, but he said that was for me to find out. Took out the piece of paper with Cricket's number on one side and the chalk girl's on the other and wrapped it around Catty's card then tucked it away again feeling rich.

A guy on the other side of Roy ordered a specific brand of whiskey and Roy told him that drinking cheap liquor quickly makes more sense than sipping expensive whiskey. The man asked Roy why he was jealous of sane people. The bartender finally got to me but I decided not to get drunk again. Roy immediately objected but I reminded him that we had to get up early tomorrow. All right he agreed by finishing his drink, then nodded at the whiskey sipper and said that it was amateur night anyway. He dropped off his stool and pulled on my sleeve, telling me to c'mon. I followed him out the front door where he stood looking up and down the street, muttering what the hell. He had forgotten that we came in the back, and when the memory kicked in he said he wasn't going back through the restaurant again so walked toward the corner, going around without saying goodbye. I went the other way toward home, my feet bigger and heavier without a beer buzz. Roy yelled hey and I turned around. He put his hands out to each side, palms up and said he thought I wanted to do something else. Like what, I asked? Just c'mon. He turned and walked around the corner not waiting to see if I obeyed, so I caught up, my feet lighter again.

He drove onto one freeway into slow traffic but a few minutes later merged onto another less busy then exited along some railroad tracks that ran next to warehouses and storage unit rentals, eventually turning up a long winding drive where we caught up with another line of cars. Ahead I saw people along the side of the road stepping between the cars and I figured they were stopping traffic. I told Roy about my jay walking ticket my first day in town. He said pay the fine or they would put out a warrant for my arrest, that there were guys doing jail time for jaywalking.

The opposite lanes were empty, making our inching along seem static but eventually we came near one of the roadside guys who held a cardboard sign. Maybe he needed a ride, but the sign said tickets, sloppily printed. Maybe I should carry around quality cardboard and felt pens and make nice signs for people like that, charge a couple bucks. The signs would increase business, pay for themselves. Roy leaned over to my side and yelled out the window, whattayagot? The sign guy said he had four in the blues behind home plate. Roy wanted two and the guy told him twenty dollars. Lemme see 'em. The guy jammed the tickets through the open window so Roy could examine them. All right. He found a twenty in his wad of bills and switched it for the blue-trimmed tickets under my nose. They sign guy stepped back and held up his sign high with one hand and two fingers up with the other. You got to check the dates, Roy said, sometimes they'll pass off tickets for an old game. He handed one to me, saying that I could buy the beer, and only then did I know we were going to a Dodgers game.

We entered an open space between hillsides giving the area a lost horizon feeling though it was just a parking lot. Roy quit the line of vehicles heading toward the stadium to park in the outermost row, the wagon facing outward, so we had a long walk across empty rows of spaces to catch up with all the other people already at the gates. He complained about a pain in his hip. Then why park so far away, I asked and he told me to trust him, he'd done this before. Instead of going to the entrance he steered me up a several flights of concrete stairs that weren't steeper than Len's fire escape, the smoggy air burning in my chest and Roy's breath getting wheezy again. I thought we might meet some monks soon.

There was another entrance at the top and we entered the stadium through a turnstile, shuffling with the crowd under steel girders finally to emerge among blue seats high above the playing field. The game was already in the second inning and I could easily read the numbers on the players' jerseys if I squinted, but above was yet another level where the fans shouted down encouragement for their favorite hitters and cursed the opposition. Roy sent me for beer and I had to wait in line, watching the game on a tv monitor bolted to the wall and breathing deeply the fried hot dog flavored air. Back at the seats I handed both to him. The other two tickets must not have been sold because he was able to set the second cup on one of the empty seats next to him. Roy informed me the team was statistically out of the running for the post-season, the attendance not large enough to sustain the wave, too many gaps and too little enthusiasm. The stadium had an announcer, but in every row was a person with a small portable radio listening to the play by play, the tinny broadcast voice of Vin Scully heard throughout the stands, occasionally drowned out by a salesman running up and down the steps screaming peanuts.

The foul balls were scattered to all sections of the level below but had no chance of reaching us, so after finishing his first beer Roy told me to follow, taking us down to an empty section of those orange seats in hope of catching one. A possum crossing the outfield was the most exciting moment of the game, and even though the Dodgers had a one-run lead Roy decided it was time to go after the seventh inning. He rushed almost dangerously down the stairs in a race with others also leaving early. There was almost as much congestion during the eighth inning exodus as when we arrived but with the wagon strategically parked beyond the other cars we were able to merge into the exiting traffic, cruising steadily back home.

Roy explained that leaving at the end of the game meant an hour just getting back to the freeway, but now we could watch the last inning at the Frolic Room. He parked on a side street past the Pantages and when we reached the bar I didn't go in, telling him again that I didn't want to get started. He called me a lightweight then said he was going to park behind Musso & Frank's for the night, don't let him oversleep. Told him thanks for a great day. He waved my words down as if slapping the compliment to the ground and went inside.

Drove to a coin laundry I had noticed while wandering and went in with a couple shirts and my other jeans bundled under my arm. There were boxes and plastic bottles of detergent in the trash but some of them had small amounts of soap in the bottom. There was a sink where I hand-washed the clothes then put them in the drier for twenty-five cents worth of heated tumbling.

The day's edition of the LA Times was scattered around, sections scattered on chairs, counters and floor. I found two pages of movie ads bragging that every film was the best something or other. An old guy came in with a can of olives and a can opener and went to the sink, saying that he would do his laundry but at the moment there was a karate class between him and his clothes. He cranked the lid almost off but kept it attached to strain off the liquid, telling the machines and me that it was probably a mistake, the good stuff was all in the brine. He pulled the lid up and pinched an olive from the can and put it on his tongue, savoring the flavor before chewing and swallowing. He looked into the can and said that he had sold his radio for two dollars and that people take advantage of you, that it was a good little radio too. The drier time ran out and I carried my still damp clothes back to the van, driving to the lot behind Musso & Frank and parking in the back upper corner against a retaining wall that held the neighborhood above in place.

The manual in the glove department instructed me how to pop the top and unfold a cot that served as an upper bunk where I spread out the jeans and shirts to finish drying overnight in the cross breeze than came through the netted canvas windows that appeared when the top was angled up. Quietly peed against the retaining wall, watching the dark stream with street lamp highlights run under the van, then went to bed in the gloom of the evening surrounded by distant human noise.

CHAPTER FOURTEEN

- -

The day the suit was finished I lurched up and down our street at dusk causing a dog to bark and a car to honk. The church had announced its annual picnic and put a request in the Sunday bulletin for a clown who might juggle or make balloon animals for the children. I volunteered to appear as the gorilla, promising not to scare the kids worse than any clown. Maybe my presence would revive someone else's memory of the gorilla in church.

I was at the church parking lot early, same as two firefighters who had brought a sparkling clean fire engine that would end up covered with the greasy handprints of a hundred picnickers just finished with buttered corn on the cob and fried chicken. For sitting inside the cab to blast the horn and siren the kids were given fire-safety coloring books that still littered the area days after the picnic. The ladies aid group was on the church lawn struggling to set up an awning in the wind but it kept collapsing and blowing toward the Methodists, which made them determined to stand it up against any natural element that might indirectly suggest they weren't god's favorite franchise.

At the other corner of the lot the architecture provided a neat square of space protected from the wind by twin jutting projections that housed the staircases at each end of the classroom's hallways. It was a weedy area in the corners where the riding mower could not maneuver. There the school janitor had set up a homemade grill made from an over sized wheel barrow once used for unloading the daily catch of a commercial fisherman until his boat sunk in the river channel after colliding with an old underwater oven that had been dumped from the bridge to save the cost of using the city dump.

A local radio disc jockey made up as Bozo had been hired for clown service and was helping the janitor light the coals. As I put on my costume in one of the stairwells, the firemen went to help the ladies wrestle the canopy unaware that the clown had fanned the coals with his giant flat shoes, sending burning embers into the air that fell in the tall dried grass where a proper fire started. He and the janitor were too embarrassed to ask for help, hoping to put it out before the firemen noticed. The janitor stomped on the flames and the clown beat down on them with his shoes, but the comedy toe extensions weren't made of leather but of some light material that was flammable. He dropped them before they burned his fingers and the janitor had two sets of flames to stomp, hopping from one fire to the other. The disc jockey grabbed a kitchen towel and slapped at them but again he just fanned the flames.

I rushed out with the mask and hands flapping loose, grabbed a can of Canfield chocolate soda pop from the big galvanized trough of ice the church always provided in place of Coke or Pepsi because it cost much less, yelling where's the can opener? The janitor pointed to one hanging from a cord tied to one of the handles at the end of the big bucket and I pried a couple triangles into the steel lid and shook it quickly, turning it into a nice little fire extinguisher though it took another can of lime flavored pop to put out the janitor's smoldering shoes.

We looked over to the firemen stabilizing the canopy. The ladies applauded and cooed, and nobody asked why the clown had burnt shoes assuming they were black and melted for comedy value. After fifteen minutes in the costume surrounded by kids I was exhausted and quit, not bothering to rejoin the picnic in my sweaty shorts and t-shirt, no condition to meet girls. Went home wondering if I ever would have a wife waiting after a hard day in the jungle, someone to help me out of my suit and hang it to dry then bring me furry slippers and a hot cup of Coca Cola.

The morning of the park rehearsal I felt the early sunshine at the end of a dream about sleeping. Turned on the radio to hear what time it was, and while peeing into a bottle heard the shocking news that weather was coming to town. Closed the camper top and changed into clean and mostly dry clothes though my skin was still grimy and crawly. Tossed the bottle into the restaurant dumpster and walked over to Roy's car. He had put cardboard up against the rear windows of the wagon so I couldn't see if he was in there sleeping with his gun in hand. Crouching against the rear bumper I knocked. He said something about hell, maybe go to or what the, or maybe he said help, so I knocked again and told him to get up, that it was time to go to school.

Watched dark clouds come in from the west, their front edges a yellow gold in the low morning sun. We had time for breakfast so I decided to get some and bring it back to bait him out of his lair. As I pulled out onto the side street I heard him yelling at me to wait, shouting wait, wait, wait! As I slowed to stop he appeared out the passenger side window barefoot and dressed in sweats, running sideways and pacing me down the sidewalk, waving his arms in case I hadn't noticed him. His hair stood up in a young punk style from sleeping on it weird but it made him look old. I leaned over to unlock the door and he opened it, still gasping the news that he was going with me. Told him I was only going to get him some coffee and donuts and aspirin. He took two steps backwards and sat on the curb, concentrating on getting more air into his lungs, then whispered that he'd wait there.

Talked him into the van and when he had come back to life asked what the panic was anyway, he could still drive himself. He said nah, the wagon was almost out of gas and all his money was gone. He couldn't remember if he drank it all or somebody went through his pockets. What, like a pickpocket? Said he had a few vodkas and must've fallen asleep for a minute. He said gawd, wiping both hands over his head to smooth down his hair as he told me he'd never live down the shame.

At the gas station store I bought him his coffee and collected assorted junk for breakfast then swung back to the wagon so he could get dressed and put on shoes, having braved the floor of the gas station bathroom in his bare feet. On the road he tried to tear the plastic on a pack of mini donuts, telling me he celebrated last night because of his idea to change Charlie's hat and mustache enough so he was just a silent film comedian in white face, that way there would be no conflict over Chaplin. That'll work, I said waiting for a donut but they were sealed beyond Roy's ability.

After a few minutes on the freeway Roy asked if my granny taught me to drive. It was a slight upgrade and the van was unable to accelerate. Well he said, good thing we got an early start. The little bottle of aspirin opened easily but the opening was too small for him to get his finger in and pull out the wad of cotton. He dug at it with the plastic stir stick from his coffee and eventually got a strand up that he could pinch between his fingers, pulling carefully so it wouldn't break away from the main body of wad. With work the strand became thick enough to pull out the rest and I sighed with relief louder than Roy. He poured the pills straight into his Styrofoam cup, stirring his coffee into a foaming mix and drank that down like a big shot of liquor, then dropped the cup onto the floor between his feet and leaned against the door with his arms crossed and eyes closed. He said to let him know if I needed him to get out and push.

Turned up the radio, a song I'd never heard about being up on a mountain just as mountains appeared on the horizon. Asked Roy what they were but he either was sleeping or faking it, though when the song was over and I turned down the volume on a blaring commercial about stereo systems he asked me if I golfed because we should golf when he got his clubs out of hock. Asked when he hocked them and he said last Christmas, then uh oh, it was too late, they were gone, hoping the new owner liked bogeys because that was all they were good for anyway. He never moved or opened his eyes.

The radio warned of rain again but there were no drops on the windshield. Another song elbowed its way between commercials about water beds and window tinting, so I turned the volume up again. The subdivisions changed into newer homes with acreage between them as exit ramps became rare, most traffic going in the other direction. A billboard announced the park's opening a mile before our exit and it was exciting, never having had a connection with a billboard before.

Beyond some low hills, the tops of several coasters and thrill ride towers peeked at us in anticipation. We drove through a gateway framed by painted murals of happy people in colorful coaster cars hurtling at the speed of excitement, giving us highlights of the fun waiting inside. The empty parking lot was long as an airport runway and it took a minute to drive across the painted hash marks of parking spaces before reaching a group of cars parked near the employees' entrance like a small herd of animals that had discovered a single spot of good grazing. A guard in the booth seemed happy to have company for the moment and checked our driver's licenses against a clipboard list, and it wasn't a Hollywood studio but I was in, working.

There was construction noise and a cloud of concrete dust in the air, worrying me that a sudden downpour would mix the two and coat us into statuary.

We were early and Leely was in the corner of a warehouse laying out papers on a table. She welcomed us and motioned toward donuts, coffee and juice at the table's other end. The building had space enough for a rock concert but it was empty except for a long cart of folded chairs against a wall, and a portable stereo in the middle of the floor plugged into an orange extension cord that went to the opposite wall. Roy grabbed a donut then a chair, trying to unfold it with one hand and his knee. He dropped his donut, laid the chair down and picked up the donut to examine it for any obvious dirt then bit into it.

Leely asked us to fill out the paperwork but Roy was getting coffee. He picked up pen and paper in one hand while holding the donut and cup in the other, looking down at his still folded chair on the floor. Gawd I hope this gets easier, he whispered.

I set up four chairs, two for sitting and two for desks. On the employee information form I used Mac and Sam's address and phone number as my own. It suddenly got darker and I looked up to see a giant blocking the light. The sliding door left an opening big enough to allow a tractor but he still ducked his head as a reflex. With legs like stilts he took small careful steps though there was nothing in his way, just afraid of breaking things if he moved too quickly. He wondered out loud with a hello. Leely good-morninged him with an extra o in the word morning to make it friendlier, keeping him calm. I thought he might turn and run as she invited him over to the paperwork, pointing at the sheets and pens. He stepped closer but was wary to touch it, watching until he was certain it was just paper, not a dangerous trick.

Roy, overwhelmed by his own page, griped to Leely about having to provide medical history and education and past employers. She told him to fill in as much as he could and Roy continued with a sigh, like it was a final exam for which he were unprepared. I examined my sheet for the bother it was causing them but it did not intimidate me. A crashing of chairs filled the building, echoing off the far end. The giant had taken one away and the rest tipped over like dominoes. Nothing was damaged but his expression made you think the building had collapsed. The chair in his hand looked like it might have come from a little girl's play set of tea party furniture. The three of us looked away as if nothing had happened and I heard him set his chair down yards away from everything to fill out his form. Would've introduced myself but didn't want to send him fleeing or stop his heart.

Almost the prettiest girl I ever had seen arrived and I became conscious of my hair and beard and lip, even the concentration of freckles on my hip that looked like a map of Alaska. I wanted to sit on the big guy's knee for security, suddenly afraid of getting hurt. I needed time to learn to think and speak and walk again, wishing I were inside my gorilla suit. It would have given me an excuse for smelling like a busy gym.

Before looking at the table she said hello to us as a group. I nodded and smiled instead of answering like a human being. Leely said hi,

Sonny, then announced that she was our princess, or fairy queen, or maybe park goddesss, she wasn't sure yet. Roy sucked in his gut, which caused him to sit up straight and he produced a new smile that made him appear younger, telling Sonny that he was our Charlie Chaplin as if every place had one. His voice was higher than usual and so melodic he might have been auditioning for a musical. The giant and I dropped our heads and attention back to our papers, a way of bowing to her.

A pair of little people arrived together, a waddle in their walk. Roy no longer could concentrate on filling out the form so leaned in, whispering that Mickey and Minnie had arrived but don't use the words dwarf or a midget, not that he knew the difference, but to refer to them as little people. Do giants not want to be called giant, I asked also in a whisper, trying not even to move my lips in case the giant was watching. Roy said nah, don't be silly.

Told him I'd play it safe and just call them Mickey and Minnie, but he snorted and said their names were Robby and Sheila, that they had played Mickey and Minnie Mouse at Disneyland. I asked if they were married and he said not only weren't they married, they wouldn't even date other little people, and to watch out for Sheila, she was the seductress type. Strange electricity buzzed my nervous system at the thought.

Two clean-cut guys with muscles enough to be gymnasts joined the cast, maybe acrobats. They got touchy feely with the little people and laughed over some inside joke about Disneyland. One caught me watching in fascination and asked what I was looking at, calling me Shaggy. Sorry I said, grateful I had bothered only a normal person, unless he had webbed feet or something. Roy informed me they had played big Disney bears until getting fired for throwing an annoying kid into a lagoon, one incident of retaliation among many but the only time caught at it.

Another guy showed up better looking than both of those guys put together. Leely introduced Sonny to her prince. I stopped worrying about my dirty tennis shoes, having just become invisible. Leely announced that the costumes weren't ready but took a blood oath they would be finished before opening day and we'd squeeze in another rehearsal in costume. The plan was a small parade with a dance routine in the middle of the day, framed by a schedule of set times for us to wander different sections of the park with breaks long enough to stop any bleeding and splint broken bones.

She blocked us out in parade positions and when she called out gorilla I stood in that spot. Leely asked if I had a name yet and I told her Exoticus. She nodded, pleased, and wrote it into her chart. One of the muscle guys said something about my appearance that made the other one laugh, but when Leely announced Pink Elephant and Lady Giraffe and they stepped into those spots, the rest of us laughed. They weren't acrobats or sword-swallowers or even clowns, just mercenaries who would shoulder any costume.

Sonny and her prince were behind me where I didn't have to look at them, and Roy didn't have a place. Leely told him he would be free to move around and work the people on each side of the parade route, but I could tell he was suspicious of being cut. For two hours we learned a stepping, hopping and circling routine to move us forward in a winding path from one end of the park to the other. Roy gave up early and sat down for a while, but after the rest of us took a five-minute break he was up and stumbling again. The Disney people learned the routine quickly, the pink elephant almost insulting it by saying it was Mickey's Birthday routine without the hard parts. I was having trouble with the easy parts, starting on the wrong foot, mixing left with right, hopping when I should have been turning, hating the music but saved by lunch.

We went out into the park where a roach coach lunch truck had materialized at the base of a coaster, the ride's supports a tangled web of iron pipe painted brilliant red as if spun by a giant Technicolor special effects spider on acid. We waited in line following construction workers with buckskin gloves in their back pockets and hard hats in their hands. When Roy and I complained about having to dance they gave us looks that were a cross between pity and envy. I bought us each a burger and drink, Roy promising to go to the bank on Monday and pay me back. The sun could be seen, a glowing spot through the gray but not dark clouds. We chanced potential rain to tour the park and see the areas we were scheduled to work. A couple of the rides were being tested, the cars whipping past without people in the seats, no human sounds of screaming or laughing, just the whoosh of wind stirred with factory noise of metal bearings and wheels at work, the sound of robots having fun.

Back at the rehearsal hall we were given a page of rules: no running, talking or beating children, no drinking, smoking or just being plain weird. We took turns rehearsing in character, miming interaction with each other, some pretending to be park guests of different age and demeanor. It was an awkward worthless hour except that we were getting paid so I didn't care if we acted out feeding noodles to martians. There were a thousand jobs worse than pretending being in my own gorilla suit shaking the hand of Roy pretending to be an eight year old on vacation from Deerwood, Minnesota.

We rehearsed the routine a few more times and suddenly the moves fell into place, like finally memorizing the combination to my high school locker and its satisfying click of success. The break had allowed the ink to dry on my brain and my feet knew what to do. Then it was back to the employees' gate where we were shown how to punch a time card correctly, something I had seen only in movies. The final segment of our orientation was a tour of the locker room divided into two areas for guys and girls, the shelves stacked with park-issue shorts and t-shirts, a box filled with all sizes of new deck shoes, and a fan forcing air through a system of pvc pipe posts to dry sweat out of costumes overnight. It almost made me cry, a miracle cure for what I feared would be a disease named after me, what I tentatively had named gorilla suit disease, but the blower and the fact there were showers in the back with clean new towels were cause for a new religion.

We were told to leave the end of next week open for that dress rehearsal after the costumes were finished, but our first checks for today would be cut with this week's payroll and be available for pick up on Monday or in the mail on Tuesday, welcome to the entertainment division of McLoughlin Park. Roy and I and Sonny and the giant still had to do a photo shoot, but the others were asked to sign a time sheet then reminded to punch it at the time clock for the next rehearsal.

I had my pack but Roy had left his Charlie case at the rehearsal hall. Leely told him he wouldn't need it, that the legal team hadn't given her a yes or no on using the tramp. He pitched his silent movie comedian idea, rising up off his heels like a boy who wanted something out of reach. Leely said it would confuse people and curled her finger at the four of us in a come with me motion. Roy muttered damn Laugh Land my ass.

We followed her upstairs to a space above the security office where four women were busy, two of them stitching bright colored fabrics on industrial sewing machines and the other pair attaching them to large forms of foam and bracing. Atop a post sat the finished head of a cartoonish dragon with mutton chop whiskers and a flat plaid cap over one squinting eye. Leely asked Roy what he thought. He looked around and said about what? About being the park mascot, she told him.

But you just told me … he began, realizing then she was talking about the head. He examined it almost in shock and asked if she really wanted him to wear this thing. Sonny stepped up to rub her hands over different parts of it. Roy looked to me for some sympathy but my eyes were on what Sonny was doing. We're calling him MacNessie, Leely said, it's a loch ness monster. She interrupted Sonny to lift the head off the post saying let's try it on, but it was clumsy and caught at the bottom causing her to lose her grip and drop it back onto its post. A bump appeared in the top of the hat. One of the sewing ladies rushing over to lift it easily then turned it upside down. She bent over inside, inspecting how much repair work would be added to her overtime. Leely assured her it wasn't bad and wouldn't show in the photo, wrestling it away from the lady and swinging it over to Roy. It landed hard on the concrete floor, which flattened out the bump again. Just try it on, Roy.

Roy turned away, took a few steps then turned back, not willing to walk out but maintaining his distance. I'll wear it, he told her, but only if I can do Chaplin. She confessed her love for his Charlie but told him that this character would be all his own, whatever he made of it. He put on the head and bounced off a few nearby things, his muffled voice complaining from inside about the smell of glue and that the shoulder braces needed more padding, but then did a little jig and we all laughed, even the giant.

The costume lady went away satisfied that the head would survive the moment, but she was replaced by one of the others who offered a blue blousy thing to Sonny and hand a brown tunic with laces up to the giant. They put them on and looked fairy tale enough for a newspaper ad. Roy asked the giant to carry the head down the stairs for him but the giant was so tentative about handling the bulky think that Roy took it back and bullied it down the stairs. A golf cart with a rolling bench attached behind rolled us out to the front gate where I put on my suit and the four of us assembled into various poses for too long while a photographer took pictures. Sonny eyed Exoticus almost as much as I had been staring at her.

Roy was quiet on the way home, arching in the seat every few minutes as if his back were bothering him. I was reliving the hot shower I had talked Roy into letting me take. He was in a hurry to get back to town and get a drink. The shower took longer than planned because there was no bar soap so I had to cross the locker room to squirt handfuls of liquid soap from the sink dispensers. Roy leaned his head against the passenger side window and I thought he had fallen asleep but suddenly he burst into a rage, swearing and slapping the dashboard and passenger door before getting quiet again. The sky grew darker as if his mood controlled the weather and the first drop hit his side of the windshield. What, I asked him, or do I have to beat it out of you, and he said damn MacNessie big piece of scheiss.

The rain fell heavy like a drive-through car wash, and the peppering of drops on the van sounded as if a posse with shotguns were shooting at us from too far away. Driving in weather didn't feel like California anymore, but same as the trip out at least the traffic was in the other direction, workers escaping the city for the outskirts. It was pouring even harder when I pulled into the parking lot near Roy's wagon, but he sat there unmoving, not wanting to get out because even in the few steps it would take to reach the door he might drown, getting drenched for certain. Told him that I didn't want to wait out the storm, it might be days, did he want to go with me to Mac and Sam's house, but he winced at the mention of rock and roll, looking like a mean Moe and for a moment I thought he was going to poke me in the eye for it.

Told him I was hoping to find a girlfriend there and he went pfft and said I'd probably be married to Sonny within the year, telling me to pull around to the front where he could get out under the awning and get a drink without needing a life preserver. I drove around to the boulevard and delivered him, the van his personal limo. He left without another word, walking with side-to-side motion, suitcase in hand and looking like Charlie even without the coat and hat.

CHAPTER FIFTEEN

Bought a case of beer and drove to Mac and Sam's, finding a parking spot a few houses away. I had been layering the deodorant thick for days and the stuff was used up beneath the edge of the applicator, so I had to dig out some chunks with a pen and smear them into my pits, believing I was clean and deodorized for a Saturday night. There was no movement at the house and the walls and windows weren't bulging outward from the severe volume of live music so I stayed in the van. Watching the rain run down the outside of the windshield was like being underwater as I drank a beer to shift into a wilder mood. The constant pounding of drops sounded like a drum roll played at the wrong slow speed and my danced-out legs throbbed to the rhythm.

When it was time to pee I left two beers under the seat and went out with the rest and my pack, running while holding my breath through the wet weather, remembering a story about a guy back home who always had his mouth open. He got caught out in a thunderstorm and drowned. I didn't believe it but I had never been out in crazy California rain either. My left foot came down in what didn't look like a puddle but it was inches deep and the splash soaked the other pants leg and shoe. Made it to the shelter of their front porch where I wheezed in a big breath of humidity, some air but most of it wet. Coughed and woke the dogs inside. There wasn't as much barking as last time. Knocked on the door, which brought the barking near the inside of the door but none of them could open it, thankfully. The porch was covered and dry, and luckily shadowed enough for me to pee off one end.

The couch was damp, which brought up some dog stink but not dead dog in the sun stink, just stinky to someone who had showered recently and applied crumbs of deodorant. I eased down into a short folding beach chair, the plastic woven strips frayed and likely to break under my weight, but they held and it was comfortable to sink low, my butt almost touching the floor. The sky thundered and the rain came off the roof in a solid sheet of waterfall. It made the porch a cave. Well into my third beer I felt warm and dry then fell asleep.

In a world before alarm clocks and morning bells, people used to be awakened by livestock, similar to a dog they called Joker licking my face. Its snout dripped snot that made my forehead shine. Jerking away I broke through the chair's frayed weaving and dropped onto the wood of porch floor, trapped inside the frame of the chair. Mac and Sam appeared under the waterfall, stopping there for one second until they recognized me. No party tonight, huh, I asked while trying to pry myself out of the aluminum tubing.

Mac shook the water out of his hair like a dog and said they were going to have their first party on Halloween. I had to fall on my side and wiggle my butt to get loose then stand as if nothing had happened. What about the last time I was here? He told me the earthquake might have made it feel like one, but when they had a party I would know it. Had to work Halloween night but maybe I could catch the party's tail. Mac said it would just be getting started about midnight.

We sat in the kitchen drinking beer while Sam pushed something sizzling around in a black iron skillet. As the food fried she spoke about putting an all-girl band together using the spatula to emphasize her plan, looking like a Rolling Stone cover painted by Norman Rockwell. The dogs motionless except for drooling on the linoleum reacted to a sound only they could hear, suddenly trying to get up and run, their nails clicking and sliding in a jazzy beat as their paws worked to earn some traction on the slippery surface. They ran toward the front door barking about trespassing. I followed, leaving Mac and Sam to eat their fried supper.

Through the window I saw a six pack of wild people standing on the porch shaking the rain off and wiping hands down over their faces, all of them too cool to knock. I stood still so they wouldn't see any movement inside, wondering how long they would wait. The dogs were fighting for position at the door to be the first to get a muzzle through when it opened. The scene remained static long enough for Mac and Sam to finish eating and come out of the kitchen, wondering what was going on.

They gave me permission to let the loiterers in, the dogs disappointed that none were unwelcome and good for biting. The group took over the living room as if they had done it before, filling it with different types of smoke. The stereo had been playing a rock and roll station that did commercial-free blocks of music, but the block was over and an equally long stream of advertisers began shouting at us. I was the only person standing so Sam told me to put on a record. I looked down at the row of albums and was afraid to play the wrong thing. One of the smoky guys might be a stick waiting for reason to pick on me, but luckily there was already something on the turntable and all I had to do was drop the needle. I was a little nervous but prepared, having practiced it at home on the portable player for 45s. Scratching somebody's album in high school was the worst thing you could do besides steal their girlfriend, which left scratching records the only thing I had to worry about.

The volume was cranked high on their system, so if I made a bad drop neighbors down the street in both directions would know my hand shook when company came, and I didn't want the nickname Scratcher, already a possibility because of wearing the same clothes for days in a row. The good part was I could start at the edge of the album where there was more room for error than aiming for the silent grooves thin as a toenail's edge between songs to play a specific cut. I touched the needle against the rim of the record creating a tremendous hiss then found the surface. Monstrous music blared on each side of me. I went back to the kitchen to escape, preferring the smell of fried food to the smoke.

The big dog had its head down in the trashcan beating me to possible leftovers. The doorbell rang and the dog dashed away without removing its head first, and running blind it slammed sideways into the doorframe. A moment later Goliath rolled a keg of beer crookedly into the kitchen, almost over a hind leg of the dog but I pulled it to safety and cleaned up the trash. He asked me what happened and I told him someone had thrown away a perfectly good dog, then asked if he intended to drink that all by himself or did he buy it for everyone. He asked what made me think he bought it.

He didn't have a tap so he had me help lift it onto the counter so the cap was over the sink, then he plugged the drain and looked into drawers until he found a big knife and a flathead screwdriver. When I realized what he was planning I grabbed my pack to keep it from getting a beer shower, hiding in the fog bank of the other room. There was some clunking and splashing and swearing from Goliath, but he emerged from the kitchen with a jelly glass full of beer though a little wet all over. Help yourself he told me.

The keg was upright on the counter and the sink was filled with beer. I sat alone at the table drinking another can from the case, saving the sink beer for later. The phone rang. It was wall mounted and aqua colored against brown wallpaper, the curly cord drooping to the floor and probably could've stretched to the front porch. Next to it was a spice rack with no spice jars, but a naked Barbie doll was posed in one shelf, a pair of leather gloves in another, and on the bottom a rolled up magazine. I got up to answer the phone but thought that might be rude so opened the magazine. It was for bikers and featured photographs submitted by subscribers displaying their naked wives and girlfriends posed on better looking motorcycles. The phone stopped ringing, and a moment later Samantha appeared. She had answered on the extension and the phone call was mine. I quickly rolled up the magazine and put it back in the rack, but I had rolled it the wrong way and it unfurled then fell on the floor.

Leely was calling with a minor emergency. Roy had called her and quit, but she could tell he was drunk and maybe I could change his mind when he sobered up. I promised to try then took advantage of the moment, telling her I had misplaced Sonny's number, that I was supposed to call her. She didn't sense the predatory lust in my voice and found the number on her information page. I dug out my little note pad and wrote it down at the table, but before I could hang up two longhaired guys came in for sink beer walking into the slack of the cord and trying to wrap each other in it. I let go of the handset hoping Leely had hung up.

Some test thumps came from the drum set in the other room. Samantha seemed to have rounded up the core of her girl band because there was an Asian woman on bass and a short guy in tights with heavy mascara and dark red lipstick playing the guitar. It was slung low either for a cool effect or because the strap was adjusted for the much taller Chase. Some of the smokers climbed out of the furniture in the living room and gathered as a small but enthusiastic audience. After plunking enough strings to sound almost in tune they played a chunky screamer, something about Eve bleedin' in the bad part of Eden, the refrain mentioning original cleavage and the final lyric ended with the words unoriginal sin. The rest was too garbled to understand but it all seemed to rhyme. A loud slow song followed about not being able to join the gang that had become a tradition in his family, unable to wear the red colors because of his acne problem. They finished with Big Girl, Little Dress.

I applauded politely while staring at the bass player, my hand clapping alone among whistles and hoots. She grinned at the ground as if shy but walked across the room and into one of the wild guy's arms. The girlish guy, however, took the guitar off and came directly at me. I turned toward the kitchen pretending I was out of beer but he cut me off friendly as a poor man's daughter, saying that his name was Angel and was I gay? Told him no, sorry, but he said oh come on sure you are, I can tell. I laughed nervously so it sounded like a gay giggle, going around him to get at the refrigerator. There were three beers left in the case that took up the entire bottom shelf. He was in step behind me and asked for one, which I handed him then grabbed one for me. The last one sat alone, the entire box to itself, a beer can's mansion.

Angel stood next to me like a sidekick so I finished the beer faster than dad ever did then pulled the tab on the last one, drinking as much as I could before picking up the phone. The cord was bunched into a large knot like a dead slinky so I had to stay close to the wall. Fumbled out my note pad and dialed Sonny's number, Angel giving me incentive as much as the beer gave me courage, but a man answered so I hung up. Mac and Sam came in saying they heard something about a sink full of beer. Samantha asked if Angel and I had met and we both nodded. They got cups from the cupboard and dipped themselves a beer as the phone rang again. They waited for me to answer it so I did and it was Leely apologizing, but Roy had called her again crying this time. He had asked her if she could call me to come get him at the bar, that he couldn't pay his tab and they wouldn't let him leave. I promised to free him, thinking of maybe creating a distraction in the suit to allow his escape. Leely suddenly was my best friend saying she'd make it up to me.

The kitchen had become a popular watering hole, biker Goliath tipping another batch into the sink, but Angel was leaning against the wall, listening to my end of the conversation. Finished my beer and handed him the empty can, telling him I'd be back, that I had to help a friend. It wasn't until I was through the front door that I noticed he was in step behind me. Asked where he was going and he said with me, that he needed adventure for his sulphuric personality. Told him that the night was definitely not going the way I had planned. We ran in the rain and he waited at the passenger door for me to get around and in, one hand over his brow to keep the mascara from running, looking like a soldier at attention saluting before a mission.

Was tempted to drive away and leave him standing there but then I wouldn't be able to return, not as a nice guy anyway, which was the only reason anybody ever let me hang around. Thought he would be talky but he sat silently with his hands on his knees looking forward eagerly the way the dog rode along, so I explained about Roy and then for some reason told about the first time I went to a bar alone and ordered a Seven Up. The bartender thought I had an upset stomach because that's what his mother had given him for a tummy ache. Angel told me Mormons kept a Coca Cola in the back of the refrigerator as tonic for cold or flu. I asked how he knew that and he said it was his job to know, and asked if I liked his songs. I did.

On street corners people were selling umbrellas for five dollars. The lot in back was full but there was another lot down the alley that had space though a sign warned it was for their patrons only. It was going to be a wet run to the restaurant and I considered driving around the block to buy an umbrella, but Angel was confessing he had been a grossly fat teen because he read that chocolate was a chemical substitute for sex. He ate three pounds of Hershey bars hoping for that feeling then almost died. I didn't want to hear another story so I chose to get wet and quickly inside.

Roy was on the inside half of a booth bench with a full glass of ice water in front of him. Sitting on the end was a big guy blocking his escape, gesturing louder than he was speaking. Roy was staring at the water like it was an aquarium with hypnotic fish. I moved sideways through the crush of bodies, Angel following my moves with his hand lightly touching my left shoulder blade as if I were one of those people who lead the blind so subtly you have to look close to notice.

I stopped at the booth and dripped there until the guy with talking hands looked up at me with argument in his face, maybe thinking I was a wet waiter ruining his crappy meal by bringing the check. Roy, still red-eyed from crying however, got happy as a first offender getting bailed out of jail.

He slid toward the big man expecting to be let out of the booth, telling him that I was the guy. For no reason he called the booth guy Sarge, who put up a hand that stopped Roy's slide, then got up out of the seat but stood there still blocking Roy. Sarge took a long moment to brush down his sport jacket with his palms as if to shoo away wrinkles and lint or maybe blood stains, finally stepping aside to allow Roy to stand. Roy shook my hand and thanked me for coming, his breath burning my eyes. Sarge took three large steps toward the bar, spreading the customers aside and creating a path for us to follow. At the bar we stood shoulder to shoulder as if awaiting sentencing from a judge.

The bartender set down a piece of paper and pushed it toward me. It was covered in a confusing handwritten code of letters and dashes that added up mystically to sixty-eight dollars. He drank sixty-eight dollars since I had left. The bartender said the last three rum and cokes didn't have any rum in them so they weren't even on the tab, but Roy was so drunk he didn't notice. Sarge said that wasn't only tonight's bill, but that he had run out on his tab numerous times. Roy laughed.

I didn't know if I had that much left, but as I dug in my pockets Angel handed a credit card to the bartender who turned away with it before I could complain. Expecting Roy to thank him I introduced Angel, but Roy mumbled uh-huh and slipped away between customers. I waited for Angel to sign the charge slip and get his card back, then apologized and thanked him, promising he'd be paid back.

Outside the rain had lessened, the flood on the pavement receding into puddles, the drops hardly a bother and only felt during gusts of wind that also carried surprisingly refreshing cool air up the alley, oxygen blown around the curve of the Earth from tropical Pacific islands. We walked over to Roy's wagon where he unlocked the driver's side door and reached under the seat for a half pint of something, sucking a noisy gulp into his mouth before saying he wasn't ready for bed, asking what are you and your freak going to do? Angel faked some high-pitched laughing in his throat, what a miniature horse might sound like. I invited Roy to Mac and Sam's a second time and he agreed to come, his resolve weakened by liquor and lack of choices.

Roy was slow catching up to us at the van and was angry Angel had taken the passenger seat. I told him about the beer under my seat and he got in back and laid himself out on the mattress. By the time we got back to the house he was snoring and curled up around the empty cans. You're a man magnet, Angel told me. I said crap, that I wouldn't have any hangover beers in the morning. He pulled a palm full of loose pills of different shapes and colors from his pocket and picked out two of one kind. Try these he said, dropping them into my hand. He told me they worked for broken bones and amputations so they would probably work for a hangover, just don't drive.

I tucked them into the little coin pocket of my Levis and we went out into the blowing mist. My canvas shoes squished out their own spray with each step. Bass notes could be heard and felt on the porch like a heart beating inside the house. When Angel opened the door no dogs greeted us, though a few heads turned as we entered and shook the rain from our heads the way the early Beatles did when they hit Little Richard's high notes. It was to draw attention to their bangs and make the girls scream, but my doing it got me nothing.

Some guy was singing drunk as if that's all it takes to sound like Jim Morrison. More people and some new females had arrived, none pretty like Sonny but strangely attractive, except for one who looked like a bird. She recognized Angel and cawed his name, hopping over. He told her enthusiastically that I was someone she needed to meet. He introduced her as Chacha who told me how happy she was that Angel finally found someone. She could have punched me and I would have been less surprised. I shook my head no and started for the kitchen hoping for something to drink, but I saw Len playing bass. The guy singing finished a refrain then ran out of lyrics for the last verse, letting loose the reins on the musicians and they finished in a runaway race to end the song.

Len had his own brown bag of beer behind the amp and dug one out for me. Sam came from behind the drums with her own glass half empty, and as I scanned the room looking for sex she told me I wasn't like the other guys just looking for sex. It didn't show because of all the years of hiding desire behind my church bow tie that made me look harmless.

Len asked if I had my van and wanted to know if I could run him over to a place, that it would take only five minutes. I was enjoying the wildlife but saw Angel and Chacha coming out of the kitchen so agreed to the trip. Len picked up his bag of beer and we mazed through the people and out the door. Before we got off the porch my new friends came out after us wanting to tag along and Len said sure, putting his arm around Chacha. Angel called shotgun so the other two sat on the floor in back, Len asking who was the dead guy in the back? Roy was still asleep but had stopped snoring. I rolled down the window and started the engine but didn't put it in gear, breathing the rare damp air to clear my mind, separating out some of the thoughts grown crowded by the menagerie gathered around me.

Len guided me west and south then said to let him out at a dark corner, telling me to drive around to the other side of the block and wait for him at that corner. He stood in a glowing sphere of lamplight, an effect created by the moist atmosphere. What is this I asked while following instructions and Angel said he must be making a buy and his dealer doesn't want cars stopping and going in front of the house all night. I remembered the first time I saw Len waiting for a call at the phone booth and what the cop told me. Chacha said the whole street was probably staked out and somebody was running my license plate. My gut jumped to remind me of drugs and money in the cushions.

Instead of driving around the block I went around a four-block section to confound and confuse any lookouts, hands sweaty on the steering wheel as I watched the rear view mirror for law enforcement. Angel asked where the hell was I going so I confessed my fear of prison. You're such a virgin, he said.

Afraid to wait at the corner I parked down the cross street where Len could see me if he looked hard enough. Chacha pulled a beer from Len's sack and we passed it around, listening to the radio but only pieces of songs as Angel spun the tuning dial up and down. Chacha spotted Len at the corner and reached past me to honk the horn. He casually walked over to us, just a regular guy on a fresh air stroll while I waited for unmarked cars to screech around the corner with wheels off the ground on one side.

The horn woke Roy who started swearing at none of us specifically, but Len paused at the sliding door until Roy moaned and rolled toward the window, maybe confused, maybe to fall asleep again.

Whatdja get asked Angel and Len dangled a little baggie of rock candy in front of his eyes like a hypnotist with a pocket watch, telling him it was crystal. I pulled away from the curb feeling like a getaway driver. The interior of the van was quiet, the drugs seeming to take over their minds in anticipation of the rest of the night. Before I reached Mac and Sam's, Roy called out that if there wasn't a bathroom in this thing I'd better pull over fast. His peeing against a palm tree in a quiet neighborhood worried me as much as my crystallized fear of being pulled over with a van full of everything I was taught not to do. He hacked up phlegm and spit so loudly that porch lights came on, homeowners wary of burglars with pneumonia.

Back on the road and cruising Sunset I felt sick so pulled into the parking lot of a liquor store to get beer. Everybody went in. The man at the register had deep eyes and foreign headwear, saying hello with a happy accent, watching with a smile as we split up and wandered different aisles of booze, beer and wine. At a wall of cooler doors I grabbed another case of beer to assure I'd get four or five myself, party math. As I paid and thanked the checker outer for my change he said it was good to be polite, that too many people used dirty languages.

One by one they returned to the van except Len. Roy sat back on the bed like a foreign ruler, drinking another half pint in a little brown bag and would have looked natural in a turban on a bed of nails. Angel slid a bottle of white wine out of a long bag and Chacha did the same with a bottle of red. I asked how they were going to open them and they twisted off the caps.

After another two minutes that seemed longer because I hadn't started drinking yet, I went back to find Len. Maybe he had been caught shoplifting or couldn't decide which wine went best with crystal, but the store was empty except for turban guy and a lady shopping with a cart. She had boxes of stuff and seven large bottles of different liquors. I told the foreigner that I had one more friend when I came in than when I left. He said there was someone in the bathroom past the coolers. There was a mop in a metal mechanical bucket in the corner there with a door on each side, one marked employees only so I tried the other but it was locked. I opened the employees door, which set off an alarm bell and the foreigner shouted wrong door. I knocked on the other. Yeah sorry, coming, Len said and I heard running water and the toilet flushing, telling him that we didn't want to leave him behind. As we passed the turbaned guy ringing up the lady's cart-full of booze I said with that sale he could buy a bigger place. He said he knew it was small but I didn't have to rub it out. Not sure if that was a joke or mangled English but I laughed anyway to keep it cheerful.

Outside the door Len took a hypodermic needle out of his pocket to throw in the trashcan. Wouldn't have noticed if he hadn't paused to use his other hand to push the flap open in the domed lid. I acted cool about it because I wanted to be cool, to know what the attraction was.

At the van Roy had focused on Chacha, making room for her on the bed/couch depending on how one used it. When Len arrived she slid into Roy to make room for him too, both pleasing and displeasing Roy. Nice party he said, and I told him this wasn't a party, when it was a party he'd know it.

Angel suggested we all drive to Vegas, causing the engine to cry. When we got back to the house not only was there no parking space, but our lane was blocked by a police cruiser, two officers on the porch. Drove around the car and parked down the street, facing the house so we could watch what happened, see if the party was going to get shut down. Angel wanted to go back in and Roy wanted to know what the hell we were doing. I told him we were drinking and we all drank. I looked at Len to see if he were bleeding or puking or dead, but he was normal, smiling with extreme content.

Sooner or later we're all going to have to use the bathroom so we might as well just go now, said Chacha. We marched down the sidewalk single file, watching the cops exit the porch and get into their car. We couldn't hear music from outside but the stereo was playing quietly when the door opened. The dogs had given up, surrendering to constant traffic. It was still smoky but there was nothing illegal in the air. I went to the kitchen where Racer, Chase, Mac and Sam were at the table where I set the case of beer. Mac said I told you so and pulled an end open. I turned to introduce Roy but he hadn't followed me. Grabbed two beers then found him on the couch on the porch. He stood up and pulled me down the front steps telling me he wanted to get out of there, that place was scary.

I agreed to shuttle him to his wagon and we strolled toward the van. As I unlocked the passenger-side door the police came back the other way, wheels hissing on the wet street. We turned to see cruisers coming from the other direction, converging in front of the house, doors opening. A small crush of cops dashed up the front steps and into the house. We drove away.

CHAPTER SIXTEEN

----

*T*he year I climbed out on the girder over the gym somebody left an electric watch on the upper shelf of a locker, and instead of turning it in I wore it under my sleeve in case the owner was eyeing wrists to find it. I checked it constantly to see how many minutes until class was over or until school let out, making the day seem twice as long. When the battery ran down I put it back where I had found it, but from then on I had the ability to picture the watch-face in my head and see the time. Checking my guesses against a clock proved I usually was within minutes of being correct.

It was raining again when I woke in the middle of the night. Knew it was between four and four-thirty. Feeling miserable I dug out one of the pills Angel had given me and drank one of the warm beers I had saved, trying to sleep again and escape the pain. As I worried about losing my mailing address in the raid on the house a pleasant warmth spread from my belly in all directions, running out of room at the tips of my fingers and toes so the pleasure backed up and intensified.

I don't know what the pill was, but it made the drinking life easier. It carried me into the morning light. I peed in the empty can then poured it out in the parking lot while noticing that Roy's wagon was gone, which was weird because he had been out of gas and cash. Another beer and the other pill then back to bed, the noise of early Sunday motion muted by the white noise of constant drizzle on every surface sounding like the static behind every song on a cheap transistor radio. For over an hour I thought about most every girl I had ever known, but eventually the magic left my system, its residue maybe gathering in my liver because I got queasy, though movement helped.

The rehearsal had turned my legs wooden, but there was no chance of working the boulevard anyway because the suit wet with rain would stink worse than a real ape, if they stank, assuming they at least carried a rich odor of rain forest rot like the smell of watering a freshly turned plot of topsoil fertilized with a mix of chicken poop and cow manure. The more I thought about it the more I wanted to know, but the library would be closed. Drove to the market and hobbled in, my walk involuntarily like an orangutan's.

Bought a peach, a Mounds and a skinny carton of chocolate milk, avoiding the beer aisle like a one-night stand seen sober under fluorescent light. Stopped at the rack of free papers to check for gorilla work ads but noticed a separate holder of pamphlets in the shadow of a bank of gum machines, their space helmet tops filled with different species of chewables in various sizes, shape and color. Got a twenty-five cent giant red gumball the flavor of hot little red hearts at valentines. Sang that phrase as I grabbed a tri-fold brochure advertising the Los Angeles Zoo located in the growingly familiar Griffith Park.

With only a single wrong turn I found Los Feliz and followed its mansioned hillside, chewing on the gob of prickly cinnamon. According to the minimal map on the back of the brochure, if I kept the hills to my left I would drive around Griffith's mountain or whatever it was, pass a golf course and find the zoo. It looked too easy to be true, and was.

Stuck the wad of gum on the dashboard for later then steered with my knees while opening the gabled spout of the milk carton. With that between my thighs I bit out a chunk of the peach, crisp and almost sour instead of sweet. The hills suddenly were replaced by parallel sets of train tracks bordered by a concrete trench on one side and dull colored windowless buildings on the other. The hills were in my mirror. With

both the milk and the peach between my legs, two left turns somehow
put me on an entrance to the 5 Freeway and trying to exit that put me
on the 134 Freeway. The next exit and a right turn put the hills ahead
of me again, but lost is lost no matter how close you are to where you
want to be.

Finished the peach while driving forward at twenty-five miles an
hour because every block had a stop sign at the intersection. Threw the
pit out the window on a curving road that surrounded a mostly empty
parking lot, and while chugging some milk saw a sign to the side that said
zoo parking. Celebrated with the last swallow then parked luxuriously
close to the pedestrian incline leading toward the entrance. Put the candy
in my pocket and the carton into the little brown bag, compressing it into
the smallest neatest piece of trash possible, knuckles cracking.

A guy wearing Jungle Jim's safari suit took my donation at the
turn-style booth and gave me a map to locate most any creature of
choice. The drizzle was light enough that if I kept moving my hair and
shoulders and the tops of my shoes remained dry, but when I stopped to
stare at a pond full of gossiping pink flamingoes the rain dripped off my
hair and down my forehead where it gathered in one eyebrow, refracting
into little rainbows if I looked at something to that side.

Expected neat rows of big cages with iron bars, the kind that gorillas
bend apart to escape from in cartoons and comedies, but the animals
had imitation landscapes, fake rocks and cliffs and ponds of concrete
reminding me of the scenery at Laugh Land. Wandering brought me
twice to the same alligator basking on a man-made island, waiting
for the sun. It was good to see it again but used the map to locate
the gorilla enclosure, which took me first through the reptile building
and out of the rain. Inside was a cross between a hall of mirrors and
a neighborhood walk-through haunted house at Halloween, a zigzag
stroll with menacing snakes and lizards behind walls of glass around
each corner. Parents told their kids to take their snotty noses off the
glass, announcing each species as if they weren't reading the plaque but
still mispronouncing the names.

There was one tank full of an unmoving turd-colored anaconda either dead or in a near sleep-state waiting to shed. Watched it for motion but was distracted by a small busy movement in the corner behind the realistic plastic leaf of an imitation rubber tree, where a large feeder rodent not only had escaped being eaten, but was grooming itself comfortably on a section of the snake's tail that had chew-marks where the rat had tasted anaconda but found it unappetizing. A forward curve of the giant reptile expanded as it took a slow slight breath. It might have been followed by the sound of a sigh through the glass.

The family caught up with me, and the kid asked why there was a big mouse sitting on the snake. Dad told him they were friends. Maybe that was true, until it shed that skin anyway.

Coming out of the reptile house moved me forward on an evolutionary timeline, out of a low dark hole to stroll a grass-edged path between okapis and wildebeests, the smell of the wet walkway mixing with the taste of animal excrement in the air, the same odor as hosed down and mopped up rest-stop bathrooms across the country's highways, paved versions of ancient migration trails.

The kangaroo was so illogical I had to stop and look for an explanation. It seemed to exist simply for being cast in funny commercials, the pouch begging for jokes, and the jumping with two feet thing more suited for laughs than locomotion. It tipped forward to sniff at something on the ground using its tail as a counterweight, the motion making it look like those freaky drinking bird toys with the black hat and water-bulb butt. Past its tail in the distance of a farther enclosure was something massive moving slowly through overhanging eucalyptus branches.

I approached slowly ignoring the excitement in my gut, pretending it was remnant nausea from the beer and pills. Behind me monkeys screeched equally excited. I leaned against the next barrier, sweat mixing with the rain on my forehead. A pair of tigers growled at me across the deep ditch designed into their space that was meant kept me from being eaten. They paced in thought as if someday they got tired of free meals of chicken, rabbit and horsemeat, they would jump across and eat a guy like me.

The black and gray animal's movement was graceful as an anchored Macy's parade balloon, a gentle motion. Rumor and film had given them a fierce reputation, so movie ticket buyers didn't pay to see a five hundred pound monster build a nest and munch wild celery. The cost of admission had to include a man thrown across a room or jungle clearing and a girl carried away for an unimaginable purpose, which is why gorilla experts hated gorilla suits, beating the drum about how gentle the giants were by nature, unless you've seen one charge in a masculine territorial rage.

I stood in front of their artificial natural habitat and watched six or eight gorillas eating, sleeping, playing tag and sometimes looking back at me. A younger one noticed how long I stood staring, separating itself from the gathering to climb down the hill and squat before me on the other side of the empty moat. It put its hand to its mouth several times as if asking for food. There was an obnoxious sign telling me not to feed the gorillas, how carefully their diets were planned and controlled, but I didn't think one piece of Mounds would hurt anything with hundreds of pounds of muscle. Casually scanned the area for zoo cops as I ripped open the wrapper and slipped out one of the candies. With a quick short hook-shot threw it across. The gorilla scooped it up, smelled it and stuck it inside its lower lip. I ate the other section at the same time, my first meal with a gorilla.

The one with the touch of gray must have been watching because it dropped out of the tree and ape-ran using all fours at the one with the candy, sending it hurrying back up the hill. Now I had the bigger one motioning to its mouth while giving me the stare down. It scared me. It was nothing like my suit, and if you threw any classic comedian in there it wouldn't be funny.

It probably had a crude conscience and some imagination. With the right equipment it might be made able to speak. There were people with holes in their vocal chords who could buzz out electrified speech, and guys who talked out of their cheeks like a cartoon duck. With money enough, someone might find a way to get them talking and hear something equal to the first words of human prehistory, odds good it would be a grunted swear word.

This one grunted and I could feel it as much as hear it. Same as my hair not getting wet when I walked the rain didn't collect in its fur either, but even when sitting still, enough natural heat there to create a hazy halo over its head and shoulders. I wanted to get close enough to smell it but only the scent of eucalyptus crossed the moat, which in the humidity was potent as a cough drop. I had read not to look directly at a male gorilla but this one either was used to it or didn't find me threatening. The reptile-house family strolled up ending our stare-down. The kid ran ahead excitedly and jumped onto the barrier to balance on his belly, the mother instinctively grabbing for his feet as she let out a high-pitched yipe. The father two steps behind rushed forward and reached both arms around her waist so as a team they both pulled him like their end of the rope in a game of tug of war, dragging him back off the wall causing minor injury to his chin and hands. He cried, the noise and action causing the animal to rise and back up. It wouldn't take responsibility for what people do, but the younger ones came part way down the hill as if a show had begun for their entertainment.

I also backed away, noticing that the sight of a human female had not driven the beast mad with lust, evidently that which separates an ape from me. Somewhere a jungle bird cried in the rain with that Tarzan movie a-wow-a-wow, maybe a mating call, maybe a complaint about having no umbrella. Nobody would want to see a guy in a gorilla suit acting like a real ape, not tossing men and carrying off women, because it would be boring.

Using the map I went around the reptile building to find the exit past acres of other animals that might crave attention but I was feeling under the weather, realizing the phrase could be taken literally, sad for my home and family. Young male gorillas sometimes were kicked out of their family group, the great silver-backed leader sending it out into the jungle to find a group in need of new blood. Dad thought he had done it for good reason, but whether good or bad it would always be an unoriginal idea.

An elephant trumpeted as I left the zoo, maybe a gag they did to honor each guest's exit. I had seen an elephant before. A small Mexican circus set up in a vacant field back home. It was during my years of radio addiction when I couldn't stand the silence of my bedroom or my thoughts, needing the radio on every waking moment even until I slept. In the middle of the night I'd wake up and turn off the static, the station also sleeping until early morning. An announcement claimed the world's longest line of live elephants had paraded from the train station down to the space along the river where the ruins of a cement works finally had been removed to make possible a new marina. Even if it were a hoax, searching for elephants in town would be adventure.

In the middle of the descending street a short guy in coveralls shoveled coconut size piles of poop off the bricks and into a rolling bin. Down on the lot four teenaged elephants loitered with their heads together deciding the next play. They constantly shifted their weight as if standing on hot pavement but it was to glance behind with a swaying motion that made it easier to look behind in both directions for hyenas or hunters with oversized rifles, and to wrap their trunks around more of the delicious long grass that had grown wildly tall since the factory's foundation had been front loaded onto trucks and used to build breakers along the eroded beach properties of the people who would dock their cabin cruisers here next summer.

The circus wouldn't open until the next day but there were more than twenty people enjoying there not being a show yet. A chestnut-colored man in an ivory suit handed out free tickets. He had a mustache shaped with wax and matched the carved detail that trimmed my grandmother's jewelry box. His shiny black hair was combed down and back on each side of his head, the part very close to center. The tickets weren't for general admission, just good to attend one of the sideshow attractions along the midway.

A woman in a tight red jacket and black boots up to her knees used a broomstick with a hook on the end to shoo the foursome of elephants into a corral made of metal fence sections. She didn't get trampled though she looked tough as if she might have been knocked around once or twice, her skin like a black market purse not of elephant, but of imitation elephant. There were no tents or trucks, only the overdressed man and woman who made me promise to tell my friends and bring my family. When the sight of elephants lost its novelty we turned to watch the guy in coveralls slowly working his way to the source of his labor.

That evening I called Jayo and told him about the elephants. He said that circuses came with tent-fulls of nasty women eager to seduce local males out of their pocket money. We had barely enough of it to buy tickets but were hopeful there might be other reasons for seduction, maybe a competition between women, something to do with wild traveling circus pride. The street-sides were parked full bumper to bumper and the cars in the street waited for escape or at least room to turn around. We walked faster than traffic, crossing streets between cars and following the smell of a fair.

The riverbank had been transformed into a tent village surrounding the castle of canvas of the big top. For the price of admission we got to see the elephants again, but the three-ring show boasting clowns and trapeze and rings of fire cost extra, same as the sideshow attractions. We walked the midway thinking of circus sex, I with my free pass to one exhibit, and we both decided to witness a girl change into a gorilla. The barker didn't say if she would turn back into a girl.

We sat in the fifth row surrounded by twenty empty chairs. The front of a small stage was visible but most of it was behind a sparkly curtain that had lost some of its sparkle with age. Eventually a family of six entered and found seats, almost filling the second row. They shared several boxes of popcorn, passing them left and right without any pattern, breathing through their mouths and putting butter and salt in the air. The barker must've given up on pulling more people into the tent because he appeared from the shadows, speaking loudly as if before packed house. His eyes scanned every row of seats as he shouted his set routine, not giving the eight of us any special attention. Maybe in his mind he saw someone in every chair, the show perpetually sold out. He was bald and wore black slacks and a gold satin shirt with a pink bowtie, carrying a shillelagh that he pounded onto the ground to put an exclamation point at the end of certain sentences. The story was a tale of animal magic and tribal secrets brought out of darkest Africa by a witchdoctor taken by slavers, the origins of juju, voodoo and proof of evolution.

Somewhere an unseen assistant dimmed the lights and cued a tape recording that began with an amplified hiss followed by tom-toms or conga drums. The barker stepped to the stage and pulled the curtain across to reveal a cage of iron-like bars. He swept his stick across the bars, accidentally hitting one and it thunked instead of clanged, so he grabbed it, jerking his arm and pulling with his body leaning toward us trying to pull it loose, demonstrating its integrity as he told us not to be afraid, the cage was escape proof, we were as safe as babies in our mothers' arms, but in case of emergency the exit was directly to our right, clearly marked with green and red glow in the dark tape.

Behold, he said, Inanna the gorilla girl. A circle of light revealed a black hairy mass inside the cage. The drumming slowly increased in tempo and volume. Inanna sat upright. She had been bent over with her forehead on her knees and her arms tucked against her chest, her black hair thick and long enough to hide behind in that position. It was also enough to hide whether she was wearing clothes. If there was any clothing there wasn't much of it, the shadows creating a deep illusion of cleavage and though her feet were bare, a bracelet of Wilma Flinstone oversized pearls circled her left ankle. Jayo elbowed me and meowed in the back of his throat, claiming her, his version of calling dibbs.

He had done it many times though he never had the courage to introduce himself. It was a warning for me not to talk to a girl. Instead of a conversation he would wait until she wasn't looking and yell marry me from a distance, turning away as if someone else had shouted. I'd get her scowl.

The light turned to strobe, flashing and causing her to writhe as if she were tied to the chair and trying to escape. We waited for the hair to move away from her body but there was too much of it. She moaned a long note like the start of a painful song. The barker was almost shouting now, still talking about escape, escaping the jungle, escaping the laboratory, but how she could not escape the animal within, that animal in all of us, the immortal beast of hunger, rage and lust. Her moan rose into a wail. His voice was too loud for our ears, too loud for the room, the drums pounding like a racing heart with his words matching their rhythm, no escape, no escape, no escape. Behind him the girl screamed.

And then the girl was there at the same time as a gorilla twice as large, the flashing light confusing the mind to what we were seeing until the strobe and her scream stopped exactly at the same time. The room went dark and silent except for nervous noises from the family and the hiss of the sound system, then half a second later a mighty roar come through the speakers as a red light snapped on to illuminate the gorilla throwing itself against the bars, rattling the cage and causing us all to skid back in our chairs. The gorilla wore the same jewelry around its ankle, trying other bars for failings. It knocked around in a rage for a moment giving us time to breathe again first then chuckle at the effect. Suddenly it charged the front of the cage again and it broke away to slam against the wooden stage floor.

Popcorn flew above the family's heads as if they had pulled the strings on party poppers. The barker was screaming escape, escape, as the gorilla roared and leapt forward to the edge of the stage. The family scrambled over each other and their collapsed or overturned chairs toward the exit. We played along and hurried out behind them as the gorilla jumped off the stage and chased us past the red and green glow tapes and out to the sunny safety of the real world where we remembered it was just a jerk in a gorilla suit.

In front of the tent we studied the tall canvas painting that portrayed the girl crouched with one hand touching the jungle floor, staring out with yellow Lugosi eyes. The ape was behind her with arms raised, claws to the sky with broken chains hanging from its wrists, its mouth full of fangs open and drooling in a bestial silent howl of rage as if maddened by the fact it couldn't be the girl and have the girl at the same time. The barker's booth was unattended, no sign alerting the times of shows, just the price of admission and a guarantee for the strangest sight ever seen by human (or any other) eyes, or your money back.

Jayo said we should sneak in the back and try to see the girl again. I wanted a better look at the gorilla. We went back to the side exit and slipped past the fold in the canvas, now blind in the darkness. I bumped into a chair and turned right until I felt the stage with my foot. Stepped up to get caught in the curtain and pulled it past me, reaching out to feel the cage. Jayo asked where I was and I shushed him. He tripped his way towards that shh as my eyes adjusted to the light creeping in at the edges and seams of the tent and burning through worn areas of canvas. Jayo bumped into me, knocking me into a big pane of glass. Imprints of my nose, cheek and palm caught the light looking like pieces of a ghost, but on the other side of the glass was the gorilla suit draped over a chair, the mask resting on that. A duplicate chair sat so the side within a wooden boxed-in area that had a lamp in the top. It was a magician's trick done with mirrors.

A little door opened in the back of the box, the light beating up on my vision again. A man's head appeared and he growled like the gorilla. I heard Jayo make a second clumsy escape to the exit. Using my hand to shield my eyes I watched the man smile and say gotcha, then he laughed proudly at the gag. I apologized, telling him I only wanted to see the gorilla suit. He asked how the hell I ever figured out it was a suit, laughing at himself again, kind of a creepy carny version of the great and powerful Oz.

Come around and hand her over, he said. I asked who and he said Molly, pointing to the mask. I handed it over and he told me to bring the suit, that he was too old to use the trap door. I scuttled through with the costume, which smelled like my cub scout knife after I used it to clean lake perch, the funky odor sticking to the blade and taking the fun out of whittling. The entire stage with the mirrored cage and box trick was attached to a live-in trailer, a tiny room with bed and closet and sink and fold down table. By comparison the suit didn't smell bad.

I turned to the guy who had put the mask on, trying to scare me with the familiar growl but it immediately turned into muffled laughter. He pulled it off still laughing, not caring that I faked my enjoyment. He looked like one of the deacons in our church who escorted people to the proper pew, keeping the congregation balanced so the gospel wouldn't flow more to one side than the other. He was mostly bald, a ring of gray from ear to ear the way Caesar wore a wreath of leaves. He might have been related to the barker, an older brother or maybe even his father.

I held the suit gently as if it might be sleeping and I didn't want to wake it. An almost hidden zipper went down the center and two boobs of a newer fur had been sewn onto the chest pad turning it into a female. Moloch had a sex change he said while laughing again, so now it's Molly. He tossed me the mask and I caught it using the suit the way firemen catch someone in a net. The face was hard leather that somehow had been molded into a crude ape face and painted black. Around its edge were holes punched with an awl or something so it could be sewn to the headpiece made of a stretchy mesh fabric that had hundreds or thousands of strands of hair tied off to the netted material. It wasn't intended to be seen close up. I knew I could make a better one, but told him I liked it.

Someone asked who he was talking to, a female with a tropical accent who called him Rico. He flinched at the name and said that he used to be Rick, but his young Mexican wife made the rules. There was a picture on the wall of a young muscular man with black curly hair posing on a high platform with a trapeze in one hand. Next to it was a matching picture of a young woman in the same pose but in the opposite direction. They looked ready to swing into each other's frame.

He said that was taken when god was young. When his wife died he did a solo trapeze comedy act in the gorilla suit. I handed the suit to him and thanked him. He threw it on the unmade bed as I turned to go back through the little stage door but he told me it would be easier to use the real door.

It was a big step down onto a little foldout metal plate that reflected the sun in my face. With both feet on the trampled grass I saw the trailer was attached to the tent in back and hitched to a large old yellow truck in the front. Next to the truck was gorilla girl in sunglasses, stretched out in a folding lawn lounger, sun-bathing in an orange dotted bikini. Next to her chair was a matching chair and between them were personal items on a towel, a bottle of lotion, a book and purse, one sweaty drink with ice and one almost empty. I felt more like a trespasser here than I did sneaking inside the tent.

She looked at me first through her glasses then over the frames, asking why don't I take a picture maybe? Like an idiot I said nice to meet you, looking for the red and green tape marking an escape route. Rick laughed from the trailer door and gripped the frame to swing down past the metal step. He eased into his chair and warned me not to try sneaking into any of the other attractions; the snakes weren't poisonous but they could strangle a grown man, and the geek carried a gun.

As I left around the side of the tent the gorilla girl asked Rick if I had wanted a better look at her. He said nah, that I was interested in Molly. Though I was out of sight she called me a gorilla groupie as an insult, rolling the r's with her tongue. Rick laughed.

Jayo was waiting by the elephants and said he thought I had been killed, then asked if I got laid. Told him I was going to make a gorilla suit. He said yeah, and he was going to get his own elephant.

CHAPTER SEVENTEEN

’d make three right turns around extra blocks to avoid a single
left turn that would aggravate drivers stuck behind me as I waited
for a gap in oncoming traffic. There was a forced left on the drive
back to the boulevard where Los Feliz turned south. My pack sat on
the passenger seat, the suit now inferior. Gargantua before his famous
circus career had been a pet gorilla named Buddy who went for drives
around Brooklyn with his lady owner showing off his new suit of clothes
and recent plastic surgery. Chimpanzees not only had appeared in films
regularly but in many they were the stars. In The Unholy Three a
chimpanzee even played a gorilla because there were no trained gorillas
in Hollywood. Maybe it had been tried and gone terribly wrong. I
needed to check the library and the classifieds again.

The boulevard was shiny from the rain and I prowled some side
streets and alleys searching for Roy's wagon or a naked lady, whichever
came first. Passed the x-rated store and remembered the low grunt of
the big male, feeling gruntish myself. I wanted to walk on my knuckles
in search of a girl. My wallet dug into one butt cheek reminding me
of the telephone numbers it held. Made a reckless left turn and drove
down to the booth.

A VW bug was parked in my usual spot staring with the same
headlights as the van, but on the enormously popular little cousin

model they appeared wide eyed. The beetle could be slept in and lived out of but only on a dare. Behind house girl's spacious four-door it looked like something waiting to be thrown into the sedan's trunk. Over by the booth the chalk on the walk had been washed away by the rain, a piece of notebook paper folded several times down into a neat square and taped to the glass. It had my name on it. Taped next to it was another piece of paper, a page ripped in half with a message for anyone thinking of touching my note. It promised a curse of bad luck beginning with pain in the genitalia, enforced by a local gang if the reader was not superstitious. It was bordered with a series of dangerous looking symbols. I was slightly afraid to take my own note.

It was news from home. Mom had tried golfing until the weather turned cold, and Dad wanted me home for the holidays to see the new addition on the house. Bring your friend, she sounds nice. No signature, just thick x's and o's added in pink chalk. I imagined taking the chalk girl home for Christmas, and if it snowed and she became inspired I would have to shovel the front walk to make writing space. Put it in my pocket and found the number that had been chalked on the patio wall, then dialed.

It was a sex chat service. I didn't know if she worked there or who to ask for, but it required a credit card anyway so I hung up and dialed Cricket's number, the wind chime girl at the beach. It needed extra coins but she answered. She wanted to go out but it was her week to have custody of the kid. I promised to call again but crumpled that number into a spitball and jammed it into the crack between the phone and the glass of the booth. Then I found the card for Catty's Attic.

A lady said a generic hello and I heard myself breathing into the mouthpiece, which meant she could hear it. Must have been nerves. I normally was a nose breather so the sound caused my thoughts to stumble, giving her a few seconds to worry if I were a dirty caller. As she asked who is this, I spoke at the same time asking if this is Catty's Attic. She told me she was Catty, and I explained about the elderly gentleman in Musso & Frank giving me the card, sounding

STUCK ON EARTH   215

perfectly squirrely. Anthony she said. I didn't remember getting his
name but I played along and agreed, wondering if the old guy were
a pimp. She asked if I wanted to take the tour and I said yes, mouth
breathing again but telling her as soon as possible. She hmmed and
told me the regular tour had been last night, but if I was a friend of
Anthony she didn't want me to wait a week, so when would be good
for me? Tonight, I dared and she hmmed again and said okay, I guess
so. She gave me the address and I hung up repeating it to myself while
I took out my little book and wrote it down, then I drove again into
the Hollywood hills.

I knew Rock Hill Road from accidentally crossing and driving it
several times while looking for other things. Followed the numbers
painted on the curbs up to her address and noticed I was driving
straight toward the lit letters spelling out Hollywood, taking it as a
shining sign, but the curbs ran out many numbers too soon. There were
still some houses scattered on both sides but set back from the street
so I slowed down to get a peek at front doors past landscaping getting
thicker. Finally reached the last house isolated at the end of the road,
with an antique ticket booth half way along the walk. Tree branches
were drooping low from the weight of rain and I almost expected to
see that slow movement of black and gray again. Pulled up behind an
American van that looked clumsily overweight compared to the v-dub,
setting the parking brake with a quick ratchet sound.

On a second better look I saw a sign attached to the ticket booth
that might have been from a circus or in front of an old movie theater:
Catty's Attic. The house seemed to be climbing up the hill, a big section
built above the entrance level. There air was still wet so I walked quickly
hoping to keep my hair dry, reverting to teenage worry of being judged
because of my hair. Skidded to a stop on slippery terra cotta tile as a
woman opened the front door, her hair bright between the porch and
interior lights. It was combed high and burned to a shade between
blond and white. She smiled through a bitter mix of residual cigarette
smoke and a recent dose of perfume meant to cover it, but it didn't.

We both faked a chuckle and shook hands with a light grip of only fingers. Nice shirt she said and I couldn't remember what I was wearing, but thanked her as I glanced down, then over at her black clothes but couldn't see detail so said nice you too. She didn't back up to allow me in her house, asking me what I did. I wanted to say you first, but told her I had a gorilla suit. She brightened as if I were working on a cure for cancer, not only backing up but pulling me inside saying she knew I'd be harmless.

Her living room was dominated by black leather furniture and enough pieces to seat a baseball team. The dining room was centered with a long glass table attended by leopard-skin chairs. She led me up a staircase padded with white shag along an unlit hallway leading toward an even darker room. My nerve endings itched and I worried that my shoes were leaving a trail of wet stink in the clean quiet carpet.

She said here we are, feeling for a light switch and must have found it. Little spotlights hung along a track in the ceiling shone brilliantly and deeply into a space packed like a storeroom with movie props and memorabilia. My attic she told me. The place was full of old friends from a youth of sitting in front of the television, a toy box that hadn't been opened in twenty years. Everything was used and familiar and smelled weird. It wasn't sex but as exciting, just in a different way.

On a shelf within reach were ray guns that had allowed various heroes from several decades dissolve space creatures and villains across the universe, though close up it was clear they never had shot even a ray to compete with a flashlight. Also useless was the screw-shaped nose of digging machine that had carried a crew through the crust of the earth to a cavernous land below. We watched that movie once a year on Family Classics hosted by Frazier Thomas, but the device was made of plastic and so fragile after twenty years that it was laced with cracks I could poke my thumb through, which I accidentally did while she was pointing out the next wonder.

A rubber head that had set the standard for Martians was crumbling and peeling paint. Dracula's Transylvanian shoes had a label inside that proved they were from a Wilshire department store. I asked to touch them and she handed me the right shoe. It smelled like old licorice, maybe something not known about vampires, or maybe Bela kept candy in his sock. Knew how an archaeologist must have felt finding a four thousand year-old bit of statue in the excavation of an ancient Egyptian trash heap. It was just junk, but special for its rarity.

I had lain belly down with chin resting on the heels of my hands too close to the tv, at least according to Grandma because it emitted some kind of dangerous radiation, and on the screen had been the shoe I now was holding, taking its turn down the steps of a mausoleum, scaring a trained rat out of its path with an added sound effect squeak. I merged with my younger self from seeing the scene on that tv to this place in movieland because of a lady named Catty whose hair matched her carpeting, but it was just a shoe so I handed it back.

There was a framed eight by ten photograph I had seen before. It was in Famous Monsters but cropped close and in black and white. This wide one was in color and of the young lady in a hairdo more painful looking than Catty's now. She was in the arms of a hairy monster that once had been the anemic scientist she declined to marry. Injecting glandular secretions from a laboratory ape into his system did not transform him into a super man as expected. Catty apologized for the hair, saying it had been all the rage her senior year. I looked close and remembered her from several bad movies, holding the photo so I could see her face then and now. She turned away embarrassed, so I hungrily said you're an actress.

Was, she said, but it hadn't started that way. She was a member of a nudist colony where Anthony the porn king got his start by making nudies marketed as short documentaries about living healthy. She ended up dating the cameraman who brought her in on the almost as low budgeted monster movies.

Attic was the proper term because much of the stuff seemed to have been saved simply because there was room for it, easier than hauling it to the curb. Catty moved through the collection as if auditioning for

Let's Make a Deal, stopping at each piece with the pointy toes of her slipper shoes coming together, her hands posed as presenting a prize, but each prop was another piece of junk obviously fake as my suit.

In the hundred-watt lighting I saw her wrinkles previously masked by the make up filling the creases. Still had an urge to grab her, but instead picked up a hand-typed script, white pages gone yellow/gray, its title matching a movie poster on the wall that guaranteed medical services in case of heart failure due to terror. The script was so full of x'ed-out words and crossed-out lines and blacked-out sections it might have been a top-secret document. I paged through it and read the notes that must have been penciled into the margins by the director during read-throughs and rehearsals: enter left to mark, hand on shoulder, cue axe, reverse angle, blood splat.

Catty interrupted the read telling me to close my eyes, which I did as she took the musty script out of my hands. She turned me around and walked me in a weaving path around some of the junk, reminding me not to look. It was like being stuck in one of the scenes with old action crossed out and edited movement rewritten in. She stopped me with her palms on my chest and I was tempted to return the move, a new kind of patty-cake. I was thinking of nudists when she told me okay open your eyes. Hoping she was naked I opened my eyes on a gorilla suit. There was a curly black wig where the head should be, but it was like meeting a long lost brother given up for adoption when a baby.

Rubbed my fingers over the dusty fur and leather chest plate that had the smell of my first baseball mitt left in the yard before the early winter of '67 and not found until the strange Christmas thaw. Look out she said. Thought she was upset about me putting my fingertips on it, but she jerked the suit off the dressmaker's dummy to wave it at me. She kicked off her shoes and stepped inside the opening down the back, enjoying it so much I wondered if a pill or something she had taken earlier was just kicking in.

The suit had been recycled as the body of a beast on a jungle planet where rocket men were stranded for two episodes of a serial that ran before the western during Saturday matinees, divorced from its gorilla mask long before. She snaked her arms into the sleeves then walked like the Frankenstein monster up and down the space between a wooden coffin and a row of prop rocks made out of paper-mache.

She asked me to get the wig that had fallen behind the mannequin, and when I bent over to reach for it she came up behind me and started humping against my butt, grunting with simulated pleasure. I enjoyed the attention and stayed in that position extra seconds, hoping it was foreplay. Told her I hoped the suit wasn't anatomically correct, turning around as I stood up with the wig between us. She put it on and told me not to worry or whine, she wasn't seducing me, I was too nice a kid. I said darn, and she said see what I mean, who the hell says darn?

She pulled off the wig and let the costume fall away from her body, stepping backwards out of the legs. Trying to slip one foot back into her slipper she tottered and grabbed me to steady herself. I became more suspicious that she had guzzled a bunch of something just before I arrived, the mystery intoxicant now taking over like a disease from outer space. I took advantage of the possibility and put my arms around her and our lips almost met, but I kissed her about half a mouth too far left. She was still off balance and fell backwards, pulling me over until I let go with one hand to grab the dummy for support while she attacked my face with teeth and tongue in a circular motion, her mouth a cave with the breath of a cave.

Holding her upright was work and she tasted like make up and pencil eraser. She noticed I had stopped kissing back and backed up her tongue while sliding her hand to my crotch, rubbing where my erection should have been but wasn't. I was more surprised. She cupped my whole works in her hand to be certain nothing was happening. With a nonsexual grunt she regained her balance and other shoe then walked away, leaving me with my arm resting on the fake female torso, a more compatible match. I hung the suit back on the dummy and settled the wig on the finial, then looked more closely at the stitching between the chest plate and fur fabric, wondering what to do next, whether to chase after her or let myself out. The worst part was that the moment she left, my excitement suddenly appeared and reached to undo my belt buckle from below.

Catty came back with a drink in each hand but stopped at a distance to look at me strangely, telling me I really was some kind of freak. She smiled and handed me one of the drinks, tipping hers to her lips at the same time. It was whiskey with ice and I pretended to sip but my throat automatically shut at the smell. I stifled the gag reflex, and when she finished her own long swallow I stepped forward and put my hand on the back of her neck to kiss her properly, moving my hand down onto her breast.

She waited patiently until I was finished with the move, then told me to look at this, continuing the tour by leading me to a walk-in closet filled with costumes, uniforms, gowns and tuxedoes all in clear plastic dry-cleaner bags tagged with sizes. She explained she still did wardrobe for independent productions and suggested we work together some time. On the way out she set her glass of ice clumsily on the glass table with a rattling clunk. I checked for cracks before setting my still full drink quietly next to it. I caught up with her at the door where she craned her head forward on her neck and puckered for a polite pretend kiss. As the door opened it pulled in sweet freshly washed oxygen, and it was good to smell again something that wasn't old and used. I thanked her sincerely, looking back as I passed the ticket booth.

She waved from the lighted doorway like an antique housewife. She was still there as I started up the van so I leaned over to put my palm against the passenger-side window, as if saying goodbye from the inside of an invention that would take me back to my own time.

Turned the van around and felt my heartbeat in my upper lip, running my tongue over it and tasting a hint of lipstick and whiskey. I was getting a bit of a fat lip from her attempt to eat my face. Could have been worse. Might have ended up part of her collection. Glancing back up the street I couldn't see the house or even the ticket booth, as if she and her career had disappeared, everything vulnerable to time except her indestructible hairdos. After many more years the collection would become important, like a bullet from the civil war, or a caveman's tooth, but not in our lifetime. She gave me the realization I had something more valuable than a gorilla suit. I had time.

CHAPTER EIGHTEEN

Had become so used to the thum-d'dum of the windshield wipers that I didn't notice the rain had stopped until the worn blades began squeaked protests against the dry glass. Couldn't see stars but the glow of Los Angeles often washed them out, the night never dark here as other places. It was light enough to drive without headlights and I realized that was what I was doing. Rolled down the window to rest my arm on the door, elbow catching the breeze. Something up the slopes had burned not long ago and the air had the sharp flavor of wet ashes. The corner umbrella salesmen were gone and the guy at the side street newsstand was moving racks out from under the awning, searching the sky for a sign that it was the right thing to do. After several random right hand turns I saw the colors above the Frolic room and pulled to the curb.

Smelled my armpits before going in and got the scent of Catty's musk on my shirt. The room was empty and I almost turned around but the bartender stood up from some business below the bar like a life size puppet. Didn't want to be the only customer, but also didn't want to hurt his feelings. Stayed because I liked getting beered-up and believing in my invisibility, but didn't know if I could take the pressure of being a solo drinker less than worthy of any bartender's singular focus, especially visibly drunk. Sat center bar, balancing the empty weight of space to each side, and ordered a Bud. Bottle or draft he said with a professional smile. I mentally kicked myself for being such an amateur, telling myself not to give up, that I could do this. Bottle.

He seemed tense. Thinking I made him nervous, laid a ten on the dry clean bar top while glancing up at the television, a sports report about some guy's injury though it wasn't clear what the sport was.

Needed to say something and prove I could make conversation. Deciding between sports or weather the bartender interrupted my worry to ask how it was going. Without thinking I told him about Catty and her collection. It relaxed him as if relieved not to have to do or say anything original, which relaxed me. That and the beer I sucked down like water. He replaced it without asking permission. On a hunch I asked if he were an actor. He smiled as if I had served him two beers.

He told me about playing a bartender in a series about a private detective until two other customers wandered in, and he was almost annoyed at the interruption. Until then I had assumed bartenders wanted to be bartenders, but we were all on a higher climb. When there were an equal number of customers on each side of me I left some singles for a tip where everyone could see them, hoping to inspire generosity.

Outside there was movement at the corner, a family of six raccoons walking single file along the gutter until they disappeared down a storm drain. They had waited out the flood and could go home again. Unfolded the message from dad inviting me home. The chalk girl might be crazy but I didn't think she would have made that up. Drove to a quiet street to sleep, but the occasional passing car sounded like an airplane taking off from the wet street, too much a contrast to the quiet so I parked again nearer the boulevard, the noise a continuous drone like waves.

When still so young that my injured lip looked as if forced through a screen door, slept some nights at grandma's house on a homemade feather bed. It was a giant pillow made from blue and white striped ticking filled with feathers hand-plucked from the thousand chickens fed to my dad as a growing boy on the family farm. Grandma was forever on farm time and needed no alarm clock, hearing a rooster in her head every morning at dawn. She'd open her eyes and light the stove.

Because the feather bed used up the small living room floor over which she had to pass to reach the stove, there was no sleeping late for me either.

When her feet hit the cold linoleum I rolled up the bed and stuffed it into the old crib wedged between the wall and the foot of her high skinny bed. Also had slept in that crib years earlier. She went sick one night and we slept past dawn. That was when my first dreams came. I flew then peed, and when I awoke was not flying but had peed a little. The secret of how to wash a featherbed went with grandma. After she died they threw out the yellowed bed that smelled like a chicken in the rain.

In the van it was morning. Escaped a bad dream about wetting the bed. Across the country most people were busy jumping into a tub of hot coffee then eating a couple sticks of butter before driving their too big too old car to the factory that built new factories for their kids to work in after eventual sex then marriage. Or else somebody was just as busy doing something else somewhere else. Instead of getting up I rolled over to free any good dreams that might have been stuck to that side of my head and went back to sleep.

Later at McDonalds there was a new sign: Restroom for Customers Only. The restaurant manager wanted the panhandling pack of runaways out front to spend their money on burgers instead of drugs. Though my routine had been to order something after using the toilet, to avoid suspicion I waited in line to buy something first. The problem was my need to go was becoming painful and the line was long and slow. I did the little knee-knock dance for the first time since childhood, putting my hand down my pocket casually, secretly squeezing off any possible accident while thinking dry thoughts and looking at anything but the beverage menu.

Somebody bumped me in the butt and I turned around hoping it hadn't been intentional. There was a toddler holding his mother's sleeve with one hand and slurping on a plastic baby bottle grasped in the other. It was enough to make me quit the line and use the bathroom, but there was a guy in a vest with a nametag who told me sorry, customers only. I promised to order when I finished. He spread the sides of his mouth in an imitation smile and shook his head. Took out a wad of crumpled bills and pulled on the corner of a five, asking if he would mind buying something for me because I had to pee in the next few seconds and it was going to be in the toilet or in the aisle, his choice.

When I came out he was gone with my money. I broke the new rule and left without eating, giving a few coins to one of the teens outside. It is good to have someone around worse off than you are. With an empty belly and five dollars closer to joining the teens, drove up the boulevard and parked in front of a pawnshop that had my attention every time I passed.

The stuff in the window was intimidating, shiny things most people wished to own, stuff easily hock-able for that reason. Shouldered my pack and opened the heavy door that rang a bell. I was surrounded by a department store crowded into a walk-in closet. A glass case the length of one side was filled with treasure. The opposite wall was hung with anything that could fit on a hook: guns, guitars, antlers, autographed baseball bats, bicycles, surfboards and swords. A man in a yarmulke behind a counter at the back of the room looked up from a newspaper and asked if he could help me. Behind him a lady working both an electric typewriter and some chewing gum stopped typing to look at me, the pause in the clacking louder than the typing. She smiled and I smiled and she went back to work.

Setting my pack on the counter I unbuckled the straps and told him I was wondering if they would loan me something on this. He leaned over the pack as I opened the flap to reveal the ape face and he quickly backed away, bumping into the typing table and causing the lady to make a mistake and say something in Hebrew that had the universal language delivery of an impolite word. She peeked around him carefully in case I held a gun or something.

What is that, a dead animal skin? Told him a gorilla suit. The lady stretched her neck to see better as the man raised his reading glasses to rest on his brow, telling me he already had one. He came forward to pull more of it into view and with a jerk of his head caused the glasses to drop back onto the bridge of his nose, inspecting the fur as if searching for fleas and running his fingertip along the stitches with a comment that his wasn't this nice. The lady made an achy sound that matched the squeak of the chair as she forced herself out of it to lean around him for a feel and a close look. She said that it smelled like it was from Western Rental. Told her I made it. She looked at me hard and suspiciously, trying to make me confess something, maybe admitting gorilla suit fraud but I didn't break. She shrugged and returned to smiling and typing.

He asked to see its feet and hands like it was a normal thing, no different than checking a diamond for flaws. I pulled the whole suit loose and laid it on the counter, a victim needing medical attention. He went over it front and back searching for holes or fleas maybe then said he'd loan me fifty or buy it for seventy-five. The lady instantly assured me that was a good deal without looking up from her work.

Asked him if he would show me the suit he had. He called out for someone named Yosh. An almost twin opened the door from a back room, leaning in to yell what. His double held up the head and shoulders of the suit so it sat there limp like a passed-out drunk ape. Unimpressed by the display Yosh said so what. He was told to bring out the one they had like it, at the end of the rack of monkey suits. Turning back to me he winked and said that meant tuxedos, kind of a joke.

Yosh returned with a tagged garment bag and dropped it on top of my suit, turning without a pause and disappearing into the back again. Inside the zippered vinyl bag was a cheap Halloween costume, unpadded and made of lightweight fun fur. The hands were leather gloves safety pinned to the sleeves like kids mittens so they wouldn't get lost. In the bottom of the bag were a pair of furry slippers and the head, a stock rubber chimpanzee mask advertised in any novelty catalogue. He asked if I wanted to trade straight across. Shook my head no so he offered ten dollars an hour for me to walk down the boulevard wearing it, telling people about his great deals. We settled on a sixty-dollar loan. After a few minutes of paperwork I was back in the van feeling as though I just had sold a family member, but it was in a safe place.

The liquor store was surprisingly busy that early, the lottery giving customers an excuse to take home a bottle and avoid the afternoon crunch. A man in a three-piece suit and shiny shoes left the counter holding his printed-out tickets like a Chinese folding fan. The turbaned guy told him to take good care from them. I went to the beer cooler and window shopped, thinking about buying a loaf of bread and having beer sandwiches for brunch.

Somebody behind me told someone else that last night he heard a skunk crying. The other guy asked how he knew it was a skunk. The first somebody said that it smelled like skunk. Well maybe the smell made something else cry. Yeah, but the odds of such an occurrence are improbable. Heard no answer as I chose a single tall can of beer. There was a rack of Hostess temptations at the cash register so I balanced a package of cupcakes on the top of the can.

Turban guy was looking out the door at a kid in the parking lot. He told me somebody had been stealing out of parked cars, and that he had accused the kid who denied it. Looking back at me he said that he wouldn't let anybody pull the wool over his ears. He wanted cops to give him a lie detective test or he would take the law out of his own hands. I asked him if he knew anything about the weather. No.

After stuffing change in my pockets and his cramming my stuff into too small a sack the kid was gone. I was lost in thought about turban guy, almost certain he was faking the accent, so didn't notice the opened sliding door of the van until I was next to it. Without looking in I kicked it closed and it was like trapping some animal, though I worried about the crying skunk. There was a thump then banging as I went around to the driver's side door as it opened, the kid sliding out head first over the front seat, spilling like laundry onto oil stained lot with the Frisbee gripped in one hand.

His voice was lower than mine as he cursed me, his back on the asphalt as if I had done something worthy of his bad words. Stepped over him and got in my seat, unable to pull out the cupcakes jammed into the strained paper bag so ripped it open. Took one twin cake out of the plastic then handed down the other still in the package, telling the boy that I had pissed in the Frisbee. He dropped it and scrabbled upright onto his butt, wiping his fingers on dirty clothing before grabbing the snack. After eating it he wiped his fingers the same way then got up and walked away. He didn't cry like a skunk, and the bad smell was the van. Thought of throwing the Frisbee at the back of his head but was afraid to make him mad.

Some people get away with more than I could hope to. Finished my half of the moment and washed it down with beer, the after-taste a little like pork for some chemical reason. I burped loudly and said excuse me, then drove over the Frisbee to the walk and spotted Roy on a side street, sitting on the dropped tailgate. He was staring at the curb with a donut in one hand and a coffee cup in the other, chewing and chewing but not swallowing like a loop of film going around and around. In white shirt, trousers and suspenders he looked like a normal person. If he hadn't been with the wagon I might not have recognized him. I parked and finished the beer, walking over to ask him how he felt.

Around that mouthful of perpetual donut he told me he felt with his hand and his heart, waiting until one was torn apart before the other, still staring at the curb. I said it was a nice cup and he told me it had to go back to the house, that he had visited his wife to tell her a check was only days away so she let him stay overnight. That didn't fit things he had told me earlier, but he said that if he lied a little here and there it was only to get the truth across, and keep things interesting. He admitted first to groveling and then to flattery and finally to making promises and she fronted him gas money.

He finally swallowed and finished whatever was in the cup, turning to open his case and dig out his little black mustache. He asked if I was going to work today, and I told him that I had hocked my suit.

Watched him costume-up while giving me dirty looks, unable to speak his disgust but the message was clear and cold. Finally he asked what I got for it, and I told him gas money. He shook his head and shuffled away more like a homeless person than the tramp.

The clouds had rolled off to the east and I stood in the shadow of a kiosk watching him work. The tourists were so hungry to see a movie star they treated him as if there were a small chance he might be the real Charlie. If one person tipped him a dollar Roy would snap it straight and fold it neatly to make certain everyone saw it so the next person would give him two or a five to gain his attention. One drag-along husband didn't care, busy searching for a pair of leading man footprints that matched his shoe size, and after finding a set he tried to reach his hand into one of the handprints but he couldn't bend over far enough. Roy saw that butt in white shorts shining like the moon and couldn't resist, giving him a little kick in the pants that might have been cute on film, but the guy fell over with an oof. He glared back up at Roy, his newcomer face already pink from the vacation sun turning rage red.

The wife hop-scotched over, superstitious about stepping directly on a signature or imprint, so another couple helped her husband stand up, his shoes again in the footprints but backwards. The four of them looked at Roy as if he were a mugger. When he pulled out a hanky to brush the guy off for funny, they backed up in honest fear. Roy wouldn't break character even to tell the guy he was sorry, so he bowed and shrugged and tramped away to a section of crowed that hadn't seen the incident.

The foursome had a whispered conference then looked around for help, sighting a security guard on the far side of the property. When they walked in march-step toward him, I warned Roy that he was tattled out. The man with a badge listened to the story then lazily crossed the cement, the four accusers following like baby ducks, but when he got close Roy quickly moved away again, threading between and hiding behind tourists. The guard intentionally made no effort to hurry, not wanting to cause a disturbance or force an actual chase. The people caught on that the badge was after Chaplin, letting him pass then closing ranks to block the way. He ordered them to let him through but it sounded so scripted that the crowd laughed, many thinking it was a standard routine. Some even stuck autograph books in his face.

I caught up with Roy at his wagon where he was already out of the hat, mustache and coat, an ordinary citizen in baggy pants. He pulled dollars out of his pockets, so much green in each hand that he looked like he had just weeded a lawn. We both rested against the side of the car and squinted in the sunshine. Reminded him that a paycheck was waiting up at the park, but I was going to wait for the mailman on Thursday at Mac and Sam's, sit on the porch and wait if there was nobody home. It was too hot to stand there against the wagon so I started up the hill toward the van, but walking backwards so as not to turn my back on Roy. Our mailman back home sometimes walked backwards to used different muscles and give his back a rest.

Roy told me to stay away from that freak-house, certain he had seen Manson in there. I said that they were the only people I knew with a shower. He called for me to wait up, dropping his baggy pants and stuffing them through the space where he hadn't rolled the window up all the way. He had a big pair of plaid shorts on underneath. He made sure his doors were locked then followed me to my van where he told me we all walk through life backwards, only able to see where we've been. In the driver's seat I took the time to write that down. Roy knocked on the other door so I unlocked it though I hadn't invited him anywhere, but he told me to head up Cahuenga.

Roy told me how he and his wife met at the open-mic night of a comedy club. After doing five minutes for the four people watching he raced to the bar. An Asian man sat next to a pair of crutches and asked Roy if he wanted a writing job, that he needed a pair of comedy writers. Roy agreed and asked who he'd be working with, and the guy said they would have to wait and see. The female comic behind him did her five minutes and came to the bar, the Asian guy asking if she wanted a writing job. After getting their telephone numbers the guy got on his crutches and promised to call, leaving on his only leg. They got together to work on ideas but never heard from the guy or saw him again.

Roy directed me along a route of several turns until we were on a curvy street of very nice homes where he told me to pull into the driveway of one that had a for sale sign on the tree lawn. Without a word or look back he went around the side of the house. I waited for a moment then got out and followed, passing through an iron gate that opened on a swimming pool empty except for a neat circle of leaves and a broken skateboard. At the other end of the pool was a smaller building that matched the style of the house. One of its slatted double doors was open. I stuck my head inside and was hit by a beach towel. Roy was standing in front of a washer and dryer, pointing to a shower on the other side of the room. There's your damn shower, kid, sometimes you stink like a poor nation.

Put all my clothes in the washing machine then used the shower. There was soap and extra towels. After using several, wrapped another dry one around my waist and put the wet ones with my clothes in the drier. Sat by the pool with Roy on white wicker lounge chairs. Roy had attended parties here before the couple divorced. She moved back north to wine country and he was living at the beach with his young girlfriend. When Roy heard they had put the house on the market he spent nights sleeping on the wicker in the laundry room, its door lockless, but now we napped in sunshine.

The nagging melody of Pop Goes the Weasel approached, the sound of an ice cream truck creeping through the neighborhood. While I got my clothes from the drier Roy went for treats. We met at the van and I drove carefully so the Nutty Buddy didn't drip on my clean shirt.

Licking food made me think of Catty for some reason so I told Roy about our meet and how I might have missed an opportunity there. He damned testosterone, blaming it for everything from my awkward night at the Attic to all wars and to his homelessness. Once it kicks in you may never have a single clear thought again he said, asking for details. When I finished he suggested that if it doesn't work out with the park princess I should go back with a bottle and a nice gift, something for her collection.

Finished the cone thinking about Sonny while Roy whistled the weasel melody, pointing where I should make more turns until we came to a drive with a guard booth. The security guard had a white mustache and heavy framed glasses. He leaned out of the booth, holding onto the doorframe with one hand. Where to?

Roy leaned over until his head almost touched the steering wheel and told Captain Kangaroo he just had to drop off today's revisions at the Miradero office, that we didn't even need to park. Okay the guard said, pulling himself back into the booth like it was his daily workout. I drove over a speed bump and asked Roy where we were. The Universal lot, he said, welcome to movie land. I asked why the guy doing pull-ups hadn't checked our identification. Roy said this isn't a bank vault. There's nothing to steal, just a thousand people play acting.

The lot had streets and buildings like a small town but fewer cars because the employees walked, rode bicycles and drove golf carts, none of them in costume. It's not like you crash the gate and can sneak into a scene being filmed and get discovered, kid, that only happens in the movies. He gurgled a self-congratulatory laugh and showed me where to park, then treated me to lunch at the cafeteria.

Ate my turkey sandwich in an athletic way that allowed me to look around the room, snapping my neck and stretching one shoulder at a time while hoping to see a famous actor, but they all must have been extras. Roy said the big shots had expensive lunches brought into their dressing room or mobile home, but didn't eat because it might spoil their drunk. He pointed around randomly and said with his mouth full that these were the writers and line producers and assistants and paper pushers who did most of the work so the actors could show up eventually and take credit for everything. I thought a college campus was less boring. He steered us out a different gate while telling me that if we drove around until we found a crew shooting an exterior then I'd understand true boredom.

We climbed back into the hills, winding back and forth along another canyon road without a canyon, getting passed by angry speedy cars until we caught up with an old truck that stole my title of slowest vehicle in a fast town. As it turned on the tight curves the name of its landscaping business could be read, hand painted on the doors: Arn's Lawn Care. I snuggled the van in behind it so cars had to pass both of us at the same time, but their anger directed at Arn. When we were up and over the hump of the hill, some of the turns gave a view of a thick brown layer of air blocking sight of the concrete panorama below. I rode my brakes and looked down at the road to be certain I hadn't missed a turn and was driving on a cloud of polluted air.

The truck squeaked almost to a stop and shakily turned into a hidden driveway, other cars still passing. An expensive model braked and skidded to a stop next to us, avoiding a head-on collision with an oncoming twin of itself that had to move onto what little shoulder there was, so we were three across at that instant. I asked Roy what the odds were of twin Porsches meeting on the road like that. Out here about even.

We coasted down to a stop light at Sunset where a woman tiptoed in leopard-skin heels between the flashing don't walk signs. She wore Laura Petrie pants and her breasts were bigger than my imagination. They were held so tightly in a tight top of orange stretch fabric that I could see not only the shape of her nipples, but the bumps in the circles around them. I tasted orange juice and breathed the word impossible. Roy said to be careful, that it could be a man. She had to stop at the corner and look down to keep her balance as she stepped up onto the curb. A honking horn behind me broke the spell and I saw the left turn arrow was green. Running a red light wouldn't have mattered because all traffic had stopped to allow the lady to cross against the light the other way, no horns.

The next sight was like a cold shower, a street person sitting on a bus stop bench wearing a too-small trench coat, each wrinkle in his face and hands filled with grime so he looked like a victim of a cruel make-up artist who used a black magic marker to age a person. Roy nodded at him and said I don't think you've met my agent, then asked what I felt like doing. I told him I wanted to go back and offer that lady a ride. He said yeah, he wanted a beer too and told me to pull over.

He jumped out and put a coin in a newspaper dispenser box, grabbing one and getting back in, no beer. I waited as he paged through, finding what he was looking for then folding the paper open to that page. It was a picture of us in costume, the ad for Laugh Land. Princess Sonny was in the crook of my gorilla arm, wide-eyed and pushing herself away from me with one hand on the shiny leather of its chest, the other touching her bottom lip as she mouthed an oh! It took my mind off orange boobs. Told Roy that he looked great, the eyes of MacNessie staring at the sky because Roy was looking at the camera through the mouth of the costume. He said thanks but it sounded like a threat and he planned to get even.

We veered left onto Hollywood Boulevard and up near the walk, but before we reached his wagon he told me to take a right and find parking. We walked up to a tall off-white building. Inside it was suddenly cool and quiet, our footsteps echoing off the lobby walls, preceding us into a barroom of marble and leather under a vaulted ceiling. A female in a white blouse that tried to contain her, a black vest over the blouse if it failed, called us gentlemen and asked us what we would like. I waited for Roy to say something rude, thinking to myself it must be national boob day, but he stopped and swallowed as if surprised at her presence. He told her he had never seen her before, curiously as if she had slipped in secretly and done away with the regular server, now impersonating a bartender.

She said her name was Sheba to settle the matter. I suggested two drafts while easing onto the tall chair with sides and back of studded mustard-colored leather, able to lean back and get comfortable. She tossed a pair of perfect unused coasters onto the bar as if she spent her spare time in Vegas as a dealer, then lifted a delicate frosted mug to the tap. Roy whispered that he had to use the can, echoing away around a post that curved up and away to meet the top of another post's arch. She set the mug on the coaster in front of me then filled the other, her eyes watching the level of foam and beer like it was a crucial measurement in a scientific experiment. She set that mug perfectly in the center of the other coaster without asking for cash or if we wanted to run a tab, just picked up a plastic swizzle stick and bit on it, crossing one arm under her breasts as she leaned back against the rear counter like a centerfold waiting to be told it was time to undo the blouse.

The glass was so cold that a bit of my lower lip froze to its outer edge, the skin stretching before it broke free and snapped back into place. I looked around and asked her where everyone was, just to be talking while hoping she hadn't seen me with my lip stuck. She told me that most of the guests were out on a bus tour looking at movie stars' homes. I cringed at the memory of eyeballing every studio employee as they chewed on their blt's and cobb salads.

Footsteps came around the corner followed by Roy, his hair wet and slicked back so it showed more forehead than before. He sat down noisily, both the chair and him creaking, then took in a big breath and drank the mug half empty. He held it crooked in the air so a beam of light caught what beer was left, bubbles rising from the bottom like an animated display sign. The three of us watched the bubbles until Roy brought the mug down onto the bar. The bartender used a little push of her back muscles to come off the back counter and slide Roy's coaster a few inches closer to his beer. He slipped it under and set one hand on each side, the right hand with bigger knuckles than the left as if beginning an asymmetrical transformation into a beast.

Roy wondered at her how much the rooms went for, but she said she wouldn't know because she didn't stay here. I finished my beer as Roy poured the rest down his throat. She raised her eyebrows and Roy and I nodded. She used the same mugs to pour us another round and I was disappointed because I wanted to get my lip to freeze to the glass again and show Roy. When the bartender got busy transferring some other types of glasses from under the bar to the counter, Roy raised his eyebrows and pointed his head toward her, kicking me in the leg but I ignored him, enjoying the one beer in me and the other in front of me, a moment of balance. Very quietly he told me that she doesn't know what I drive yet, that I should talk to her. From the other end of the bar she said that I was the guy living in the VW van.

We stared at her again but for a different reason. She said it was the acoustics, that in the right spots you can hear people whispering on the other side of the room, pointing to where the walls curved into the ceiling. Roy cleared his throat with a growling sound, drank as much as he could in one swallow without taking a big breath first, then excused himself, tap-tappa-tapping away. She asked me if she was right, that I was the guy in the van. I nodded and she said that her friend had told her about me. I also tried to finish most of my beer quickly and got an instant headache. Putting the mug to my temple I finally asked who her friend was.

Before she could answer, a tall guy in the same shirt and vest entered and went to the cash register, looking through a stack of receipts skewered on a spike next to it. He jotted something down on a pad and said okay. She told him that everything was filled but they were low on some brand of something in back. He threw a towel over his shoulder and asked me how I was doing. I was broken hearted she left without telling me anything more.

More footsteps approached and we both looked over to see who would appear, but the footsteps faded away as if an invisible person had crossed the room. He told me that it happens sometimes, the acoustics. I stood up off the stool and asked how much I owed, but he said that I didn't owe him anything. Stuck some dollars under the mugs and looked for Roy, the brightness of the buildings reflecting the low sun bringing back the pain in my temple. He wasn't at his wagon or Musso & Frank but I sat down at the bar there anyway. Leaned back expecting the mustard leather from the hotel bar and lost my balance, kicking my feet out to keep from falling backwards. They thumped into the bar-front as I grabbed the rounded edge that trimmed the bar-top. The other customers look over expecting me maybe to start singing drunkenly, but I held my hands out in a calming motion to inform them I was fine, show over. The tan man was working and served me a beer in a room temperature glass. Had to pay for it. Such was the sunny side of the street.

Anthony was at the end of the bar in conversation. When it stalled and our eyes met I raised my glass and asked how Catty was doing, feeling local. He lifted a hand like it were made of lead and waved me over, telling me that she was digging out slowly. He wished he could help but at his age he was useless as a one-inch weenie. I understood the weenie part but not the digging out, asking him what that meant. Mud, he said. Half the hillside had come down on her attic room.

CHAPTER NINETEEN

---

he first white settlers of Michigan asked the native people about the large tree-covered mounds and overgrown earthen ramparts, but they confessed ignorance about them. Earlier locals had built them, probably as some kind of burial ritual. The massive piles of dirt and stones were untouched out of respect. First thing white men did was dig into them hoping for treasure, but the ojibwe had guessed correctly. They were tombs with skeletons in a stone chamber at the bottom center, the bones so old they crumbled when moved, buried with beads of shell, mica ornaments, stone pipes and copper bracelets, treasure enough for back then. One farmer removed a dead tree that had lived on the mound, its roots grown down throughout as if reaching for treasure. It had five hundred growth rings, living five hundred spring and summers on the mound, but nobody could know how long the mound had existed before the tree first sprouted then took root.

After another generation the mounds were gone as the land was cleared for farms and towns. Probably will happen to all of us, buried beneath the mound of years until getting cleared away by future people. Drove back to Catty's thinking of buried treasure, planning to grab a shovel and get my clean clothes muddy. The street was blocked off, a sign posted to keep me out of danger. The hill above was bare and brown-black ugly. No people were around so I ducked under the caution tape and walked up toward the ticket booth. The big van was gone and so was part of the room on the hill. There was another danger sign tacked to the booth but I braved past it up to the door where a notice told me no entry. Nobody answered when I knocked, and the door was locked so I snuck around the side, stopped by a wall of mud. The blob again, in black and white. Stepped onto a section, afraid my shoes might get eaten, and wondered how much memorabilia it had swallowed.

As I walked back down to the van her neighbor was in front of his mud-free house straining to see if I carried any loot. Asked if he knew where Catty was staying and he shook his head no, but said she was with friends. He stared across the sky as if looking for anything that might fall on his home, a meteor or tumbling aircraft, but there was nothing but a chunk of moon visible in the still-light sky. Satisfied it was staying up there he turned and went back through his open front door. As I stepped up into the van I noticed my shoe rimmed with mud, realizing I had left my prints just like the ones at Grauman's.

Roy's paper was between the seats. Unfolded it back out to the front page and there it featured an article about mudslides, but focused on a different area where people were dead under the hillside. This slide could have come down on us when she was bent over me wearing her ape-monster suit. Our bodies would have been found in that position, like things from the tar pits or the embracing victims of Pompeii. Males animals hungry with desire had prowled the area for tens of thousands of years, getting caught awkwardly in sticky places, some leaving only footprints and others sinking down and leaving their bones.

Starting the van I worried that the mud had been my fault, the sound of my engine that night maybe enough to trigger the slide, and now that I was thinking about it maybe there had been a strange vibration and slight rumble as I drove away that night. Cruised down the hill needing a distraction and some kind of thought-killer. It was Monday, anniversary of the side door club with the midnight band, so steered toward Len's building then parked in the alley.

Waited the length of two oldies on the radio for anybody to tell me I had to move the van, then got out and went up. There was a nice view of rooftops mostly unused but some had lawn furniture and potted plant gardens, one with an Astroturf putting green. I stood in the open doorway rubbing the rust off my palms, trying to remember the number of Len's room. Called out his name but no answer so went inside, aiming for the door that seemed to be the correct distance from the fire escape landing. The hall lights were off and I followed the ray of light beaming through the crack of door jam, shining a path along the dirty linoleum hallway floor.

Said Len's name again but still with no answer. There was a morlockian clunk from below and I heard a crowd of birds somewhere high on the building, their noisy chatter falling down a chimney or vent pipe. Something crunched under my feet, the floor not swept in a decade. Could have been bits of plaster fallen from the ceiling or brittle sections of loose flooring, or maybe dead roaches that finally found conditions too poor for survival. Used my fingers to find the door and trace out the numbers 314, which I remembered now so knuckled softly, the memory also reminding me that he might be in jail. Whispered Len's name and listened for movement but only heard more clunking from floors below, the sound of old plumbing, its arterial piping reacting to miniscule shifts of the building's old walls and floors settling this way and that around a skeleton of old steel beams failing in geological time. The birds suddenly went silent, abandoning the roof in one great flock and I felt panic as if the place might crumble down around me. Left before I bothered anyone.

Parked near the library then retraced our trail from the other Monday, back toward those fifty-cent drafts. Wanted the safe and protective embrace of beer. And there was Len. He had not been spending much time at the apartment, preferring to sleep in garbage bags on Mac and Sam's porch couch. I asked about the raid, if they had gone to jail, but he said that when the cops told them to keep the sound down and left, it was only to double check for warrants on a guy

they saw wasted in the living room, a known local villain. They called
for back up because of the crowd and the dogs. Len said the worst part
was that they also called animal control and took all the unlicensed
animals. Then he said no, worst part was that to be on the safe side he
had to stuff his drugs up his butt.

We drank a few rounds and nibbled on some stuffed doughy things
that tasted like a combination of French fries and oil paint, and when he
asked me if I had any spare cash I told him I'd pay here and at the club
later if he wanted to go. He chewed and nodded like a motorized exhibit
and told me that was cool. I wanted it to be cool, telling him about my
suit and that maybe he had something to pawn. He had a bass guitar
stored at a guy's house but no shop would give him a loan because they
were stuck with too many unredeemed basses that wouldn't sell. He
doubled the speed of his motion with the beer and I realized he needed
to buy drugs, finally noticing the stare in his eyes and shakiness in his
fingers as if fearing something ahead. I wanted to be cool, to cool for
Sunday school, like an out of place wild furry thing in church. Told him
I could get him something.

Bought a case then dropped him off at Mac and Sam's telling him I
had to go alone. Drove around a couple of corners until I found a dead
stretch of street where an iron fence and a wall of shrubbery hid property
from the street, but also hid me from the property. I raided Jayo's stash,
hands shaking with adventure as I unzipped the naughahyde to get at
the pot and cash, unwrapping the money bundle to peel off some bills,
then the pot. My heart was a hammer as I re-wrapped the stuff and
hid it again. Before driving back I waited for a mudslide or meteor or
tumbling plane to punish me, but a minute of nothing proved to me that
nobody was watching, nobody was in charge, didn't even care.

Len was on the porch drinking a beer, an empty can already crushed
next to his foot. He was up and leaning forward as I reached into my
pocket. He set the can on the railing and held out both hands like Oliver
Twist to make certain nothing would get lost. He accepted the gift of
weed and bills, looking at me as if I had given him communion.

Inside I saw that the empty keg had been turned into an end table by putting a piece of plywood across the top. Mac was on the couch playing his Strat' unplugged so all you could hear was thin spider web sounds. Len held his closed fist out in front of him until Mac stopped playing and cupped his hand so Len could drop the pot into it, telling all of us he'd be back, not bothering me for a ride this time. Maybe I had done enough, for now anyway. A dog that hadn't greeted us at the door came from around the lounger. It wore a collar with tags and had survived the other night's roust, sniffing along the bottom of the closed door for the smell of animal cops. It learned that hiding was safer than greeting people at the door.

Mac laid the guitar down on the couch with its headstock on the armrest like putting his kid to bed. I followed him into the kitchen to find one of my beers. He asked where Len got the pot and I told him I just wanted everyone to be happy. He stretched his mouth into a big fake smile while he dug into a junk drawer for paraphernalia, finding a little metal pipe. He smoked and offered me the pipe the way it's done in cowboy and indian movies, but I shook my head no. He told me that Samantha got a job as an assistant to a woman who had inherited her father's patent on a type of coin-operated binoculars used at scenic lookouts and observation decks on the tops of skyscrapers, which had made them rich one quarter at a time.

About an hour later Len was back and somewhere along the way he had found Angel and Chacha. Angel was dressed like a guy except for the mascara, and Chacha was in a yellow and gray vintage dress and wearing big work boots, looking like a depression-era farmer's wife. Mac said hi and offered his pipe. They were quick to take it. With everybody high and me getting drunk I asked if they knew about the mudslides. Angel told me they come with the rain after the fires. I had missed the fires. He said that those come with the Santa Anas. I had missed those too whatever they were.

Mac played a chord and sang about too much change in the weather, not enough in my jeans, love like something when we're together, together like rice and beans ... or kings and queens. Angel warned against using the word love in a love song, or the word blues in a blues tune. Mac said never write anything down, because if you can't remember it then it isn't worth remembering. Now the good stuff, you can't get that out of your head.

Chacha came in from the bathroom to announce that Len couldn't find a vein. Mac said that he couldn't either as he set the guitar down against the couch to smoke more. I asked him how the bike was coming along and he said he was waiting on parts. Angel reached over for the guitar and sang about a catalogue of parts to repair batch of broken hearts. Len joined us wearing a satisfied home run smile. I went for another beer to keep up with them but it seemed futile as a dog chasing a car. Len went over to sit on an amp and play the bass guitar, so Chacha jumped up to strap on an off brand Les Paul-style six string and strum with her thumb. I asked if everybody around here played guitar. Mac said it wasn't much harder than learning to talk, the problem being that most people didn't know what they were talking about, same with guitar.

There was an electric pop and buzz as a toggle switch was flipped. Mac had sunken so deep into the cushions that he had to kick his feet out to sit up before standing and joining the others. Without speaking they played a blind and ragged stumbling thing that eventually found its way to walk then run. Angel hung some of his lyrics on different sections. Somehow they knew

when to finish at the same time. At that moment my life became simple and I didn't want to become a man, I wanted to be in a rock and roll band.

Mac asked if anyone had anymore weed, looking at me so they all looked at me. It was getting dark so I went to the kitchen and turned on that light and got another beer. Back in the dining room they hadn't moved, lit on one side like that Beatles album cover. Said that I had to pee.

I chugged at the same time I went, like a circulating beer fountain. There were candles on the toilet tank with jar lids for holders, books of matches all around from different clubs and motels. More on the windowsill and along a tiled shelf in the tub area, all mostly melted down to stalagmites. The roomed seemed like a religious memorial to the invention of indoor plumbing. In our bathroom back home Mom had a scented decorative candle on a doily on the toilet tank lid, but it never was lit, dust gathering on the wax so if someone ever put a flame to the wick the entire candle probably would catch fire. I had stared at it while peeing tens of thousands of times. When I came home from college it had been replaced by a ceramic outhouse circled with plastic flowers. I didn't own an unused candle, but had time to burn, making certain if ever I had a toilet lid there would be something useful and used on it.

Flushed, lit what was left of the candle then stepped over to the sink and looked in the mirror, my reflection almost familiar. Against the door was my shadow in profile, larger than life and dancing because of the flickering light, my dark side until the door opened. Sam was home from work and didn't know anyone was in there. It felt like she caught me doing something naughty, but she said sorry before I could.

Stepped past her and told them I could get more marijuana. I said it and that was it. The money I'd have to account for but I wasn't going to baby sit his pot, not if it would guarantee me a seat at the party table with people who took drugs like candy and wrote songs on their feet. They would get what they wanted and I'd get what I wanted, law of the jungle. Ask any jungle lawyer.

Drove back to the blind spot and pulled a larger wad loose from the bundle, looking too late for something to put it in so jammed it in my pocket. The stereo was filling in for the band when I returned, all of them in the kitchen where Sam was boiling water. Chase and Blanca were against the counter, Blanca behind with her arms around his chest so it looked like he had four arms. I pulled the wad from my pocket and dropped it on the table, a green mound like a Christmas centerpiece. There was light applause as Angel asked if I was picking this stuff out of somebody's garden. I shrugged and got another beer.

Dinner was macaroni and cheese and I ate my portion using a spoon out of a coffee mug decorated with a crab and the word Chesapeake because there weren't enough forks and plates for everybody. When the food was gone Chase took out his wallet and gently removed a folded piece of paper, setting it on the table next to the green mound. He told me to look inside. I unfolded the top part like opening the cover of a book and inside was a long thin piece of striped paper like a filmstrip with a little picture of a skull in each frame. He told me not to touch, that it was acid. Didn't make sense that paper could burn my fingers and I told him I didn't get it. He said if I touched it the acid would rub off on my skin and be wasted. I turned to Angel who said it was LSD.

The stuff sat there like the opening ante in a card game, but after supper settled they began smoking again. I drank at a speed of four beers per hour knowing the case wouldn't last long. Goliath and Racer arrived with a pack of wild women that reminded me of the missing dogs. Racer raised the bet by adding a bindle of powder to the mix of drugs. When the beer ran out

I sniffed some off Racer's knife tip again, asking him what it was. He asked back how did I think he got his name?

Later they used tweezers and tiny sewing scissors to cut up the paper strip. Those participating opened their mouths like baby birds to accept the little tab directly onto the tips of their tongues, curling them back inside as if eating fire. Mac and Angel ganged up on me to try it. It felt good, peer pressure, like a girl pushing you toward the bedroom. A week or even days before I would've joked about it and left, but my brain had changed. It had grown claws and fangs and horns, and I craved to sniff the wild dog's butt. I picked up a square with my fingernails hoping some of its potency would be lost there. I rubbed it against the saliva of my tongue where it caught, and then I swallowed, waiting for the sound effects that followed when Curly swallowed a horse pill. Nothing happened except for pats and punches of congratulations.

Back home during the summer months there were touristy attractions along the bluff with arts and crafts and music and food.

I had a habit of holding my breath when people walked past unless it was an attractive female, disappointed with the smell of cigarette. Walking through a crowd like that I would have to breath in quick deep breaths between long distances of regular looking women, causing hyperventilation, dizziness and the need to sit or squat or lean against something. One time it was five-foot tall boulder that I leaned against, a monument to the explorer LaSalle who claimed territories like brides for his harem.

A hippie on the other side of the rock asked if I wanted to score. I asked what, meaning I didn't understand but he thought I meant what was it I might score. Acid, man. I looked around to see if anybody else had heard and he told me to be cool, that there were narcs around. I asked him who were the narcs, and he used his eyeballs to point to a man wearing black rubber snow boots. I knew the guy. He lived at the end of my street. He had survived the Nazis and planted little trees all over his small yard, making the house look huge compared to the tiny forest. He wore those boots every day of the year. A real cop appeared and told me to get off the rock. When I looked over the acid man was gone.

And it was good my drug use occurred far from home. I snuck away, climbed a tree in the back and took off my clothes. If I had done that in Ravinia it would have been considered bad behavior. It would've gone unnoticed in Hollywood if I had stayed up there, but saw a wandering light and climbed down to follow it with the belief it was guiding me somewhere important. The police caught up with me at the patio bar where I was reciting verses from the Bible. They acted as if happened every night and did their best to learn where I had left my clothes, simply wanting me to get dressed. When I couldn't cooperate they cuffed me and put me in the back of their car. At the station another cop took my pulse and blood pressure, politely asking for my address so they could get me home. It might have been a trick to get me to lead them to Mac and Sam's so I told them nothing.

Believing I was starring in an old movie, expected they eventually would beat the truth out of me, but they dressed me in a paper jump suit and delivered me to a dark basement room someplace where male nurses strapped me to a bed. Cartoons were projected onto the wall but the only sound was a lady singing. In the morning a nurse traded me juice for a blood sample. There were other beds in the room, some occupied by other troubled minds, but no projector or singer.

Later a nurse asked if I wanted to hurt others or myself. I did not and told her about the party toxins. I was given a cheap pair of flip-flops and lunch. The doctor came back with my blood work and recommended their drug therapy program, asking if I had health insurance. When I told her no she suggested I enter one of the free programs offered by other institutions. I could go if I signed a release form so I signed. Outside it was sunny but cool, or maybe it seemed cool because I was wearing paper clothes. If it had happened back home I would be in jail, then forced to go to church.

Stuffed my copies of the paperwork in the first trashcan then asked the nearest guy which direction was Hollywood. He pointed the way and told me I was sure dressed for it. Crossed a freeway on an overpass and recognized the view of hills, realizing I was up in the valley. It was a long walk that took me past the Hollywood Bowl, which I had never noticed when driving. The air stayed cool on my sweaty skin and the paper stuck to my butt and belly. Blisters grew between my big and second toe and my feet ached from trying not to lose the thongs. The town that had been getting smaller now was too big to cross, but without money or the van there was nothing to do but shuffle along. I didn't look at people or into store windows, only at the seams in the sidewalk, two steps per square, one square after another. The sun burned my nose and cheeks and forehead until they were too sensitive to wipe off sweat, so it trickled down my neck. The thirst hurt. If I had found a puddle I would have drank from it. The journey was like crossing the world's busiest desert.

At dusk I was at Mac and Sam's. Drank from the outside faucet and soaked my head, then had to climb the tree again with bloody feet to retrieve my clothes. The muffled sound of heavy metal music throbbed from inside the garage and light shone around the edges of the t-shirt used for a curtain. The pounding beat was like a giant's footsteps as I shinnied up the trunk, Jack up the beanstalk, ripping my paper suit in several places. The magnolia hadn't been so tall the night before but everything was safe, my shoes hanging from laces neatly tied around a skinny limb. My wallet, loose cash and the van key were still inside the pants pockets. Dropped them to the ground and followed, descending to the grasslands to become re-civilized.

As I dressed behind the tree trunk the garage side door opened and the bare bulb hanging inside spotlighted me. Mac stepped into the doorway and his shadow hid me again as I finished buttoning my shirt. He welcomed me back, but instead of wondering what I was doing behind the tree he asked me to help him mount his front wheel. I saved my story because he had one that was more serious. Len had seizures and they dropped him off at some free clinic. Calling around today they learned he had hepatitis and might not live. His parents were flying out and I was supposed to gather his stuff. Asked if he had a flashlight.

Mac held the fire escape door as I went to tap on 314, praying for no answer. Tried the knob and it wasn't locked so I opened the door, announcing that I was a friend of Len's, that Len was sick, that Len wanted me to get his things, making it clear I knew Len. The apartment was empty and I called for Mac, shining the light ahead of his feet so he could follow. Shone the light on the light bulb cord and he plugged it in. In the corner was a dark green military duffle bag. I wrapped the radio and some kitchen items in the sleeping bag while Mac dragged the duffle into the hall. Thought maybe we should leave a note, but we heard the ghostly faraway sound of a girl yelling, not angrily because she also laughed, then yelped and it was quiet again. Mac said we should get out of there.

As we pushed the stuff out the gap in the fence a man and woman slowly walked past on the sidewalk. When they saw us we stopped, looking guilty of something so they stopped. Mac asked them to help and they walked away faster. I told Mac that if this had been a burglary we'd have gotten away with it, then in the van asked him if he minded taking a quick detour. Thinking about Len, my conscience reminded me I had parents and I wanted to check for messages at the phone booth.

The booth was wrapped in two kinds of tape, yellow and red, because each panel of glass had been beaten with something until it cracked or shattered. The phone unit was loosened from the metal backing so you could see some of its guts. I parked and got out to walk around the damage, chunks of glass grinding under my shoes. Mac was busy searching AM frequencies for his kind of music, so I jaywalked over to the girl's house while searching my pockets for a ten-dollar bill. Knocked on the door and when it opened the dog smelled my legs for a moment, but was more interested in the yard. Handing her the money I asked if she knew what happened to the phone booth. She said somebody treated it like their only child who didn't live up to expectations and embarrassed them in front of company because she was too shy to speak so she had to wear long sleeves in summer to hide the bruises left by her father's strong fingers when he grabbed them to shake some sense into her.

I thanked her and waved bye to the dog. Mac was listening to a Mexican song heavy with accordion, playing drums on the dashboard. He said that he forgot to tell me I had a phone message at the house about a parade rehearsal on Thursday, and oh yeah, they got a gig to play at the Palomino. I told him congratulations.

CHAPTER TWENTY

ayo wasn't a tough guy. The engineers of a recent subdivision had drained a swamp and plowed the landscape into high ground and low ground, transforming the worthless wetland into a neighborhood. The cloned homes sat on hilled plots above streets that curved gently between man-made ponds connected by underground spillways. The floodwater of spring thaw and rains fed into the river instead of basements finished as dens and rec-rooms. We had been snake hunting along the riverbank until we were stopped by the new construction, a concrete and steel framed series of white water rapids. To get around it we had climb the bank and enter that neighborhood past the keep out sign.

Some kids saw us trespassing into their neat world and cut us off before we could exit between the twin brick towers that sat like sentries at each side of the two-lane entrance. A big kid told us we could pass unharmed if we each paid him a buck. We didn't have even one dollar between us so he changed it to each of us had to catch them a frog, pointing to the nearest pond. That meant getting into the cold water among the weeds, but he didn't want a frog, he was just being a stick. I took off running for the road and the big kid came after me but couldn't catch up. The rest took it out on Jayo, herding him toward the pond. Most of the kids were about his size or smaller, a pack of pests. They pushed and poked at him until finally he was standing in enough water to cover his shoes. He couldn't run and he wouldn't fight. He should have thrown a few elbows and kicked at least one of them in the stomach but he started crying, so they let him go. As he walked away looking at the ground they circled him and pretended to cry like babies, not nearly as mean as the kids in town but it hurt worse because they were good rich kids, most of them attending the big new church across the river road, kids who had seen Disneyland, who would get cars for their sixteenth birthday. And we hadn't even seen a snake.

When I saw they weren't coming for me on bicycles or mini-bikes I waited for Jayo. He passed the big kid bent over and breathing too heavily to be a problem. Jayo wasn't crying but his face was that embarrassed puffy. Each step squirted spurts of pond water out little riveted holes in the sides of his shoes. So when I called home collect using Mac and Sam's phone, and my parents told me about the weather, that a cousin had a baby, and that Jayo was on his way to California to find me, I wasn't worried. He could have his van and contraband and I'd work harder and drink less and rent a corner of a room somewhere in town.

I had slept well out of extreme exhaustion from the wild night, the weird morning and long walk back, but Wednesday morning I was more jittery than rested, already thinking of drinking a short cut back to feeling good. Needed another shower and clean clothes but didn't know how to find the house with the pool and cabana, so it was another breakfast at McDonalds with a paper towel sink bath.

Found a parking spot on the boulevard near a trashcan and slid open the side door to clean out the van, getting it ready for the inevitable turnover to Jayo. Trashed the torn paper jump suit but saved the flip-flops, then moved his box of framed antique Latin phrases to get at debris under the driver's seat, and while I was on my knees reaching for cup lids and paper straw wrappers and pop tops somebody asked me what these were. It was a tourist and his wife peering in at the priced items, burdened with cameras and shopping bags but looking for more junk to buy. I told him they were secret words of ancient wisdom. The lady asked if like are they for good luck, so I agreed. They might have been with friends or part of a tour because others soon arrived to begin a jostling contest while picking out a good one for themselves, which brought over random people passing by, none of them wanting to miss out on a one of a kind opportunity. Within an hour I had one hundred and thirty extra dollars cash.

Got my suit out of hock. The pawnshop guy said he was sad to see it go, that it would've looked good in his window. The lady at the typewriter said it was like losing a member of the family, on his side. Asked him if I could sign over my paycheck to the shop but he told me to take it to a liquor store, giving me a good excuse to go there. Nobody was at the register but a tanned blond-haired guy was in an aisle pulling bottles from a carton and lining them along a bottom shelf in perfect rows. He asked me how it was goin' as he shoved the emptied box away and slid a full one next to him, opening the cardboard flaps with a popping sound. He was fast and robotic, singing in a quiet falsetto voice.

I got a quart of beer then waited at the counter with my paycheck, reading a stack of long thin yellow fliers that advertised a month's worth of double features, revived films cleverly matched such as Godzilla paired with The Giant Gila Monster, or a Dean Martin movie teamed with a Jerry Lewis flick after their break-up. The blond guy alerted me he was on his way. I saw the red turban on the stool behind the counter. It was pre-wound and could be donned same as any hat. I stood on my tiptoes and leaned over the counter to see if the foreign guy had fallen out from under it. Blondie came up behind me and asked what I was looking for, stacking the empty cartons in a corner. Told him I was looking for the owner of the turban. He went around to the stool, put on the turban and with his special accent said here I am. It was some kind of extended joke I guessed. Told him I don't get it. He shrugged and gave me change, telling me not to spend it all on one place.

Drank the beer in the parking lot and thought maybe I was doing life wrong, that I should be somebody else. The quart made me thirsty but I didn't want another performance. I remembered passing a saloon on my long walk down from the valley, one I hadn't noticed before, but at that time my money had been in a pants pocket at the top of a tree. The saloon had a vertical sign that promised cocktails and an arrow pointing the way inside so its customers wouldn't enter the Chinese restaurant next door by mistake. Both the sign and the arrow were the red of a wino's nose. It needed exploring. There were unused parking spaces along the curb in front but I didn't want the van to sit out there alone and vulnerable to busy traffic. Turned into an alley past the entrance and parked along a steel fence that enclosed an auto body shop where cars were parked so tightly the doors barely had room to open. They must have employed a very skinny person to squeeze inside when one needed moving.

Threw the pack over my shoulder, a team again, and from a distance the van blended in with the rest of the cars on the other side of the fence, maybe visiting a loved one stuck on the other side. There was inviting laughter from inside the bar. A speaker should have been mounted on the front of the building blasting that sound for people driving past to suck in business. Maybe I would suggest that to Leely for the park entrance. Going in from the brightness of day gave me familiar bar blindness so as my eyes adjusted, waited inside the door. One of the laughers sounded like an old car engine burning oil, and the smell also was a bit oily maybe from guys who breathed auto repair air all day.

The bar itself was short and centered in the room, surrounded by dark carpet and walls painted black. Unable to see the shadowed floor, walking forward felt like floating, so I shuffled my feet in case there were a step up to trip on or a pit for new customers to fall into as a joke. The guys at the bar watched me choo-choo forward as if waiting for a reason to laugh again. The bartender looked like a customer who had been promoted that day and given the previous tender's shiny black shirt. It was at least one size too large. Later learned he had cancer and was shrinking so didn't care about new better fitting clothes.

He was filling shot glasses that sat next to each guy's other drink. Still pouring he reached down blindly and came up with another shot glass and filled that too, only then returning the bottle to an upright position. He set that shot on the corner of the bar near me then held his hand out to show it trembled, asking if I could believe he used to be able to straight-arm a new tire for five minutes. I nodded to be agreeable and he told me it was on the house.

The laughing guys picked up their shots then waited until I stepped up and lifted mine. They toasted Tom and Frank, throwing their heads back to dump the liquor directly into their throats. I imitated them recklessly and almost drowned, my throat muscles refusing to play along. I wanted to say gak but a mouthful of licorice-flavored booze was in the way. Willed myself to swallow and wiped the tears out of the corners of my eyes, not daring to say smooth like in the old joke because it felt about to come back up again. When finally I could speak, in a burnt voice asked who Tom and Frank were. They had invented breast implants.

They used their other drinks as chasers and I croaked for a beer please. Able to see better I looked around. Two glow in the dark velvet paintings decorated the wall opposite the bar, women with pink lipstick, industrial eyelashes and cleavage enough to make me wonder if they were products of Tom and Frank. One of the laughers ordered me to pull up a stool, his blue work shirt advertising the body shop in the alley. I moved a little closer to him and he put his chin against his collarbone as if that made it impossible for the others to hear him as he spoke, asking me if I had ever seen a botched-up boob job. I shook my head no and he scowled in pain at the memory of one, adding no further information.

He looked over to the others to see if he had spoiled the party, but their attention was focused on a fly at the edge of a drop of booze, seeming to be drinking. Body shop guy turned back to me while lifting a beer bottle to his lips. Instead of tipping it back he spoke quietly into the neck that the lady he was seeing now had a breast reduction. His eyes went wide as if worried about speaking heresy, but added thank god, you should've seen those things. Then he drank. He got the little bit of beer that had been mostly foam in the bottom of the bottle, then sucked as if there might be more stuck up in there, his lips getting pulled into the vacuum. He pulled loose with a mousey squeak and clunked the bottle down where the bartender had been standing, but he wasn't behind the bar. Behind us he was straightening one of the portraits.

Auto Body yelled how 'bout some service, telling big shirt that there was nothing wrong with the picture. He confided to me again, this time about the bartender having cancer, but also that the guy never thought any pictures were straight, adjusting them constantly at home and at the hospital. He had been banned from several art galleries.

The fly took flight and was lost in the darkness so the other laugher joined our conversation, saying it began when he caught the cancer, as if cancer is contagious. The bartender was temporarily satisfied with the artwork and crossed back to the bar, ducking and swatting at the fly that buzzed around his head as if wanting another drop of drink. He pulled up a bottle and levered it under an opener attached to the work counter. There was a light crack of bent tin, a quick hiss of spit, then the cap clinked into a can below. He put it in front of Auto Body then raised his eyebrows at me. Told him I'd have the same. Crack, hiss, clink.

I dropped my pack and put one foot on it in a cowboy pose, elbows on the bar, shoulders hunched up near my jawbone. Tipped the bottle of beer to let it flow like a cool mountain stream. The thin line of outside light that spilled in under the front door grew faint. Two guys dressed in dark clothing entered and sat at a little black table that I hadn't noticed. They came in while the bartender was in the bathroom and when he returned didn't notice them because they were perfectly camouflaged.

When he served us another round we all heard them grumble. That startled the bartender, but when he heard specific words of gripe they also offended him so he purposely ignored them. They got up angrily but before they could say anything more the two laughers sang happy birthday. When the song ended the angry guys tried to complain again but the laughers sang another verse. They caught on and politely asked for drinks and everyone smiled, friends.

After carrying my pack to the bathroom several times someone asked what was so valuable that I couldn't take a piss without it. Showed them, and they were excited as if it were full of fake boobs. They talked me into putting it on and I drank my beer through a straw. They laughed themselves onto the floor and ordered me more drinks until it seemed like a brilliant idea to get me out front. If the bar filled up because of me I might never have to pay for another beer. Careful not to step into the street and stop traffic, I walked the curb like a tightrope as drivers played their car horns, the different tones and notes like warring geese. The guys from the bar laughed from inside the doorway because they weren't allowed to take drinks out of the building.

Whether it was simply the sight of me, or the belief that I was trying to cross the street, one driver braked to a burning rubber stop. Traffic in the far lane slowed down too quickly for those in the rear who couldn't see that something unusual was happening. I don't know which car hit which first, but it set off a change reaction of fender benders, each slam and crunch increasing the amount of trouble I was in. Rushed toward the bar to hide but the guys there were jammed three across and three deep, and none wanted to miss the show by backing up to allow me inside.

Drivers were getting out to inspect damage and blame others, and before they traced the original collision to me I ran around to the alley and pulled off the gloves, letting them hang, then pushed the mask behind my head. Undid the suit to reach in and dig out the van key. Driving with gorilla feet was like the first time for drivers-ed in the school parking lot. As I let out the clutch the van lurched and stalled. There were no villagers with torches in the rearview mirror so I took more time and got rolling. The other end of the alley let out on a curved street so I knew I was in the maze at the bottom of the hills. No sirens warned me of being chased but I could hear the guys' laughter in my head.

Weighing one thing against another it had been a good night. Parked at the dark end of a cul de sac in an unlit spot equidistant between two homes and passed out while waiting for sleep.

In the morning went back for my shoes and pack but the bar wasn't open yet. The morning sun made a thousand broken bits of automobile damage twinkle along the street. Had to go to work in my crazy flip-flops, carrying the suit as a rolled-up bundle of fur like a trapper ready to do some trading. I was early and showered until my skin was white and puckered. Because I was alone in the locker room I stood before the mirrored wall with a white towel around my waist, my face and arms Hershey-colored in comparison to the rest. Behind my reflection Exoticus watched from the pvc blower stand, inflated and billowing enough to seem almost alive.

Put on work clothes, shorts and t-shirt, tube socks and deck shoes, then bought crumb cakes and chicken broth from vending machines. A group of other new employees passed on their orientation tour, ticket takers and ride operators. Pretending to stare at my breakfast I secretly searched the female faces for someone to fall in love with, trying to keep my thoughts clean. Followed them at a distance into the park and watched a test run of a corkscrew roller coaster.

Went back to the employees' entrance to punch in at the scheduled starting time. Magazines and the day's newspaper were there for waiting time. A picture of crashed cars in front of the bar made me wait. In the article nobody mentioned a drunk in a gorilla suit, blaming instead an animal or wild man that had wandered down from the hills, displaced by the fires and mudslides. The writer even speculated it might have been a publicity stunt to promote a horror movie that went horribly wrong.

In the next section there was that same advertisement for the park that included Exoticus. I folded the two pages to put the photos side by side, the gorilla and the real-life bumper cars with their ends crunched together in expensive kisses. Fingers mussed the hair on the back of my head and I expected Roy, but it was Sonny. She was always friendly as someone needing money, but it was genuine. As she punched in I showed her the paper and asked if she had seen this, meaning the ad but she took the section with the accident article and asked if I had something to do with it. Told her it was caused by a wild underdeveloped thing to which rules did not yet apply. She confessed to crashing a Volvo while eating a sundae and trying to steer with her knees, but it was okay because those cars were known for their crashability. It would almost be a waste not to have an accident in one.

Half an hour later we were all going through the parade routine again, everyone doing a different version at first but by the first break we were almost in synch. Roy sat limply in a folding chair as if waiting outside an emergency room. The Disneyites were gathered around the cooler of Gatorade talking about Peter Pan's funeral, so I went back to the vending machine on a mission for Roy. I was sweating stale beer and breathing heavily, smog scraping the inside my lungs, each wheeze the sound of measuring out a scoop of dry beans. Leely and Sonny were in the shade of one machine, sweating lightly on their brows and noses like they might've run through a sprinkler instead of dancing for two hours.

As I fed change into the Coke machine Leely pulled on a dry area of my t-shirt sleeve and asked if Roy was feeling better about everything. I guessed he was since he was here, but that didn't mean he wasn't going to have a heart attack if we kept rehearsing. I bought two cans of pop and smiled at Sonny as I passed, inhaling deeply to catch her scent but there was too much fresh asphalt in the air. Leely called out to my back, hoping my costume hadn't been hurt in the accident. Turned around and walked backwards to see them nodding with that I know that you know look, cheeks up under their eyes without really smiling. The unfamiliar rubber heel of the deck shoe caught against the blacktop and I had to turn forward again to keep from falling, using my knuckles on the ground because of the cans in my hands.

Roy pulled the tab off his can and it sprayed my new shoes with soda, but they were already damp from sweat-soaked sweat sox. He sucked the excess from inside the rim then chugged half the can. The little man warned us about drinking carbonated beverages but we both braved the full twelve ounces. Roy asked me how was he going to carry that head and dance. We were going to rehearse the parade route in costume after the break. As if on cue a cart arrived pulling a trailer covered in plastic. The driver parked and unzipped one side to reveal the sea creature staring at us with its lidless cartoon eyes as if it wanted to pick a fight. Roy stared back and muttered an obscenity only I could hear. He tossed his empty can into the garbage without breaking eye contact, suddenly energized by the challenge. As he stood up he sucked in his gut and stuck out his chest.

Two against one wouldn't be fair so I went to get my suit from the locker room. In the park we inched along the route following Leely with the portable tape deck, stopping regularly for costume problems and the fallen. Roy seemed to do better with the head than he had without it. Old strengths are the same as old injuries, he told me, they come back easy. At the end of the course the trailer with zippered sides was waiting to reclaim the costumes with the heads mounted on poles like giant Pez dispensers. It had brought the giant jug of Gatorade and fresh towels for everyone. We wore them around the back of our necks like boxers, slumped on the break area benches like contenders who had gone fifteen rounds but didn't get the decision.

When everyone had checked their boot blisters and shoulders rubbed raw by the weight of the heads, and when our heavy breathing lessened enough to hear her, Leely announced the schedule. Half hour to dress before sets in the park with breaks before the noon parade, break, then sets before the afternoon parade, and another paid half hour to shower and change back into street clothes. Roy would work with the prince and princess. Somewhere an old classmate was picking out his first three-piece suit or pacing a maternity ward, maybe submitting a scientific paper for publication, but I was assigned to work with a pink elephant and purple giraffe.

Other cast members skipped the shower, changing clothes quickly and giving a one size fits all good-bye without waiting for a response.

After another marathon shower and using six towels to dry myself, asked Roy if he thought we could sleep there. He didn't want to spend the night in a locker room, he wanted to get a drink. I didn't want to drive back to Hollywood, so he said that with all the trailer parks in the area there had to be a bar nearby.

I dressed over a clean pair of shorts and t-shirt, then fresh sweat socks and another never been used pair of deck shoes. Left my suit drying on a head post then rolled up a clean towel and carried it out under my arm. There were still hours of light left but the sun had lowered into the dirty zone of bad air over the city, turning it red like Krypton's sun under which Superman lost his power or went crazy or something. Pointed that out to Roy, feeling weaker than usual myself. He pointed to the other side of the sky where a bulging but not full moon was sitting on the horizon like a special effect prop that had been built on the rise of ground behind the oak trees, their leaves hanging down like reddish brown bats as if they knew it was almost Halloween. He said that our power was in the moon.

Roy drove because by some miracle his older legs still worked. Doing Charlie at Grauman's was easier, but he couldn't let us kids see him give up. It was a steady job and the worse thing that could happen was he'd get back in shape or die. Not far down the road was the yellow slashing arrow of an In & Out Burger, almost as magnetic as the red cocktails arrow of the night before. The cars were backed up causing traffic on a road without no other traffic. Roy said the park would do good business if they just caught the overflow from the busy franchise.

On the opposite corner was a bowling alley, Presidential Lanes, set back behind a large weedy parking lot that was waiting patiently for bowling to become popular. The sign was lighted so I said we probably could get a couple beers there. Roy parked near the only car in the lot, a white Triumph. The door of the alley was open and the crashing of wooden pins echoed through an atmosphere of used shoes. A lone bowler rolled the evening away like a background extra, oblivious to whatever dramatic events might occur on the diamond patterned carpet of the entrance way.

There was a barroom to our left and a sign labeling it the Executive Office Lounge, more velvety than presidential, crushed fabric walls and blood colored naugahyde seats bought secondhand from a Las Vegas casino renovated in 1970. Roy slid into a booth, the scene looking like a vintage postcard. A guy in Buddy Holly glasses came in from the lane rental area and asked if we were drinking and bowling or just drinking, clapping his hands together and holding them there while waiting for our answer. I told him we were just drinking. Got it he said and clapped his hands another time, the world's shortest applause. He left the room as I thought about burgers then moments later he appeared behind the bar through a curtain that filled the doorway to another room. One end of the bar began against one wall then curved to meet the adjacent wall with no way to get behind from our side.

We ordered from the booth and he plunked down the drinks on the bar, but instead of doing his disappearing trick again, waited there until I got up to retrieve them. That's the way they built it don't ask my why, he said and exited through the curtain. Roy raised his glass and said from battle to battle you never know how life will attack you next. I thought he was making a toast but he was pointing his glass at the unfinished portrait of George Washington, the same one that decorated my kindergarten classroom. I toasted to revolution and clinked my beer against his glass.

Asked him why the little people would quit Disneyland to work here, or were they also fired? They quit to be actors. After Star Wars there was enough creature and costume work to make a good living, but then came a wave of little people flooding Hollywood. There hadn't been so many small actors since the Wizard of Oz. Then the work ran out. He said the female employees at the park would play both Mickey and Minnie, but the guys never played Minnie. I thought it was because the legs didn't look right but he said no, they didn't want to make Walt's ghost angry.

The clapping guy came into our side of the room to refill our drinks by kneeling on a stool and hanging over the bar, knowing they were reachable from the front, but warned us that it was league night and we'd better drink up before the rush. The rustic sound of the ball against the pins had come about every forty seconds, but before our glasses were half empty the crashing was continuous. People in gala embroidered shirts shuffled into the room, one hand gloved but with the middle fingers bare as if made for Spiderman to trigger his web shooter. A country song suddenly blasted from an unseen jukebox as a female bartender with tortured hair appeared theatrically through the curtained doorway behind the bar. The bowlers shouted her name Dixie, and she knew all their names and drinks. Soon the bowlers were so deep at the bar that people had their butts hovering over our table, the brand of jeans easier to read than the name of their teams across the backs of the shiny shirts. We excused our way past the hind ends of the Spare Me's and the Wild Turkeys, leaving the Executive Office Lounge and entering the main space full of Gutter Snipes and Sweet Rolls and Strike Force team members, even the mysterious XOX'ers.

At the end of every over-waxed hardwood floored lane the pins tumbled like frozen penguins in an earthquake, violent expressions on the hurlers' faces after their flip of the wrist roll of the ball, some finishing in a statue moment as if waiting for a modern Michelangelo to ask them to pose for their own trophy. Roy said he had been on a team at The Lanes on Crenshaw just so he could tell people he played the Hollywood Bowl. He went up to a guy doubled over in a plastic lunchroom chair lacing his orange and gray saddle shoes, asking the guy if there was another bar around here. The guy finished his chore then sat up and exhaled, unable to breathe while bent over. After taking a fresh suck of stale air he asked rhetorically, well what about The Aces out on Villanueva past the plant? Roy echoed him saying the plant. Yeah you know the plant, the guy said reassuring himself. Okay thanks. We went out against the incoming tide of shimmering pastel shirts boasting of being Pick Me Ups, Fast Laners and Lynch Pins.

CHAPTER TWENTY-ONE

The wooden screen to my bedroom window was held in place by two metal doohickies that turned on a simple nail driven into the window frame. I could remove it from inside by sliding it up past those stays then pull it diagonally into my room. One summer night I snuck out to creep around the neighborhood, curious about what went on after dark, why I had to be home and safely inside. There were no burglars in black lone ranger masks peeking into windows or trying to find one mistakenly unlocked door, no wild animals roaming the yards or gangsters leaning against the light pole on the corner, all the things I expected. Even the big kids were home watching tv. What I saw was the full moon through a gap between broadleaf maple trees. I had seen pictures but we never had met face to face. It was better in real life and made me understand a stupid poem we had to memorize in third grade.

Later that summer I told a buddy about sneaking out and we agreed to meet at that spot because I wanted to show him the big fat moon. He never made it, getting caught trying to go out the back door, but neither did the moon. I couldn't understand, expecting it would be in the same place every night the way the sun was high in the sky everyday at noon. That was the first time I felt the pain and fear of not knowing, and everyday after there was something else I discovered I didn't know.

When we exited the bowling alley the moon had risen above shoulder height into the night sky, smaller but still chubby. The lone bowler was sitting in his little sports car now drowning in a sea of vehicles. His head was back with eyes closed listening to a lady singing opera. The guy was probably replaying his game, the soundtrack elevating his mistakes out of the gutter. As Roy opened the wagon door he asked the guy how to get to Villanueva and The Aces out by the plant. The guy sat up and looked around, re-adjusting to reality and saying the plant. Roy said yeah, you know, the plant.

Opera bowler started up his toy car, its go-cart engine threatening the world the way a tiny dog barks at anything. He told Roy to follow him, letting out the clutch to steer backwards and almost sideways out of his space, disappearing between the rows of taller cars. Roy had to back up then make a three-point turn to get after him, unable to see the sportster. We heard it getting more distant, buzzing now like one of those flying model airplanes on a leash, then reappearing out on the road. Roy got impatient trying to find the driveway and drove across a shallow grass ditch to get to there, both of us leaving our seats on the bounce. A new rattle came from under the wagon and didn't go away as we caught up with the kiddy car. Asked him what do you think that sound is. About a hundred dollars give or take.

Miles of pipes of many sizes curving and connecting rows of circular holding tanks must have been the plant. The array shone from hundreds of lights strung along every part, making acres around it glow as if the desert were radioactive. It reminded me of a movie about miners on a moon of Jupiter. Watching it was the first time I thought not only of leaving home and getting out of town, but maybe getting off the planet to fight giant spider rats with bat wings. The Aces was definitely outward bound in that direction. It was built of cinderblocks in the middle of bumpy brown dirt not glowing but still maybe radioactive. The parking area was unpaved and limited only by where the farthest car might park among those same low alien-looking plants I had parked near my first night seeing Los Angeles.

Hadn't known then there might be something giant and dangerous all about the place.

The bowler parked directly before the double door entrance as if waiting for us to swing them open so he could drive inside. He listened to another snatch from the soprano then hopped out over the side, telling us that he wasn't a big fan or anything, it was just that he couldn't hear the tape as he drove and was eager for the whole mess to end so he could say he had listened to it, a gift from a friend. His bowling bag sat in the other seat, a tubby ochre passenger settled into maroon upholstery. I asked wasn't he worried somebody might steal his ball, and he said they could have it, that it was cursed. Roy stepped ahead and opened the door on the right, pulling the sour smoky air of the bar around us like decompression chamber event, a stage to prepare for the toxic atmosphere inside.

The bartender stood still at the empty bar, staring at three young customers around one of four tables in the room. They chattered in voices too high to be regulars in any saloon. Roy and the bowler went to the seats directly in front of the bartender in case he wasn't able to move, and even if he were mobile those seats would eliminate any time wasted by unnecessary distant drink fetching. Scanned the cinder block box for any irregularity that would indicate a bathroom. The jukebox and long shuffleboard table had been placed in positions to detract attention away from a dark corner walled off by life-size Lincoln logs, and on the shadowed wall was a sign with geometric images of a man and woman with cowboy hats added later using magic marker. I walked over trying not to step in time with the beat of the cowboy song playing, but it was difficult and I probably looked silly anyway.

The bathroom was clean and smelled like an indoor pool. The toilet water was blue and I turned it green. The toilet paper roll was so new there was no start sheet hanging loose. I had to rip the paper across and ended up with several layers of unwind that clogged the toiled when I flushed, but there was a plunger sitting ready and I plunged the wad down before much water overflowed. The paper towel dispenser had been filled recently, stuffed so tight I couldn't pull a sheet loose without ripping little bits off. After putting enough torn pieces of towel into the puddle I gathered up the wet mess and dropped it in the tiny wastebasket, mashing it down with my foot and getting it stuck. Had to sit on the toilet seat to use my other foot to pry it loose. The floor had become patterned with my dusty footprints made muddy so the paper couldn't wipe them clean, just smeared them into swirls. Gave up when there was no more room in the overflowing basket. Didn't wash my hands for fear of something else going wrong.

On my way back to the bar something was flapping around my feet so had to stop and pull a piece of wet paper towel off the bottom of my shoe, stuffing it into my back pocket. Roy and the bartender were both staring at the chatty table where the bowler had moved. Artists, the bartender informed me, motioning towards them with my bottle of beer before he set it down, adding that there was an art school over the hill. The kids had discovered the bar so recently that they were assumed an invasive species requiring watching. All wore t-shirts with different designs across the chest, maybe created as an assignment in t-shirt design class. Two had partial beards and mustaches that required talented attention with scissors and razor. All had intentionally messed their hair to give them the wet feathered look on a baby chick's head.

As if just remembering we had come in with the bowler he stepped back to get a better look at us. He seemed to be viewing a painting, wondering if it might be a forgery. He asked what we did and Roy told him we worked at the new roller coaster park. The bartender thought it over and decided that was good enough. He put out his hand and said to call him Ace. As I shook it he leaned in and confessed it wasn't his real name, but it was easy for the customers to remember, then bragged about his clean john. Most bar bathrooms were literally shit holes. Customers who cared about drinking from a clean mug could be just as particular about where they pissed it back out. I nodded but turned away so he wouldn't see my cheeks turn red, drinking my beer while he announced to Roy that he owned a motorcycle, a guitar and a horse all the same two colors of white and brown. He seemed unable to stop talking and we suspected the bowler and his artsy friends knew the hazard for sitting at the bar.

A worry about having a hangover for work the next day rose in my mind, but the alcohol kicked in and convinced me that more was not only harmless but necessary, making it a pleasure to do nothing but stare at the lights of the jukebox while mechanically picking Spanish peanuts out of a wooden bowl, choosing only those still covered with their thin papery brown husk which I removed before eating, assured that the nut itself had not been touched by others' fingers. I ate no pretzel sticks for that reason.

As a reward for listening without complaint or inventing a cheap excuse to move to a table, Ace poured us two shots of something flammable and touched his lighter to the surface of each while suggesting that we drink them quickly. In the mood for a dare I tossed mine into my mouth sloppily, trusting that it was done regularly and that the fire was for show. I could see blue flame near my eyes as I swallowed, more pain from the liquor in my throat than the slight heat on my lips and chin where I had dribbled. As I rubbed away the burn Roy slammed an open palm down on top of his, extinguishing the flame. He quietly mentioned that I was supposed to put it out first. He sucked his down, ah'ed, then shook his head and laughed.

Enough time passed that some league bowlers came in, a mix of different teams but all sitting at two tables pulled together, their shirts clashing. Two were women, Donna and Deirdre according to the names stitched above their left breasts. Roy said dear dear Deirdre. After serving them, Ace whispered behind us to watch her work. She used a cocktail stir-straw to sample others' drinks, sucking the alcohol from the bottom where it settled, heavier than the carbonated mixers. It took her only fifteen minutes to get drunk. She ordered a rum and coke for herself but Ace left out most of the coke in hope of something we all could imagine.

Roy asked if I knew how to play shuffleboard, the table conveniently behind her chair. He led me over to the long game with its shiny hardwood surface like a miniature bowling-lane except it was sprinkled with sawdust. With one eye on the ladies he lifted a silver puck and moved it forward and backward on the table top, getting a weighted feel for the proper speed, then whisked it down the table hard enough to fly off the end of the gaming surface and bang into the backstop where I leaned against it with my belly. I reflexively jumped back and my butt bumped into Deirdre's chair. I apologized with a whoops but she hadn't spilled her drink so she didn't mind. I glared at Roy who got big eyed and waggled his body in a confusing display of victory over my making contact with her.

I returned to the bar as Roy slid the rest of the pucks more carefully, hoping his talent would get Deirdre's attention. I reached for more nuts but the bowl was empty and Ace was gone. Finished my beer and watched the jukebox. Ace came from the bathroom swearing and accusing the artsy farts of messing up his bathroom. I shook my head in sympathetic disgust. Deirdre yelled out for Irving to bring another round. He flinched as if she had thrown something at him, telling her to call him Ace or he would put a measurable amount of coke in her next drink.

Roy switched to the other end of the table to play back, explaining the rules and motioning me over to play a game with his eyes on Deirdre. Tiredly I slid a puck into one of his then asked if he were ready to go. With both hands he slid rest of them in a widening display of game over and told me yeah, let's get out of here. Deirdre's preference for bowling over shuffleboard was a disappointment to him, and outside under the high partial moon he confessed that he was going out as Charlie the next day, that they couldn't stop him. I told him they could fire him, but he said Leely wouldn't do that as long as he wore the other costume in the parade.

We could smell the burgers at the In & Out but the drive through line was longer now. Roy's shirt pocket was bulging with peanuts from the bar so he shared them with me. I was too tired to care about whose fingers had touched them. He parked next to the van and we got out on each side of the wagon. He said g'night as he walked wearily to the back, and I answered g'night as I opened the sliding door. The slam of my door was followed by the slam of the tailgate. Used the fresh towel as a pillow then as a blanket, and dreamt of being late for school while searching my old room for a clean pair of pants.

In the morning I couldn't move my legs, revenge of the rehearsals. Had to pick them up like prosthetic limbs and throw them over the side of the mattress. Waiting for blood to feed the muscles I rubbed the memory of another night of drinking out of my eyes. The need to pee got me on my feet, wobbling like a rusted tin man. Had no choice but to go in a can again. Walked like a monster for a few short steps in what room there was, then finally got them to bend enough for me to step down outside. A couple slow motion laps around the van gave me hope of being able to work later.

Knocked on the window of the wagon and heard Roy make a dying sound. Gave him a couple minutes to come back to life while I walked the can of pee to the edge of the lot and poured it under some kind of evergreen, stomping the can flat and burying it under the wood chips used for mulch. After bothering Roy again he kicked at the inside of the window and promised to kill me, but he was a master of recovery, flipping a switch in his head and forcing himself into the day. Minutes later we were able to hobble toward the gate with hot showers and vending machine breakfast as incentive.

Under the rejuvenating rush of hot water Roy seemed to sleep again, his forehead against the tile wall, but instead of snoring he spoke. There was an old guy who was a regular at Roscoe's Bar, both the guy and Roscoe long gone. He sputtered through the stream down his face, the words under water. So this guy worked for a studio in the story department finding books that would make good movies, option the property and maybe lure the author out to write a draft. Roy's voice was an oracle from a wet cave sharing a secret, telling me that Bill Fields was big reader and the guy would deliver him boxes full because Bill wouldn't drink if he had a good book. I asked who Bill was and Roy peeked around the edge of the shower to look at me drying myself, his expression asking if I might be drunk. W.C. Fields he said. That's what I thought, I told him, just that I never thought anybody might call him Bill like a regular person. So this guy lugs a liquor carton full of novels up to Los Feliz but Bill already had been in the bottle that day and wanted company more than a book. Fields told the guy he was crushed that his wife didn't think he was funny. They had been separated for years by then. She married him because he was successful, but never laughed. He worked hard on every movie to win her back by making her happy, get her to laugh.

Roy came out of the shower but didn't dry himself, just let the water shed and puddle the outdoor carpeting, telling me he knew how that felt. He couldn't make his wife laugh, not anymore. It was worse than being a lousy lover he said, the confession making him nakeder than naked. When he watched Bill on the late show he saw a man working not for laughs but for love. That's why he was going out as Chaplin, for love. I saw his Chaplin clothes waiting patiently in the open locker as Roy dried himself, but instead he grudgingly got into his McNessie suit.

It was always hot inside the costume but with kids pulling and hugging, the heat had its own weight and it seemed I carried the extra pounds of a real gorilla. Opening day was a success and there was a constant mob around me, its members changing every few minutes. When some parents told their children not to hurt the monkey it had the opposite effect, becoming a competition to see who could hit the hardest while others kicked me on my blind sides.

The giraffe and elephant knew how to work together for their own safety, finding a small space in the shade where the park guests could only get at them from one direction, tucked out of view from people passing on their way to the big ride. I was stranded in the sunlight, seen from far away so the kids came running ahead of the parents, which allowed them time to pull at my arms and climb my legs until mom and dad caught up to put the word hurt in their heads. Only the endless demands for us to stand still for a picture saved me a continuous beating, every parent carrying a camera as if without a photograph of it, the event never happened.

The other characters tapped out a signal with their feet. Beneath the fur of their paws were work boots, the soles trimmed with crescents of steel at the heel and toe for that purpose. It meant nothing until I was left alone with thousands, when I easily broke the Disneyland mystery code. It was break time. Had to bully my way through, ignoring hundreds of requests in several languages, demands and desperate begging for just one more picture. Some had figured out my exit route and gathered at the baffled wall that was the employees' secret escape. It was white and reflected the sun, intensifying the heat at that spot, and the crush of bodies made it impossible to catch the breeze. I was stewed in my own sweat, my mouth working like a fish's in the bottom of the boat as I tried to swallow oxygen. There were probably dozens of photographs taken of smiling kids and the passed out gorilla before a ride operator coming on shift dragged me to the break area, possibly saving my life.

Soon after I finished making the costume back in Ravinia, decided to be a gorilla for one day. Made a bowl of cereal and used a long handled spoon meant for tall glasses of iced tea to reach my real mouth. Tried to ride my bike but the crotch was too low and the bottom of the legs pulled away from the feet, exposing my human ankles. Exhausted from less than an hour of motion, sat with my feet on the coffee table and watched a cartoon on tv. Before it ended I was breathing heavily and feeling dizzy so I pulled the mask off in surrender before I passed out on the couch. Crazy is never as much fun as it sounds.

When I woke up in the Laugh Land break area somebody had removed my mask and Sonny was dabbing my face with a wet blue bandana. Had a momentary thought that now she knew my real identity until I remembered it wasn't a secret. Embarrassed I sat up too quickly and needed to lie back down, but waved her away, not wanting to be treated like a kid. She asked if somebody had hit me and I shouted no, that I felt fine. Sat up slowly and told those gathered around in a mix of boredom and curiosity that I often took quick naps in costume.

The water fountain towered over me like an Empire State Building and I began climbing up the side. It didn't take all of the break time remaining. It wasn't beer but it was the next best thing. Pulled my gloves loose and pressed the magic button. The steady spurt of water probably was enough for ticket takers in short shirt sleeves, but the pee-sized trickle barely covered my tongue so I collapsed on it in a vampire move and sucked until I saw one of the Disney guys slowly lift the long giraffe headpiece onto his shoulders. He had spent the entire break bunked out full length on one of the benches and seemed angry already at what wasn't even a full time job. It made me feel better. While my heartbeat still showed in my temples, he and the elephant did a death march toward the park entrance. I dragged myself after them and got in step, pulling my hands and mask back on.

The crowd had dispersed but like a few angry bees, the buzz of those who were lucky enough to witness our appearance stirred up another swarm. This set we were scheduled in a farther section of park and my coworkers sped for it like football players running through a determined defensive opposition. We traveled so quickly I barely could keep my eyes on the low-neck tops of young mothers. By the time I caught up they had backed themselves against a low fence where only a few guests could reach them at any one time. Trying to make wheezing part of the character I signed some autograph books, a few park maps and one forearm. At the sound of tapping I left in mid-pose as a dad too slow on the shutter button finally clicked a photo, capturing a blurry photo of what might have been a Bigfoot passing his kid, but just as easily an out of focus shrub.

I arrived in the break area one long moment behind the other guys but already they were neatly undone and lounging against their costumes as if just awakening from a nap. The giraffe asked what took me so long. Sweat squished between my toes with each step, producing an electrical tingle up my spine that made me grit my teeth, which was odd because my back felt as if several vertebrae had been removed during the pulling and posing and signing autographs with furry fingers in a hunched over posture. Something was sprained between my shoulder blades or maybe I had been stabbed with one of the oversized pencils with the MacLaughlin logo.

Leely stopped by to see if we had major injuries, commented on the redness of my face and told us to get lunch at the rehearsal hall. Removed my costume so it might dry out before the parade while realizing this was it, my job in show business. It was probably harder work than making burgers, and unimportant compared to joining the Peace Corps, but the families loved my gorilla.

As we approached the hangar-size doors Roy came from the other direction carrying that huge serpent head across his shoulder like a lumberjack coming in from the woods holding his beloved axe. He looked strong and happy. Maybe he'd been drinking. Because I hadn't spoken all day didn't realize I had lost my voice until I tried to say hello. The stress from straining my neck on the lookout for young terrors, and grunting yes's and no's to questions had ruined my throat. He must've read my lips, at least for the word tramp. You want to know when I'm going to change into Charlie, right? I nodded as he lowered the head onto one of the extra tall stands that were for the serpent and the giraffe. He's coming, when you least expect him, besides I'm having a ball with this stupid thing. Nobody knows what the hell it's supposed to be so I just wander around and sneak up on the tourists, scaring the crap out of everybody.

He turned as Sonny and her prince caught up behind him and he yelled hey here they are, automatically giving her a hug like sudden family. I wanted to slap him away from her. Though I hadn't become the third musketeer, it felt a little like the Disney guys and I had survived a battle together. The prince stared without expression but he was simply tired of smiling. He pulled out a make up compact and I believed he was going to powder his nose, but he moved the mirror around his face checking for damage from several angles, then snapped it closed with one hand and slipped it in a holding place at the small of his back.

Over a build-it-yourself sandwich from the deli spread out for lunch, Roy told me that the prince had been bachelor number three on The Dating Game. He was chosen over bachelors one and two by an ex-cheerleader from Wisconsin whose ambition was to act but currently was employed in the cosmetics department of The May Company. They won an all expenses paid weekend on Catalina Island but because he had done the show only to get a video on himself, offered to sell his half of the package to the girl to take someone else. She wouldn't sell and went on the trip with her co-worker from the next counter who sold a rival brand of war paint.

Roy laughed at his own telling and was in such a good mood I wondered again if he had a bottle hidden in the costume, but he confessed the park guests were the best audience he ever had, and the big head was perfect for shtick. The sight of the top-heavy creature doing a simple time step brought instant applause. The elephant and giraffe hefted the serpent head, comparing its weight to their own. Roy proudly told them to get their sweaty hands off his head.

A marching band arrived wearing tartan uniforms, our musical accompaniment that would lead the parade. They honked and tooted like strange water fowl, getting in tune or maybe nervous. All they had to do was march in time as they played but they were young, probably a local high school that had won a regional title but weren't ready for show business. Behind them was a used pirate ship float to fill out the parade and beyond that a small fleet of odd carts and construction equipment customized to work on the rides, anything that rolled on wheels.

Almost asleep by start time, forced myself awake and back into the damp gorilla, which smelled too much like the unwashed me. Park loudspeakers welcomed the guests to the historic opening and announced the inaugural parade of MacLaughlin stars. Roy's character got top billing and he didn't miss the fact, looking as if he might cry until he saw me watching so rolled his eyes in self-mockery. Stepping out to the music made me wish I had practiced the routine during lunch, but the crowd didn't know or care what steps we did, and dancing down the open lane was easier than fighting kids. About halfway through the park the toe sweat squishing got louder than the band, but I stayed in step wet as it was. Scanning the panorama of happy faces gave me a burst of energy and I felt good, comfortably in the world. Suddenly Jayo was standing in front of me.

To anybody else he was just another coaster nut wanting an autograph, but he put his face close to my mask to make certain I saw his raging bloodshot eyes that were like two promises of violence, one a little wonky. In a squeaky voice that was too tight with anger to be the manly threatening noise intended, he informed me of how many days he had spent on a fumy bus without real sleep. He waved a torn scrap of paper where I could see it, the park advertisement with my picture in it. Tired again, too weak to dance around him I shuffled forward hoping he wouldn't be willing to walk backwards for the remainder of the parade.

With lack of patience oozing from his pores he grabbed me by the fur and in the same tone but an octave higher he asked me where was his van. I gave my legs a break and sat down, which broke his grip on me so he began pulling at my mask. I hugged my head as the other characters performed a turning step in the choreography and saw me being attacked by a crazed hippie. I had been silent hoping Jayo might doubt that I was inside the costume but when I saw the elephant and giraffe charging, told him he might want to take a look behind. He didn't have time to process my advice because they hit him at the same time, knocking me onto my back as he hit the pavement behind my head.

He was scraped and stunned but got to his feet not knowing if the cheers and applause were for him being taken down, or for getting back up. Roy's unit had caught up with us, and Jayo stood unsteadily in front of the giant. I could read the giant's thoughts. He was afraid this psycho was going to try and climb him, but Jayo didn't know that and stumbled to the side before he got trampled, but directly into the path of the even taller serpent. Roy bent over and charged using the head as a battering ram. He ran blind and only clipped Jayo on the shoulder, but knocked him spinning back into the gallery of parade watchers. Some oohed, some laughed and he got an echo of applause nothing near as loud as the first ovation. We hustled to catch up with the parade, not bothering with the routine.

Finally it was over and we collapsed as a group in that first break area, reviving one at a time for a turn at the drinking fountain until a maintenance worker drove up with the big dispenser of Gatorade on ice. We regained control of our limbs and stood at the back of the cart like office workers around the water cooler. In a wheezy voice Roy asked me who that guy was. Old friend I said, then thanked him and the two Disney guys. No problem, Ex. A pleasure, Exo. I had been accepted.

CHAPTER TWENTY-TWO

ecurity was spread throughout the park looking mostly for kids getting high before riding the coasters, but none guarded the characters so Jayo was able to stake out the location where we had disappeared into the scenery. He was waiting when we reappeared. We were to travel to a different location in the park and the other guys set the pace again, jogging ahead. When they were safely away he approached me carefully this time, apologetic. All he wanted was the van. Told him it was in the parking lot though his mom didn't agree that it belonged to him. He left and I assumed he had a spare key. I was relieved, homeless and stranded, but happier than I had been in a long time.

We finished the last two sets and during the break I told the guys parts of the story of driving out and living in Jayo's van, and we became friends, working together like a small pack of vulnerable animals to survive the endless herd of dangerous humans roaming the park. Instead of rushing home as the giant and prince did, they hung around the locker room and laughed as I took a shower still wearing the suit to wash out sweat, stink and anything beyond my imagination. Roy was quiet as he showered then toweled-off and dressed, maybe feeling left out or simply tired and content. Leely brought a message for me from the office, that I was supposed to meet someone at the front gate. Thought it would be Jayo but a man and woman were waiting in matching sunglasses, the lady with a leather organizer against her chest. They looked like detectives and I feared they were there to cuff me either for causing the accident the other night or for having a van full of drugs and money.

Before I put my hands up in surrender the woman opened her cowhide notebook, removed a card and handed to me. The guy saved me the trouble of reading it by telling me they were talent agents and wanted to represent me, me in the gorilla suit or maybe me and the gorilla suit, sitcoms and commercials. They asked me please to call them soon and we'd take a meeting, then left without a word back from me. Maybe that was how things were done out here, no words wasted.

And then there came Jayo again. He was stuck outside the entrance, more angry than when he interrupted the parade. In his hurry to find the van he hadn't got his hand stamped to get back into the park, refusing to pay for another admission. He called me a liar, screaming that the van wasn't in the lot. The ticket takers threw worried looks at each other as I calmly told Jayo that the van was in the employees' lot behind the park, pointing the only direction he couldn't go. He had the surprised look of a nocturnal animal caught on a back porch when the owner came home, then ran sideways looking back over his shoulder until I was out of sight, maybe thinking I might rush there ahead of him. I stood still wondering if I ever really knew the guy.

Back at the locker room I showed Roy the card. He looked at both sides and said it was the real thing, cursing at himself for not doing the tramp that day then left without another word. By the time I did punch-out at the time clock both Roy's wagon and the security guard were gone. One of the ticket takers had notified in-park security about the suspicious person racing around the perimeter. They radioed the guard in back and in moments he saw the suspect running up and down the aisles, jumping up to look over the many rows of vehicles in hope of spotting his fairly rare van, but there were several similar and at the top of his jump he saw a wrong one and zigzagged between cars, bouncing off some of them and causing minor damage.

The job of the security guard back there was to check our identification on the way in and to keep us from exiting with a roller coaster hidden on our person. He didn't chase down Jayo as much as intercept him, and even then all he did was stick out an arm to block the way, catching Jayo in the throat as if playing dirty in a game of red rover. That didn't stop Jayo, but he gurgled as he got up and ran. The guard wore his arm in a sling for several days.

To save him more grief and prevent more injury either to people or things, I called out to Jayo and pointed him in the proper direction. He still attempted to run but now was slower than most walks. He pulled at the door but it was locked and I realized he didn't have a key. While digging in my pocket to give his back to him, he desperately elbowed the vent window, busting through the wire and tape of my repair to reach in and unlock the driver side door. With no key to start and drive it, and still in his weird breathless panic he decided his stash was the important thing. Not having time to unzip the troublesome zippers on the cushion or mattress he grabbed them and fled before any other badges arrived, the mattress dragging like an anchor.

The recently returned guard in the booth wedged the phone between his ear and shoulder and used his good arm to call the town police. Ten minutes later they found Jayo hiding under the entrance sign behind a row of shrubs, unable to cross the busy traffic arriving for nighttime thrill rides and fireworks. He could run no more and had not learned the power to stop moving cars by stepping off the curb. He might have been brought back to park security for a trespass warning except for the package of pot peeking from his waistband, too large to hide in the small space of his crotch. The mattress had been shoved under a car that also was too small to hide it. It had not been unzipped and an officer brought that to the security guard who allowed me to reclaim it, more worried about his sprain than would-be cushion scams.

Lied in the van with all the windows open, half-waiting for the return of Jayo, afraid to drive away in it in case he told the cops it was stolen. Fell asleep listening to the radio and woke up in the middle of a windy night, a snake of cold crawling over my still sweaty clothes, giving me a snotty nose and a shiver as if I caught a cold. Tried to start the engine to run the heater but the battery was dead. Without my suit for a blanket I put on a layer of dirty clothes over my work shirt and shorts and listened to a single distant cricket having trouble getting its chirp up to speed in the change of weather.

Because the cops had not returned for me or the van I assumed Jayo didn't want them knowing about the cash. With cold stiff fingers I had the same trouble Jayo did with the zipper but having more time worked it open and dug out the brick of bills, stuffed them down my pants in tribute and went to punch in. The empty locker room was empty of Roy but there was a cardboard box of combination locks available, their combinations written on a piece of tape across the back, so wrapped the bills in a small towel and locked them in my locker. Washed my jeans and old shirt under the hot shower while singing the numbers of the combination over and over in my mind to remember them like lyrics, then flushed the piece of tape down the toilet with the mess of my morning meditation.

I put the wet clothes on a blower next to Exoticus who was clean and dry, looking fresh as a mail order monkey, the advertised one I failed to buy. On our way out the Disney guys came in and called me a vulgar name as a good morning, their way of showing me we were still friends. Had a Coke and candy bar for breakfast, but they still weren't ready when it was time to go out into the park, a Disneyland tradition I was told, so I went out alone. The attendance was light for Halloween at noon, most guests planning on visiting near dark. There were posters made from the photo used in the paper, our characters' names overlaid so some people called me Exoticus, some called me King Kong. One set of parents claimed to their kids that they had already seen me on television many times.

Sonny, the Prince and the Giant passed and I waved them over, asking quietly in her ear where was Roy? She told me he hadn't shown up. Wondered aloud if maybe he was sleeping it off in the parking lot but she didn't understand, not knowing we were drunks living out of our vehicles. They moved off toward their scheduled place deeper in the park and most of the guests followed them like baby ducklings. There was a larger crowd over by the entrance and I moved into a shadow before they saw me, but the group had their backs to me. Curious I snuck closer then stood on a bench to see what held them together. Charlie Chaplin.

Backstage the Disney guys were setting their heads on the stands. They reclaimed the benches as beds so I sat on a cardboard box of vendors' merchandise, watching Leely slog toward us wearing the serpent costume, its legs bunched up at her ankles and lugging the head on her bent back like a refugee. She let it fall to the ground, too unhappy about the situation to care. In a threatening tone she asked me where was my friend? I pointed toward the park and told her he was working. She understood and borrowed a walkie-talkie from some kind of manager guy passing through and requested someone on the other end to page Charlie Chaplin inside the park and ask him to exit at the parade start area.

She looked at me as we waited as if I were to blame. We heard laughter from over the wall. It came closer as he reached the break area, balancing groans of disappointment as he left them to step lightly into our view though there was some applause. Leely used both hands to pull off his derby and mustache and it worked like kryptonite. Roy seemed to gain ten years and twenty pounds, slapping his hand over his upper lip in pain, and for some reason calling us whores.

Leely put the hairpiece in the hat and handed them back to him. She untied her boots then unzipped the costume body and let it fall in a pile around her, telling Roy he could do what he was hired to do or sleep in his car days too. She stepped out from inside the bunched up serpent, but before she could leave victoriously he told her she didn't mind his being Chaplin in bed. She opened her mouth but had nothing to say and I wondered if instead flames might shoot out. Roy threw his derby at the serpent head and asked if she wanted him to show up tonight in that one now. Do whatever you want she sighed and he said all right, all right he'd wear it. Hadn't he been wearing it?

I had drifted away, suddenly fascinated by anything else until I heard the giant ask if he could play MacNessie. The Princess unit had returned from their set and heard only Roy's last words. I turned back with new interest. We heard that he had not found the courage to speak to any park guests so he had become known as the silent giant.

She took advantage of the shift of attention and acted as if Roy not only hadn't said what he said, but didn't exist. She pulled the velcroed serpent feet off her boots and tossed them to the giant, and then she removed two big safety pins from the shoulders of the costume where they worked as a temporary hem for the too-large suit, shortening it by seven inches. The giant removed his tunic and tossed it away like a big rag. He wrapped the serpent feet around his boots and put on the body, having to slump his shoulders and stoop over slightly to get the bottom of the scaly legs to reach the top of the webbed clawed feet. Then he lifted the head and disappeared inside it as if going back into the warmth and safety of a womb.

Roy had snuck up behind me and whispered that we might be witnessing the birth of a new era for Laugh Land, thank god. The giraffe guy put his head on to see which character was taller. The serpent now towered above the giraffe. Because he was now hidden, the giant became bold and reckless, manically working the suit as if it were filled with acrobatic monkeys rather than a slow and clumsy ex-wallflower. As we watched his improvised performance Leely punched Roy in the side of his gut and told him he could be the tramp until somebody sued.

The rest of the day passed easily. High thin clouds dimmed the glare and heat of the sun. After the parade the park became filled with guests celebrating the day in costume and we were no longer a novelty. The guys signaled that we were finished and most of our last set was spent traveling back toward the locker room break area with only several stops for families, literally a walk in the park. Because enough photographs had been taken there no longer was competition for attention, the mob mentality evolving into something more humane. The kids stopped beating on me, so instead of following the guys off set I lingered an extra five minutes to allow everybody to shake a hand or hug a costume or take a final picture. Work was over and I had the party at Mac and Sam's.

Gave the suit a piggyback ride to the locker room where only the giant remained. With his new identity as the creature he was still excited from the afternoon and finally needed to talk, finding the courage to pepper me with short sentences, long pauses between them as he struggled to compose something new. Cool job, right? The kids are a riot. The park smells new. Are you coming back for Christmas?

I had been nodding and answering yeah as I removed my regular clothes from the drier stumps and hung the suit there to dry out a little, but the last question stopped me. Turning to tell him that I wasn't sure put my face level with his chest and almost into it. With his careful way of moving he had snuck up on me in silence. He put out his giant hand and said that it was nice to meet me as if it were his first chance after all these days. I put the clothes in my left hand to shake his, watching it disappear inside what could pass as a baseball outfielder's mitt. I looked up to smile at his chin bone then back at his hand, slightly worried mine might not reappear from within his grasp.

While in the shower I thought to invite him to Mac & Sam's, both to be friendly and because it would be fun to show him off, but when I came out he was gone. The locker room seemed twice as big without him. As I dressed in my blown dried clean clothes, sang back the combination number for the lock to get the money, putting it still wrapped in the towel into my pack with the damp suit.

Planned on asking the security guard for help getting a jumpstart for the van but Sonny was waiting at the time clock. She had my time card so knew I hadn't punched out. She said she was beginning to

wonder if I was going to spend the night in the locker room. The idea
that she for whatever reason had been waiting for me caused me to
sweat again as if in costume. Said she saw my card un-punched out and
thought we could walk out together, but that had been twenty minutes
ago. The only words I could find were those I had prepared for the
security guard so I blurted that my battery was dead, could she give me
a jump? She shrugged sure, so I said do you have jumper cables. She said
sure again, proving I was an idiot.

We walked under the buzz of parking lot lights that created
a perpetual dusk only a shade brighter than the evening sky above,
stopping at a yellow Volvo that was scarred along the driver's side.
She opened the door that didn't want to open, having to force it past a
creaky sticking point after which it swung freely out of her hand to hang
open far wider than originally designed, then it sagged as if coming
off its hinges and I stepped back to protect my toes. We watched it for
further motion but it was done scaring me. Sonny let her big bag slip off
her shoulder and threw it across to the passenger seat with a clank, then
rubbed her hand along the largest scar, which was filling with rust at
its deepest part. Said that she got an insurance check to get it fixed but
seeing the damage reminded her to drive carefully, and she was using
the money for rent.

In the back of the car besides a spare tire and an extra spare, there
was a unused car battery, two cans of fix-a-flat, a fan belt still in its
cardboard sleeve, a tube of emergency radiator repair, a box of spark
plugs, three cans of oil, an army surplus two-way radio, and a set of
jumper cables. I asked if her dad owned a gas station.

She told me about her car breaking down near a place called Oxnard
where she accepted a ride from a young executive-type in a steel-colored
Porsche. He drove her against her will to meet his mother in Bakersfield
until she escaped at a Sinclair gas station amid acres of nut trees where
she paid a Mexican field worker ten dollars for a ride to the bus station.
She wasn't afraid of him because he sat on a flat wooden box to see over
the steering wheel and had a friendly small dog she could threaten to

throw out the window if he tried anything crazy like the other guy. She stopped eating candy bars with nuts because they stirred bad memory.

She got in the driver's seat and asked for help with the door. It closed halfway then became stuck again so I stood with my back against it and butted it closed, slamming hard enough to make the car shake sideways on its springs. She turned the key in the ignition and there was a rattling of fan blades under the hood then a smell of hot oil, very sexy. We cruised a few aisles over to the van, her enormous purse sharing my lap with the suit, which was still too wet to put in the pack. Her bag was embroidered with a Mexican peasant couple framed by two larger colorful parrots that seemed ready to eat them. It weighed as much as a suitcase and I asked her what all she had in it. She gave me permission to look inside. It looked as if she had emptied a toolbox into it, screwdrivers and pliers and a socket wrench. Besides the emergency supplies in the back she was learning roadside repair from an oversized and overdue library book also taking up purse space. Evidently it didn't inform the reader which end of a VW holds the engine because she pulled the Volvo up to the van nose to nose.

After repositioning her car and getting my engine running she asked to see the inside of the van. We made out until Roy saw the two vehicles with hoods open as if in conversation, the jumper cables looking like red and black licorice whips being eaten by the Volvo. He slapped the sliding door with an encouraging roar causing our front teeth to click against each other's. I invited her to the party but she didn't take time to consider, saying she had a date. All I could say was oh. Roy knocked more politely and asked if I was driving into town tonight or getting married. I let Sonny out who collected her cables, closed her hood and with both hands struggled the door closed. She waved then backed away with a snaking motion, the lane between the two rows of parked employee vehicles just wide enough to accommodate her reverse swerving.

Roy whistled that wedding march tune as I rolled the passenger side window up on the arms of the suit so it could dry during the drive into town, telling him about the party, informing him more than inviting him. And I told him that he could save the tune, she had a date tonight, keeping the ache out of my voice. He got back into his wagon also parked in the aisle with the engine running and I backed out and down the lane with Roy following.

Out on the road he passed me but drove slow enough that I could keep up. Enough pumpkins had been lit with candles to put the smell of cooked gourd in the air, and though none were in sight I heard snatches of kids' voices yelling trick or treat. I could still taste Sonny's spit as the radio played songs about evil, devilish and witchy women. A tree that might've been transplanted from the Midwest was attacked by a piece of wind, causing a flock of orange and yellow leaves to fly across the road in front of me. One clung to the windshield as if showing off its fall colors then lost its grip, sliding from view toward the roof. All the way to town I wondered if it was still hanging on up there the way my suit held tightly to the window.

Roy passed all the boulevard bars and continued driving beyond the party house. My mouth went dry with extreme beer thirst. He went almost as far as the beanery where the road was blocked by portable red and white barriers with blinking yellow lights. He turned up a side street then over a few blocks where we parked facing down the hill. He said that tonight was the one time a year he had to visit this side of town. I rolled up the now dry suit and put it in the pack, carrying it along as we went down the sidewalk and crossed a few streets, merging with a growing stream of foot traffic. You should see this, he said, promising me I'd never look at a beautiful woman wearing too much make-up the same again. We became part of a crowd that lined the sides of another main boulevard and through the spaces between the heads in front of us I could see a parade of ladies, some in gowns, others in costumes but all gorgeous as if they stepped out of a single male's fantasy, pretty as a dozen Sonny's. I said the last thought aloud and Roy told me to look closer, it was tricks and treaters every night of the year down here.

I excused my way between several layers of spectators to get a better view and must have angered someone for cutting in front, because I was pushed out into the street from behind, directly into the path of two paraders, one The Queen of Hearts and the other Glenda, good witch of the east. They were at least six inches taller than I, had bodybuilder arms and manly voices, picking me up as if I were a stray dog loose in the street. They carried me along the route, arguing over which one would get to keep me. I desperately called out for Roy and could hear him faintly far behind, promising he'd find me. Some kind of cat-woman guy approached and asked them what they had found and one of them said dinner. He tried to steal me from them and they had to let me go to fight him, throwing real punches but that seemed to please cat-woman man who hit and kicked like the real character. I ran into and through the crowd, the song Lola by the Kinks in my head, but now I was on the wrong side of the street from Roy.

Lifted myself onto the top of a cement wall to sit and rest my heart. It beat nervously, unable to settle on a single time signature. I had the wall to myself, watching the parade again from a safe distance. It looked as if a Broadway musical dam had broken upstream, sending a torrent of showgirls to flood the street. Fresh waves beauties strutted past, each a trick on the eyes, forcing me to swallow my urges and remind myself they were men, men with more muscles than any bully back home. There were some male characters but by the same reverse logic and the look of their hands I realized those were women in costume, women uninterested in me. I wondered if some gorillas preferred other gorillas of the same gender.

Parade weary, my attention was drawn instead to a pair of Mexicans with their arms crossed in matching gray shirts who stared back at me instead of the event. After a few moments they framed my dangling legs with their backs to the wall, looking toward the street but one said something in Spanish then glanced up at me for a response. The other one translated, telling me that he wants to know if you can read. Before I could ask why, he pointed toward large letters painted in lavender along the wall, three feet tall and almost invisible in the ambient light of the street lamps. I saw two e's in a row then read saw the k on one end. KEEP OFF WALL. One read it loudly to me, then they shouted something foreign at the same time, maybe Chinese as they both lifted a foot to pushing me over backwards. There was a patch of dead grass on the other side that the recent rains had not brought back to life, but because of the recent soaking the ground wasn't hard as it might have been.

I was at a driveway that led into parking spaces built under the apartment building above. I expected them to climb over after me so I tried to run away. It was difficult to move quickly before my ability to breathe returned. There was a sliding iron gate that might have opened from the weight of a car approaching from this side, but I was at least a thousand pounds too light. I hurried through the underground parking hoping it opened up at the other end. Every space that didn't have a car had a matching oval oil stain, the air stale breath of older engines. There was a short set of stairs at the other end that led to a side door entrance to the building. Through a short but scratchy maze of landscape shrubbery I found the main entrance and a gate that unlatched from the inside. The twin shirts hadn't come around to catch me trespassing so I hurried down the street that paralleled the parade one block to the south, Stray bunches of kids in costume were working the occasional houses, sometimes calling to let into the gated apartment buildings, their shouts of trick or treat bringing my thoughts back to normal. Then something shattered in the street.

I didn't see it hit but something exploded in the street, looking like a firework but only by reflecting the light of street lamps. A few sparks tickled my legs. I stooped down to examine the damage. There were bits of glass stuck to my jeans and sparkling the sidewalk. Another explosion popped behind me followed by a new rain of shards. I stayed in a crouched position, looking around for mean kids too old for trick or treating but only saw a mom with two masked children crossing the next street half a block away. Randomly checking the variables I looked up and saw something meteor-like streaking down from the heavens, crashing close to the first impact. Turning my back to the expected shrapnel I looked up again, scanning the balconies of what was either a fancier apartment building or a hotel. Heads tiny in the distance peered back at me like gargoyles as an arm tossed something into gravity. Like a high fly ball to deep left I tracked it long enough to see it was a champagne goblet tumbling in the night, crashing on the roof of an innocent car to leave a dent, but giving it a momentary halo-like crown of stars.

I jogged ahead to escape the falling glass of party people, reaching the intersection where the Halloween threesome had stopped for the same reason. The backs of the parade watchers were visible up the block, but instead of music and hooting and clapping there was angry shouting and the blare of a car horn, longs blasts interspersed with short beeps as if it were a coded message. The crowd parted and a pair of headlight beams proceeded Roy's wagon. He had driven around the barriers and bullied his way through the spectators and paraders, several of whom were punching and kicking the sides of the vehicle, one man in a dress riding the luggage rack on the roof. Away from the parade he looked silly up there, alone in his femininity on a dark side street. I, and two kids in plastic cartoon masks stared at him as he climbed down and searched for lost incentive.

Roy leaned across the seat to unlock the passenger side door. As I opened it his laughter drifted out on the smell of old clothes and bad breath. Get in he told me, before the cops come. I hoped he hadn't run over too many people.

CHAPTER TWENTY-THREE

---

*T*he van was on the other side of the spectacle and we didn't know how far ahead or behind were either end of the parade. Roy asked if I dared him to drive across again, but instead I guided him toward my liquor store parking lot where we could wait out the event. Roy yelled out the window at trick or treaters, telling them to get a job, ya little beggars. Turban guy was working the check out and greeted us with a bow of his head. Roy waved and said hey, Benny. When there was an aisle between us asked in a whisper if Roy knew that guy. He said everybody knows that guy, don't you watch tv? He almost shouted the words so I ducked a little, embarrassed.

Roy explained the guy had a part on a sitcom, that he had known him since the stand up comedy days. Then what is he doing here? Roy shrugged and made the circles with his finger around his ear to tell me the guy was crazy, reaching for a bottle of something I'd never seen or heard of. So what country is he from? He looked at me as if I were nuts. He's from right here; that foreign crap is his bit. He lives it.

At the end of the aisle was a mountain of beer, 24-count cartons neatly stacked like bricks to create a towering wall like the inside slice of a pyramid. The bottom row was the width of the back of the store, skulls and spiders and limbless rubber feet and hands on the shelf-like steps up the outer edges leading to a psychotically laughing plastic pumpkin

atop the peak box. If I had been in my suit I would have climbed it.
Carefully slid one carton from the middle of a row just over my head.
Those around it followed, creating a graduated bulge in the center of
the structure. Wasn't certain if the groan came from myself or some of
the beer cans also feeling the moment's stress.

Took a step back then tried to push the case I had chosen back in,
but a dangerous sound of pond ice popping under the weight of skaters
came from the windows behind. Behind me Ray asked why didn't I
just grab a cold one. He aimed the bottom of his bottle toward the row
of glass door coolers along the sidewall. I tugged a case out of the chill
and fast walked to the counter, afraid of an earthquake however small
at that moment, no place inside the store would be safe.

Already at the counter Roy asked Benny if he wanted a swig,
holding his bottle in front of the guy's face. Benny scowled and said he
wouldn't touch it with a ten-dollar pole. Roy told him he didn't have
the kahunas, trying the same accent but it sounded goofy. Benny stared
deadpan as if there were no such thing as humor. Back in the parking
lot I asked Roy if he had made up the story, but he assured me the guy
was rich and famous, smart as a wimp. Then I asked if he was going
with me but he had other plans, swinging the bottle from its neck like
a hypnotist's pocket watch, as if that action supplied details. We waited
for nothing and drank, Roy telling me that I was going to turn into one
of them. One of them what? He sucked on another sip then suddenly
relaxed, settling into the seat like a bag of sand as he said a drug addict.

A big guy and a fat guy went into the store and I trembled slightly,
hoping it was a nervous reaction and not a vibration from all that weight.
Something clicked internally and Roy sighed, burped then started the
wagon and put it in gear. Saying that's enough, he drove away, and I was
almost certain there was no distant crash or crushing sound.

The parade was over but people mostly in regular clothes still
walked the boulevard, now in all directions. Roy honked his way
through, stopping and starting about twenty times, but delivered me
to the van. He drove away talking to himself then laughing at whatever

he had said. I put the case on the passenger seat and safely belted it in place, then let the van coast down the hill, popped the clutch and started the engine. Police cruisers spinning their colored lights were sweeping the road clear of people, and behind them vehicles carefully crept onto it in both lanes.

At the party there were more motorcycles than cars parked along each side of the street. From the opposite direction two grumbled slowly past, prowling for their own space. Finding none they turned at the corner and drove up the sidewalk's handicap ramp, then along the walk to use the lawn as others had. I would have tried the same move but there wasn't room for the van. After parking on the other side of the block I dressed up, the inside of the suit slick with dried sweat residue that made it easier to slip on, but after a few moments of body heat it became sticky with the smell of fat fish- bait worms.

Loping down the sidewalk gave me an irresistible impulse to crouch, stopping occasionally from habit to touch my knuckles against the concrete and look around for food or predators. The weight of the beer pulled me from one side of the walk to the other as I changed hands carrying it, making me walk drunkenly and giving me a headache up the back of my neck, a hangover long before the morning after.

Before reaching the corner I cut across lawns and driveways to shorten the route, fearing watchdogs and shotgun owners who enjoyed staring out picture windows instead of at television screens. Near the house two more riders jumped the curb and throttled carefully through a maze of look-a-like bikes that could have been siblings born of a single pair of parent motorcycles. I stepped behind the next-door neighbor's tree but one guy saw me just before he had braked to a complete stop. He wobbled and stuck his leg out for balance, kicking his partner in the leg, which caused that guy to lurch forward against the stairs, coming to rest with his front tire on the second step. He turned to his buddy who pointed in my direction as an explanation.

Too tired to run away with the beer, came out from hiding and showed it to them as a peace offering. Though the guy angled up the steps had lost some amount of long and carefully collected coolness, a gorilla offering beer repaired the damage. They smiled and reached into the open box for a couple cans without speaking, not knowing what to say to a great ape, but as beer drinkers enjoyed the weightlessness of a twelve-ounce can as they raised them to their mouths and swallowed all of the liquid whole. In a weird reverse ritual they touched the empty cans together to toast after drinking and tossed them into the darkness, not caring that they clunked off someone else's hardware. They dismounted and flexed their bodies, the leather sighing, and I presented the case again so they could grab more beer. They gripped the cans so greedily it dented them even while they were unopened, as their other hands grabbed me by my upper arms and escorted me inside like a prize, or maybe a prisoner, thinking I was a crasher.

One whispered at me not to worry, they wouldn't let anybody hurt me, though no blood was circulating below my elbows. A few people turned as we came through the door, but instead of letting the crowd react my bodyguards cheered our entrance as some kind of victory, then pushed me forward to enjoy the party. There was an unenthusiastic echo from some of the partiers who weren't certain if my presence was worth the noise, but didn't want to miss out on the moment just in case. Many of them punched me in fun same as at the park, some of them hurting me despite that promise of protection.

Allowing a few to grab a beer lessened the assaults and I reached a clearing in front of the live band in the connected dining room. It was a threesome playing something that was probably titled Ain't Did Nuttin' because those were most of the lyrics. D'evil was scrawled on the front of the bass drum, but the female bass player announced that they were No Biting. She wore a lone ranger mask and black boots, bra & panties as her costume, or maybe she always dressed that way just without the mask. Somebody yelled at me to do the funky monkey, but luckily the song ended. Bra girl leaned into the singer's microphone to tell us remember, forbidden fruit also makes excellent jellies and jams.

The crowd shouted approval and a couple sexual suggestions, for which she thanked them as if it were applause.

Mac and Sam were in the backyard babysitting a keg on a square of concrete that once was the floor of an out building but now was being used as a patio. They might have been dressed up as Bonnie & Clyde or maybe a pimp and his prostitute, stoned and high and drunk so they didn't act or talk in character, just nodded to the beat of the music. The band was playing another song but only the bass and drums could be heard out there, loud enough to make people do everything in rhythm, the nodding, drinking on the down beat, laugh in key, walk as if in a rock musical. Mac bent close to look at my eyes behind the mask, asking if that was me in there. I pulled my gloves off, then the mask, asking if he ever knew anybody else with a gorilla suit.

Set the case down next to the keg and popped open a beer, looking over the lip of the can as I chugged a third of it. Everyone was staring at me. Sam said a silent clown had showed up earlier and they wondered if that might have been me. I was kind of insulted and told them maybe it was a narc. They looked at each other seriously until Mac shrugged and said it didn't matter, they had used up all the drugs.

A pirate walked up and tried to fill his empty cup at the keg, but the spigot only hissed and spit foam. Sam needlessly told him it was all gone, but he was sincere as if sharing a secret. The pirate noticed the can in my hand and I realized what the others had been looking at. I reflexively glanced down at my case, which made him look at it like his buried treasure chest. He released the spigot and that hand fell onto the pommel of his plastic sword. Before he could say argh and run me through I offered him a beer. He said thanks and I watched him walk away to meet up with his partner, a wench in bell-sleeves and a tight leather vest that gave her own chest the illusion of being treasure. He showed her his twelve ounces of booty and she looked at me and smiled. I stacked as many cans as I could on the top of the keg and stepped away with the rest. There was a murmur of oohs that sounded like cattle drives in movies, and the herd gathered around the keg to water.

A lady devil appeared from behind my naked tree, dressed in a red leotard with a tail sewn onto the butt that ended in the shape of an arrowhead. Her horns were attached to a headband and she wore black lipstick. She might have been an athlete or a dancer because her body seemed to want out of any clothes. She glanced at me so I offered the mostly empty carton and she dug out a can, then asked if she could have one for her boyfriend. Told her okay, though it wasn't. Sharing the rest of the beers with Mac and Sam I eventually asked about the bass player. She belonged to a biker.

Settling for getting drunk, asked if there was beer in the refrigerator. Mac said no, just spoiled food. Defrosting it with an ice pick, he had punched a hole in the freezing element, releasing the Freon. Asked him how long the party would go on and he said until cop-o'clock, or when the beer runs out. I suggested more beer. He pulled a set of keys from his picket and jingled them, offering to drive if I would buy. I said deal and followed him to the front yard where he stopped to look up and down the street. Asked what he was looking for and he said that he wasn't sure. He started walking in search and told me to go the other way, to shout out if I found a kind of truck thing. There was one small truck on the next block but not worth a shout, then a truck thing raced up behind me with its horn shouting as it skidded to slightly crooked stop. Mac was at the wheel so I got in.

He told me it belonged to a cousin of either Jan or Dean, he couldn't remember which, but the guy left with a group of ladies and asked Mac to take care of his vehicle. I asked if we could make a detour to the traffic accident bar on Cahuenga first, that it had velvet boobs. He told me hell yeah, as long as I was buying. There was a non-party there, a dozen drinkers but none acted as if they recognized me even though I was still dressed in most of the suit. Two bartenders were dressed as vampires, but neither were cancer guy from the other night, their costumes out-numbering the only costumed customer who wore a robe, his beard and long hair making him look like Jesus but he wasn't carrying a cross, and without a crown of thorns he could've been anyone ancient and famous.

As Mac admired the art I ordered two beers and asked about my canvas pack. One vampire told me to check the cardboard box that sat on the lower rack of a rolling coat rail in the corner, the kind they use in hotels. There was a black cape and an army jacket on hangers, and in the box a yellow knit cap, one work glove, and my pack with the stinky shoes.

Uninspired by the company and jukebox selection we drank most of our beer in a few swallows to rush back toward what was left of Halloween. Steps from the vehicle I noticed Mac had one of the paintings tucked under his arm. Darkness is good he told me. We rushed faster.

There was a different liquor store on the way back so we didn't have to risk the avalanche of the mountain of beer. It almost brought a tear to my throat. I was too tired and already buzzed enough not to crack open another can, looking at the occasional carved pumpkins with their candled insides gone dark and dead. Mac drank as he drove. In the middle of a block he braked hard again and stopped the truck thing, no horn this time but I fell into the dashboard as some of his dropped beer splashed me. Though I was hurt, asked if he were okay. He said he hit a kid. I said no he didn't, not that I knew but was hoping he hadn't.

He opened the door and got out saying it was a kid dressed as a ghost or a ghost. I rubbed my arm, shoulder and head, looking in the rear view mirror for blood then got out too. There was no kid in the street, not under the truck, not on a sidewalk or lawn. No blood either. Mac confessed he was on acid, that he might have been seeing things. I asked if he wanted me to drive. He told me no because that guy left the vehicle in his care and he couldn't take the chance of me wrecking it or something.

We left the scene of the non-crime, Mac driving so slowly that I could have raced him back to the party and won. He told me he used to sell acid outside rock concerts with his older brother and got arrested, learning in jail how to carve a skull from a bar of soap using the broken handle from a plastic spoon, trading the soap-skulls for cigarettes. Made me almost want to go to jail.

The street was still crowded as a liquor store parking lot so Mac drove between the bikes on the lawn and the cars in the driveway to park in the backyard next to his row of sinsemilla plants. Some guests still stood around the dead keg in tribute, so we rewarded them with living cans of beer. A person in a nice three-piece suit with dress shoes and necktie, wearing reading glasses and a fake mustache approached and put out her hand, so I put a beer in that one also. In a fake low voice she said she had meant to shake my hand, moving the can to the other to offer me her it again.

It must've been some sort of secret handshake because it trapped my middle finger while hers curled under to tickle my palm. She leaned in and whispered if I wanted to go to the bathroom. Told her I was fine and she said she meant with her. I could see the bulge of breasts framing the tie and asked if the mustache were real. She said a real fake anyway, and that she liked my suit. We had to wait in line so long that when we went in together I had to pee, but didn't think it could happen with an erection. As she locked the door I began to undo my suit but told me to stop, that she wanted me in costume, gorilla sex.

That was impossible unless I cut a hole in the crotch. She unlocked the door and told me to get a knife, that she would wait. I reached for her breasts hoping for compromise or at least get a feel, but she grabbed my wrists, her mustache almost touching my nose as she told me to get a damn knife or scissors or something. Suddenly it was disappointingly possible to pee, so I did. Didn't get a knife, just snuck behind the sinsemilla plants to water them. Curiosity made me go back inside. The line for the bathroom curved around her. She was asleep on the floor, most of her suit untouched by the vomit staining her nice shirt & tie. Stopped looking at the ladies, tired of hope. Salvaged two beers from the bottom of the case and went back to the van to drink them then sleep. It wasn't many hours until dawn, but when you're drunk and lonely they seem to stretch near forever, or at least those minutes until sleep.

CHAPTER TWENTY-FOUR

----

*T*he highways were built in the decades after world war two to make the soldiers feel good about buying big new cars using their G.I. Bill loans. Those wheeled-boats cost more than the farms they had lost during the depression before the war. When the section of interstate outside our town was finished it included a rest stop between the lake and Kalamazoo. We drove out there like it was a new Disneyland attraction, something futuristic that soon might exist on the moon for wilder travelers, but more importantly a place where people were not allowed to litter. The word litter and a place without trash were new to us same as the Frisbee and instant photos, so we had to see it. On the way dad drove so fast we had to roll the windows up halfway so the wind wouldn't blow any of the paper crap littering our car out onto the highway.

The scenery was exciting because it was all new, then seen and gone unlike the repeating background rocks, trees and hills of cartoons when the characters are moving. Old farm roads were cut in half like worms, government barriers of steel giving them two dead ends, yet they still squirmed away in opposite directions. The cool April wind stung our cheeks recently sunburned during Easter break at the egg hunt along the bluff, the budding branches of trees providing little shade without their broad leaves of summer. This is it I thought, road to the future, short cut like a slide on a board game where you pass go to get ahead, no seat belt holding you back, just speed to the newest and cleanest place of rest ever invented. The rest stop exit was closed.

Some guy in a Galaxy 500 had taken the exit too fast and gone to the biggest and final rest stop. Dad pulled over anyway, braking to a stop that threw us forward into the uncomfortable parts of the interior, every family member for themselves, leaving twelve feet of stinky black skid marks on the shoulder of the immaculate highway.

We walked over like a family of ducks to the bathroom built of taxes, needing to pee because none of us had gone before the drive purposely so we could wet the new facility. Nobody had seen the accident but there were tire tracks in the dirt between the exit and the crash site as if the Galaxy 500 had tried to reach orbital speed and live up to its name, but wasn't ready for more than a flight shorter than the original Wright Brothers' success.

The wreckage had been towed away but there were pieces of evidence left, shards of metal and neat chunks of rubber and glass along a scar near the bathrooms. I found a tapered thing of steel and traced its edge, which cut the tip of my finger, then went inside. The toilets and urinals were pristine but the porcelain no cleaner than our well scrubbed old Lutheran receptacles.

Having to pee in the morning is an alarm clock that never stops ringing. Woke up daydreaming about that rest stop. Mac & Sam's door was unlocked and the house quiet except for the guy sleeping on the couch. He breathed through his mouth with a moaning wind sound. Used the bathroom and the flush brought Mac out of the bedroom. While he peed I cleaned up some of the mess then asked him for a jump. The other guy's truck was still there and we searched it for jumper cables, finding an unused set in a special compartment that also held a fire extinguisher, flares, and orange and black reflective warning markers.

Asked Mac if he wanted to go to a hangover bar, but he planned on sleeping all day. You can do that if you have a bedroom I said, thinking about my old bed, my old bedroom, my old self. I missed the first two.

Found Roy's wagon and a spot to park a couple cars away. Climbed onto the roof and the bird poop, groaning not only for fun but hoping to wake Roy. Might have slept for a minute or an hour but know I slept because I woke up from a dream about high school wondering where I was. I elbowed the car and called out his name. Did it again and he screamed some bad words, opened the side door and got out, looking around in angry confusion. He said damn and began to crawl back inside but I said hey Roy. He looked up and over at me and stared, looked down at his feet then across the back of the buildings, then back at me. He said I was the second weirdest person he'd ever met and almost smiled.

He wanted to go to a hangover bar. The bartender was alone and though we seemed to be interrupting his day with our orders he served us because we outnumbered him. If I had come in by myself he probably would have ignored me. When Roy came back from the bathroom I confessed about wasting too much time and money in saloons, but he told me it was money well spent. When people are drinking you get to know them in minutes. It could take years of sober church events for a clue what somebody might be like. Told him about Sonny and the pirate wench and devil girl, and he told me to put on my thumb-sucker glove and stop whining. He said that years equal women, that I had plenty ahead of me, and that it's easier to keep track of time by the women whether they have sex with me or don't. We finished our drinks quickly but the tender didn't care, busy staring at something in the opposite direction. I waved at him but Roy grabbed my hand and forced it back to my side, saying let's go, I know a better place. He drove south past the 10 Freeway.

Something was in the seat crack against my spine, and though I shifted around it couldn't get comfortable so reached back and pulled it loose. It was a plastic container of pepper. Here's that pepper you were looking for I told him, and he didn't even glance at it, saying keep it then telling me it was for self-defense. Not everybody deserves to be shot. What do you do, I asked, put too much on their salad? He said if you throw it in anybody's face, game over. When he was young and picked on by gangs in school he carried a bunch of one-dollar bills and would throw them down. While the bullies dove at the sight of cash he ran away, but ran out of cash so invented the pepper trick.

Told him because of my lip I got picked on so much that I got used to it. What do you mean, your lip? I pointed to my scar and he leaned closer, one eye on traffic and the other on my lip. He said that he never would have noticed without me pointing it out. Then he said you know it looks just like you. I asked what and he said the gorilla's face, then told me he needed something to eat. It was some historic restaurant in Chinatown and the food tasted historic, but history was not my favorite subject so drank Chinese beer. On the way back told him that Jayo made fun of my lip, chipped tooth, weird walk, then asked Roy how to bail someone out of jail. He said don't do it, unless he himself ever got arrested.

Back at the parking lot he left to do personal things. I found a gas station that sold beer and bought a gallon and a quart. Drove with the windows up trying to catch a breath of the night before, but only smelled my bad self. Played the radio recklessly just to use up electrons, agreeing with juvenile lyrics enough to sing along with a crappy song.

Found a phone booth, feeling as if I were cheating on the other beat up one and called the agents. A robot machine answered, but after I said uh and gave my name a lady picked up the phone. She said that they were anxious to see me, giving me an address up in the valley for lunch. With over an hour of free time I used the phone book attached to a cable to look up the bail bondsman Roy recommended. Another female voice told me that bail may have not have been set yet, and to get Jayo's arrest number. I thought that would be a good name for a band. Made other calls enough to learn he already was out of jail on his own recognizance to report back to the court regularly before his court date.

Called information for Jayo's mother's number. After many rings she answered angrily as if she deserved sleep more than another piece of bad information about Jayo. She told me to bring back her van, but nothing about Jayo.

Drove to the clean hand Mexican garage and washed myself in the bathroom, fearful of leaving a trace because it was still cleaner than my grandmother's good dishes. Went west on Ventura Boulevard smelling my fingers, maybe because of the gas station soap, maybe because of what I had been into before that.

Found the address but had to make several turns to get back to it with drivers honking insults at me, finally pulling up to the sandwich sign that told me where I wanted to be, which included a cartoon sandwich with eyes and a smile for the illiterate.

The sign was two boards leaning against each other dependently in the shape of an upside-down v, but I thought it would've been better if they had been contoured like slices of bread, being a sandwich sign for a sandwich place, making the artwork cleverly redundant. The bottom line of the red-on-white text bragged of valet parking though there was no valet, but there was space enough at the curb to park. I parked then noticed the no-parking sign, its shape nothing like a sandwich either. Just as I turned the steering wheel to leave, a valet parker in a white shirt and black vest jay-walked across the street and up to the door of the van, jingling a round key-ring big enough for a jailor.

Left the van running and got out. He gave me a piece of paper with a number in trade for the van, chewing gum as if angry I didn't drive something better. Told him to take good care of it and he almost smiled, revving the engine to forty rpm's.

Inside I was worried about a dress code, but most everyone looked more unemployed than I. The girl at the podium who seats people asked if I were a party of one. Yeah, told her, but that I also was meeting people and she said ain't we all. Looked at her reflection in a framed night photograph of the restaurant as she pulled at the neck of her sweater, nervous about being herself. We searched the dim place lit by candles even though there was daylight through the window up front. Because I didn't see my hosts she sat me in the back where I couldn't even see that window. Within half an hour a good-looking guy told me his name was Skylax and did I want water? I ordered a beer then followed sweater-girl's trail back toward the light to wait for my people.

Eventually a newish silver car arrived and the valet ran to the passenger-side door chewing with more energy than the last time I had seen him. With his help, the lady agent groaned her way up out of a deep leather bucket seat. He reached back inside for her purse almost big as my wallet though she held it as if it weighed more than she could carry. The valet almost jumped the hood to meet the driver, accepting the car keys as if they were a tribute from some ancient ruler. I stepped into view and waved. They looked up as if in hope and saw me, nodding that I was real, then gave their attention to getting up the three stairs, maybe wondering why an escalator hadn't been installed. Past them I saw the valet throw a caloric smile at me as he dropped into the addictive luxury of their car, revving it loud enough to wake rocks.

After the three steps up with the help of her husband, the lady agent faked a kiss about ten inches from my cheek. The guy agent held a thin briefcase in his right hand, so shook mine using his left. He had the grip of an old rubber band, but a smile that promised me a car like his.

The sweatered seating-girl asked if we were three, so I told her that I already had been seated. She was confused until I said ain't we all, then led us back through the obstacle course of dark eastern Siberia. My beer was waiting. As the agents took less than a year to sit down and get comfortable arranging and rearranging their butts, I chugged it.

The agent guy finally leaned in with his hands folded on the table and sighed a so. I echoed him hoping he was going to ask me if I wanted another beer, but before he could speak his wife brought up the brief case and used it to move the empty beer bottle to my edge of the table. It seemed to weigh less than her purse. She added a third so, but before she could finish the thought a waitress stepped to the end of the table, pretty but with so much make up she might have been trying to cover up the fact she was beautiful and maybe irresistible without it, needing tips more than unwanted attentions until the right producer or director saw through her disguise.

Her tag bragged her name was Cassiopeia. It almost sat flat on the top of her left breast, maybe not even pinned on, just balanced safely there. She asked if we were ready to order and I could smell her lipstick. As I pulled a menu from the little rack behind the napkins, the agents kind of bowed toward me to order first, so I pretended to speed-read it, each offering having some kind of movie title then a bunch of ingredients I had never eaten. I shrugged and told her a cheeseburger and another beer, setting the bottle on the corner of the table. They asked only for coffee and water. Feeling like a drunken pig I put the menu back into its rack, noticing a card next to the pepper that explained there was a drought, so customers had to ask for water. I imagined a failing reservoir in the hills being drained one specially ordered glass at a time.

The waitress promised she'd be right back and we all watched her walk away, probably with several different thoughts. The lady came to her senses first and introduced herself, nudged her husband back to reality and introduced him, explaining they were from the William Morris Agency. Before I could be more confused than impressed she added that they had left to manage talent on their own. I still was impressed because they hadn't left our meeting to chase the waitress. Peeked over the open top of their briefcase and saw a small stack of papers, a box of business cards and two fountain pens, one brown one blue. She carefully separated two stapled papers off the stack, which severely reduced its size, and handed them to me. The large elegant print at the top claimed they were the Blohn & Waistburn Agency. The rest was paragraphs, each one a list of conditions and promises that meant less at first scan than the menu. I took a moment to glance at the second page and saw the lines for signatures and wondered who would be paying whom and for what.

The guy told me in a calm voice that it was a standard contract, but I didn't have to worry about signing anything today or ever. They were casting for a fast food chain making new commercials for national markets, and if after reading and researching the terms on my own time there was a good chance I'd be cast in a costume character. After that it wouldn't be difficulty to find work for the gorilla. He continued about percentages, unions, royalties and residuals as I resisted grabbing for one of the pens and signing. Luckily the waitress returned with my beer and their beverages, so I calmly chugged it slowly, dragging it out in six or seven swallows.

As their attention went to peeling back lids of tiny cups of cream, a stranger brought my burger, apologizing that she had taken over the earlier waitress' shift. We didn't accept the apology but the burger also was lovely. I offered the agents a portion, plus some fries and my pickle but they hugged and sipped their coffee. I tried to think of an intelligent question, biting and chewing to give myself extra time, but before I could take a second bite heard myself tell them I didn't have to think about it, I was ready to sign. We all smiled, everyone satisfied with the water and coffee, burger and beer, costumes and contracts, the only thing missing being Cassiopeia.

We signed and they finished their coffee before I was half-done with the burger, begging me for permission to leave for other business. I bowed thanks to them as they left a twenty under one of the cups. Their water was untouched so I hoarded both glasses over to my side knowing none of it would get back to the reservoir, using it to wash down the pickle and last of my fries. Traded my slip of paper for my van and tipped the parking guy five dollars. He asked what I did for a living and told him I was in commercials, and that I almost always parked my own vehicle.

Three days later without shaving or showering, after too much beer and little food I stank again, people dodging me from many feet away not wanting to get close enough for the thought of a collision. The manager at McDonalds reversed his rule and wanted me to use the bathroom sink and not stay to order food. I slept at weird times and woke up at all times trying to remember if a dog had bitten me because I was afraid of water and maybe had contracted hydrophobia.

Beer had become the only liquid I could tolerate, so brushed my teeth and washed my face, hands and armpits with it in the morning. At Mac and Sam's the dead refrigerator stood at the curb surrounded by black garbage bags that slouched against each side, seemingly gathered in a suicide to join their kitchen-sharing friend in the next life. There wasn't a party but some people were hanging around the porch and a couple corners inside. I must have become literally stinking drunk because some lady again lured me into the bathroom but before I could close the door male muscles escorted me into a tub of soapy water and held me down, threatening exotic methods of violence if I didn't sit there until the album ended. It was Woodstock.

I woke up hours later from a nap, the water drained and damp towels over my wet clothes for a blanket. Used the toilet and on my way out said thanks to anybody left over, and inside the van changed into something less clean, but dry. Drove out to the park to pick up my paycheck. Without my employee identification the shack guard had to call payroll to verify it was there, but couldn't get anybody to bring it out. He looked around guiltily, made me swear a blood oath not to linger or loiter or go inside the park proper, then waved me backstage.

Leely's little office was unlocked so I found Sonny's number in the Rolodex and used the phone to call her, humbly bragging to say I had an agent, well really a pair of agents. She was angry it had taken me days to call but then said good for you. Asked her about the date she had and she confessed it was to break up with a guy. I almost kissed the phone while doing a sideways sliding butt dance on the seat of the office chair, but then noticed a scribble pad with the park logo at the top. The characters names were listed, and all circled except Roy's and mine. His was crossed out, and next to mine were the scribbled words: ordered better suit from creature shop, Studio City, get bigger guy. Sonny asked if I was still there, but I couldn't speak so gently pushed the hang up button down to cut us off without a click, then hung up the handset.

Somewhere a coaster was being tested at speeds only park workers and jet pilots experienced. Somewhere in Studio City a better gorilla suit was getting made. Somewhere a bigger guy didn't know he would have a job this Christmas and probably for years to come, working with Sonny. My check wasn't even at payroll, mailed out to Mac and Sam's the day before. I hadn't known what day it was, and now knew less about tomorrow.

Inside the van motes of dust moved in a beam of sunshine like a school of fish. The top edge of the dash was covered in dust that wasn't dancing. I drew a wavy line through it, my fingertip turning dark as pencil lead. My fault, I was rotting, wasting away and at the same time killing the van from the inside out. I breathed in and it smelled like dying. Found a self car wash with a vacuum hose and sucked out the dead matter, then gave the interior a bubble bath with the sprayer. When I put my clothes and the suit back inside the rotten smell returned. Put more quarters in the slot and sprayed my clothes and costume, then laid them out the roof of the van to dry while I drove slowly in the sunshine with the windows down and the sliding door open.

After an hour of bad thoughts and cruising the curved streets of a subdivision at a speed so slow that an ice cream vendor had to pass me, pulled over in a tiny park with tiny toys where tiny kids tentatively used the short swings and a slide almost tall as a sunflower. Everything inside and outside the van was dry and the bad smell almost gone. I gave the dead microbes a moment of silence then drove down to Hollywood.

There were metered parking spaces in front of a barbershop that I had driven and walked past many times with a feeling of mocking victory. Parked and fed the meter, then stopped before going inside to read a flyer in the window. It was red and green on white, advertising the Christmas Parade featuring somebody in a vest and cowboy hat from the old show Bonanza, Mickey Mouse and Santa Claus, like the Halloween parade but with friendlier costumes.

Above it was my reflection. Felt for the scar on my lip through the hair, centering my face in the middle of the letter O painted on the inside, surprised to see a barber looking out at me. I must have looked like an ape having an epiphany, a shocking thought that sharp flint might be used not only to cut up an ibex or an enemy, but maybe shave off some of the hair that collected too much of the fat and blood when eating a fresh kill. It could drive wild women more than wild.

Went inside to chat. The barber walked me back out to examine the van, asking if it was for sale. He was going to drive back to Brooklyn for the holidays and it would save him from getting motels. Told him no, but he walked around it. Told him my thoughts about the first hominoid shaving with the edge of a rock. He inhaled my words as if they were oxygen. What a wonderful world that would be, everyone covered in hair. He looked at me as if I were almost edible, smiling as the scissors snickered with an unconscious reflex while nodding at my hair.

He was bald except for the back of his head, worrying me that he might be jealous of his customers and in a moment of anger take revenge on some heavily forested scalp. I looked around for help but for some unlucky reason the boulevard was empty of pedestrians. With nobody to rescue me, told him just a trim.

The place smelled of medicine and damp magazines. Across the wall opposite the chairs and mirrors were pictures of men who looked like movie stars but maybe never got an agent or contract, men with the best hair in the history of the world. Highlights shone off their heads as if haloes came not from purity but from a quality cut by a skilled barber at a reasonable price.

When I sat he draped a large bib over me with a magician-like flair, preparing to make part of me disappear. He cranked up the seat then dropped it back while holding the scissors where I could see them, a short but effective thrill ride. He clipped my hair and beard in a rhythm that soothed me, humming one note as if trying to think of the rest of the song but afraid to get the next note wrong. He asked if I followed politics and I said not really. He said they picked the smartest Democrat and Republican to get together in private and finally solve the country's problems. I asked what happened. He said that nothing happened, they couldn't agree on a time or place to meet. Bicker bicker cotton picker, he sang on that single note.

He switched to an electric razor and shaved the back of my neck, and then for some reason part of my cheekbones. Felt the buzz vibrating my skull more than I heard it. In college I shaved with an electric razor and always thought the phone was ringing, but nobody ever called me. When finished he sat the chair upright and spun it toward the mirror to present my reflection. It reminded me of me.

CHAPTER TWENTY-FIVE

----

ne summer of Fridays Dad woke me early to ride along on his beer delivery route. It was forced on him during my school year, a go to work with a parent thing, but on the last and busiest day of his workweek he wanted company, maybe just to have someone tote the empties back to the truck while he flirted with the daytime women bartenders. We didn't talk, listening to one country music station while looking at the brief downtowns then the orchards that separated them, occasionally hearing about baseball and weather from those making adult small talk at the crossroads stores where I'd steal a Twinkie or Suzie-Q. Life then almost was a television show but without the funny parts.

In the back of one store was a carton filled with trinkets that stocked the vending machine out front, its cardboard split open crookedly by some kind of razor. The box was gutted like a fallen piñata, its dying wish a party of kids but I was what it got. Helped myself to a pocket of treasure, casually keeping my hand over the bulge on my thigh for the rest of the day. The prizes were a rubber octopus, a fake coin, a pink plastic ring that might fit a fairy's finger, and a once inch comic book. For years I put a nickel or dime in that machine to repay the owner.

The barber shaving the back of my neck gave me a new sensitivity. Felt as if I had a haircut all over myself, a naked ape. Yeppa deppa salt and peppa he said as I looked in the mirror seeing something new, almost the way I saw older humans. He cleaned me with a midget vacuum, my leftover hair and shirt collar also sucked into it for a moment. Avoiding my reflection I had a vision of the rest of me following, sucked up into wherever, but felt my own gravity.

Went to the van and gave him the photograph from the park. He said it would make a good before and after picture when he got a picture of my haircut. It was almost a joke so I laughed.

Back in traffic a bus at the curb blocked me so I used both lanes to steer lazily around it, one hand rubbing the back of my neck. Felt fearless as a teenager so didn't stop at stop signs, didn't use the turn signal, went double digits over the speed limit. Finally nearing a yellow traffic light a sports car downshifted to pass me, its engine calling me a beginner at driving recklessly.

There was a parking spot open near the bookstore, and as if it were a penny in the street I picked up that needed space. Following fate I chanced the bookstore, wandering aisles looking for a book with a good cover contrary to the old phrase. Found an African book with photos of naked people living anciently. The women were fixed up in weird ways to get a man but not a man like me so I didn't interfere. It reminded me to go to a saloon and hopefully meet someone fixed up in a weird way familiar to my culture.

The bar before happy hour was the usual thin scatter of guys looking up at the tv, then down at their drinks every few moments to assure themselves they had a drink, necks getting sore so they rubbed them as I had earlier. Something at the base of our brains aches for touch from the outside world. They secretly glanced at each other to see if anybody else was bored by the sports channel with no sound because the bartender I had seen before used quarters from the till to play songs he loved in high school, and songs he hadn't like then but now they improved a once bad memory of almost having sex at band camp. All of them were waiting for the same woman, the one who never entered nor ever would enter the bar.

The light I brought in with me through the open door made them squint in hope then turn away for another swallow of beer or booze or both as their eyes adjusted back to the easy glow of the television.

There were two or three stools between each guy but after more drinks the songs sounded better and during the commercials and more neck rubbing we all began smiling and nodding at each other until one guy said something about the female commentator. A living voice surprised me and he had an accent so I didn't understand what he said, but I nodded. To thank him for his effort I told him my name and that I had a gorilla suit. He got smiley. That's the joy of the bog, he said almost singing, you never know what you'll find.

He told me the guy on his other side was called Ladies. They had sarcastically called him a ladies' man for so long that it had become shortened. The guy Ladies used to brag that he dated so many blondes he might be addicted to bleach, but he must have left them outside the door because nobody ever saw him with one. Told the accent guy I had crossed most of America to sit here. He said it was sixty miles from Kilkenny to Cork, that he should know because he had walked every step, then picked up his tumbler and toasted the fact. Yet here I thrum, he said then added something maybe in gaelic about Dunnerdee. We drank and he stopped moving to make a tender noise in his throat, staring forward without the smile as if something bad might have happened in Dunnerdee, or maybe that a good thing had happened so long ago it wasn't simply far away now, but unreachable even in memory.

Ladies said amen, and though we were five guys in there with at least ten or twelve thoughts among us, we said nothing more, waiting.

Woke in the morning to a hard working engine of a dump truck and its louder brakes. The smell of garbage might have been me. I was parked across the street and peeked through the curtains to watch two men in blue coveralls and big yellow gloves contemplate the refrigerator. One worked a toothpick in his mouth. Maybe it was stuck between two teeth and he was trying to free it. He shook his head and picked up a garbage bag with each hand and waddled over to swing them into the hollow back of the truck. Walking empty handed back toward the refrigerator he still waddled, too big to put one leg directly in front of the other so moved like an upside-down pendulum.

The other trasher wasn't big but not skinny either, no Laurel to a Hardy. He was just short enough for contrast and used a hunting knife to cut through the duck tape bindings. The smell hit him hard but he took it like a boxer, then counterpunched by opening the fridge door beyond its limits until it snapped off. Though he was a professional the evil smell made him turn away from his work, almost an art. He jaywalked across the street. It was his good fortune that the cars seemed also to smell something bad enough to slow down, giving him room enough for escaping injury or death on Fountain Avenue.

After thanking the sky he went back for the door and slid it into the truck, then tested the stinky weight of the body, but toothpick told him it wouldn't fit. They finished with the bags and the truck screeched ahead fifty feet to the next pile of human embarrassment. I hobbled past the stinking carcass of the fridge, its insides black and green the texture of cottage cheese. Maybe it used to be cottage cheese.

For a science fair Jayo made a battery out of potato, slightly lighting up a tiny bulb. With less energy than that potato I knocked on Mac and Sam's door using my fingertips, unable to form a fist. I was suspicious that getting my hair cut had cost me power, some old testament samsonian type of strength. The new dogs barked as if rehearsing a bad rendition of the Jingle Bells novelty record. Chase opened the door with a fried chicken leg in his teeth. He nodded and gnawed waiting for a sales pitch. Hey, Chase … it's me. He held the almost meatless bone higher than the dogs could leap then smiled, backing up to allow me inside. Commercial man, he said, didn't recognize you. The dogs stayed close to him in case his arm got tired.

Bathroom, I asked. He turned sideways and waved me toward it. The bedroom door was closed with quiet behind it so I aimed for the side of the toilet bowl to make no noise while peeing, leaning my head back with my mouth open and eyes closed, almost a yawn. When the stream lost pressure it hit the rim and made a yellow splash of mess. Used as little toilet paper as possible to clean up any evidence of my presence, wondering why he called me commercial man.

Back in the living room the dogs used their prehensile tongues trying to get shards of chicken bone from between their teeth. Chase was on the floor playing a dead electric guitar. Even without an amp he made it sound good. When I asked him about my nickname he pointed to a note stuck to the wall with a piece of chewed gum. I got the commercial, call for the info. A muffled arguing sound came from the bedroom, or maybe an agreement, so I went out on the porch to sit in the sun and stare at the note, enjoying daydreams I never had been able to afford before.

Soon Samantha slipped through the front door followed by a dog's snout sniffing for a more edible world. She closed the door slowly so it had time enough to pull back inside. I couldn't see around her so didn't know if maybe it got cut off anyway, the black nose snapped loose to bounce around on the porch.

She wore nothing black and carried a colorful purse almost big enough to contain the files that stuck out of it. Told her she looked nice and she said so did I, and that there was a message for me. I waved it at her. She said congratulations and that she also had a job, just a few blocks up and over on Sunset. I offered her a ride and steered her way around the leftover appliance as she said that good news comes in threes, that she was pregnant. Told her she didn't look pregnant and she pouted out her lower lip as if I had insulted her. You're bad as Mac, she said. I heard Bad Ass Mac, good name for a band. Asked her if she knew they served beer at McDonalds in Europe and she asked me how much would I get paid for the commercial. Both of us shook our heads as answers.

She steered me left on Sunset then pointed to a tall office building on the other side of the street. Made an illegal turn almost in the shape of a u and skidded the side of the front tire against the curb. It was my first time chauffeuring anybody pregnant so I was too careful to drive well. She thanked me and got out. I leaned over to lock the door. It wasn't necessary but I wanted to smell where she had been sitting, wanting sex that sounded like arguing that soon would produce some kind of mutual agreement.

Drove down to the old phone booth to call home with good news, but it was gone, the corner bright with new concrete and wheelchair ramps instead of curbs. At one seam where the new stuff met the gray and gum-spotted old stuff was a message traced with a finger in stone while it still had been wet. Graffiti girl had written the word goodbye, maybe to me, maybe to the world, maybe to writing on the sidewalk.

The sedan also was gone and the area looked so different that I looked up at the street sign to know it was the same intersection. I must have been standing there too long with the posture of a condemned man because a voice asked if I was all right. I said yes and looked around but didn't see anyone. Up here, the voice yelled. There was a man on the roof looking down at me so I asked what was he doing. He said he lived up there, what was I doing, so I told him about the phone booth gone missing. He told me there were others and backed away from the edge. I continued to look up at the sky for a few moments, wondering what he might have seen the past couple of months. He might know something about me, my quantum of fame with the satisfaction that I was not an invisible person or a secret.

I yelled up at the roof asking if he had seen the black dog. A passing car stopped as if I might be yelling at it, a blue Vega with too much exhaust for a small car. A sickly guy puffing more smoke than the car used an enormous amount of effort to unbuckle his seatbelt and open the door to pull himself up and out of the crushed seat so he could stand with one foot on the street, speaking to me over the sun-bleached hood. If I wanted help we could go to an AA meeting together. Told him I wasn't even drunk yet. He said he had seen the black dog too and howled at heaven from random street corners. I told him this wasn't random, that it was my corner, freshly poured and handicap accessible if he felt like a howl.

He chuckled which brought up some phlegm and a spasm of coughing. Being bent over while hacking, he used the posture to reach into his car, coming back out and up with several different pamphlets. With the engine idling poorly he put his other foot on the ground then shuffled over to me, neither foot ever leaving the ground. He handed me free secrets about his sober god, the end of the world and how to beat it, then slid his feet along the pavement back again, the backs of his loafers crushed under his heels, forcing them to become slippers.

The engine began coughing, maybe mocking him, and he dove in foot first to land on the gas pedal, which made the car almost flip sideways and the motor roar with pain. He closed the door with a plastic thunk then shifted back into drive before losing any of those rpm's, so the car jumped forward as if in a street race nearly out of control. He had to zigzag over the centerline for a few car lengths before winning the only race between the world's slowest hotrod and nobody else. Only the lack of oncoming traffic kept him from a head-on collision, his sober god saving him from sideswiping any parked car.

A minute later I drove away in the opposite direction, worried he still somehow might crash into me. My engine sputtered, maybe having caught something from the Vega. Went up the boulevard and turned east past the McDonalds, the barber shop, book shop, porn shop, pawn shop and saloons, crossing Western where the blocks of houses were normal with no stars on the sidewalks or footprints in the concrete. The brownish green hill to the north dotted with cream-colored turrets and red clay shingles fell away to reveal the northern sky. Reached a neighborhood where the freeway passed through it, over it at an angle. It was supported by concrete supports decorated with hieroglyphic graffiti signed and dated almost old as I. Trash filled uneven gutters no longer connected to storm drains because of those massive stilts larger than any useless uprights at Stonehenge. The oldest debris was unrecognizable, just industrial confetti in all colors faded toward gray.

An old chain link fence meant to keep people and freeway traffic separated had failed at that purpose long ago, subjected to a steel bending force by something that wanted or needed to get past. It was concave, the bottom edge curled up four feet from the hard packed ground like it was dying there the way a dying leaf turns in on itself.

A pack of bicycle boys pedaled around the corner then past the pylons, skidding to a stop in unison with their bikes at a forty-five degree angle to the ground, more of a small herd than a bunch of kids. The bikes didn't have kickstands so they laid them down in the dirt then climbed under the fence up toward the freeway. Maybe it was their playground the way ours was dirt roads, wooded hillsides and train tracks. One kid stopped to pick up a stone and throw in my direction, maybe at the van but it didn't matter, he couldn't throw. I drove past their bikes until the street curved because of some geological deformity in the flat landscape. Same as a stream finds a river, the lane led me to a larger and straighter street.

There was a parking lane with humble businesses but it was still as a movie set after hours. A phone booth stood on one corner as if flagging me down for a ride. I pulled over and got out as a primer-painted car passed, music loud out the darkened windows lowered only an inch to trade inner volume for outside oxygen. I heard staccato trumpets over a busy accordion. The car slowed to watch me dig in both pockets for coins. I waved and the car stopped, revved its engine then burned rubber to screech away, leaving its parallel black tracks next to the van, marking territory. I smelled long-dead dinosaurs.

Called home in hope there might be room for me again, and time enough to plan another adventure, maybe a job in Africa. Dad answered and I asked how the house was coming along. Who is this, he said. I explained and he apologized with a laugh, telling me he was busy thinking about weird stuff and the voice didn't click. Some voices just don't click, I thought, and maybe mine was one of them. Told him all my good news, hoping he agreed it was good but worried that maybe he still wasn't certain who I was.

The dark windowed car passed again in the other direction. Maybe they considered it their booth the way the other one belonged to Len.

Drove away but a few blocks later saw it creeping up behind me. Busy watching the mirror I ran a stop sign and an accusatory horn caused me to stop in the middle of the intersection. It honked again only longer so I drove ahead, glancing in the rear view mirror. The creeping car turned right and I never saw it again.

The cross street was Los Feliz so I drove back to Hollywood, afraid of anyplace else. Parked behind Musso & Frank and got out but my legs were asleep. Grabbed the iron rail above the back stairs and the vibrations from my suddenly shaking hands made it hum. Everything glowed as if I had induced an electro-magnetic field. Some guy using the stairs asked if I was okay, but my vocal chords had tightened and though I could have forced an answer it would have come out like a trick high voice used only by ventriloquists or Saturday morning cartoon characters. I let my head use the vibrations and nodded a rhythmic yes. Got so tired I couldn't hold on and fell to the ground as if sex was over and it was time to lie still. The desire for beer got me up on me feet and down the stairs.

Waited at the end of the bar behind a seated guy who didn't notice me, but the bartender saw me without looking and brought me a beer. Drank it in the walk-through between sections. A waitress asked if I wanted to sit but I told her if there were going to be an earthquake that this was the safest place. She didn't laugh or even smile, bored of crap talk after a long shift full of it. With the beer inside me went back to the bar and stood next to a small pack of men who crowded the space between the stools and the tables. After more drinks and the day's scores and myths about women I interrupted to ask if any of them knew Roy, taxi Roy, Charlie Chaplin Roy.

A guy with a birthmark on the side of his nose said yeah, he didn't know him well but Roy was a character, always good for a laugh. I asked if he knew where Roy was tonight and he stared at me for too long then said maybe … maybe heaven. Roy just had died.

The ambulance had left but cops were still out front for no reason because the body was gone. A witness said he walked out of the door laughing and dropped dead on the sidewalk. Instead of a star there was a rectangle of orange cones and yellow police tape. I walked like a zombie down to the Chinese theatre, looking for Chaplin's footprints, thinking of playing hopscotch across the squares, and the outlines of hands spit-painted onto ancient cave walls, and dinosaur tracks along the Rocky Mountains.

Somebody pushed me down from behind and I scraped my palms and knees on the fossilized scrawled name of Edmond Purdom. Looked up at Jayo. My hands and knees left no imprint, just a smear of blood. Asked the inside of my skull why the best talent had to go down on their hands and knees to make an impression. Asked Jayo who was Edmond Purdom.

He said shut up, where was the van. Asked him how answering were possible if I had to shut up. He kicked me a little and I told him honestly that it was near, and that Roy was dead. He said cool, probably about the van not Roy. He bragged that in jail he met some dudes, that it was a small world. Other guys stepped up behind him, his only strength. Told him that this town was a smaller world. In the van we drove to the Frolic Room. Though my palms were bleeding the bartender took our order.

Paid then gave Jayo all the money in my pockets, put the van key on the bar, and asked if he would buy me a drink, telling him about the commercial shoot the next morning. He drank his beer in ten seconds then bought a round for all of us with a burp I first had heard in ninth-grade social studies, suddenly with his arm around me as if holding me up, maybe thinking he had helped me up, bragging to his new friends about how I used to stay up all night thinking of something funny to say in school the next day. He lied about the size of our water snakes and the boobs of girls we lusted after. He and his new friends got drunk quickly, but when that redundant novelty wore off they suddenly didn't like each other, pushing and grabbing and accidently spitting while talking tough face to face.

I backed away with what was left of my third beer and watched from a corner at the window. They made friends, hugged and called each other nasty things then did shots of Southern Comfort, chugged a beer each and within minutes were arguing again. One of them with an imagination picked up a beer bottle and in one ambitious swing tried to hit all the others at the same time.

The bartender had been on the phone already and as they wrassled each other to the floor two cops came to break up the playground nonsense. I recognized one of them. Some were told to leave but Jayo had to prove he was Jayo and screamed some old hippie nonsense that barely counted as political free speech so they handcuffed him. He tried to drink the rest of his beer using no hands then kicked the cop who looked familiar. As they took him back to jail the familiar cop smiled and nodded at me.

I moved into the space left, picked up the van key and left the tender to clean up the bottles, glasses and spills. Walked to the little grocery to use its bathroom, washing my face, hands and knees. It was still early but I went to the van and tried to sleep but only could rest, forcing my neck and shoulders to relax. They resisted and I got a cramp in my brain. Every few thoughts it got worse from fear of not knowing the future. Others who made stable choices knew what the next day would be like, maybe matching exactly the schedule they had written before bed. They could plan with good probability of accuracy weeks in advance, and with age months and years. I imagined them looking back on a lifetime that had happened as planned. It made me relax finally with relief that life was better as a surprise.

Dreamt about trying to sleep but couldn't get comfortable in my dream, then woke up comfortable. Seemed to be near dawn, the promise of light leaving only a few visible stars or planets, but I was no expert on nature. It could've been the advance glow of a distant atomic bomb, its sound and radiation eventually to follow, but decided it was better to die awake than asleep so got up. Almost felt good not having a hang over, and it brought back memories of waiting for the bathroom some mornings, mom and dad with a mysterious amount to do in there with the cabinets full of bottles, tubes and hand held-devices that would've made good props in a science fiction movie laboratory. Some of those days I peed out through the bb holes in the window screen wishing I had my own little toilet in the room.

Later I found the studio. It took me several tries around two blocks, a one-way street taking me in the opposite direction. Tried to cut through an alley but it dead-ended at the massive butt of an old building painted dead dandelion yellow. If there had been traffic I would've been late, but there was little movement except for a heart-shaped man walking a dog that was trying to run. They covered so much ground I passed them four times. Would've asked the guy for help but by the third time he reined in his pet to squint at me and the license plate, and the fourth time he stared me down the entire time I was in view, his hand on the dog's collar as if about to turn it loose on me.

The color of the security guard's tiny booth made me notice the small gate. It was up a short driveway that could've been to any size residence, and was that same sad yellow as the alley building. I pulled in and the gate opened. The guard was eating a glazed donut, and when I asked is this the studio he said of course, pointing to a sign that had some letters and parts of numbers showing from underneath morning glory foliage. He took a bite and with his non-donut hand checked a clipboard for my name, smiling me in. He finally swallowed and yelled stage two, the big yellow building. Every building was yellow, some with a red tile roof, the biggest one in the back looking over their tops. The studio must've been built after the original neighborhood, taking half the houses, half of one alley, and somehow taking half of one direction to create the one-way street. Hoped it wouldn't take away half of anything mine.

There were no marked parking spaces so I pulled behind some other cars and carried the suit to the building that had a red number two painted over its

white wooden doors big enough for a small airplane. Didn't know how to open them so walked around to the side and found a normal door. It had a red light over it and a sign on it that said do not enter when red light is flashing. It wasn't flashing.

Coffee and more glazed donuts were on a long table. Past them through the dark was a pirate ship under changing lights, every change happening after somebody yelled out suggestions. There was movement to the side so I wandered over where a small lady was helping an even smaller lady into a french-fry costume. While waiting, looked at a rack of other costumes of edible characters. The smaller lady asked through a circle of french-fry colored mesh if I was the new guy. I said yes and the bigger small woman welcomed me with a handshake and then a quick hug. Without letting go of my arm she led me to the costume rack telling me her name was Cille. I asked what it was short for and she said it was short for Cille, saying it again but with a long, drawn out southern vowel.

She checked tags attached to garment bags then put her arms around one and lifted. The hook of the clothes hanger came up off the rack's bar and she turned to let it fall toward me, telling me to try this on. I traded hers for mine and at the same time we both asked what is it? Told her it was my gorilla suit. She said cool and that she'd take care of it, then went back to the big french fry.

There were folding chairs scattered in the large sections of unused spaces so I sat down and unzipped the bag. Inside was a red costume, kind of a coverall with gloves, socks and hood. My thought was what is this, but must have said it out loud because Cille's voice told me that I was ketchup, that she was still waiting for mustard. I was going to be red, that's all, just red.

We jumped on a big foam rubber beef patty, mustard, ketchup, pickles and lettuce, in that order. The only good thing was that mustard was female and pickles and lettuce weren't big guys. The french fry was the only animated fry among a bunch of look-a-like props. The milk shake had to do a spin and was the only reason we needed more than one take. I don't know why they started early in the morning because even with the waiting we were done by noon.

Traded the red suit back for my gorilla, expecting a Hollywood party or sex or something, like after a wrap in theater only better, but everybody had regular lives and went home to them waiting for a check in the mail and another job. Bought a can of spray paint and drove east again. At that dead end I sprayed the name Exoticus on the side of the overpass support, then found a road that continued east.

By evening my left arm already looked paler. The air was cool but the setting sun was a warm color in the rear view mirror. Through the windshield the full moon was rising ahead, bluish gray, and by moving my head I could see them next to each other. Moving farther caused a lunar eclipse, and thought I also was eclipsing, one self for another.

The years of being part boy and part man had been taking so long that I worried about being an intermediate freak all my life, or at least until retirement age when I might become part man and part woman. Now they were ending too quickly. Having played along with church, school and dating, dressed accordingly, it wasn't until my job that I realized all clothes are a costume, and the organized rituals of tradition do not guarantee an evolutionary step up into society as an upright member of civilization. The eternal chaos that allowed the chance of chemicals to replicate on a young planet earth was the same chaos that caused me to go naked in public, same as the first humans, same as any newborn human.

Wearing the Hollywood t-shirt I was allowed back into my parent's house for sentimental reasons, though they charged me rent to sleep in the new addition while I waited for residuals from the commercial. Didn't tell them anything they wouldn't have wanted to hear, so made up some stories to fill in the gaps. During happy hour at the Idle told the stories again. By last call confessed some of the real stuff, but nobody believed me. Began reading more than drinking, at the library in bad weather and the beach in good. Paid my rent and saved enough to go back to college. There was a rumor around town the day I left again, someone claiming they saw a gorilla in church.

Today a guy called me old man, not as a joke or insult, but because I got old. That and he didn't know my name. I've never been old before, not in public. What doesn't change is living with change, automatic as time regardless of our personal weathering and crumbling, though many teenish desires are surprisingly resilient.

Now a mountain is out the western window instead of a great lake. They both freeze over in winter but in moments of forgetting where I am it's as if that blank gray horizon of a fresh water sea too big to see across has grown tall and rugged while I was busy with desirable things that seemed more important than geology or time.

Maybe this is where the mound builders went, their namesake works a simple message left behind to inform any person of wonder. If ever that need to learn something new gets me up off my butt and out of my chair again, hope it's to another place that has a shining sign on a hill to give me direction. Maybe Africa, or better another planet of giant waters and mountains, but for now still stuck on earth.

End

Printed in the United States
By Bookmasters

Printed in the United States
By Bookmasters